HOTTER IN THE HAMPTONS

TINX

Bloom books

Published by Bloom Books, an imprint of Sourcebooks
P.O. Box 4410, Naperville, Illinois 60567-4410
(630) 961-3900
sourcebooks.com

Cataloging-in-Publication data is on file with the Library of Congress.

Printed and bound in the United States of America.
LSC 10 9 8 7 6 5 4 3 2 1

For my best friends.

Chapter 1

IT WAS A minor decision before a major meeting, but Lola Fine felt paralyzed by it: her trusty pink Miu Miu flats—scuffed and worn from years of city sidewalks, bought at full price after her first major brand deal—or her black Prada slingbacks, a recent, lavish gift from a publicist that hurt like hell but looked insanely chic.

The flats were definitely less sexy, but they were practical. Plus, they reminded her of a Lola from long past: that starry-eyed, aspiring fashion darling who worshipped at the altar of Sienna Miller and dreamed in dress patterns, who'd moved to the city by herself to see if she could also be part of that glittering, exclusive scene she'd read about in magazines.

But which version of her would be more likeable today—and more importantly, which would be more *forgivable*? The aspirational content creator with seven-figure savings and in-season style, or the earnest fashion girl who doesn't try too hard? She wasn't sure.

The one thing she *was* certain of: the Pradas gave her blisters.

Did she really want to limp her way from Soho to Brooklyn? No. She did not.

Ten minutes later, the trusty flats squeaked on the concrete floor as she breezed through the airy lobby of her apartment building. It was the right choice. She felt like herself. (Though she'd also stashed the Pradas in her bag, just in case she decided on the way that she *didn't* want to feel like herself. It was best to be prepared.)

She waved to the graying doorman, Hector, who greeted her with a warm nod.

"No packages for you this morning, Miss Lola," Hector said.

"It happens," she replied breezily, trying to hide her frown.

Last year, the building's management had bought a new cart just so the doormen could take Lola's mail up to her. Otherwise, her daily onslaught of packages—PR gifts of varying designer clothes, shoes, high-end beauty products, luxury home decor, up-and-coming books, the occasional athletic gear—was unmanageable.

But this week, there had been no packages at all. Not that she really cared about the gifts themselves; the thrill of brands sending her free stuff was long over. Designer bag blended into designer bag, something that would have been unthinkable just a few years ago. Though she'd become famous for her personal style, these days, she felt as if her entire aesthetic was decided by various marketing teams that selected pieces for her to promote on their behalf to her five million followers.

No, it wasn't the lack of packages that bothered her—it was the implication of their absence. It had been a hard few days.

The cream ruffles of her new Chloé maxi dress swished against her waxed, self-tanned legs as she made her way to the exit, her gold bracelets jangling on her wrists. She'd put her favorite pink Guerlain lipstick on, expertly obscuring the tiny scar on the top of her lip. If nothing else, she thought, she looked great today. She smelled great too; she'd sprayed Daisy Wild on her pulse points, relishing the fresh scent. On regular days, the fragrance made her feel like she was prancing whimsically through a field of jasmine, her head floating through the clouds. Today, though, the scent seemed to poke cheekily at the low thrum of anxiety in her chest, urging, almost aggressively, *perk up, babe!* She was forcing herself to listen.

Ever the Virgo, she supposed she was controlling what she could. And if she couldn't make strangers be nice to her online, she could at least make herself look perfect for the task at hand. She was determined to fix her mess.

Hector held the door open for her, and she stepped out onto Mercer Street.

New York summer always felt like a hot bath. Across the street, a horde of young men in tailored three-piece suits—Goldman Sachs interns, she guessed—looked ready to drop dead of heatstroke. The air smelled like steaming garbage. Her feet immediately started sweating in her flats, and though she'd gotten her hair blown out at Jenna Perry the day before, she couldn't resist throwing it into a quick topknot, her neck already damp beneath her blond mane. She'd take it down before the meeting, but for now, there was literally no way she'd survive her hair plastered around her throat. The thought alone made her shudder.

And yet there was something that felt like magic about Manhattan in June, when the chilly, unpredictable spring days finally unfolded into the blazing heat. Lola was born and raised in Los Angeles, so the East Coast's shifting seasons were still novel, those tiny changes that built on each other until suddenly, one day, everything felt new. She hoped she never got used to the romance of it. It made her feel invincible.

She'd wanted to take a Citi Bike to Fort Greene, a quiet, hip neighborhood in Brooklyn with historic brownstones, a leafy park, and a smattering of exquisite little restaurants and bars. She'd always preferred a bicycle to taking taxis or Ubers or, in more recent years, brand-sponsored Uber Blacks. In fact, riding a bike was one of her favorite parts of living in Manhattan. She loved whizzing past all the people, feeling like she was flying through the veins of the city itself, the wind in her hair. When she first moved here, her old bike was how she learned the streets, memorized the grid and the neighborhoods, falling more and more in love with the pulse of this place by the day. It was *her* city, she felt. And she was New York's.

But even she knew she shouldn't attempt to bike over the bridge in couture. She needed to make a good impression, which meant she couldn't risk getting bike grease all over herself, as she was prone to do.

Not to mention the heat. She didn't want to arrive to her interview with the famous Aly Ray Carter looking sweaty. No, it would be an Uber for her today. She needed air-conditioning like she needed Aly to write a redeeming profile of her.

At least that was what her team had been telling her. A flattering profile would turn things around. And Aly specifically needed to be the one to write it. No one else had that kind of cultural cachet with the fashion-obsessed women who followed @LolaLikes on Instagram, TikTok, and X (which Lola had never stopped calling Twitter).

As though she'd been manifested from Lola's thoughts, a teenage girl wearing a Marine Serre T-shirt and cargo pants—a living billboard for Gen Z—walked by. They made eye contact, and Lola offered her a smile. The girl smiled back, looked away, and then whipped back around, recognition flickering across her face. "Oh my god, wait, sorry, Lola Likes?"

Lola, who was waiting in the doorway for her Uber, smiled, unsurprised to be recognized on the street. She was, if anything, a little bored of all the fanfare, though there was also some relief to it in this moment; at least she still mattered. At least what she'd done was not bad enough to prevent a random Gen Z on the street from wanting to talk to her.

"Yes," she said. "Hi!" She expected the girl to ask to take a picture with her. She always said yes when asked.

"Rough week, huh?" the girl said instead. "I would *not* want to be you."

Lola's heart sank to the sidewalk. Usually, girls in their twenties told Lola the exact opposite. They were jealous of her life. They wanted to be her. But apparently, not anymore. She felt a small flame of embarrassment lick up her stomach as she tried to keep the smile firmly in place.

The girl looked Lola's outfit up and down. "Slay, though."

Then she turned and kept walking.

Slay, though? She blinked back tears. How could two words—two stupid words at that—be so cutting? She'd just been read to filth in a matter of seconds, and Lola was shocked by the sting of it. She'd never had an encounter with a fan like that, and she couldn't help but wonder how many people were now out there hating her. Every time she tried to tell herself it wasn't a big deal—that no one other than a specific slice of the internet knew what was happening—she was proven wrong.

The black Land Rover pulled up to the curb, and she felt grateful for the privacy it would give her.

"For Lola?" she asked, sliding in. She felt herself briefly relax in the dark, quiet, cold safety of the car, with its tinted windows and classical music. No Gen Z could hurt her here.

Lola's phone started vibrating. It was Ryan, her best friend. A picture of him she'd taken at Coachella popped up, grinning at the camera, his brown curls loose in the breeze, the pink mountains and palm trees behind him, a dirty martini in his hand.

"Howdy, babe," Ryan said.

"Hi, gorgeous," she answered, slightly perked by his small-town Texas drawl. "Do you think *slay* can be used pejoratively?"

He laughed. "Definitely. Especially if it's being used by a teenager."

She groaned. "Why are you literally psychic?"

"It's my gift." She could hear him smiling on the other end. She envisioned him as he often was, puttering around his Lower East Side studio in his Free City sweats and Gucci fur loafers ("house shoes," he called them).

"What are you doing today?"

"Equinox before work, and then I'm going to the wrinkle doctor on my lunch break," he said. "I need to freeze my face before East Hampton."

Lola had recently asked her own dermatologist for injections. The doctor had refused, rolling his eyes as Lola pitched the idea of "baby Botox" for her nearly invisible crow's feet, telling her she didn't need it—and this gave Lola a renewed appreciation for the effortless, smooth glow of youth still on her face, even while she knew the sun was rapidly setting on her twenties.

Her thirtieth birthday in September already loomed large. She had always assumed that by thirty, she'd be happier than she felt now—more confident, more excited about her life. As it was, she mostly just felt kind of bored, like she was going through the motions of what was expected of her. And at the same time, she felt a confusing sort of desperation to hold on to what she had, despite how little joy it recently brought her. She'd worked so hard to get to this place. And she'd come a long way—when she'd first started out, all she'd had was an obsessive vintage habit and a blog she'd poured her heart into that got barely two hundred clicks a month, mostly from her parents. Now she was someone who had her whole closet curated for her based on which brand cut the biggest check, with the clout to get into any fashion week event, restaurant opening, or club VIP. With millions of followers who wanted to be just like her…except, did they still?

That scathing Gen Z sure didn't.

Regardless, she wasn't sure who she'd be without her lifestyle and the many, many people who followed it. When you stripped Lola Likes away from Lola Fine, you were left with just…fine. And Lola hadn't worked this hard to be just *fine*.

"Don't get too much Botox," she said. "You're perfect as is."

"Exactly. I'm trying to maintain it. Listen, will you *please* reconsider coming to the Hamptons with me this summer? You are the only bitch in NYC who would say no. Giancarlo didn't leave me his house keys and car so that I could drink rosé alone."

She laughed. Ryan was a publicist at the Lede Company, and Giancarlo was one of his wealthiest clients. His Hamptons home would be, without a doubt, stunning beyond reason.

"So there's part of me that does want to, but I really feel like it's important for me to be *here* for the next few months. Plus, I can't leave Justin for that long, and you know how he feels about going east instead of west." Her boyfriend, Justin, was from LA too and took every opportunity he could to go home and see his family. Whenever she asked him about going to the Hamptons, he always countered with, "Why not Santa Barbara?"

It was a fair question, but it made her bristle. She loved her family—and his too, for that matter—but something about going back home always made her feel like she was going backward in time. Her life was here. New York was here.

Lola examined her nails. They were almond shaped and freshly painted with her go-to shade, Ballet Slippers. Simple but still a statement, just like the delicate heart tattooed along the side of her right pointer finger.

"You say that every year," Ryan sighed. "You need to get your FOMO checked by a doctor."

It was true. Lola hated leaving New York. But she feigned innocence. "Do I?"

"Yes. You wouldn't come with me even if you *weren't* canceled."

Lola bristled, though Ryan was the only one allowed to joke with her about the fate she'd recently brought upon herself.

The Uber was on the bridge now, and the crisp Manhattan skyline cut across the clear blue sky, looking like a still from a rom-com.

"Yeah, but now I really mean it," she said. "I can't come. Plus, Justin and I have that Capri trip in July."

"Y'all's life," he sighed. "I wish *I* had a Justin to go to Capri with."

"Maybe you'll find one in the Hamptons."

Ryan had a never-ending stream of gorgeous lovers, but like many people who hadn't become confident until later in adulthood—he'd grown up chubby and been incessantly bullied for it—he had trouble committing to any of them. His fitness addiction and the attention it brought him didn't help the fact.

"Girl, I doubt it!" he yelled, loud enough that Lola had to pull the phone away from her ear. "There are no gorgeous Black doctors out East. The Hamptons are full of WASPS and wannabes. That's why I need you with me. You, me, and this perfect Nancy Meyers cottage. What could be better?"

"Maybe I can come out for a weekend," she conceded, and she could sense his eye roll. "I just feel like if I'm not here, who is going to fix things?"

"Is there anything I can do? To help rehabilitate your image?"

Lola sighed. "I wish."

"I still maintain it wasn't a big deal. And I was there."

"I know."

The day her life fell apart, Lola had been on Instagram live while she and Ryan tried on clothes at a trendy new boutique in Nolita. Salesgirls were plying them with glass after glass of chilled champagne until the clothes and the bubbles and the smell of her perfume left her smiling and dizzy. Lola had connected her iPhone to the speakers and was playing her favorite early-2000s pop playlist while clothes, bags, and shoes piled up around them. Everything she and Ryan did together felt like a movie montage—a whole party broken into dazzling still images and open-mouthed laughs—and this had been no exception.

As Lola swirled back to the changing room in a particularly flowy maxi dress, Ryan had handed her a serious-looking olive-green pantsuit. It was not her usual style at all. She tended to lean boho, kind of a 1970s-rock-star vibe; a Zillennial Daisy Jones, as her followers often pointed out. But Ryan had insisted. "You're legally obligated to try on the most expensive thing in here," and she found that idea so funny, she couldn't resist. She was also more than a little buzzed.

She came out of the dressing room in the suit, her body swallowed by the aggressive structure of the straight-leg trousers and oversized blazer.

"Oh, Lola," Ryan gasped, putting his champagne down. "Mother is *really* mothering." He held the phone pointed at her so her fans could see. Ryan was always pushing her to be edgier in her fashion decisions;

sometimes she trusted him, and other times she wasn't sure if he was just messing with her for a laugh.

"Really?" She turned around, doubtful, looking at her ass over her shoulder. It was hidden beneath the blazer—a shame, given it was usually the star of the show.

"Lola no likes?" he asked.

The words that ruined everything left her mouth before she even gave them a second thought: "It's just very lesbian chic, I think."

From the look on Ryan's face—panic—she instantly knew she'd messed up.

She tried to correct: "Not that that would be a bad thing! I just feel like, this suit? It's, like, very menswear inspired. Which is great. It's just not really me. It's almost giving Ellen."

"Not *it's almost giving Ellen*," Ryan whispered, equal parts amused and horrified. "Girl, we're still live."

"No, wait, I love when people are lesbian chic. It's such a good look," Lola said, becoming flustered and starting to sweat, the suit all of a sudden feeling heavy and hot, claustrophobic. "It's literally *chic*. Lesbian *chic*. It's just not *my look*." She wondered how many times she was going to say the words "lesbian chic" before someone stopped her.

She hated that she couldn't see the comments as they rolled in, but she already knew in her heart what they would say.

"I love *all* gay people! I'm here with Ryan! My best friend! Who is gay!"

Ryan groaned, laughing. "*Lola*." He slid to the floor.

"Okay, that's it for now! See you guys later!" She'd grabbed the phone and ended the livestream. "Shit."

"Oh my god," Ryan said, nearly hyperventilating with nervous laughter.

"Will you tell me what they're saying?" She whispered, giving him back her phone.

"Gird your loins," he sighed.

She held her hands over her face.

"Okay, I'm in your DMs. Here we go. *Why do you hate lesbians? Why are you so homophobic?* Yikes, y'all. Everyone needs to calm the fuck down. I'm not reading you all of these. Sorry. Oh, wait, here's a good one: it says, *Lola I WISH you were a lesbian!* And this one says, *Show me your feet.* See? Not all bad."

Her hands still over her face, Lola said, "Is lesbian chic an offensive phrase?"

"Not objectively, my dear, but we live in strange times," Ryan said.

Over the course of the next day, Lola lost twenty thousand followers.

The comments on her posts devolved into heated arguments over who is allowed to say what.

The boutique got in on it too, captioning a photo of a model in the suit IT'S JUST VERY LESBIAN CHIC. It got around seventy thousand likes, while the boutique itself only had twelve thousand followers.

The top pinned comment on the post was Not it's almost giving Ellen!

As she lay in bed scrolling through the damage, even Lola had to laugh at that—it was brilliant marketing—though she was also weeping with embarrassment. It was such a fine line between being popular on the internet and being the main character. And you never, ever wanted to be the main character.

The suit sold out within hours, and the brand announced it would be donating 100 percent of the profits to the Trevor Project.

Her team called an emergency meeting the next day.

"We can fix this," her manager, Todd, had promised her.

"I'm so sorry," she'd said for the hundredth time. "I didn't realize that it was a problematic thing to say."

"It doesn't matter if it is or isn't," Todd said. "It's about perception."

"Can't I just match the donation to the Trevor Project?" she asked.

"You should definitely do that," Todd said. "But that's just the beginning."

It was her publicist's idea to pitch a profile to Aly Ray Carter.

ARC, as her friends and fans called her, was famously stylish, intimidatingly smart, and deeply well-respected. An entire generation hung on her every word. A freelancer, Aly wrote for *The Cut*, *Vanity Fair*, *Vogue*, even the *New York Times Magazine*, where she penned scathing runway critiques and brilliant cultural commentary. She was often coining new phrases that were quickly adopted into the lexicon—things like *STF*, which stood for *secret trust fund*, to call out the way some influencers so obviously lived above their means, and *Bushwick University* to describe how everyone in a certain part of Brooklyn appeared to be eighteen. Aly's catchphrases were often printed on T-shirts and sold by *The Cut*, though Aly was not big on social media, so it was unclear if she understood her own impact.

She was also a nepo baby but had been so open about it that no one could use it against her. Her parents were both editors, her dad high up the masthead at a tech magazine and her mom an executive in book publishing. If anything, Lola thought, this made Aly *more* alluring—hailing from a long line of tastemakers.

If ARC could write something generous about Lola, it would turn things around. All Lola had to do was make a good impression, something she'd been trying to do in various capacities her whole life.

Besides, the fact of the matter was that Lola was not homophobic. She'd grown up loving and loved by LGBTQ+ people, had only ever lived in places where the queer community was thriving and visible, a regular part of her life. The phrase *lesbian chic* did not have negative connotations for her.

But according to her audience and subsequently her team, it was not her phrase to use, and a Notes app apology post would not do. Which was how she got here, in an Uber on the first truly hot day of the year, hoping Aly Ray Carter might feel like saving her career.

There was a reckless voice in her head urging her to skip the interview altogether and ride the wave of scandal into obscurity. Maybe she could just start over. If she was honest with herself, that didn't sound half-bad. But then again, if she was *really* honest with herself, if she had been all along, she wouldn't have said yes to the series of deals that launched her into the stratosphere in the first place. Honesty would mean admitting that the more successful she became, the further away she got from her reasons for wanting to do all this. She had never wanted to take photos of *herself* for a living. But here she was, known for it.

And anyway, the louder part of her was more logical than that. There would be no point in throwing away what she'd built.

"I love you," Ryan said on the phone. "Good luck. God, it's such a classic publicist move to get a lesbian journalist to profile you."

"But also kind of brilliant, right?"

"Oh, absolutely. It's what I would do too. Tell ARC I say hi."

"Does she know who you are?"

"I mean, I wish? God, she's cool. Those Tom Ford sunglasses kill me."

"Agreed." Lola smiled, knowing exactly the ones he was talking about. "She's like, very…" Lola trailed off, searching for the right word. "Hot."

"Oh, she's, like, the hottest hot person ever. Total heartbreaker too. The stories I have heard would make your blood run cold."

"Yeah?" Lola was suddenly and inexplicably curious to know which hearts Aly had broken—and when and why and how.

Just then, the car pulled up to the restaurant.

"Tell me after. Love you."

"Be careful what you tell her," he added quickly. "She's famously a Scorpio."

Aly was waiting for Lola at a table for two tucked into the corner of Evelina, an Italian bistro near Fort Greene Park, which was mostly empty but for a couple nuzzling into each other over coffees and the young, attractive waitstaff folding napkins and slicing citrus at the bar. The first hot day of the year would mean a horribly crowded happy hour, everyone dying for chilled orange wine and Blue Point oysters, and Lola was glad they were meeting in the morning, when they could have some semblance of privacy.

"Lola," Aly said as Lola approached, standing up.

Lola gave herself a moment to take Aly in. She was the epitome of intellectual luxury in black linen pants that hung loosely on her lean frame, a perfectly cut black T-shirt, and black leather Celine loafers; her long, brown hair was pulled into a low ponytail with a nineties-inspired tortoise-shell claw clip—or, Lola thought, maybe the clip was actually vintage. Aly's infamous Tom Ford aviator sunglasses were on the table next to a Moleskine notebook emblazoned with her initials and a recording device. A canvas *Paris Review* tote was slung over her chair.

Lola tried to swallow and found that her mouth had become dry.

It was terribly intimidating, how beautiful she was in person. An off-duty Kristen Stewart, with longer hair, as charming as an A-list actress and as cool as… Lola actually couldn't think of anyone who instantly appeared cooler. Aly was in her own league.

Lola's stomach did a backflip as she realized how overdressed she was in her ruffled maxi dress. She wondered what Aly thought of her, if she found her aesthetic charming or cheesy. *Smile*, she told herself. *Be likeable.* At least she hadn't changed into the heels.

"So nice to meet you," Lola said, and she realized with a flash of embarrassment that she sounded breathless. She had no reason to be out of breath. She'd only walked about twenty feet from the car. Still, her heart was pounding as though she'd just run a mile (not that Lola was a runner—she hated nonessential cardio).

Aly was a couple of inches shorter than Lola, which wasn't surprising. At five feet nine, Lola was used to being the tallest girl around. Aly was smaller in general too—while Lola had something of an Amazonian figure, Aly was slender and narrow.

Lola wasn't sure why she was so fixated on the physical differences between them. She wasn't usually one to compare herself to other women.

"Oh, we've met before," Aly said, shaking her hand, her face neutral and unreadable.

"I'm so sorry, of course we have," Lola said, trying to cover up the faux pas by lying. "I just didn't think *you* would remember *me.*"

She quickly ran through all the possible places she could have met Aly, but there were too many to count. She wasn't sure how it was possible that she could have forgotten, but then again, she was sometimes in a different mode, too distracted and in her head to catalog every introduction. She felt rising panic at the thought that Aly might already find her rude.

Aly simply raised one groomed eyebrow, a half smile flickering across her face. "Please, sit down. I have a cappuccino coming, but I wasn't sure what you'd want." There was something kind of old-school about that, about her order, about her. Like she was from another era.

"Oh, I'm good with water, thank you." Lola was too nervous to eat. To compensate, she concentrated on switching over into Professional Influencer Mode, taking a breath to shake away her nerves. She sat up straighter, batted her eyelashes. She prepared to be fun and funny and nice—nothing more, nothing less. It was the persona her team knew well, the one her brand clients loved. It had never let her down before.

"Thanks for coming to my neck of the woods," Aly said.

"Oh, do you live around here? I love this neighborhood."

Aly nodded. "Near the park."

"How lovely," Lola said. This neighborhood was all brownstones, trees, and charm. A different kind of New York. One more intimate and unique. Kind of perfect for the girl sitting before her. Lola, on the other hand, was made for Soho, the beautiful chaos of it, the luxury, the ongoing identity crisis.

They had both found their places, it seemed.

Lola couldn't help but let her gaze skim over Aly again as she flipped open her notebook. Aly had soft brown eyes framed by dense, dark eyelashes. It didn't look like she was wearing a drop of makeup across her high cheekbones and sharp jawline. She was gorgeous but in such an understated way, it struck Lola as distinctly unfair. She wondered if Aly even appreciated it or if her prettiness was a burden, if it prevented people from taking her seriously. And Aly seemed like the kind of person who wanted, if nothing else, to be seen as serious.

The wind blew in from the open French doors, and Lola was hit with a waft of something delicious she couldn't place. "Oh my god, what is that smell?"

Aly blinked. "Hm?"

"You don't smell that? It's, like, woodsy but also citrusy? It smells like summer. Fuck, what *is* that?" Lola felt almost intoxicated by it, enough that her professional mask momentarily dropped.

Aly grinned sheepishly at her. "Oh, that's probably just…me."

Lola's cheeks grew hot. "You have to tell me what perfume it is."

"It's called Molecule 01," Aly said. "It's supposed to blend with your natural scent or something."

"Wow, you must have a great natural scent, then."

"Thank you," Aly said, avoiding her eyes.

Lola wanted to apologize, then start over, try to have better boundaries—or at least just not mention how good Aly smelled, for god's sake. Could she sound any thirstier? Would Aly think she was flirting?

Was she flirting?

Still not looking at Lola, Aly turned her recorder on and flipped a page, tapping her ballpoint pen on a sheet filled with indecipherable scrawls.

"Whole milk cappuccino?" The server placed Aly's drink in front of her, the foam cresting pleasantly over the edge of the white ceramic mug.

Lola fought the urge to take a photo of it. "Whole milk," she remarked. "So classic."

Finally, Aly looked at her, sending a little jolt through Lola's whole body when their eyes met. "I tend to feel like the plant-milk situation has gotten out of hand. I mean, do we really need to be milking oats?"

Lola laughed. "I love oat milk."

"Of course you do," Aly said.

Lola didn't how to take that.

They stared at each other for a few moments. Lola felt her heart skipping around in her chest. She wasn't sure why she was freaking out so badly. She'd done plenty of press.

"So, Lola. This is a profile, okay? I want to get to know you."

"Okay." Lola smiled nervously. "You're going to have to be more specific."

Aly laughed. "Sorry," she said, and by the way she said it, Lola had the odd and surprising thought that Aly might actually be nervous too. But before she could consider this further, Aly said, in a voice so professional she sounded like she should be on the radio, "You were one of the first fashion bloggers to turn your Instagram account into a multimillion-dollar business. What made you want to become an influencer in the first place?"

Lola noted Aly's tone shift with a small smile. *We can both do that*, she thought before reciting her own mantra: *Pause. Breathe. You are Lola Likes. Act like it.*

"Content creator," Lola corrected and ignored Aly's barely concealed eye roll. Her Professional Influencer Mode flipped back on. "It started in college. I got really into thrifting and repurposing clothes. I started buying used clothes and giving them a second life. I became kind of known for it. People would constantly stop me and ask about my outfits." She paused, wondering if she was going too far back in her own lore, but Aly was listening and appeared to be rapt. "Then I met Ryan in class, and he convinced me to start a blog about it, which is how Lola Likes was born. I had a few series—Lola Likes, Lola Loves, Lola Hates— which were all pretty much what they sound like. Then I did Lola Loots, which were basically haul videos, and Lola Listens, where I answered questions. Eventually it made more sense to do all that on an Instagram account versus keeping the blog going. I think my first big tutorial to go viral was how to turn your Target T-shirt into the Row."

Aly raised an eyebrow. "How *do* you turn a Target T-shirt into the Row?"

"You'll just have to watch my video." Lola winked, a little awkwardly. Her foot hit something soft under the table, and Aly flinched. "Oh, fuck, sorry. Did I just kick you?"

"You did," Aly said, a flicker of humor in her eyes.

"I'm so sorry," Lola groaned, her mind scrambling for the composure she had moments ago. "I don't know where I begin and end sometimes."

To her surprise, Aly laughed. She had a nice laugh, a warm sound deep from her belly. Lola liked the sound, but more than that, she liked knowing she had caused it. Like she was winning at some undefinable game.

"Go on, though," Aly said. "You were telling me how you got your start."

Lola moved her foot away from Aly, though under the small table, there were only a few inches between them. Maybe she was losing it, but she was almost certain she could feel heat radiating off Aly's leg. She took a breath, struggling to find the thread of what she'd been saying. "Okay, yeah, anyway, things kind of took off from that first viral video."

"Say more," Aly urged. "What did it look like when it took off?"

"Well, I started getting invited to actual runway shows. I went from being a fashion outsider to someone who was welcomed on the inside. Then came the spon-con, the brand deals, and the real, actual income. I didn't even have to get a full-time job when I graduated. Not that this isn't a full-time job—it's basically twenty-four seven, but you know what I mean. I was never a W-2 girlie or whatever. So to answer your question, I wouldn't say I ever set out to be a content creator, but I had content I was creating, and people liked it, so…yeah. That's how it happened."

"A W-2 girlie," Aly repeated and wrote something down in her notebook. "So now instead of telling people how to make things look like the Row, you're just…" She paused, catching Lola's eye. "Wearing the Row."

Lola winced. "It sounds much less fun when you put it like that. But yeah. Now I get the Row for free."

"So how would you describe your style now?"

"Bohemian chic," Lola said, her stock answer.

"Yeah?" Aly said, not buying it. "What does that mean?"

"Um," Lola said. She did not know how to answer. What *was* her style? What was the name of the style of *Free Everything All the Time*? Beyond wearing the latest trends before their release, she didn't know what made her style any different from anyone else's. She gestured to her ruffly dress. "It means I look like this."

Aly checked her notes, and Lola had the sudden sinking feeling that she had somehow disappointed her. She pasted on her most accessible smile as Aly looked back up. "Tell me about your personal life. The people you spend most of your time with. The person in the video with you—Ryan Anderson, the fashion publicist? That's the Ryan you mentioned meeting in college?"

Lola nodded. "I don't know what I'd do without him."

"And your boyfriend?"

"Yeah, Justin," she replied, though for some reason, it bothered her that Aly knew she had a boyfriend. "He's a pediatric oncologist."

"How'd you meet?"

"We went to high school together."

This seemed to surprise her. "Really? You were high-school sweethearts?"

"Oh, no, no," Lola corrected. "That's how we *first* met. We reconnected when we were older." She hesitated to tell Aly more. It didn't seem relevant. And she didn't want Aly to think of her as Lola-with-a-boyfriend. She wanted her to just think of her as Lola, her own person, not tied to a man.

"And I read he's also on the board of USC's Black Alumni Association," Aly said.

Lola nodded. "He's very involved. He mentors a bunch of college students, and he's always helping organize fundraisers and whatnot."

"Okay, perfect man. So how serious is it? Is he *the one*?" There was something condescending about the question—as though the idea of soulmates was laughable to Aly—that Lola chose to ignore.

"We're just enjoying each other for now," Lola replied, terse. "I try not to overthink it."

Aly seemed to accept this and moved on. "So what do you do for fun?"

"For fun," Lola repeated, laughing.

She was having a hard time remembering; by documenting every moment of her life, she'd turned every waking second into a commodity. But damn if she was about to admit that to Aly.

"I go out, I guess. Ryan and I like to try the dirty martinis at different bars around the city." She knew she was probably drinking too much these days, but she wasn't sure what else people did when they went out at night.

Aly nodded. "Okay, tell me about your brand partnerships."

"Which ones?"

"Whichever one you like the best."

"Sorry, I probably can't do that? Contractually, I can't say I like one brand better than another. Pick one, and I'll tell you about it."

"Okay." Aly nodded, checking her notebook. "Tell me about… Lola for Rêver."

"Oh, yay, French robes." Lola tried to sound more excited than she felt. "Washable silk. They made a custom pink just for me. They're twenty percent off if you buy them through my link in my bio. I love them. They're very popular." Lola was not passionate about robes. But it was a lucrative deal and not a lot of work on her end.

Reading Lola's mind, Aly tapped the edge of her pen. "How much of your income comes from brand partnerships at this point?"

"I mean, all of it?"

Aly made a note. "So what are you working toward?" she asked. "What's your five-year plan?"

"Oh, I mean, I don't know if I really have one." Lola shrugged. "I can barely think about the next month, not to mention the next five years. Things have been moving so quickly for so long that I don't really have time to plan. I just go with it."

Aly considered this for a few beats, her pen still tapping on her notebook. "How do you decide who to work with? You've got your luxury robes for the stay-at-home audience, the aviator sunglasses for the cool girls, the vitamin-B supplements for the wellness junkies, the cowboy boots for the…well, I actually don't know who is wearing cowboy boots right now. And that's just last month. I'm trying to find some connecting thread in your clients, and I can't really see one."

Because there isn't one, Lola wanted to say, heart thumping. *Because I just say yes to everything my team tells me to. Because they want me to appeal to as many people as possible.*

Instead, Lola said, "Look, I'm just trying to make a living like everyone else." Aly's questioning had pushed her into a rare moment of frankness, which was, perhaps, the point. She wasn't sure she liked how it felt.

"Huh," Aly said, her brow furrowed. She looked like she was dissecting something vital, trying to solve an impossible equation.

"What?"

"I mean, look." She put the pen down and clasped her hands on the table. "I'm listening to you. I'm hearing your story. And it just kind of sounds like you're not doing any of the things that you originally loved. You're just getting free things and putting your name on products. You studied fashion, but you're not really working in it."

Lola's stomach twisted into a knot. "Ouch," she said, laughing but incredulous. "What the fuck, Carter?" Maybe it was too familiar, addressing her like this, but the criticism was so personal, she couldn't help it.

"I don't mean to be an asshole. It's just, I don't really think what you do counts as working in the fashion industry, you know? Unless you want to call it freelance marketing. Like, I asked you what made you want to be an influencer—sorry, content creator—and what you gave me was more of a *how* you got here, not why."

Lola cringed. She didn't have an answer to *why*. It had just happened. "Is there a question in there?"

"I'm sorry. Yes. I guess what I'm trying to ask you is: In a life of free stuff, how are you supposed to know what you really want?"

Lola's heart sank. That *was* the question, wasn't it?

She felt stripped bare by Aly's read and was surprised to find herself fighting back tears.

But instead of showing how painfully real this all was, she shook her head and rolled her eyes, trying to project confidence—or at least attitude. "Wow, ARC. I guess this is why they pay you the big bucks, huh?" She was less than convincing, though. Her voice cracked and trembled as she spoke.

The truth was she had no idea what she really wanted. She just didn't know anyone else could tell.

"Hey, I'm sorry," Aly said and looked like she genuinely felt bad for pressing. "Just food for thought. You don't have to answer that one."

There was a long pause. Lola, still trying not to cry, pretended to examine her fingernails.

Aly offered a tentative "Are you okay?" before reaching a hand across the table and resting it on Lola's forearm. She gave her a warm, little squeeze.

Lola looked up. Their eyes met, and for a brief moment, Aly's face looked open, imploring. Like she was actually concerned that she'd hurt Lola's feelings. Which she had, of course, but her soft hand on Lola's arm was weirdly helping.

"I'm okay. Just feeling a little...naked," Lola said, a weak smile tugging at the corners of her mouth.

Aly's cheeks turned the color of a strawberry, and she pulled her hand back, as though suddenly aware that they were touching.

"I mean, not literally naked," Lola corrected herself quickly. "Obviously. It's a metaphor." And then, in a moment she'd soon come to regret, she threw her hands up in the air, knocking her glass of water over on the table.

"Oh my god, fuck," she yelped. "Sorry, sorry, sorry."

Aly jumped to her feet as the ice-water tsunami spilled toward her, narrowly missing getting totally soaked. A waiter appeared with napkins, mopping up the table and Aly's chair, and all the while, Lola held her hands over her mouth, wishing the ground would open and swallow her whole.

Aly sat back down, no longer blushing, a good-natured grin on her face. "Well, you didn't have to throw your water at me about it," she said, laughing.

Lola groaned. "I'm *so* sorry." And then she added, with more than a little bit of sass, "But that's what you get for reading me like that."

"Fair enough," Aly said, holding Lola's eye contact.

Lola felt something loosen inside her. Yes, it *had* been a bitchy question to ask, but she wasn't wrong to ask it. And she hadn't been *afraid* to ask it either. No one in Lola's life was that honest with her. Justin—and Ryan, for that matter—liked to couch feedback in flattery. Even though it hurt her feelings, she had to admit there was something deeply attractive about being called on her bullshit.

Actually, it was kind of hot. She crossed and uncrossed her legs, suddenly too aware of her own body, of Aly's body on the other side of the table, and the distance between them. She wondered what else Aly might say to her, what else Aly could see.

They continued talking, and Lola pushed away the confusing swirl happening in her head. So what if Aly could see right through her? She was a journalist. That was her job. It didn't mean that they understood each other in any sort of unique way. Unless…

Meanwhile, Aly asked Lola her thoughts on the latest runway shows, algorithm changes, and microtrends. Lola did her best to sound cute and interesting, though she had absolutely no idea if Aly was buying it anymore. She would have given anything for a chance to look at Aly's notes.

The restaurant was slowly starting to fill up with people on their lunch break, which was how Lola realized that they'd been there for over an hour.

"How'd you get that scar?" Aly asked.

"Oh god, you can see it?" Lola was sure she'd covered it effectively.

"I've seen photos of you without lipstick on." Aly said smiling patiently. "It kind of pulls your upper lip up a little? And makes your front teeth show." She paused as though unsure whether to continue, and then she said, "It's cute."

"Oh, um, thank you," Lola said, growing warm, the hairs on her arm standing up.

Aly had been looking at pictures of her. Lola wondered what Aly had thought, scrolling through her countless selfies. She wondered if Aly had a type.

It occurred to Lola suddenly that her hair was still in a topknot. So much for the nice blowout. She pulled it loose, and it fell softly in golden waves around her face, a few strands sticking to the sweat on her forehead. She noticed Aly's eyes and self-consciously tucked it behind her ears.

"I was snowboarding," she said. "In Big Bear, on a high school trip. I did a total face-plant and ruined my chances of making out with anyone."

At this, Aly grinned. "I pegged you for more of a ski girl."

"Please!" Lola cried. "I am a very cool snowboard chick, thank you very much."

Aly laughed. "Okay, I can see it, I guess. Though for some reason, it's easier to picture you drinking hot chocolate in the lodge. I'm seeing a cable-knit sweater, a fuzzy beanie, maybe some knee-high UGGs?"

"I do love an après-ski," Lola admitted. "But my version is less J. Crew catalogue than you're describing. I'm pretty chic after I shred a mountain."

"You know what? I believe you," Aly said. And then she grew serious again. "So speaking of which, the elephant in the room: let's talk about *lesbian* chic."

Lola nodded. Her team had prepared her for this, and she launched into the statement they'd rehearsed. "I'm so sorry to everyone I offended by appropriating a phrase from the queer community. I have a lot of queer people in my life who I love, and sometimes I forget that their words aren't mine. I am constantly learning and growing, and I hope that people will give me the chance to do better."

"Yes, yes, I'm sure. But how did it *feel* to get canceled like that?" Aly pressed.

"Horrible," Lola whispered. She felt totally vulnerable under Aly's piercing stare.

"I have to tell you," Aly said, softening, as though she sensed how upset Lola was becoming. "I really didn't think it was that big of a deal."

"You didn't?"

"No." Aly laughed again, that warm, generous sound. "And I watched the video many times. It just seemed like you weren't really thinking."

Lola nodded vigorously. "Exactly. *Exactly!*"

Aly continued, "I'm far more interested in the response to what you said than what you actually said. I mean, I'm not super online, so I feel like an anthropologist watching this unfold. They really wanted to burn you."

Lola nodded, relieved to get sympathy. "They sure did. And like, I said the wrong thing. We all say the wrong things sometimes, you know? But it doesn't mean I'm homophobic. I mean, the only porn I watch is girl on girl!"

Aly's mouth fell open.

Lola wanted to die. She could not believe the words that had just come out of her.

She put her face in her hands. "I shouldn't be allowed to speak," she said. "I can't request something be off the record after it's been said, can I?"

"No." Aly started laughing then. "Sorry. That's just not...what I was expecting you to say. It takes a lot to shock me. I'm almost impressed."

Lola removed her hands from her face. "I'm nothing if not full of surprises," she said with chagrin.

"Good to know," Aly said, her pretty face tilted to the side. "But just to confirm, for the sake of"—she paused, looking like she was trying to fight a smile—"for the sake of my fact-checker, you *are* straight, right?"

"Right."

Lola wondered if Aly was *really* asking for the sake of her fact-checker or if there was another reason she might be curious about Lola's specific sexual orientation—a personal reason. She wondered what it might change for Aly if Lola had said something else besides "right." But she wasn't sure what else she could have said.

Lola had never told anyone about her specific porn habit, and now here she was, offering the info up to Aly like it was nothing. Aly, the alleged heartbreaker, who was writing a story that would likely be read by tens of thousands of people, including Lola's parents. And Justin. And—probably the worst of it—Justin's parents. Her thoughts swirled. She couldn't believe she was talking about porn with Aly Ray Carter. Did Aly watch porn? Lola's mind raced.

"Well, for what it's worth," Aly said, interrupting her panic, "you *did* look pretty lesbian chic in that suit." A half smile twitched across Aly's full lips, and something devious glinted in her eyes. "Which is, of course, a compliment."

"Thank you," Lola said. Her heart started to pound again. For reasons she couldn't understand, she felt like this was the nicest thing Aly could have said to her.

Lola glanced at Aly's lips. She had a perfect Cupid's bow. *Very kissable.* The thought flickered across her brain before she could stop it.

She swallowed. It was not appropriate to think about kissing the journalist interviewing her. She was basically objectifying her. But...

what would it be like? Would Aly use tongue? Teeth? Would she dig her hands into Lola's hair? Would Aly need to stand on her tiptoes?

Lola had to force herself to stop looking at Aly's mouth.

Meanwhile, Aly turned the recorder off and knocked back the last foamy sip of her cappuccino, and then she raised her hand to get the waiter's attention. Lola caught a glimpse of the smooth hollow of Aly's armpit just beyond the cuff of her T-shirt.

Get ahold of yourself, Fine, she thought. *We are not going to ogle this woman's goddamn armpit.* It was too late, though. She'd already stared.

The waiter brought the bill, and Aly tossed a ten on the table. Lola couldn't remember the last time she saw someone pay in cash.

"Well, talk to you soon," Aly said and extended her hand as she stood up. "Thanks for your time."

Lola looked at her hand, confused. The sudden formality was like getting splashed with cold water. *Thanks for your time?* She'd expected a hug after all that. Maybe an air kiss on the cheek, European style.

Aly's hand, waiting for Lola's in the space between them, was slim but strong looking. Her nails were short and bare. She wore a few plain gold rings; a mixed metal chain was fastened around her pale wrist.

"Oh, yeah," Lola said, finding her way back to the present moment, taking Aly's hand in hers. It felt cool. "Thanks for your time too."

Aly squeezed her hand. A spark of electricity traveled up Lola's arm and into her stomach. Lola did not want to let go. But she did, reluctantly.

And then Aly left.

Lola took a breath. She inhaled; she exhaled. She put her palms on the table and tried to ground herself.

But she couldn't. She felt like she was levitating.

Long after Aly was gone, Lola could still smell her.

Chapter 2

THERE WAS ONLY one other time in her life Lola had felt anything close to the kind of electricity she felt while talking to Aly, and it was when she and Justin reconnected five years ago.

She'd recognized him immediately across the crowded Chelsea gallery that was hosting her friend Min's newest collection of paintings, a series of abstract portraits in soft hues of blue and purple. Min and Lola had gone to high school together, so it wasn't surprising that there was someone else from Harvard Westlake there; what was surprising was that it was Justin in particular.

It was like seeing a local celebrity.

He'd been the star hot guy of their high school, which was a feat, given almost everyone—with the exception of a few like Lola—was the offspring of the rich and the famous. But even in that crowd, Justin stood out, with his entertainment lawyer parents and Brentwood mansion. He wasn't just gorgeous; he was a varsity athlete, took AP everything, and was genuinely nice, beloved by everyone. Plus, he always had an equally hot girlfriend. Everyone knew he was destined for greatness.

Justin and Lola had not been friends in high school, but given their shared propensity for being on good terms with everyone, they weren't *not* friends either. The popular crowd just wasn't really Lola's scene. She grew up in a bungalow in Laurel Canyon, the only child of her costume designer mother, Jeanette, and her cinematographer father, Roger. While Justin went to parties, Lola was going to set with her parents, where Jeanette taught her how to sew and mend, how to tell if something was real or fake, and what made something look expensive or cheap. Roger taught her how to make anything look beautiful, how lighting was everything.

She became obsessed with aesthetics, with people whose jobs were curating the way things looked. While her friends went on group trips to Cabo with their maids, Lola was home, honing her sense of style and studying the history of the looks she loved best. It was the one thing she and her parents fought about. They wanted her to spend more time being a real teenager; she ached to grow up and have a career. But even when they fought, she was glad she was theirs. She could see how unhappy her friends and their parents were, despite their mansions and their chef's kitchens and their pools. She wouldn't have traded what she had for the world. Ironic, given the fact that her life now more closely resembled that of her rich high school friends than that of her parents.

She knew it had broken their hearts when she moved to New York to study fashion, but they also supported her unconditionally, and they visited as often as they could. It was important for her to leave LA, to leave them. Otherwise, she'd never have become her own person.

It took two years after she graduated to run into Justin at Min's opening, and she saw him before he saw her, which gave her a few minutes to observe him unencumbered. His trousers were perfectly tailored; his white T-shirt and gold chain necklace told Lola he was trying to look hip for the art party. But he was a little too clean-cut to get away with anything resembling edginess. Lola liked that—she was sick of all the scruffy downtown guys with their ratty jeans and sneakers and stoned monologues about *Infinite Jest.* Justin was classy. He looked exactly like the person he was supposed to become.

She downed a glass of champagne before approaching him. His eyes widened as she walked up, looking her up and down so quickly she almost missed it, but it had definitely happened—Justin had checked her out. He was grinning by the time she was in front of him, which meant he liked what he saw.

"Hello, Justin Wilson," she said, grinning back.

To her surprise, his eyes grew large as he exclaimed, "I have no idea who you are, but I'd like to."

They both erupted into laughter, struck by the brazen way she'd assumed he would recognize her and how frank he had been about the fact that he didn't.

"I'm Lola Fine," she said. "We went to high school together. You're two years older than me."

It took him a minute, but it seemed like he remembered. "Lola." He snapped his fingers. "Well, goddamn. You look different."

She knew she did. She'd always been cute but had only figured out how to be gorgeous in adulthood; after years studying actors and models, she'd finally learned how to dress for her own long, curvy body, how to play up her makeup so that her cheekbones glowed and her doe eyes looked bigger. It was like having a superpower, being able to make herself look exceptional. And Justin was clearly hypnotized.

"Tell me everything you've done since high school," he said.

"I studied fashion at Parsons," she told him. "And now I'm a fashion blogger."

"You know, that's kind of perfect," he replied. "You always had the best style. And isn't your mom a costume designer?"

She nodded. She couldn't believe he remembered that. She was touched by it, even if she didn't agree. Her style in high school had been as bad as everyone else's, complete with low-rise jeans and going-out tops. "Okay, your turn," she said. "What has become of the one and only Justin Wilson?"

"Well, I'm in medical school at NYU."

"Of course you are." She beamed. She had this odd sense of already being proud of him.

"Where do you live?" he asked.

"The LES," she said. "But it's getting pretty loud over there these days. You?"

"Murray Hill, but it's getting kind of basic." He flashed that perfect smile. "Where would you want to live? Wait, should we say our dream neighborhood on three?"

She nodded. He counted. "One, two, three..."

"Soho," they said together, erupting into laughter.

People looked at them then, laughing so close together in a corner, and Lola loved the attention—from him and everyone else. They were having the kind of meet-cute she'd always dreamed of.

"I like living in Manhattan, but it's not forever," he said. "I've always known I wanted to end up in LA, be close to my family, start a family of my own. But this is fun for now."

Perhaps it should have given Lola more pause, that he didn't want to be here forever and she did. She had already fallen in love with the city. But all she could think about was how badly she wanted him.

"So you want kids?" she asked, surprised by the openness.

"I want, like, so many kids." He grinned. "I think I was put on earth to be someone's father."

Lola had never really considered motherhood one way or another, hoping to at some point feel more strongly about it, and it had been attractive that Justin was so resolute.

"What about you, though?" he asked. "Should we just skip to the part where we tell each other all our hopes and dreams?"

This question had given her—as the girls on *Love Island* would say—fanny flutters. No New York guys had ever talked to her like this; but then again, Justin was not from New York.

"I've been obsessed with fashion my whole life," she admitted to him. "Being here, making a living in the industry, it really feels like I've accomplished something."

He seemed impressed with her, which felt like a miracle. If only she could go back in time and tell her teenage self that one day *she'd* be impressive to Justin Fucking Wilson.

The more they talked, the more the rest of the world melted away.

Their first kiss was in the cab back to his apartment, his tongue in her mouth the exact mix of gentle and firm that made her melt. Lola's only concern was that she was pretty sure she was ruining her underwear. That was how attracted she was to him, how wet she already was. Like her skin was on fire. It was all Lola could do to keep from ripping his clothes off in the lobby of his building. They had sex all night and again in the morning—and then again almost every day for the next five years.

Lola and Justin. Justin and Lola. Even their names sounded good together. She loved him completely. She was by his side when he grad-uated medical school and began his first residency. He clinked his glass to hers every time she made a new brand deal, pushed her to explore new opportunities.

He was still the man of her dreams after all these years. A hot doctor who spent his free time doing volunteer work. He wasn't just good in bed—he was a good person.

Though sometimes, if she let herself, she felt a creeping worry that they were on borrowed time. He meant what he'd said about New York not being forever, hard as she'd tried to put it out of her head. Thinking back on it now, she felt annoyed that Aly had asked her about her future with Justin when she was putting so much energy into *not* thinking about it.

Besides, she was turning thirty, not forty-five. For city girls, thirty was the new twenty. In New York, she was still a baby. She had her whole life ahead of her. Why did she need to think about *forever* at this point? Her life had only just begun.

She and Justin would cross that bridge when they came to it. It wasn't like there was anyone else she wanted to be with. Nothing had ever come close to the sparks she'd felt with him that first night.

That was, of course, until this morning with Aly. But it was probably just nerves, she told herself. It was easy to confuse being nervous around someone with being attracted to them.

Anxiety felt an awful lot like lust.

Instead of going right home after the interview, Lola had her car drop her off at the Bloomingdale's on Broadway. There, she looked for Molecule 01—just to see what it smelled like in the bottle, she told herself, to find out if it really did smell different on skin.

"Texas Hold 'Em" was playing through the speakers, and she began singing along with Beyoncé under her breath. She had the odd feeling that at any moment, everyone around her might break out into song and dance, though she also thought flash mobs were very 2014.

Tell me the deal with ARC, she texted Ryan while she scanned the cosmetics counters.

He replied immediately.

Okay the tea is she tends to pull straight girls. And then kind of discards them when she's done. She leaves a trail of bodies. A TRAIL OF BODIES. OMG tell me how the interview went!!!!!!!!

The text made Lola freeze in the middle of the floor. A shopper bumped into her and gave her a dirty look.

She could see how easily it might happen, straight girls falling for Aly. You did not have to be gay to see her appeal.

She couldn't find the perfume, and an interaction with a sales associate would just be awkward. She knew she'd come on too strong in her current supercharged state. She left Bloomingdale's empty-handed, mulling over Ryan's text.

It was a short walk from the department store to her apartment, the perfect amount of time to call her manager and then get off the phone, but she just wasn't in the mood to talk about business. She wanted to talk about whether it was possible for a perfume to mix with someone's natural scent.

She shook off the daydream and tried to bring herself back to earth.

She dialed Todd's number and looked at the clouds while it rang and rang.

Todd had swooped in when Lola was twenty-two and just starting to get real attention. Because *he* had found *her*, Lola had never been able to shake the feeling that she owed him her career, though for the past few years, he'd admittedly just been riding her coattails, collecting his 10 percent. Ryan—who moonlit unofficially as her career coach—sometimes urged Lola to find new representation. After a few years in fashion PR, he knew his way around influencers and their various teams of managers, agents, and lawyers. He thought Lola should have the best of each, and while Lola appreciated this sentiment, she was also a creature of habit. Todd already knew her, and she knew him, and that familiarity counted.

"Lola," Todd answered finally. "Tell me how it went."

"Good, I think," she said. "She doesn't seem to think the lesbian-chic thing was a big deal at all. She seemed much more interested in *me*, actually. She asked a lot of personal questions, wanted to know my backstory."

"Great to hear," Todd said. "And she just emailed the team to say *The Cut* accepted the pitch, which is perfect. Hopefully we'll get a nice juicy profile out of her."

The Cut made Lola a little sweaty—those girls could be so, well, cutting. But she trusted Todd. This affected everyone's livelihood after all.

"When do you think it'll come out?"

"She's fast," Todd said. "And this has a news hook, for better or worse. By the end of this week would be my guess."

Lola thanked him for setting it up. He promised to let her know if he heard anything else.

After she hung up, she walked by a large, gold-framed mirror that had been brought to the curb and paused, looking at her reflection. Her dress was billowing in the hot breeze, and her hair floated dreamily around her head. Her fingers itched to take a selfie. This outfit was too good not to go on her grid, especially if she could get the angle right in this mirror with the city in the background.

Instead, reluctantly, she kept moving. Her team had told her not to post until everything blew over. She was especially not supposed to post anything that seemed superficial—which, she realized as she tried to think of what might work, was basically everything she ever put on her feed these days, save for the occasional inspirational quote.

She imagined Aly looking at her Instagram and cringed. She didn't know why she was so desperate for ARC's approval. She'd been doing just fine without it. But also, she did know why she wanted it. The problem was she didn't know what to *do* with it. So she put it in a little box in the back of her mind and closed the lid. There were a few such boxes collecting dust back there, and it had never really been a problem before.

When she got home, it was just after 2:00 p.m. She heard the sounds of Justin in the shower—the running water and his adorable belting. Like always, he'd left the bathroom door ajar. That was how Justin was, all open doors. Nothing to hide. No little boxes tucked away for him. Always—even without words—inviting her in.

It wasn't a surprise that Justin was home on a Monday afternoon. He had probably just woken up, since he worked night shifts at Mount Sinai, a rite of passage for young doctors going through residency. Lola was a different kind of night owl. After he left to go save lives, kissing her through her LED light therapy mask, she liked to go out, bouncing from party to party in glamorous, gifted couture, making appearances at trendy events around the city. She didn't mind being out late and sleeping in the next morning; she didn't have a schedule, and she didn't really need one. Schedules were for people still trying to make it. She didn't need alarms anymore.

Justin was only home one or two nights a week, during which she was usually glued to him while they cooked dinner, watched TV, and went to bed.

It was a sweet ritual, but one or two nights a week was the most she could stand to hide away. Any more than that, and she'd go stir-crazy.

She kicked her flats off—Justin hated when she wore her shoes inside—and went into the chaotic cave that served as her office, which felt smaller every day. There were clothing racks loaded with ruffled gowns and long coats, Louis Vuitton Takashi Murakami bags in Perspex display boxes, bedazzled water bottles, Chanel-branded skis, a box of Venus et Fleur forever flowers that spelled out *LOLA*, and a stack of terribly uncomfortable gifted shoes from Net-A-Porter still in their boxes, unworn. In all likelihood, she'd probably just end up giving them to Ryan for his lucrative side hustle reselling freebies on The RealReal.

Unless of course no one ever sent her anything again after she'd ruined her career.

No, she thought, shaking it away. *That's what the Aly interview is for. Everything will be back to normal in no time.*

She stepped farther into the office, wading through the mess.

She had painted three of the walls pink and covered the fourth in floral wallpaper. The space was lit with a vintage crystal chandelier she'd found at a flea market in Paris, a treasure that had cost her more to ship than to buy. She thought the piece deserved to be in the living room, but it was too gaudy for Justin's taste.

Against one of the walls, a bookcase spilled over with self-help books, like *The 5 AM Club* and *Outliers*. She often got *very* into whatever kinds of ideas were being offered in each new book she tried but, because she could also never manage to finish any, would abandon the dogma after a few weeks and move on to the next.

There was *some* order to the space. One corner was devoted to the prototypes of her various brand collaborations—the Lola for Rêver robes and the branded razors with her name on them and, more importantly, a series of gorgeous, gauzy maxi dresses she helped design for Shopbop. The Lola Likes Dresses line was the partnership she was most excited about, and she wished she could have mentioned them to Aly Ray Carter. It was the only thing she'd actually designed, the only work that spoke to her passion. But she was still under an NDA while they ironed out the deals. It would be announced at the end of summer, just in time for New York Fashion Week.

In the center of the room was the pile of barely there DÔEN beach dresses, straw hats, Monday Swimwear bikinis, and strappy sandals she was saving for Capri. She was going for a kind of *White Lotus* season two vibe, inspired by the wardrobes of the girls who played the sex workers more than the show's resort guests.

Someday, she thought, looking around at all her things, she'd turn this room into a well-organized Carrie Bradshaw fantasy closet. But that day was not today. Nor was tomorrow, for that matter. And maybe not the day after that either.

The mess in her office was the exception; the rest of their apartment was immaculate. Justin was a clean freak, something Lola loved about him, and she did her best to abide by his many rules. After all, mess stressed him out more than cleanliness stressed *her* out, so it only seemed fair. She was fine to compromise, to keep her things hidden away in her own space where they wouldn't bother him.

Justin's own spotless office, on the other side of the apartment, was filled with top-of-the-line workout equipment, though he preferred going to Barry's or playing pickleball. He was, in fact, down to try just about any workout—he'd once gone to Pilates with Lola as a joke and fell in love with it (she, on the other hand, never went back).

The effort showed. His body was a work of art, and at six foot four, he basically looked like the statue of an ideal man—broad shoulders, washboard abs, biceps larger than Lola's head, and hardly any body hair. If he wanted to, he could have had a lucrative career as a menswear model, but he wasn't vain enough to have considered it. He dressed well too; he had a closet full of pressed and tailored Armani suits, plus a healthy collection of pieces from Bode and Ralph Lauren. Everything about him was refined and cool, including his attitude—he was easy. If he was ever in a bad mood, he'd simply go to the gym and take it out on the bench press. Lola was the moody one, something she hated about herself—she could never predict when her dark and stormy emotions would hit. Justin didn't seem to mind, though, and in turn she appreciated how simple it was to please him. There was no mystery to Justin, and that was comforting.

She smiled to herself, thinking of Justin's chiseled body in the shower. Come to think of it, she could use a shower too. Aly Ray Carter had really made her sweat. Or maybe it was just the New York City heat. She stepped out of her dress, tossing it into her dry-cleaning pile, and slid out of her thong. She made a small noise of relief as she unhooked her bra and threw it onto the back of her desk chair.

She was totally naked as she walked down the hall toward the bathroom, her feet hardly making a sound on the original hardwood floor. She floated past the framed photos of Justin's annual family vacations to Mauna Kea for Christmas. He had taken it upon himself to hang the photos on the wall, and as a result, Lola didn't have as many of her family on display, but that was okay with her. Jeanette and Roger were creatives through and through, happier behind the camera than in front of it.

The bathroom was filled with dense, fragrant steam.

"Hi," she said, getting into the white marble shower. Justin's soap smelled like amber and sea salt.

"Well, hi, yourself." He grinned, that warm, easy smile she loved so much. He dropped his loofah to the ground and wrapped his arms around her. "How'd the interview go?"

"Like, so good," she said, trying to sound convincing while smiling as his hands grazed her back. "I think we really hit it off. Hopefully the piece will come out this week, and then I can start posting again without everyone yelling at me."

"I'm so happy to hear it," he said, and she knew he meant it; Justin was as invested in her success as she was.

"How are you?" she asked.

"Better now. I was worried I wouldn't get to see you before I leave."

"Oh, fuck, your LA trip," she said. She'd completely forgotten. "I can't believe that's already this week."

Justin was taking a red-eye to LA to attend USC's graduation. He was being honored with an award for all the scholarship money he'd raised. She would have gone with him, but there'd been so much chaos surrounding her social media drama that he'd told her it was okay to skip it.

He laughed, but she could tell he was a little annoyed. "How do you forget something like that?"

"You know me," she sighed. "Just in my own little world."

"You do have a lot going on," he conceded, his tone nicer, always so quick to forgive. "It's fine. Just don't forget about the other trip this summer."

She gasped, feigning shocked. "I could never forget Capri."

"Oh yeah? When do we leave?"

"July…second?" she guessed, emphasizing her upspeak to sound cute. The truth was she had no idea.

He laughed. "My gorgeous little space cadet. I'll put it in your calendar."

"Thank you," she said.

She stood on her tiptoes as they kissed under the rainfall shower-head, the hot water mixing in their mouths. Not for the first time that day, she wondered what it would be like to kiss someone shorter than her. To have the other person lift on their tiptoes. *Her* tiptoes even. The thought turned her on, and with Justin naked in front of her, it was easy to imagine that he was the one responsible for her arousal. She bit his lower lip, ran her hands along his biceps, touched the well-defined six-pack that she knew would be there regardless of his lifelong commitment to sit-ups.

"Oh really?" he said.

She felt him grow hard against her. "Mm-hmm," she said.

His big, strong hand slid between her legs. "Fuck, you're so wet," he said.

She laughed into his mouth. "I've wanted you all day."

This was, perhaps, not *exactly* true, but she wanted him at that moment, and that was what mattered.

She always thought that people in long-term relationships would, at a certain point, stop wanting to fuck all the time. But that point had never really happened for Lola and Justin. They were both, it seemed, perpetually horny for each other. She couldn't blame herself: Justin was, for all intents and purposes, the most attractive man she'd ever seen. Most days, she couldn't believe she was his.

He lifted her arm up and smelled her armpit. "Lola stinks," he teased. "Let's get you clean first."

Justin's eternal, obsessive cleanliness was only mildly annoying because it meant that he wanted to be the one to wash her.

When they got out of the shower, after he'd lovingly scrubbed every inch of her, Justin picked Lola up and carried her to the bedroom.

She squealed as he threw her onto the California king bed.

He crawled up her body, pausing to worship her ankles and her hip bones, her belly button, and her nipples, until his mouth met hers and she pulled him inside her, letting out a gasp. That first moment of penetration was always intense, especially since her decade-long commitment to birth control meant they hadn't used a condom since their first few encounters. She'd never had unprotected sex before him, and it still felt like a forbidden pleasure.

She usually loved the feel of his substantial body weight on her while they had sex, but it wasn't what she wanted at that moment. She wanted more control, more freedom. She felt a little smothered, couldn't move as freely as she wanted with him looming over her. She pushed him to the side and got on top, straddling him and arching backward.

His eyes rolled back in his head as he let out a series of curses. She loved making him groan. He put his hands on her hips, trying to control her speed, but she moved them up to her breasts. She wanted to set the pace.

She started rubbing her clit.

"Let me do that," Justin said, his voice husky, pupils flooded. But she stopped him.

"No," she said. "I want to."

"Fuck," he groaned, laughing. Despite his offer, she knew he loved watching her, especially while he was inside her. And Lola loved being watched—loved the feel of his admiration across her skin, his focus locking on her fingers as they moved, faster, tighter around her clit. It was one of the many ways they were perfect for each other.

"Fuck," Justin said again, his breathing getting louder. "You're so fucking hot."

He didn't necessarily speak poetry while fucking her, but that was okay. She cared more about the way he touched her than what he said to her, how his body felt against hers. And it felt good. It always did.

There was a chest under the bed filled to the brim with restraints, vibrators, even a cute little flogger. They'd tried it all. They'd licked chocolate off each other, role-played as gruff handyman and bored housewife, taken turns being blindfolded, masturbated while staring deeply into each other's eyes. And while it was always fun to try new things together—they made each other laugh as often as they made each other orgasm—they both agreed that there was nothing better than the simplicity of skin on skin, no accessories required.

"Lola, please," Justin said, moving his hands down her body and finding her hips.

"Fine," she said, as though she didn't love when he took control.

He smirked as he pushed himself deeper into her, faster now, more urgent.

Her eyes were glazed now, appreciating the way his muscles rippled below her, but she was also thinking of someone else: smug smile, Tom Ford sunglasses.

None other than Aly Ray Carter.

Maybe not the sunglasses, she thought. The Aly in her head—Fantasy Aly—wasn't wearing more than the T-shirt she'd had on this morning. Even her shiny, brown hair was free of its claw clip.

Fantasy Aly was looking at Lola with a kind of unbridled desperation. *Please let me go down on you*, she could hear Aly begging. *Please. Lola, I'll die if I don't taste you.*

She imagined resisting. *We can't*, she said to Fantasy Aly. *I have a boyfriend. I love him.*

I don't care, Fantasy Aly said. *I've never wanted anyone so badly in my life.*

Fine. She pictured giving in. *If you really need to. But be quick.*

I do need to. I need you.

She imagined feigning modesty as she opened her legs and allowed Fantasy Aly's pink tongue to push gently into her clit.

She imagined…nothing else after that. She started to come, and her thoughts turned blank. She couldn't even hear how loudly she was chanting "Oh my god, oh my god, oh my god."

Her orgasm felt like being launched into zero gravity. The most intense heat followed by nothingness. Infinity. Floating. She collapsed on top of Justin and then rolled to the side, trying to catch her breath.

"Wait," Justin said, laughing. "I'm not done yet."

It was true; he was still hard. She shot him a wicked grin. "Oh, I am *so sorry,*" she said. "How can I make it up to you, babe? Do you want to come on my tits?"

That was, in fact, exactly what he wanted to do.

When at last they were both finished, Justin fell asleep with his face pressed into her neck. He'd always been an easy sleeper. She knew he'd pop out of bed in exactly thirty minutes, pull on clean Moncler sweats, and make a protein smoothie while he packed for LA. She loved his rituals, his predictability.

Meanwhile, Lola stared at the ceiling, her Aly fantasy idly continuing. While she knew exactly what Justin would do next, she had no idea what Fantasy Aly would.

Lola had never told anyone how often she thought of women during sex. She was not ashamed of this habit—she just didn't think it mattered because it didn't mean she wanted to fuck men any less. And she loved fucking men. She always had, ever since she lost her virginity to Benson Campbell at his family's Malibu beach house when she was seventeen.

She and Benson didn't go to the same high school, but their parents had been industry friends, so for as long as Lola could remember, her family had an open invitation to the Campbell "cottage," the cute way they referred to the ten-million-dollar summer mansion. During those long, hot, adolescent days in Malibu, things between them were platonic and innocent; they would play beach volleyball and tan and go to Malibu Yogurt. But the summer before their senior year, something unnameable changed between Benson and Lola, a sudden spark that hadn't been there before. She couldn't ignore how cute he'd become. They spent August exchanging lingering glances. Finally, in September, Benson invited her out to the beach house when no one else would be there, and she eagerly agreed. They were in the hot tub discussing what movie to watch when he kissed her.

They soon fell into bed, and while it wasn't very romantic, it still felt safe and special, which was what she'd wanted out of a first time. Better still was the discovery that Lola loved having sex—how it made her feel so feminine yet animalistic, like she could really be herself, wanting what she wanted without apologizing for it.

She couldn't wait to do it again with all the guys she'd meet in college.

That was part of the reason she and Ryan had become so close at Parsons: they were both boy crazy. One of their favorite things to do was exchange phones and take turns on each other's apps; Lola would swipe through his Grindr, and he'd swipe through her Raya, which she'd finally gotten off the wait list for once her blog took off. There was nothing they wouldn't do for each other, no boundaries between them. Once, sophomore year, he'd helped her bleach her asshole. They were still sending each other their nudes for approval.

And then came Justin.

Justin was the only boyfriend who'd ever met Lola's parents, who'd come over Christmas Eve and seen the bungalow she grew up in, with its built-in bookshelves overflowing with hardcover classics, everything cozy with warm light and cooking smells and cashmere throw blankets. He'd stayed with her in her childhood bedroom, the walls still covered in pages ripped from fashion magazines. They'd had sex in that little bed, pretending they were in high school, trying hard to be quiet while her parents watched a movie downstairs. The memory made Lola blush.

No, she thought—her body still pulsing from the orgasm she'd had while Justin was inside her—*thinking about women is completely beside the point.*

Still pressed against her, Justin started to snore. She untangled herself from him and threw on a pink Lola for Rêver robe, then tiptoed to the kitchen to retrieve a coconut LaCroix from the fridge.

She flopped onto their cream boucle Rove Concepts sofa, cold seltzer in hand, and stretched her legs onto their new cement coffee table. The living room furniture was not necessarily comfortable, but it definitely photographed well, especially since it was styled with a copy of *Chanel: The Impossible Collection* and a hand-blown glass vase that she always made sure was full of fresh flowers from the overflowing buckets in the flower district.

She loved their space, with its floor-to-ceiling windows looking out over Soho, though if it were up to Lola, it would all be drowned in patterns and colors and textures, tapestries on the wall and Moroccan rugs on the floor and fuzzy throw pillows on *everything*, more bohemian kaleidoscope than minimalist restraint.

But partnership was about compromise. The walls remained white, crisp, and clean. In exchange for giving up her ideal interior design,

Lola got to live with someone who cared deeply about her. It seemed like a fine trade-off.

The afternoon sunlight was casting a golden glow on Lola's already tan skin. Soon, after enough days in the summer sun, all the hair on her body (well, the hair on her body that she permitted to stay) would turn white blond, making her feel like a beach goddess.

She checked her phone and realized she hadn't texted Ryan back yet.

She ignored what he'd said about a trail of bodies. She didn't want to think about the many straight women who had fallen under Aly's spell.

The interview was amazing, she texted him. **I, like, love her? She was kind of mean to me but in like a refreshing way. I don't know. Like she was really seeing me. I just have a really good feeling about it.**

He sent back a series of hearts and then: **Babes are you coming to the Violet Grey event tonight? Would make me look good to get a photo of you there.**

She paused, considering it. Ryan had rented out Cervo's, a dimly lit Portuguese-Spanish restaurant in Dimes Square, which meant the party would be incredibly fashionable *and* have great food. She'd been looking forward to it—she'd even asked to borrow an outfit from Collina Strada for the evening, which sat in a garment bag in her office. But despite all that, she was still scared to be seen in public, what with her scandal still trending.

I really want to, but I think I need to lie low until ARC saves my reputation.

Understood, he wrote with another series of hearts. **Ok can't talk, getting face frozen in time.**

Everything would go back to normal soon, she knew. All she had to do was hang out and wait until Aly's piece came out. In the meantime, she was content to think back on their conversation, on the energy that had buzzed between them, and on the way Aly's hand felt in hers when they shook goodbye.

———————

Lola was still lying on the couch when Justin emerged from the bedroom.

"Do you have to pack?" she called to him.

"I did already." He smiled at her, and then he went to the fridge and started tossing food on the sparkling black marble island. "You hungry, babe?"

Justin had recently gotten into gourmet cooking—or at least into coming home with $500 worth of meat and cheese from Eataly and upgrading all the appliances so that everything was professional grade, complete with Le Creuset pieces in sage. Of all the hobbies Justin had tried out, this was the one she found the sexiest. Lola hated cooking, but she *loved* eating.

"Starving," she said, her mouth already watering. "Tell me it's steak." Steak was her favorite food, though she also felt deeply conflicted about animal cruelty. She often said she was a vegetarian in spirit, not in practice.

"It's steak."

"God, I love you." She made her way to the kitchen and planted herself on one of the island's barstools, swinging her legs as she watched him prep dinner. "Can I do anything?"

He laughed while shaking his head. "Please don't. You'll just mess it up."

There was no point in pretending that this hurt her feelings. He was right. Instead, she pulled up Spotify and started playing their joint playlist through the surround sound while Justin put some potatoes in the oven.

He started chopping vegetables for a salad, pausing at one point to toss a cucumber to her. She tried to catch it in her mouth, and instead it bounced off her nose.

"Try again," she said.

They spent a few minutes like this, Justin softly lobbing radishes, carrots, and peas at Lola's face, none of which went into her mouth. A pile of vegetables was forming on the ground around her. She was laughing so hard that tears leaked out of the corners of her eyes. The harder she laughed, the more determined Justin became.

When a tomato hit her in the eye, he said, "We need to work on your technique."

"All right, coach," she said.

"But you're benched for now. There's more salad on the floor than the cutting board."

She crouched down and started picking up the vegetables. Thanks to Justin's insistence that they always wear house slippers, the floor was probably clean enough to eat off of, but she took the veggies over to the trash anyway.

Keeping the floors—and everything else—clean was a major theme in their relationship. One of their only ongoing disagreements was over whether to get a cat. Lola desperately wanted one; Justin couldn't deal with the potential cat hair and litter-box smells. She respected his wishes enough to not just come home with a kitten, and so far the floors remained pristine.

"How was your day?" she asked when everything was clean again. "I mean night?"

"It was pretty quiet," he said as he sizzled butter in a pan before dropping the raw steak into it, dousing it in herbs. "A couple of really sick kids, but nothing too horrible."

She appreciated that he was vague when describing the horrors he saw at work. She didn't have the stomach to hear details, and he knew it. He was always looking out for her in little ways like this, sparing her from the information that would haunt her.

He continued, "Now that it's nice out, I bet things will pick up. Everyone goes so hard in the summer."

"Except me," Lola said, stretching her arms over her head. "In the summer, I become a sloth."

"A beautiful sloth," he said as he checked on the potatoes in the oven. "Oh, and my mom called. She says hi and that she's sad you're not coming home with me this week."

Lola bristled, annoyed at the secondhand guilt trip. "What did you tell her?"

"I told her to meet us in Capri if she wants to see you so badly."

Lola laughed, though she also felt some trepidation. Meeting them in Italy on a whim was exactly the kind of thing Justin's parents would do. Not that she didn't love them, but sometimes a girl just wanted a sexy vacation with her boyfriend, even if she couldn't remember the exact dates of their trip.

"My car to JFK comes in an hour," he said, checking his watch. "I think I timed this perfectly." They high-fived.

Justin carefully made their plates: a perfect piece of steak, a glistening pile of roasted potatoes, and a green salad with homemade dressing. She poured two large glasses of Bordeaux and lit a candle.

When they sat down to eat, their feet touching under the table, Justin made her taste it first. "Watching you eat my food is the best part," he said.

She beamed at him with her mouth full, a little bit of grease trickling down her lip.

They'd started dating because of their chemistry, but they'd stayed together for half a decade because of simple, sweet little moments like these. She knew it was rare, what they had—how easy it was, how loving they were.

She wished she could freeze time, stay in this moment, not change a thing. But she couldn't. All she could do was look forward.

But everything was going to be okay. How could it not? She had the love of her life with her. Her career was about to be saved by a splashy profile for the whole world to see. She wasn't sure what more she could possibly want.

Chapter 3

THE CUT

June 9, 2024

Lola Is Fine. And That's The Problem.

How the influencer economy is causing a cultural blandification.

By Aly Ray Carter

THERE ARE TWO types of people: those who have been following Lola Fine, aka @lolalikes, since she was a scrappy Parsons student claiming you could turn your Target T-shirt into the Row, and those who just heard about her a few days ago when she asked her gay best friend if a suit made her look "too lesbian chic" in front of an audience of five million.

It was the lesbian chic heard 'round the world.

The pile-on was predictable, instantaneous, and if we're being honest, a little bit tired. It made me wonder if people online have simply run out of things to yell about. Because she didn't really say anything wrong, did she? Lesbian chic is not—as she herself insisted in the moments after uttering the phrase—an inherently problematic idea. It's just specific.

I spent time with Lola earlier this week, and after our conversation, I really don't believe she meant to be offensive. In fact, I don't believe she was thinking much at all.

See, the problem with Lola is not that she's homophobic. She's not. The problem is that she's not really anything.

And this is perhaps the issue with all these influencers who started out with a strong personal brand and eventually turned into shills for other bigger brands—they not only lose the reasons you started following them in the first place, but I think they lose their sense of selves. Which is much sadder.

Lola has (or had?) the potential to be something special. Maybe it was too many million-dollar deals or too much free stuff, but somewhere along the way, she became hollow.

She's someone who wanted to be a designer, who has a keen eye for vintage, and who once believed in the power of mending versus buying new but who now chooses to only post about the clothes she gets sent for free and the brands paying her to talk about them. She makes three million dollars a year, according to *Forbes*, but she doesn't appear to support any causes other than her own expensive lifestyle. She watches girl-on-girl porn (yes, she told me that) but insists that she's straight.

She's the most boring version of herself. And I don't blame her: I blame the ecosystem.

You'd think that someone with five million followers would be amazing, that if that many people cling to her every post, she'd have unique takes, her own impossible-to-replicate aesthetic, or just something original going on in any respect. But that's not the world we live in: the algorithm doesn't want its biggest stars to be different. On the contrary, it encourages a kind of blandification. And Lola Fine, with her perfect blond hair and enviable body and wardrobe straight out of an advertorial for Coachella, is the product of it. She might as well be AI. Even in person, she speaks the language of social media (at one point, without a hint of irony, she mentioned she'd never been a "W-2 girlie").

We can't fault poor Lola for being like this, just like we can't fault her for accidentally borrowing a phrase from the queer community. It seems she's lost the ability to be able to tell where she ends and her audience begins. She's so in the moment that she's not even thinking seriously about her relationship, though she's been with the same man for five years. She is, after all, nothing but the sum total of what people want to look at, who people want to hear from. She represents all of us and none of us at the same time.

And in that role, she's perfectly fine. She just keeps posting her oat milk lattes and her Miu Miu flats and the sun setting over Soho, and we keep consuming what she tells us to.

The ultimate question is not should we cancel Lola for saying something we didn't like? No. What we should be asking is this: In a world where fashion has supposedly been democratized, is Lola Fine really the best we can do?

To support independent journalism, subscribe to *New York Magazine*.

Chapter 4

#BLANDIFICATION HAD BEEN trending for twenty-four hours when Lola decided getting out of bed was no longer worth it.

With Justin still in LA, her bedroom had become a graveyard of Dim Sum Go Go containers and empty Avaline wine bottles. The curtains stayed closed. The only light she wanted to see was from her phone, which she couldn't look away from while she festered in her Free City sweatpants.

The backlash was relentless.

On TikTok, a teenager gripping a mini microphone in front of a green screen screeched, "This is why we should *all* be anti-blandification!"

Another recited a list: "Here are the five blandest influencers I'm unfollowing this week."

Someone else made a video called "A day in the life of a W-2 Girlie."

Another video called for the death of everything Lola had

recommended to them over the years—Saint James iced tea, DÔEN dresses, Onitsuka Tigers sneakers.

Someone else dueted with the video and staged a funeral, dropping products into a hole in the ground.

"Miu Miu flats are dead," the girl in the video said solemnly. "May they rest in peace."

Time started to lose its meaning. Lola slept when she was tired. She woke up when she couldn't deal with the nightmares anymore. She went back to sleep when the nightmare of being awake became too much.

On Instagram, people combed through Lola's grid, commenting, *Wow, I never realized how bland this all is.*

And *IS this the best we can do??*

And *Lmao she really does look like AI.*

Her DMs overflowed with nasty comments from girls who, just a week ago, had hounded her for links to buy every last thing she owned.

How quickly they'd turned on her.

On the media side of things, articles were written in response to Aly's and published in well-respected publications like *Vanity Fair* and *The New Yorker*. Lola watched as notable intellectuals engaged with Aly's ideas. Which meant her downfall wasn't just trending—it had become *the discourse.*

Even her parents, who were chronically offline, called and left a voicemail. She couldn't bring herself to listen to it, but the transcription read "Honey, we're worried about you. Call back when you can."

She didn't call them back. She was too ashamed. Their sympathy would not feel good; it would just remind her of how badly she'd failed.

Because Aly, of course, was right. About everything. Lola *had* become bland. She *was* nothing but a corporate shill. She'd lost herself in an ocean of brand deals until there was nothing about her life that really felt like hers. And now the world knew. She knew too. She couldn't lie to herself anymore when the truth was there in print.

And she was alone in it, the shame and the failure. Every choice she'd made had brought her here. She couldn't blame anyone—not even Aly. Aly was just good at her job.

She ignored calls from Justin. She couldn't stand to hear him feel bad for her. Instead she let it go to voicemail and then texted **sorry, napping** or **call you back in a sec**, never following up.

After she'd been in bed for two whole days, there was a knock at the front door before she heard the familiar sound of Ryan letting himself into the apartment. "Lola," he called and then sang, "Lolalala."

"Bedroom," she wailed.

Standing in the doorway, his arms full of Loops Beauty face masks and a fresh bottle of Chopin vodka, he sighed. "Oh, babe. Have we decided to just bed rot through this?"

She put a pillow over her face and groaned into it. "I'm trying to pass away."

He sat at the edge of the bed. "No, you're not. This will be over in three to five business days, tops."

"No, it won't," she said. "Stop being a publicist, and just be my best friend."

She grabbed a mug from the nightstand. It had a dried tea bag in it, which she plucked out and then dropped on the floor. She held the mug out to Ryan, and he dutifully filled it with vodka, a grimace on his face.

"That fucking bitch," he said, taking a sip directly from the bottle. "I can't believe she did this to you."

"Did you see that *blandification* is still trending on Twitter?"

He rolled his eyes. "Babe, no one cares about Twitter."

"Media people do!" she cried.

"Yeah, and who the fuck cares about media people?"

He was trying to get her to laugh with him, but she couldn't.

"Ugh," she said. "I just feel like the whole lesbian-chic thing could have blown over on its own. It was, like, very downtown NYC niche drama. But now it's like…a national emergency. A *national emergency*, Ryan! Soon we're all going to get an Amber Alert on our phones about it."

He tilted his head to the side. "Have you been abducted?"

"I wish!" She put the pillow back over her face.

"Do you want to do a face mask?"

"Okay," she said meekly into the pillow.

They were sitting next to each other in bed, face masks on, watching *Love Is Blind* on Lola's laptop when Lola's phone pinged. She reached for it, but Ryan snatched it away.

"Let me look," he said. His face fell.

"Oh god," she said. "Just tell me."

"It's Delaney Summers."

Lola braced herself.

"She says… Fuck, are you sure you want to hear this?" Lola nodded, and he continued. "She says, 'Thanks a lot, Lola. I was about to close on a deal with Athletic Greens and they just told my team they're looking for someone less bland.'"

"I want to change my name and move to Japan," Lola said.

"Unfortunately, I do think they know who you are in Japan. You have another one. Do you want me to read it?"

"Just tell me everything."

"'Hi Lola. I was going to buy a house for my aging parents with the money I was making from my Amazon storefront, but no one has gone to it ever since I got put on a list of the most boring influencers.'"

Lola started to cry. She didn't hold back; she just sobbed into her hands until she got hiccups.

It was bad enough people were coming for *her*, but these messages meant the discourse was impacting influencers across the industry too—girls who were her friends, or at least girls she was friendly with. Everyone was being trolled, put under the microscope, criticized using this new filter Aly had designed. Lola could *almost* handle being the sole recipient of the internet's rage. But the fact that she'd brought this storm down on everyone? That was unforgiveable.

"I should stop. This is too much. I'm sorry, Lola."

"No," she said between sobs. "I need to know what they're saying."

They were all mostly the same, though—influencers who had come to yell at her as though she'd done any of this on purpose.

She fell asleep with her head on Ryan's shoulder.

When she woke up, it was 3:00 a.m., and he was gone.

She grabbed her phone, swiping past the hundreds of alerts that crowded her home screen, and then without thinking twice, she deactivated her Twitter. It hadn't ever brought in any money anyway.

"Fuck you, Elon," she whispered.

She got a carton of vanilla ice cream from the freezer. She took it back to bed and ate the whole thing before falling back asleep. The empty container slipped out of her hands and fell to the floor, next to the dried tea bag.

Can I do anything? Justin texted. **I'm so sorry I'm not there.**

It was morning—or at least, morning for some people. For Lola, it was just another moment in one long endless horrible day.

No, she said.

I love you, he sent. I'll be back in a few days.

Thanks, she replied and pulled the covers over her face.

He texted back a question mark, and she ignored it.

He texted again: Are you mad at me?

No. Just want to die.

Please don't die, he replied. I need you.

She didn't know what to say.

She was grieving the death of her reputation but had skipped the denial phase. She was in complete acceptance.

She wondered if all this would feel as bad if it had been written by a journalist she didn't want to impress. But she really respected Aly. She'd thought they hit it off. She'd thought they *liked* each other, could maybe even become friends. She'd even thought of Aly with Justin inside her. And Aly had turned around and said the most hurtful things she possibly could. It was one thing to call her out to her face. It was another thing to declare it to the world.

Though Aly was right that Lola had lost her sense of self. She tried to remember the last time she felt truly alive, in love with what she had. It had been years. It maybe hadn't been since the beginning of her relationship with Justin, back when she was still making her own clothes and doing her own styling. She had been making maybe an eighth of the money she made this year, but it had been more fun, hadn't it? Hadn't she loved digging through thrift-store bins to find the perfect pieces, refurbishing them, getting to share photos of her creations with equally passionate people online? How had she let all that slip away? Did money really matter that much to her? It was a horrifying thing to realize.

Meanwhile, Justin texted her updates from LA. His parents said hi, his sisters said hi, his friends from high school that hadn't known

Lola's name back then said hi. He sent her pictures of palm trees and avocados and the beach. She replied with hearts, unable to muster enthusiasm for the familiar scenes of home but not wanting to hurt his feelings more than she already had.

Soon enough, Justin stopped asking her if there was anything he could do, which was a relief. There was nothing he could do. There was nothing anyone could do.

One evening while she and Ryan watched *Real Housewives of Salt Lake City* during his now-daily post-work "Lola-life-crisis-time," Lola joked, "What if I did a 'get ready with me' about getting canceled?"

He laughed.

"Or!" she said. "A day in the life of a *cancelita*. And it's just me in pajamas crying."

Ryan laughed again but then furrowed his brow.

"I don't think you should do that," he said.

"I was kidding," she whined, switching the TV to *Girls*, a scene of Hannah and Elijah doing cocaine before clubbing filling her laptop screen.

"That's so us, babe," Ryan sighed fondly.

"It used to be us," Lola said. "Now we live in bed."

"*You* live in bed," Ryan corrected. "When I leave here, I have a whole entire life."

He was just joking, but her eyes filled with tears. "What's that like?" she whispered.

Before he could answer, her phone started ringing, startling them both with its loud buzz on her nightstand. "Jesus Christ," Ryan said.

She looked at the screen. "Fuck, it's Todd."

"Answer it!"

"You answer it." She put the phone in Ryan's hand.

He answered but then gave it back to her. She sighed and held it up to her ear.

"Hi, Todd," she said in a voice so pathetic, she should have felt embarrassed, but instead she felt nothing. She was becoming numb to her own tragedy.

She should have known better than to assume this was the worst it was going to get.

"Lola," he said, as brusque and businesslike as ever. He did not say *how are you?* He also did not say *this is not a big deal.* Instead, he said, "We need to talk."

"Okay." She put him on speakerphone so Ryan could hear.

"I just got off the phone with Shopbop."

Fuck, she mouthed at Ryan, whose eyes went wide.

A call with Shopbop could only be about one thing: the Lola Likes Dresses contract. The thing she was the most proud of, the first line of clothing she'd ever helped design. The deal that was supposed to bring her back to her original goals of becoming a designer.

"They've decided to put the project on permanent pause."

Ryan grabbed the Chopin and started chugging it.

"What the fuck does 'permanent pause' mean?" Lola cried.

"It means they adore you, but they don't think you can move product."

"What?" She was yelling now. "Of course I can *move product.* That's my whole fucking thing!"

"It *was* your thing," Todd corrected. "And you were great at it. You had your followers eating out of the palm of your hand. Those girls would buy whatever you told them to."

"But now?" Lola asked, though she knew the answer.

"And now, I hate to say it, but you've lost your audience's trust," he sighed. "They want to be told what's cool, not what's…" He trailed off.

"Bland," she said flatly.

"Right. Not what's bland or basic or boring, whatever you want to call it. And you know, Shopbop is very it girl, very new, very now. They want their customers to come to them for things that are interesting."

Tears began pouring down her face before she even registered them. "I'm not interesting enough for fucking *Shopbop*," she sobbed. "I'm not interesting enough to put my name on goddamn *maxi dresses*."

She could hear Todd's uncomfortable breathing through the phone. Ryan squeezed her hand.

"Look, Lola," Todd said. "I've always been honest with you, and I won't stop now."

"Obviously," Ryan mumbled.

Todd continued. "This summer is going to be rough. There aren't going to be a lot of deals. I don't know how useful it is for you to have me hanging around while you ride this out."

Next to her, Ryan's mouth fell open.

"Wait," she said. "Wait, wait, wait." She had broken out into a cold sweat.

"I'm sorry, Lola," Todd said. "I think we should put our working relationship on ice for the time being."

"Todd, what the fuck are you talking about? We've been working together since I was twenty-one. *You* found *me!* You negotiated my first deal. Do you even remember?"

"Of course I remember," he said. His voice softened. "Three posts to your grid for $250 and a pair of Birkenstocks. Man, those were the days. And look at you now! We've made millions together. For a lot of people, that would be enough."

"Enough?" Lola was flabbergasted. Ryan's mouth still hung open. "Enough as in it's over? I should quit because I've made some money?"

"And look," Todd continued, ignoring her, "we might as well get it all out there. I spoke with your agents this morning, and they think it's best if we all take a step back."

Lola was suddenly filled with a rage so blinding, she wasn't sure if she could survive it. She threw her phone with all her might across the room. It dented the wall with a loud thud before falling to the floor.

"You still there, Lola?" Todd's voice sounded tinny and faraway through the speaker. "Talk soon." He hung up.

Ryan leapt to his feet. "That motherfucking traitor," he spat. He began pacing around her bed, muttering to himself. How angry he was on her behalf almost made Lola feel better. Almost.

Ryan grabbed an empty Stanley cup from the floor and filled it with more vodka.

"Can you do me a favor and tell me if my phone is shattered?"

He picked it up and examined it. "Just a cute crack," he said. "Honestly, I'm impressed you made it this long without breaking it. I can't believe you don't have a phone case."

He handed over the cracked phone, and she immediately dialed her publicist, Veronica.

"Good idea," Ryan said while it rang. He splayed across her bed and looked at the ceiling.

"Lola, hey," Veronica said when she picked up on the third ring.

"Todd is *leaving me*," Lola said, barely getting the words out before she began to spiral. Ryan put a hand on her leg.

"He's not leaving you," Veronica said with a heavy sigh, and it struck Lola that Veronica sounded like she was talking to a petulant baby. "You're just on pause."

"Wait," Lola said, the walls closing in on her. "You knew about this?"

Ryan covered his face with his hands.

"Look, Lola," Veronica said. It sounded like she was walking. Where could she possibly be going? What could she be doing that was more important than talking to Lola about the death of her career? "You know I love you, but the fact of the matter is—"

Lola cut her off. "Not you too? *Veronica!* We took mushrooms together at Carolina Herrera Fall/Winter twenty-two! Did it mean nothing to you?"

Ryan stifled a laugh. Lola hit him with her pillow.

"Lola," Veronica said in that same patronizing tone. "You're still my favorite client. We're still friends. I just can't ethically take your money if there isn't going to be work."

Veronica's retainer was $10k per month.

This fucking bitch, Lola thought. And then it hit her.

"It's your fault that all this happened," Lola said, her voice rising. "You were the one who wanted me to do an interview with ARC. *You.* Not me. You set this whole thing up. And now you're abandoning me?"

"It was worth a shot," Veronica said, so matter-of-fact that Lola thought she might barf. There was no apology, no remorse, no taking accountability.

"You know what?" Lola said. "You can't put me on pause if you're fired."

Veronica sighed. "That's really what you want to do?"

"You're the worst publicist *ever*," Lola said. "I'm better off without you."

"If that's your final decision," Veronica replied, and from the way she said it, Lola could tell she was relieved. Lola understood: no one would want to represent her in this state. She had nothing to offer anyone. She hung up the phone and curled into the fetal position.

"Welcome to my flop era," she whispered.

Ryan started to pet her greasy hair but quickly pulled his hand away, barely hiding his disgust. "Babes," he said. He was so drunk now that his words were slurring. "I have to oversee a gallery opening."

"Now?" she wailed. "You have to leave me *now?*"

"You know I would never leave you. But it's a client. It's for work. I gotta go."

She buried her face in the pillow.

"Maybe you could try showering while I'm gone," he gently suggested.

"There's no point," she said.

"Call me if you need me," he said.

"I do need you," she whispered, but he was already gone.

———

It was almost noon when Lola woke up to the sounds of Justin finally getting home from LA: the front door opening and then his suit-case rolling across the floor. In the night, she had pulled all the white Parachute sheets tightly around herself, trying to mummify.

He stood in the doorway, sweat glistening on his skin. "Hi, babe," he said. "I'm here. I'm so sorry I've been gone." His face was full of concern. Then he noticed the state of the room. "Jesus Christ." He whistled, looking at the nest of garbage around the bed. "Lola, are you okay? I tried calling you so many times. Why didn't you pick up? Have you just been here"—he gestured at her mess—"like *this*, this whole time?"

"Everyone dropped me," she wailed. "Todd, Veronica, everyone."

His mouth hung open. "Babe, what?" He perched on the edge of the bed. "Sorry, I'd come closer, but I don't want to get my airplane clothes on the sheets."

She rolled her eyes so hard she nearly saw stars, and then she told him about the phone calls, about Shopbop, about firing Veronica. This was not how she wanted to greet him after he'd been gone for a week. She wanted to leap into his arms and sob into his collarbone. But that kind of affection was reserved for someone who was worth loving. And she didn't feel worth loving, not anymore.

Justin said, "Do you want to call my parents?"

"Why would I want to do that?"

"Because Todd owes them. They've helped him out of way too many messes for him to just drop you like this." He sounded furious on her behalf, which was nice.

"No, thank you, though. I don't think that would help."

"Okay, Lola," he sighed. "I am just so fucking over all this bullshit."

She lifted her head up. "Which bullshit?"

He gestured to the window, at the sprawling city below them. "New York. All these fucking pretentious assholes thinking they can say whatever they want about you. About us."

"You mean Aly Ray Carter?"

"Yeah, I mean Aly Ray goddamn Carter. Like, how dare she? I *hate* her." His hands were balled up into frustrated fists. "Who does she think she is?"

Lola sat all the way up then. "I mean, it's not Aly's fault. She was just doing her job." Lola wasn't sure why she was being put in a position to defend Aly. All this just felt very bad.

Justin was incredulous. "Her *job?* It was her job to say that you don't stand for anything?"

She returned to her fetal position, whispering, "Well, she was right. That's why it's so devastating. She was *right*, Justin. What do I stand for? I'm a nothing."

"Was it also her job to tell the world that you don't take us seriously?"

The reality of Justin's anger slapped her in the face. "Oh my god!" Lola cried. "That's not what I said!"

"Do you have any idea how embarrassing that was for me? For my family?"

She put her face in her hands. This had nothing to do with what Aly said about her and everything to do with what she'd said about *him*—and them as a couple.

"Look, Lola," he said, sounding like he was gearing up for a speech. She braced herself.

"Maybe it's time we leave all this behind."

"Leave all this behind?"

"Maybe we should just go back to LA."

Her heart caught in her throat. She always knew he'd say this to her someday, but she never imagined he'd say it now, like this. She didn't want to hear it. Not yet. Not now. Maybe not ever.

"My parents offered to give us the WeHo house. That means I could take my time looking for a good job, one where I could work during the day. Maybe even open a private practice. We could start over. Have a nicer, easier life, close to family and friends who have known us forever. Don't you want a situation that's a little..." He searched her face. "A little kinder?"

Lola tried her best to remain composed, but she was dangerously close to having a total meltdown. She balled her hands into fists, willing herself to be calm.

If he noticed her reaction, he ignored it. "You're almost thirty. I'm thirty-two. We've been together for five years. I know you told ARC that you don't want to, but I think it's time we start thinking about next steps."

"Next steps?"

"I want to get married," he said plainly. "I want to start a family. You know I do. I've always wanted to. And I don't want to do it here, in this goddamn mess of a city, where we have zero family. We have an out, Lola, a way to leave all this behind and be near people who love us. Why wouldn't we take it? This was always the plan anyway."

She looked at his face. His gorgeous, symmetrical, flawless face. A muscle in his jaw was pulsing. His T-shirt didn't have a single wrinkle in it. He even smelled good. He was still the man of her dreams. But the words coming out of his mouth terrified her.

He said, "Why do you think I went to LA without you?"

"To get an award?"

He shook his head. "To get my grandmother's ring."

Her mouth hung open. "Her *ring*?" she repeated. "Her engagement ring?"

This was not how she imagined a proposal would go.

"I'm tired of our life here," he said. "You know I am. On nights I'm off work, it's all I can do to make dinner and collapse in bed. I'm ready for something new. Something quieter."

She was silent for a long time. She thought about all the signs she'd missed—how burned out he was. How he wanted to stay home with her while she yearned for wild nights. How had she not noticed this growing schism between them?

Was it possible she loved New York City more than she loved him?

No, that wasn't it. She could love them both. She could speed around on her bike and go to glamorous events and still want to come home to him. But marriage? Was it that she just wasn't ready to settle down or that she would never want to? That she just wasn't the type?

"I don't want to leave New York," she whispered.

He stared at her, confused, and then he furrowed his brow. He looked furious. "Why not?" he demanded.

"It was always *your* plan to leave," she said. "Not mine."

"You should have told me if it wasn't what you wanted. All this time, Lola! All this time, I thought we were on the same page about our future."

"I just don't think my time here is over. There's so much I want to do. And I don't think we should get engaged just because you're mad about what some journalist wrote."

"You know that's not the reason."

She sighed. "I'm sorry. I'm just really in my own head right now."

"In your own head?" he repeated. "Lola, you are *never* in your own head. You are so in your body that you've stopped thinking. All you do is eat expensive food and wear beautiful clothes and feel the sun on your skin and have afternoon sex and go to the spa. You haven't intellectualized one damn thing."

She felt her skin flush, nails digging into her palms. *"What?"*

"I'm sorry," he said, backpedaling. "That was way more harsh than I meant it to be. But Aly Ray Carter *was* right about a few things. You've been doing what brands wanted for so long that you don't even know what you want anymore. When I met you, you dreamed of being a fashion designer. Where did that girl go? I never thought you'd want to be an influencer forever. You've lost yourself, Lola. And now I'm giving you a chance to find yourself, and you don't even want to take it?"

She shook her head in disbelief. "Are you trying to neg me into marrying you?"

He threw his hands up in the air. "I'm just trying to be honest with you. I know you're not happy. This isn't living, what we're doing here.

It's an empty existence. You've always known I wanted to go back to LA eventually. I told you the night we reconnected."

The worst part of all this was that he wasn't off base.

Lola *did* feel empty. She *did* feel as though she'd lost herself in a sea of sponsored content and brand partnerships. But was the answer to her problems abandoning her life and becoming Justin's housewife? Popping out a few babies and vanishing into wealth and obscurity? How would that be *finding herself?*

It wouldn't be a terrible way to live, she knew. The WeHo house, which Justin's parents currently used for rental income they didn't need, was a mid-century modern stunner. And it *would* be nice to be close to both of their families.

Maybe she could delete all her social media and live completely off the grid, just a regular civilian, not ruled by the algorithm. Hell, maybe she could even throw her cell phone away and get a landline, something cute and aesthetic, like a pink rotary phone with a curly cord that she could wrap around her wrist while she talked to her mom and wandered around the first floor.

She could start wearing beige linen sack dresses and get really good at braid crowns, learn to grow herbs in their abundant garden and make hummus from scratch and maybe eventually put out a cookbook with a photo of the two of them laughing over salad on the cover. It would be called *Lola Likes Greens*, if the Lola Likes brand wasn't totally dead by then. Maybe Alison Roman could develop the recipes with her. Or maybe she could resist monetizing her new gardening hobby and just be happy to do it, not try to turn it into a publicity opportunity.

And then what?

She imagined having two or three daughters—scheduled C-sections, most likely—and then having to navigate their doctors' appointments and school schedules, their sports practices and music lessons and math tutors, their playdates and the other moms. God, those other moms, with their Land Rovers and their spray tans and the jewelry they'd wear to compete with each other at morning drop-off.

As if Lola would be able to wake up early enough to make morning drop-off.

And where would Justin be during all that? Seeing patients? Doing something that mattered while she still didn't have a purpose?

Her heart was pounding wildly. She had broken out into a cold sweat. She tried to breathe normally, but it was getting harder and harder.

She slipped deeper into her spiral, wondering, what would she even do with herself when the kids were at school. Mend their clothes? Start drinking orange wine with two ice cubes every day at 3:00 p.m. in a big straw hat, staring at the hills?

Cut her hair into a sensible, chin-length bob?

Sign up for a pottery class just to feel something?

She had the urge to flip over all the furniture in the apartment.

She knew that other women would jump at the chance to be kept like this by Justin, to live for free and do nothing but vibe in the sunshine. She wished it were appealing to her—she really did.

But it wasn't appealing. It was nothing short of repulsive.

It felt like admitting defeat.

She had been in Manhattan for over a decade and hadn't become a fashion designer, the one thing she'd set out to do. The one thing she still *wanted* to do.

"Justin," she said, her voice full of all the love in the world. "I don't want to move back to LA. I'm not done here. I need to fix my shit. Just because everyone is giving up on me doesn't mean I'm giving up on myself."

His face fell. "So you don't want to be with me."

"What?" she gasped. "No, I didn't say that."

"If you wanted to be with me, you'd come to LA."

"No, babe," she insisted. "I want to be with you *here*."

But Justin shook his head. "You've always known this is what I wanted to do. If you aren't ready to take the next steps with me, I think we need to reassess."

"Reassess what exactly?" Her heart was hammering in her chest.

"Us," he said, looking at her with huge, sad eyes, as though he already regretted what he hadn't yet said. "Maybe we need to take a break."

It was like getting slapped in the face. "You want to *take a break*? What does that mean exactly?"

"I mean maybe we should spend the summer apart and both think about what we really want—and if what we want is each other or something else. Personally, I think I really need someone who is ready to get married and have kids. Our twenties are over, Lola. It's getting to be that time."

"Not you bringing up my biological clock," she retorted. "I can't believe you just went from wanting to marry me to wanting to take a break. It's really all or nothing for you?"

"I want to spend the summer in LA," he replied. "I got a visiting resident position there. You're welcome to come with me. In fact, I wish you would—but not if you don't want to."

"I can't believe you're so willing to throw all this away," she said.

"I am okay with this life as long as I know it's leading somewhere," he responded, all the fight wrung out of him, and for the first time in this conversation, she realized how sad he sounded. "I love taking care of you, because this whole time I've been thinking that someday you'll be my wife. But if you're not going to be? What is it all for, Lola?"

She couldn't answer. She didn't know how.

He stood up. That was when she noticed it: his suitcases were by the door.

She said, "Wait, you're leaving right now? Did you know you'd be leaving me when you started this conversation?"

"I'm not leaving you," he said. "I had this whole plan to fly in, propose to you, and sweep you off your feet back to LA with me. I thought it would be romantic. But I guess you're not coming."

"What about Capri?" she cried.

"The tickets are refundable." He shrugged. "It's just not the right time for us to go on a romantic vacation. Not when we don't know what we're doing."

"Okay, wait. Define *break*," she said. "Will you be fucking other women? Is that what this is about?"

"I don't want anyone else," he said. "I want *you*. I want you to realize you can't live without me. And I don't think you can do that with me here."

"I already know that," she insisted.

"Sleep with other people if you need to. Personally, I don't." He said it so matter-of-factly, no secret meaning or hidden agenda to unpack. No tricks or *we were on a break* mental gymnastics to maneuver. So simple. So Justin.

And it broke her a little inside.

He walked toward the door. She felt her heart cracking in two, an actual sharp pain in her chest.

"Justin, please," she begged.

He turned and looked at her one last time. "I love you," he said.

"Yeah. I love you too."

He gathered his Louis Vuitton suitcases, tossed his spring jacket over his shoulder. He put his pristine white sneakers on, crouching to tie the laces as tight as they'd go. And then he left.

Lola wanted to cry, but she couldn't. She was too angry.

Chapter 5

LOLA FINALLY FELT ready to take a shower.

It would be an everything shower, she decided. She'd stewed for long enough.

She turned the water on as hot as it would go, trying to scald the week of misery off her skin. She washed her hair twice, the Oribe shampoo sudsing satisfyingly on her scalp, and did a hair mask while she shaved her legs and armpits. She even broke out the body exfoliator for a final polish, scrubbing her elbows and her knees with probably too much force.

She did not think about Justin walking out on her.

She did not think about the horrible-yet-true things Aly wrote about her.

She did not think about Veronica and Todd dropping her, nor of the five million people who had turned from fans to haters in the blink of an eye.

She just focused on the hot water as it pounded down on her, on the fragrant steam that filled the air.

Afterward, her skin so pink it was maybe more raw than fresh, she wrapped herself in the fluffiest white towel she owned and made her way to the kitchen. There, she poured an enormous glass of Chardonnay and took big gulps while she looked around the kitchen and, beyond that, the living room.

It was all just so damn clean. So minimal.

So...*Justin*.

There were no signs that this was her home at all.

She'd compromised and compromised and compromised until she'd made herself so tiny that there was almost nothing left of her other than what she could squeeze into her little office. The rest of their "shared space" just reflected his taste, his preferences, his...everything.

She felt a surge of fury.

How dare he minimize her like this? How dare he leave her after making her so small?

She finished the rest of her wine in one gulp and then dove into her closet and found the shortest, tightest dress she owned—a floral pink Isabel Marant halter—and fastened a huge, studded belt around her waist, channeling Kate Moss at Glastonbury. She put on her highest Larroude wedge sandals. She wanted to be as tall as possible, show as much of her legs as she could. She let her hair dry naturally, the humidity giving it extra volume and body. Then she grabbed a Fendi Baguette from her collection, the one with sequins.

Without skipping a beat, she dug around in her desk drawer until she found an ancient pack of American Spirits that she'd been saving for emergencies. This was indeed an emergency. She stuffed the cigarettes into the Baguette. It was going to be that kind of night.

Finally, she texted Ryan: Meet me at Fanelli's. We're going out.

Lola knew that she looked out of place sitting at the corner table at Fanelli's in Soho, but she didn't care. Surrounded by tourists in fanny packs and mom jeans and baseball hats, she looked like she got lost on her way to a red carpet. She had to assume that was why everyone was staring at her; she did not want to presume that they knew who she was.

When Ryan finally arrived, his eyes grew wide as he slid into the seat across from her. "I didn't realize we were serving cunt this evening."

She grinned. And then as quickly as the smile appeared, it fell. Though she'd left the house angry, having to tell Ryan what happened just felt sad. "Justin dumped me."

He grabbed her hands across the table. "He *what*?"

"Well, not exactly dumped? He wants to take a break. It's all…very unclear to me what is actually happening."

"You better tell me everything," he said.

They had each polished off their second martini by the time Lola finished giving Ryan a detailed play-by-play of her conversation with Justin.

"I'm so sorry, babes," he said. "These drinks really aren't cutting it, huh?"

When the third round came, they clinked their glasses. "To having no future and no one to love me," Lola declared.

"I will absolutely not drink to that," Ryan said. "To starting fresh."

"To being the queen of the bland. Captain Blandet. Cate Blandett?" She was drunk now. Lola always found herself to be very funny after three drinks. She could tell, though, that Ryan was losing his patience. "Okay, okay, enough about all this shit. Tell me about *your* day."

"I was wondering when we'd get to me." He grinned. "So I started talking to this guy named Emmett who's going to be out east for the summer too."

Lola squealed. "Show me right now."

He pulled up Grindr and showed her a photo of a torso so toned and hairless, it almost looked fake.

"Jesus Christ," she gasped. "Does he have a face?"

"Who cares?"

"True," Lola said and then looked around them. She wondered if there was a set of abs here, waiting for her.

But everything was off about the restaurant: the lighting too bright, the conversations too loud, the waitstaff too cheery. It wasn't what she wanted. She wanted to be somewhere dark and sexy. Anonymous.

"I want to go *out*," Lola said. "Like we used to."

"The sun hasn't even set yet," Ryan laughed. "Plus, I leave for the Hamptons tomorrow morning. I don't want to be hungover and in traffic on the Long Island Expressway. That's my personal hellscape."

"I can't believe you're leaving tomorrow," she whined. "Don't you want to have one more night out with me before you go?"

"I'm going to East Hampton, not *dying*," he replied. "I have to pick my rental car up in"—he checked his watch—"twelve hours."

"Please?" She wasn't above begging. "It's Friday night. I want to dance and meet new people and escape my real life and just be fucking invisible."

Ryan raised his eyebrows. "Sweetie, in those heels, you're six feet tall. Not to mention you're internet famous. I don't think *invisible* is in the cards for you, at least not below Fourteenth Street."

She rolled her eyes dramatically. "Please. Take me out. Let's go to where the cool people are. I want to see boys. Hot boys."

"Maybe you could eat something first."

He was right: Lola had forgotten to eat all day, very off-brand for her. They ordered a basket of mozzarella sticks, and Lola knew without having to ask that they were just for her. Ryan didn't touch dairy, especially not if it was deep fried.

She ate one, and then another, and then another, the grease smearing across her fingers. She couldn't stop. She wanted to eat a thousand mozzarella sticks, their salty, breaded crust and hot gooey insides and—

"Oh my god, is that Lola Likes?"

She heard the girls before she saw them.

There were four of them at a nearby table, with tiny sunglasses perched on their heads and slip dresses over their T-shirts and chokers around their necks.

She met their eyes as she chewed. They gaped at her in horror. She wiped her mouth on the back of her hand and stared back, unblinking.

Let them see me, she thought. *The real me.*

"Okay!" Ryan said a little too brightly. "Maybe we *should* go somewhere else."

Because he was a good friend, he took her home.

Lola woke up in her bed, though how she got there, she couldn't be sure.

Ryan was passed out next to her, his arms over his face. It was too bright in the bedroom, too hot. They were both drenched in sweat. She realized they must have gone to bed with the blinds open, something Justin never would have let happen, and the sun had filled the room and cooked them in its light.

The headache hit her then. There was no glass of water on her nightstand. She was going to have to get up.

She stumbled out of the bed, trying to be quiet. She still had last night's dress on. At least her shoes were off.

Lola chugged two glasses of water in the kitchen and took some Tylenol from the bathroom. She was glad Ryan was sleeping in her room. Without him, she'd be totally unmoored. Then she remembered he was leaving today for the whole summer. It wasn't a breakup, but the result was the same: another person she loved gone. How was she going to survive the next three months alone in this apartment, in this city, where everything she did was a reminder of all she had lost? The solitude, she felt, would consume her.

For just a moment in her delirious, hungover state, it occurred to Lola that being alone might be good for her, that she'd never let herself be alone, and that maybe that was why she'd ended up here, with a life that felt all wrong.

But she quickly pushed the thoughts away, desperate to avoid the sting of loneliness, afraid it was a black hole that she'd never find her way out of.

If that meant a summer in the Hamptons? Well, she could do worse. The decision had made itself.

She took her dress off and tossed it onto the floor. And then, in just her bra and thong, she sat at the kitchen table with her laptop and pulled up the Blade website.

"Isn't traffic to the Hamptons the worst?" the website of the private helicopter service read. This made Lola smile: the hyperbole, the marketing. It was funny. It was *fun*. She'd have fun again.

There'd been a time when Lola would have gotten a promo code to get a free ride, but those days were over. Now that she was canceled, she'd be paying full price for a lot of things. *Might as well get used to it,* she thought, grabbing her Amex. Within minutes, she'd booked the flight for later that same day.

So what if she had no income coming in? She had a large chunk of cash she'd been saving for a rainy day. What was this if not a metaphorical rainy day?

In her office, she surveyed her pile of stuff for Capri. It was everything she'd need for a summer in the Hamptons. Without folding a single thing, she stuffed all of it into her largest suitcase.

By the time Ryan woke, she was showered, drinking a La Colombe cold brew, and rolling out her forehead with her Skinny Confidential roller.

He rubbed his face in the doorway as he eyed her suitcase by the door. "Lola, what's going on?"

"Giancarlo left a car at the house, right?"

He nodded, blinking slowly. "Yeah, his Jeep stays out there."

She grinned. "So we don't really need two cars, do we? We could, perhaps, travel there in a little more style?"

His mouth fell open as he realized what she was saying.

"Cancel your rental car," she said. "I'm going with you."

Chapter 6

LOLA HAD USED up the entire supply of complimentary barf bags by the time the helicopter landed at East Hampton Airport.

At a certain point, it felt less like she was working through a hangover and more like she was exorcising a demon. Several demons, probably.

She wished she could have enjoyed the helicopter trip more; the views of Long Island and the sparkling Atlantic below them would have been, on any other day, incredibly beautiful. She at least could have gotten some good content out of it. But all she could do was retch into a bag until there was nothing left in her stomach but regret.

In the Uber from the airport to Giancarlo's cottage, Ryan rolled the windows down with an apologetic smile. "Your breath, babe," he said. She winced.

The driver handed her a bottle of Fiji water, which she gratefully accepted, marveling at how little dignity she had left.

They drove in silence down the quiet, tree-lined streets, mansions hidden behind verdant hedges.

Main Street was bustling, and Lola peered out the window at all the summer people doing their little errands. East Coast beach living was WASPier than Malibu; there were more polo shirts and boat shoes than she was comfortable with. With a pang, she realized how homesick she was for the down-to-earth surf vibes of the summers she'd spent with her family at the Campbells' beach house.

But she was here, decidedly not on the West Coast, and she was determined to enjoy it.

They drove past familiar shops with storefronts rebranded to be more beach friendly: Intermix, Brandy Melville, Nili Lotan. In between the retail spaces, summery ice cream parlors and wine shops and restaurants dotted the walk, their chalk signs and quaint awnings beckoning people in from the heat. Then the car turned off the Main Street and onto a narrow road toward the beach.

"We're almost there." Ryan nudged her. "The house is walking distance from all that stuff."

"Good thing I made you cancel your car," Lola said.

Ryan rolled his eyes, but he was smiling. "Good thing one of us can afford to travel by helicopter, you mean."

"You're welcome."

The car came to a stop with a view of the water before them and, centered in the expanse of open sky, a house that took Lola's breath away.

"Ryan, are you kidding me?" she gasped, flinging open her door.

The cottage had weathered brown shingles, with white trim skirting a classic cross-gable roof. A stone chimney rose from its center, evoking images of cozy summer storms and rain-soaked beaches, and the large windows dotting the sides seemed to beg to be thrown open. Overall, the place was big but not huge, the perfect size for two friends who were charmed by a homey aesthetic but would also perish without their own separate bathrooms over a long summer. It felt steeped in the promise of quaint romance.

The front yard was lush with blue and purple hydrangeas and pristine, freshly cut grass. She stepped away from the car and was hit with the smell of salt air. She could hear the ocean. Two bicycles leaned against the house as if waiting for them, and a white Jeep was parked in the driveway.

"Oh, Ryan," she gushed. "It's perfect."

"I told you!" He laughed. "No one has better taste than Giancarlo."

"I can't believe *he* didn't want to be here for the summer."

"I can." Ryan winked. "His other beach house is in Santorini."

The driver took their suitcases out of the trunk and wheeled them to the curb, tipping his hat in goodbye.

"I'm literally so excited," Lola said. "This really feels like we're doing the right thing."

They dragged their luggage up the cobblestone path.

Ryan unlocked the front door, and Lola gasped. The door opened into an elegant parlor lit by a crystal chandelier. She could see straight through to the sliding glass door on the other side and, through that, the yard, which had a pool, and beyond it, a private beach.

"Giancarlo!" she cried.

They abandoned their luggage in the entryway and wandered around the first floor of the house. She trailed her fingers along the soft, oversized, cream sofas. The decor was more classic than trendy, designed to withstand the test of time, not go viral on Instagram. Lola reveled in the solidity of it, taking in the sparkling clean surfaces, as though the housekeeper had just finished polishing. For a moment, Lola let herself feel sad. Justin would have loved this place.

Just then, she heard the sound of a distant door creaking open and closed. Out the window, she could see the neighboring cottage. It was all white—white shutters, white trim, white roof. It was possibly even lovelier than Giancarlo's house, with a yard full of red rose bushes and low hedges.

A thin, pale woman in a black one-piece was standing turned from Lola in the doorway. Lola took a moment at the window, inspecting the suit, a classic cut across the woman's trim frame. She couldn't help but admire the composition before her—black fabric against pale skin against white siding and roses. Lola wondered if that ease in posture was what summering in the Hamptons promised a person as the woman swept back her long, brown hair with a pair of sunglasses.

No, not just sunglasses.

Tom Ford sunglasses.

Lola's stomach plummeted as she dropped to the ground.

No no no. There's no fucking way.

She army-crawled behind their suitcases, her heart pounding in her ears.

It couldn't be. She peeked back up and got a glimpse of a slender silhouette, hands now working a tortoiseshell clip firmly in place. The woman turned, and Lola felt like vomiting again.

What the fuck was Aly Ray Carter doing in the house next door?

She heard the sounds of Aly going back inside but found she could not move from her spot on the ground.

A few moments later, Ryan was standing over her. "Lola, what the fuck are you doing?"

"Get down," she hissed.

Ryan sighed and crouched next to her. "Are we having a menty b *already?*"

"It's Aly Ray Carter, Ryan."

"It's okay, Lola. You're safe. The scary journalist can't get you on Long Island." He laughed, starting to rise.

She grabbed his wrist and yanked him back down. "No! Our next-door neighbor *is.* Aly. Ray. Carter." Lola was hyperventilating.

"Oh my god." Ryan rolled his eyes, wrenching his arm free. "I cannot hear one more thing about this girl, Lola! There is no way it's her. Journalists can't afford the Hamptons. You are *obsessed.* You are *hallucinating!*"

"I'm not," she whispered, but at the same time, she wondered, *Am I?*

"Well, whoever it was, she's gone now," Ryan said, standing up.

Lola cautiously stood. It was true that the woman was gone, leaving only an expanse of white siding in her wake.

Ryan went to the kitchen and began opening the fridge and the cabinets. There was a bottle of Minuty M Rosé on the counter and a note from Giancarlo welcoming them to his home.

"I'm going to drive to Citarella," Ryan announced. "We need sustenance."

"I think I am going to take a nap," Lola said, her hands still shaking, suddenly realizing how tired she was.

She made her way to the second floor, where she chose the smaller bedroom. All the blankets and sheets were white linen, and it was like slipping into a cloud. She was fast asleep as soon as her head hit the pillow. She didn't dream.

She awoke sometime later, the afternoon light trickling pleasantly through the window. Ryan was not back yet. She drank some water in the kitchen, eyeing the rosé.

It was not Aly next door, she decided. That would be insane. It was probably just some random girl with a claw clip and good taste in eyewear.

Lola dug around in her suitcase until she found a bikini and changed into it right there in the kitchen. Then she grabbed the wine and headed to the neighbor's house. She was going to prove to herself that it wasn't Aly. And maybe she'd even make a new friend in the process. It would be fun to befriend someone this summer. They could get manicures together. Veg by the pool. Critique each other's tans. Not talk about their social accounts.

She knocked, catching a glimpse of her reflection in the glass door. She looked messy; it was clear she'd just woken up. But it was a beach town. *Everyone looks messy at the beach*, she told herself.

The door opened. "Lola? What are you doing here?"

She was still wearing her black bathing suit. An unreadable expression played across her face—something between shock, amusement, and annoyance.

It *was* Aly.

Lola heard the Minuty shattering on the floor before she even realized it had slipped from her hand.

Chapter 7

LOLA AND ALY froze, staring at each other, Aly's mouth half-open in surprise.

"It's you," Lola said when her brain came back online.

"It's *you*," Aly replied, sounding just as shocked as Lola felt.

"What the fuck are you doing here?"

"Me?" Aly cried. "You're the one smashing bottles on my doorstep."

Reluctantly, Lola broke eye contact and looked down. Her legs were covered in sticky wine, her feet wet. The remains of the bottle were scattered in sharp shards on the ground.

"Oh shit, your foot."

Her foot indeed. The side of her big toe was sliced red like a rare steak. Blood had soaked her Hermès Oran sandal, spilling out onto the wooden step.

"Ouch," Lola said, though the pain hadn't fully registered.

She looked back up at Aly and then down at her foot, then back up again.

If this was some sort of sick cosmic joke, she sure wasn't laughing.

"Jesus," Aly said. "Can you just come in? I think we need to apply pressure to that."

Aly reached out and pulled Lola by the elbow through the doorway. Her hand felt cool on Lola's hot skin as Lola tried to relieve pressure on her injury, using her good foot to step inside.

The entryway was freezing, air-conditioning blowing her hair off her sweaty neck. A round, antique table held a bouquet of red roses from the garden, and next to it sat a bottle of sunscreen, a paperback, and Aly's phone. It smelled like salt air and flowers and Molecule 01. Lola glanced furtively into the living room, which looked straight out of a *Dwell* magazine cover story, bright pops of color and big sofas and overflowing bookcases. The corner had cubbies filled with sneakers and sandals and canvas tote bags and dog leashes. Everything was chic yet comfortable, artsy—like people who loved each other lived there. The walls were a perfect juxtaposition, lined with abstract contemporary paintings and framed children's art. It all made Giancarlo's cream-colored haven feel almost sterile in comparison.

There was music playing, some sort of hip, female-fronted indie rock that Lola couldn't place. She felt a begrudging curiosity, being swept into Aly's space like this. She wanted to freeze time so she could examine everything closely…and then smash it all on the floor.

She put her busted foot down, and that was when she felt it. Pain shot through her toe and up her ankle.

"Fuck!" she yelped, hopping back onto her other foot, but not before blood spattered onto a light pink doormat. "Fuck," she said again. "Your rug. Oh my god. Ow. Shit."

She was sweating profusely. How in the world was this—Aly *here*, her bloody foot, the red drops on Aly's rug—really happening?

Maybe, she thought, she was still asleep, having one of her insane hangover dreams. Maybe in a few minutes, she'd hear Ryan singing in their kitchen, back from his grocery run. She could peel the sheets off and wander downstairs and tell him all about this crazy nightmare she'd had while he threw his head back and howled with laughter, accusing her again of being obsessed. Then they could shower and go get lobster rolls and later take a midnight skinny-dip in the pool, and everything would be back on track—she'd be back to having the perfect summer. She just needed to force herself to wake up.

She closed her eyes tightly and then opened them again. But she was still in Aly's foyer. And Aly was still staring at her, still wearing a black one-piece that showed off her slender legs and her clavicle and her perfect little boobs.

Lola's cheeks grew hot. "Fuck," she said again. "I'm so sorry."

"Hey," Aly said, so steadily that Lola wondered if they were living in the same universe. "You're fine. It's just a rug. Can I help you into the kitchen?"

Lola nodded meekly and allowed Aly to help her hobble through the foyer and into a kitchen with emerald-green tiles and a sparkling pink marble island. Long, leafy plants hung in the windows, making the whole space feel both curated and wildly untamed.

"Colorful," Lola observed, appreciating the eclectic taste of whoever designed the space.

She bent down to examine the cut. Her sliced skin was flapping gruesomely. She stood up quickly. Lola didn't have a strong constitution for this sort of thing, and she should have known better than to look at it. A wave of nausea hit her, and the room started to tilt. Suddenly, her sweat turned cold, the edges of her vision blurring. Maybe it was her hangover-related dehydration or the sight of blood or the shock of seeing Aly—or all three—but she was pretty sure she was about to tip over.

If you faint, I'll never forgive you, she said to herself.

What came out of her mouth was "Um? I think I might need to…" She couldn't finish before she rocked forward.

Aly grabbed her arms, steadying her. Lola hung her head as she focused on her breathing. She wasn't sure what would be worse: passing out on Aly or puking on her. Both were feeling likely. Maybe if she fainted, she could just stay unconscious until this was all over. A coma-on-demand. She focused on the pressure of Aly's hands.

"You're okay," Aly said, voice cool as fresh cucumber water. "Let's sit you down."

Aly deposited Lola on a barstool and then grabbed a crumpled white T-shirt off the counter, pulling it on. It was long on her, the hem stopping just at the top of her thighs.

Lola's own near nakedness felt very loud in comparison.

She didn't have time to dwell on it, though, because her brain was already cooking up ways to get the hell out of ARC's kitchen. She could simply bolt, though with the dizziness and the bleeding, that might be a challenge. She could fake an emergency phone call. But then suddenly Aly was crouching before her with a wad of paper towels, taking Lola's sticky ankle gently into her pale hands, and Lola realized she was, at least for the moment, stuck.

"I'm going to try to stop the bleeding, okay?" Aly peered up at Lola with wide, imploring eyes. Lola could only nod and then winced as Aly pressed the paper towels to the wound. The only thing distracting her from the pain was the way Aly's eyebrows were knitted together in concern. Lola had the sudden impulse to reach out and smooth her brow, but she resisted. Even she knew that would be a very inappropriate thing to do, worse than leaving shards of broken glass in her entryway or spilling water across a café table. Instead, she took in the difference between their skin tones. Aly's hands were like moonlight next to Lola's golden legs.

"So what are you doing here?" Aly asked. "It's kind of biblical to come all the way to the Hamptons just to bleed on my doorstep."

Lola groaned. "I'm staying next door for the summer."

Aly paused a moment, looking up at her with surprise. "Not Giancarlo's house."

"You know him?" Lola couldn't believe it.

"I've only known him my whole life." Aly was shaking her head, as though she shared Lola's thoughts on their new living situation: annoyance, dread, disbelief.

"No." Lola's eyes went wide, taking in the decor, the signs now obvious. This wasn't a rental cottage; this was a home.

"He's best friends with my parents," Aly said. "What are the chances?"

Lola didn't answer, because she was suddenly worried that if she opened her mouth, the word *fate* would fall out. And she definitely, *definitely* didn't need to talk to Aly about whether this was fated. This moment might have been Lola's personal hell—sure, her embarrassment alone could recognize that—but there was also a teeny, tiny part of her that felt a strum of intrigue at Aly's closeness again. It made the idea of *chances* feel very complicated.

Instead, she said, "I was just bringing a bottle of wine to my new neighbor. Trust me, I was not expecting it to be *you*."

"That was nice of you," Aly said. "I'm sorry it turned out to be me."

"Yeah," Lola said, shrugging, trying to mirror Aly's no-fucks-given energy. She knew she was probably not very convincing. On the contrary, she found she had never given more fucks than she did around Aly Ray Carter. But damn if she was going to let Aly, who so easily brushed off their new circumstances like she wasn't responsible for Lola's demise, know that.

"Are you okay to hold this?" Aly asked, and Lola nodded, taking over the task of pressing the towel into her broken skin. When Aly stood back up, her knees cracked; Lola couldn't help but take note of it, perhaps only because it reminded her that Aly was actually human, not some ethereal being made of unaffected poise and unsolicited opinions. "I'm going to get the first aid kit. Don't move."

As if she could have. Alone in Aly's exquisite kitchen, bleeding out, Lola let the embarrassment wash over her. She was never the most graceful person in the world, but she wasn't usually this disastrous, dropping the goddamn wine bottle, almost passing out at the sight of her own blood. *Very smooth, Fine.* She recalled the glass of water spilling during their interview and winced. When Aly was around, Lola didn't know her ass from her elbow, and the worst part was Aly could probably tell. Lola put her face in her hands.

Despite the aggressive air-conditioning, a river of sweat ran between her boobs, marking the flimsy bikini that was just barely holding her in place. She glanced down. Thank god she'd remembered to shave her depression bush before coming here, but still, little bits of light brown stubble were starting to appear around her bikini line. She wondered if Aly would notice, if Aly cared about the length of someone's pubic hair at all. Lola should really make an appointment to get waxed. Ryan would definitely come with her to that. In the Hamptons, they probably offered a full spa experience. They could make a day of it.

But in the meantime, she would have done anything for something to cover up with. A robe, a towel…a garbage bag.

Aly returned holding some hydrogen peroxide, gauze, and a Band-Aid. "This is going to hurt," she noted apologetically.

"I'm a big girl," Lola replied, but when Aly started cleaning her wound, tears pricked her eyes. She appreciated that Aly didn't notice—or at least didn't mention if she did.

"Oh shit, I think there's a little piece of glass still in here."

"Leave it," Lola said, trying to pull her foot away. She didn't want to risk Aly seeing her squirm.

"Hold still," Aly snapped back, gripping her firmly, and Lola blushed, immediately obeying as a keen awareness ran up her spine.

She loved being told what to do.

With tweezers from the first aid kit, Aly deftly removed the chunk like a skilled surgeon. She held the glass up to the light as though it was a prize. "Got you, you little fucker," she said in triumph.

Despite herself, Lola laughed. Aly smirked at the sound before returning to her task. When Aly seemed satisfied that the cut was clean, she held the gauze to it and then wrapped the bandage tightly around Lola's toe. "I don't think you'll need stitches. The bleeding has already slowed."

"Thank you, doctor," Lola quipped and then reddened, hit with a sudden and specific longing for the last person who had played doctor for her: Justin. She wondered what he was doing on his break from her. If he was thinking about her at all. If he would think it unseemly if she bled all over his doormat. She shook the thought away.

Meanwhile, Aly balled up the bloody paper towels and the rest of the trash, tossing it into the garbage before washing her hands.

"Are you some sort of ex–Girl Scout?" Lola asked.

"I babysat a lot in high school," Aly said, drying her hands on a dish rag. "Kids make you learn this stuff fast."

Lola could not picture Aly with children. She seemed too cool for wiping runny noses and playing pretend. As if she could read Lola's mind, Aly shrugged matter-of-factly. "I like kids."

"Me too," Lola said. "Though I think I need another five years to decide if I want them."

"That's funny," Aly said. "I've always really wanted them."

Lola felt a tender pull in her chest, not unlike the first time she heard Justin say the same. She had not bothered to imagine Aly as a mother, but seeing how nurturing she was, it made sense to her, somehow adding seamlessly to the picture of the cool girl in the long, white T-shirt before her.

"Can I get you some water?" Aly asked. "Or, like, some vodka?"

The mention of vodka made Lola's stomach flip as she suddenly remembered the booze-soaked day that had led her here.

Their first meeting, sizzling with chemistry.

The article, brimming with cruelty.

The fallout online, which she'd never recover from.

The series of phone calls from her team as they abandoned her.

Justin, breaking her heart and then walking out the door.

Aly had been the source of all of it. Aly, who had just pulled a piece of glass from Lola's foot. Whose brow Lola had just thought about petting. Whose skin was glowing in the fading afternoon light. Who, underneath that white T-shirt, was wearing a high-cut one-piece bathing suit that felt burned into Lola's mind.

It was awfully confusing to hate someone so hot.

And she did hate her, she reminded herself. Or at least she'd been devastated by her. Wasn't that one and the same? Or was it something closer to absolute vulnerability?

Before she could think twice, Lola reeled back. "You ruined my fucking life."

Aly held Lola's gaze with her chin slightly raised, as though she was ready to take whatever Lola was about to dole out.

"Well?" Lola said, her voice sharp. "You can't seem to shut the fuck up about how basic I am when you can hide behind your screen, but in person, you have nothing to say to me?"

Aly considered her for a beat, her face thoughtful. "Has no one ever criticized you before?"

Lola scoffed. "Of course they have."

This was a lie, and she realized it as soon as the words left her mouth. Lola had spent her whole life trying to be so inoffensive that she was literally offensive to no one. No one ever had anything bad to say about her because she didn't give them any reason to. She'd contorted herself into various pleasing shapes for as long as she could remember—just as Aly had written.

The fact that Lola agreed only infuriated her more.

"I'm sorry you were hurt by it. I was just doing my job." Aly's voice was maddeningly even, almost patronizing in her refusal to rise to Lola's bait.

"Was it your job to ruin my life?"

"It was my job to report on what I observed. What my research told me. What my gut was saying."

"What would get the most attention," Lola added, and then something clicked. She grinned somewhat manically. "You know, what we do is not so different. You're over there on your high horse about writing the truth, but the *real* truth? You took me down so you could have a viral headline."

"Oh, please!" Aly said, visibly bristling. "You think how well my stories perform impacts me at all? I get paid a flat rate. Do you even know how journalism works?"

"Ugh, spare me."

"Lola, your shit hit the fan before I wrote the article," Aly pointed out. "I was reporting on what already happened. You put your own foot in your mouth."

"And you made it so much worse. You *used* me to critique my entire industry."

"Don't you think the industry needed critiquing? You can't tell me you think influencing is still exciting at this point. When fashion bloggers first came on the scene, it was so cool. They were democratizing fashion. They took something exclusionary and made it their own. But now? All those same girls have just turned themselves into advertising platforms."

"I'm a *person*," Lola whispered. "I'm not a representative of a problem or an angle for a story."

Aly paused, her head tilting at Lola's words. The truth was that Lola was not ready to have this conversation with Aly. It would mean cutting open parts of herself that she wasn't prepared to touch. But anger, anger she could do. And Lola leaned into it, letting that burning in her stomach take over, pushing back all the other shit to those dark corners where she wanted them to stay.

Lola took a breath, letting her words land heavily. "You were mean and spiteful, and I wish I never agreed to meet you."

"I'm sorry you feel like that," Aly said, and Lola stiffened at her word choice. Not *I'm sorry for what I did*. Not *I'm sorry for what I caused*. God forbid she take responsibility. "I hope you won't let it ruin your summer," Aly added. "I'm sure you and Jason will still have a lovely time at Giancarlo's house, and soon you'll forget all about what happened."

"Justin," Lola snapped, her anger flaring once again. "And no, we won't have a lovely time at Giancarlo's house. He's not here."

"No?" Aly arched an eyebrow. "Not his scene?"

"It's over. He dumped me."

Because of what you wrote. She allowed the thought to swell in her mind, to become the reason even though she knew it wasn't *quite* true.

"What?" Aly looked genuinely shocked. "But you guys are, like, Mr. and Mrs. Perfect."

"Yeah, well." Lola picked at her cuticle. "Your article was…" She trailed off, still not sure how much detail to divulge. "Let's call it a major turning point."

"I don't understand why he'd break up with you based on what I wrote. Shouldn't he have his own opinion of you?"

"It's not that simple. And I really don't want to talk about it with *you* of all people."

Aly looked searchingly at the ceiling, giving Lola the opportunity to study her. Aly had a long neck, Lola noticed. It had been hidden under all that long, brown hair. She was like a swan. As mean as a swan too. As untrustworthy.

"So you're here alone?"

"No, I'm with Ryan."

"That's good. I'm glad you won't be alone," Aly said, which was irritating.

Lola did not want Aly to be nice to her, to be reasonable. She wanted them to continue yelling at each other. "Are *you* here alone?"

"Oh, me? Yeah," Aly said. "I needed a break from all the bullshit. I have some friends nearby, though. On Fire Island."

"All the bullshit?" Lola sighed heavily and then took in the quiet luxury around her, the custom built-ins and the spotless surfaces and the view of the ocean. Aly didn't belong in this place. "Shouldn't you be holed up in some sort of Brooklyn writing warehouse for cranky hipsters? I doubt Jack Kerouac spent his summers in a mansion on Private Beachfront Property Lane or wherever the fuck we are."

Aly winced. Under normal circumstances, Lola would have never dreamed of letting this much snark sail freely from her lips. In fact, she usually went far out of her way to avoid stirring the pot. But she wanted to hurt Aly—maybe as much as Aly had hurt her.

"It's my parents' beach house," she said, the defensive edge in her voice hard to miss. "We came here every summer when I was a kid. I'm not going to apologize for the way I grew up."

"Oh, right, I forgot that you're a nepo baby," Lola said, unable to stop the disdain coming from her lips now that she'd started. "Amazing that you choose to spend your time critiquing a lifestyle you were born into and still apparently indulge in. Do people know you live like this, daughter of publishing royalty? A true beacon of democratized taste, I'd say."

Aly's face turned splotchy and red. She folded her arms across her chest.

"Why haven't you written the next great American novel by now? The great ARC must have something important to say, right?" Lola had the sudden sense that she had won a battle, and a fleeting swell of victory rose in her chest before quickly deflating as she took in Aly's face.

"You can leave now," Aly said, her voice hardly more than a whisper.

Lola felt the sting of the dismissal. "Oh, I'm leaving," she blustered, calling forward the indignation Aly deserved. Because she did deserve this after everything she'd done, Lola was sure. But as Lola reached the door, stepping over the scattered glass, she couldn't help but turn her head, taking in Aly still backlit by the kitchen. "Thanks again for the emergency services," she added, a bit softer this time.

"Anytime," Aly said, but she'd turned her back to Lola and stayed that way while Lola limped out of the house.

She heard Aly's door slam closed behind her.

Lola exploded back into Giancarlo's house.

Her heart pounded in the silence. Ryan was not back yet.

She hobbled up the stairs, kicked her ruined sandals off, and collapsed on top of the unmade bed, still rumpled from her sweaty nap.

She tried to make sense of what had just happened. Of all the cottages in the Hamptons, Aly's was right next door. Lola would have to spend the whole summer dodging her. Their backyards were separated only by short hedges. If she was in the pool, Aly would be able to see her through the kitchen window. There would be nowhere to hide.

She briefly wondered what Aly did for fun out here, if they'd be at the same parties (that was if Lola even got invited to parties this summer; she wasn't sure if her status as a *cancelita* extended out east). But she and Aly were rarely at the same parties in Manhattan, so maybe Aly had a different world here too. One that was cooler than Lola's. Aly would probably be at private poetry readings and homemade sushi experiences, something pretentious and cringey like that—the kind of party Lola would secretly love to be invited to and probably never would.

She couldn't wait to tell Ryan that she'd been right.

Across from her, there was a painting on the wall of a naked woman smoking a cigarette and looking at her phone. Lola hadn't noticed it before in her delirious nap state. The woman's eyes were unfocused, as though she'd recently gotten railed. Her breasts hung low over her stomach. A dog was curled by her feet. The scene looked intimate, as though maybe the artist had been the one doing the railing. Giancarlo had good taste in art.

Lying on her back, Lola took stock of her body. She was slick with sweat. Her foot hurt like all hell. Her headache threatened to blossom into a migraine. Her bones were tired.

And most of all, she was still completely riled up from the fight with Aly, a low thrum of anger left pulsing through her.

Which probably explained why her vagina was throbbing too. Mixed signals from her brain to her groin.

Plus, Lola always got horny when she was hungover.

Her hand wandered down her stomach and slipped underneath the waistband of her bikini bottoms. It didn't take long before she was completely wet, her clit stiff, standing at attention. She cupped her other hand onto her breast as she started to rub herself furiously, not so much for the pleasure of it but so she could get the orgasm over with and move on with her day.

The door to the bedroom was wide open, but she couldn't stop to close it. Didn't want to.

She heard a distant door slam—Aly was back outside. Lola's skin hummed.

She heard Aly's voice command her: *Hold still.*

She felt the cool pressure of Aly's hands on her arm, her ankle, her foot.

She saw the absolute concentration on Aly's face as she pulled glass out of her cut. Grasped her heel in her palm. She watched Aly fold her arms across her chest, heard her voice as she raised it. She felt the fury rising in her chest at Aly's pretention, at how condescending she was.

Lola took her hand away, panting, trying to slow herself down. She tried to remind herself what Aly had taken from her. How cruel her writing had been. How hurt Lola was that after all the chemistry between them, Aly only had horrible things to report on her.

But she couldn't focus on any of that. Instead, she remembered Aly's knees cracking when she stood. Her familiar, musky smell, so intoxicating up close.

Maybe this was the equivalent of a hate-fuck, she thought as she resumed touching herself. That would be reasonable.

It didn't take long until the feeling was building again, almost too intense to bear.

She didn't even realize how loudly she moaned when she came. Briefly, she lost all senses. The room turned spotty, and her ears rang. The only thing that existed was the blood in her body as it rushed to her clit.

Her heart was pounding loudly in her chest, bringing her back to earth. She held her hand over her throbbing labia, afraid of moving.

What the fuck was that?

She tried to catch her breath. *It is totally normal to masturbate after conflict. This is fine. I'm fine.*

The bed beneath her was damp from her sweat.

This was just my way of releasing tension.

With her free hand, she tugged her nipple absent-mindedly.

I do not actually want to fuck Aly Ray Carter.

On the contrary, it was less like an orgasm and more like a purge.

That was it. She'd binged on conflict with Aly, and now it was leaving her body.

Anything else—anything more than that—she simply did not have the capacity to examine further, not right now. She was nursing a heartbreak, mourning the death of her career. To have an actual physical attraction to the person who had wrought all that was unthinkable.

There was nothing greater than her love for Justin, nothing bigger than the hole he'd left in her heart.

Besides, if it really came down to it, she wouldn't even know what to do with Aly's body. She reminded herself that she was, at the end of the day, straight. She always had been.

And straight women jerk off to thoughts of other women all the time. The first woman she ever masturbated to was her high school volleyball coach, with her long, blond ponytail, muscular calves, and a whistle that she blew with abandon when the girls weren't making their digs. Lola used to love imagining Coach Lisa standing behind her, teaching her how to serve, guiding her hands into position. It wasn't a fantasy about sex. She was aroused by the thought of Coach Lisa helping her. She wanted Coach Lisa's approval, and sometimes, under the covers in her childhood bedroom, she made herself come just thinking about Coach Lisa saying, "Good girl, Lola."

What would it sound like for Aly to say *good girl* to her?

She heard the Jeep pull into the driveway, Charli XCX blasting from the speakers. Ryan. Finally. She wondered how long it took to go to the grocery store in this town. It felt like he'd been gone for years. Long enough for a whole side plot to come in and hijack her summer before it even started.

The front door opened and closed. "Lola!" he screamed. "Lola?"

After a few moments, he started singing to himself. Like Lola, he had a habit of falling in love with whatever was on the radio at the moment.

She should go downstairs and greet him. She should help with the groceries, Venmo him for half or maybe all of it. She should ask him about the guy from the app that he was so excited about. She should look up where to get dinner and drinks and go dancing. She should make an appointment for them to get waxed. She should express gratitude that he'd allowed her to come with him to this beautiful house in this stunning place.

She should, she should, she *should.*

The problem was that she was still so turned on. She had the girl equivalent of a boner. A lady boner? There was no cute name for what was happening to her body. She was not fit to be seen by anyone in this state.

She got up and closed the bedroom door as quietly as possible, careful not to put too much weight on her bad foot.

Back in bed, she lay on her stomach.

Her hand wandered back down between her legs. This time, she started slowly, lightly. She was still so sensitive from her first orgasm. With her mouth pressed into the pillow to silence her own groans, she traced gentle circles. Her thighs began to shake.

She was ready for the fantasies now.

In an alternate universe, she imagined that she'd knocked on Aly's door and not dropped the bottle of wine when Aly opened it. Instead, she said, "Well, hi there, neighbor," in a way that was totally calm and collected.

It was Aly who was unable to play it cool now. "Lola?" Aly gasped. Aly, who in this fantasy world was wearing a string bikini, not a one-piece. Her stomach was flat, her hip bones pointy. "Is it really you?"

"The one and only," Lola said. "Fancy a drink?"

She was not sure why she sounded British in this fantasy, but she went with it, surrendering control to the vision playing behind her eyelids.

The scene continued. She made her way into the foyer. Aly took the bottle out of her hands and placed it on the table. "Actually, I had something else in mind," Aly ground out before pushing Lola into the door and pressing her entire body into Lola's.

On the bed, Lola writhed, pressing harder into her hand. She could almost feel Aly's torso thrust into hers.

Meanwhile, Aly let out a moan as they kissed, their tongues melting into each other. Aly bit Lola's lip. Lola reached down and clutched Aly's ass, which was mostly bare thanks to the cut of her suit. Aly was standing on her tiptoes.

"Lola, I want you," Aly said and then brought her hands to Lola's chest, softly teasing her nipples through her bathing suit. She felt the touch radiate out, chanting through her: *I want you. Lola. I want. Want.*

Lola pulled the string of Aly's bikini top until it unraveled and fell to the floor. What did Aly's boobs look like? She tried to imagine them. Perky, probably. Pink nipples. She wondered if Aly would let her touch them.

Aly pressed her pubic bone into Lola's leg. Lola could feel Aly's wetness through her bathing suit, and the feeling shocked her, turned her on. How novel, to have someone without a dick pressing their groin into you. She wondered if she'd ever experience it in real life. She wondered if she actually wanted to or if some things were better kept in fantasy, as fiction.

In bed, Lola gasped.

Her orgasm came out of nowhere.

She hadn't even been trying to come, but she hadn't been trying not to either. She'd been in another place entirely. A place where Aly was feeling her up, moaning with need for her. A place where… Her back arched. She was going to come for a third time. She hadn't come three times in a row since the early days of her and Justin.

Not only that: it was the best orgasm she'd ever had. She felt it surging up and down her body, rocking her in waves of pleasure. She felt she was dying and being reborn over and over. She stuck two fingers inside herself to ride out the final wave, moaning into the pillow as her body did things it had never done before.

Lola had never felt this kind of desperate, feral longing for another girl. This was not the same as blushing because Coach Lisa tightened her ponytail in a certain way. This was something else. Something new. Something…terrifying. Of all the people in the world, did she really have to feel this way about Aly Ray Carter?

Lola fucking Fine, she said to herself. *You will not harbor a secret crush on the girl who ruined your life. You will not.*

As soon as she caught her breath, she fell into a deep, dark sleep.

She dreamed of volleyball practice.

Chapter 8

IT TOOK LOLA a moment to realize that the sound of waves crashing on the sand was coming from the actual ocean outside her window and not from her favorite white-noise soundscape on the Calm app.

She opened her eyes and smiled. As if to greet her, a nearby seagull squawked loudly.

Sunlight streamed through the white linen curtains. She felt good—much better than yesterday. She stretched her arms over her head, shaking free of the blankets that were now a tangled mess around her ankles. Three orgasms plus ten hours of sleep had done the trick. Her hangover was gone. She grabbed a cotton waffle robe from the dresser, wrapping herself in it.

Ryan was in the kitchen, drinking coffee and reading the news on his phone.

He looked up at the sound of her footsteps and then grinned as he assessed her. "I'm sorry, I'm looking for my friend Lola? I don't know if you've seen her."

"Lola?" she murmured, floating to the coffee maker. "Hmm, sounds familiar, but no, I don't think so. I am Lo*la*, lady of the vacation home." The coffee steamed thickly as she poured it into a mug and then drowned it with half-and-half.

"Yes, bitch," Ryan squealed. "You are so back. What happened? You look refreshed and *amazing*."

"I had a really nice night with myself." She smiled into her mug. It wasn't just the orgasms; it was the anger she'd unleashed on Aly. It had felt really good to yell at her. Cathartic. Suddenly she wasn't carrying around all the dead weight of resentment. She was, for the moment, liberated. She should really yell at people more often. "Oh, and I have something to tell you."

"Spill."

"I was *right*."

He put his phone down and arched a waxed brow at her. "You're going to have to be more specific."

"Our neighbor."

He thought for a second, then gasped. "No!"

"Yes. Aly Ray fucking Carter, next door to us for the whole summer."

She was savoring this. Her run-in with Aly might not have been a delight, but letting Aly have it—and getting to gossip with Ryan about it now—absolutely was. At the very least, she was vindicated.

"How do you know?" His voice came out frantic, somewhere between panic and laughter.

"I went over there to introduce myself. With a bottle of wine. That I then dropped on my foot." She held her bandaged foot out for him, and he recoiled. "It was a whole thing. Anyway, that's my story! What happened to *you* last night?"

"No, no, no," he said, as she knew he would. "Sit your ass

down and tell me exactly what happened, start to finish, and spare nothing."

She laughed and did exactly that.

Well, not *exactly* that. Her story for Ryan ended when she left Aly's house, not when she retreated into the depths of a hot hate-fuck fantasy in the guest bedroom.

"Girl," he said. "Aly living next door and tending to your wound is *crazy*."

"Crazy," she confirmed.

"And what kind of journalist can afford a house out here?"

"Well, it's her parents' house," Lola said. But then, not wanting to seem suspicious, she added, "But, yeah, I know. Nepo babies, right?"

"Isn't her whole thing being, like, an antiestablishment socialist or whatever? Like, does Diet Prada know the creator of #SecretTrustFund has a secret trust fund? I feel like they should know!"

Lola laughed. "I don't think they'd care, but I love you."

"I'm so proud of you for laying into her," he said. "That fucking bitch."

And then Ryan's face did the thing it did when he wanted to be real with Lola but was afraid of hurting her feelings—a passing frown, a pulse of the vein in his forehead.

"What?"

"Lola, listen," he said. "Does Aly staying next door mean we're about to spend the whole summer talking about her? Because I would die for you, but that sounds really boring to me."

That stung a little. "Mean."

"I'm not trying to be *mean*. I just really want to relax, and I don't know if I can relax if you're freaking out, and if she's always twenty feet away, how are you going to not be freaking out?"

"I promise you, it's not a big deal." Lola lied through her teeth. "I am fine and chill. I was just excited to tell you I was right, but beyond that, who fucking cares?"

"I mean, that's what I'm saying. She can go kick rocks in Birkenstocks."

Lola laughed. "I think you mean old Celine slides."

"Not you memorizing her shoes," he groaned. "Do we hate her, or are we in love with her?"

Lola clenched her jaw. He didn't really think she was in love with Aly; after all, she had her history of heterosexuality on her side. So there was no reason for him or anyone to think that. Especially since it wasn't true. Definitely not true.

She changed the subject. "What do you want to do today?"

"I want to get a deep, dark base tan by the pool and play Nicki too loudly."

Lola considered this briefly, but there was no part of her that could lie still today. She was practically vibrating with energy. "Hear me out: What about instead, we go into town?"

"Town?" he groaned. "With all the *people?*"

"When did you develop agoraphobia?" she shot back.

"I just thought we would be doing a little more lying low and a little less seeing and being seen," he said. "At least on day one."

She pouted.

He sighed. "Okay. What do *you* want to do?"

Lola studied her nails. "Coffee, shopping, lunch, pool, nap, alcohol, dinner, more alcohol, maybe drugs? In that order?"

"Ambitious," he said. "But fine. Only because I love you and I want you to have your perfect day."

"With my perfect friend," she replied.

"Maybe someday we can have *my* perfect day," he mused.

"What would your perfect day entail?"

"Something a little more X-rated than errands on Main Street."
He grinned.

It was eighty degrees and sunny out, if a little chilly in the shade, but as Lola pulled clothes from her mess of a suitcase, she thought not of being comfortable but about what she'd most want to be wearing if someone important spotted her. Anyone important. Anyone she may want to impress with her city-meets-Hamptons chic look.

A SIEDRÉS halter dress would do the trick. She assessed herself in the mirror, her hair still damp from her much-needed shower. With a plunging V-neck and a hemline that fell just past her ass, even Lola knew it was a lot of skin. But it was summer. Hell, she'd probably look appropriate wearing her bikini on the sidewalk.

Lola tossed her wallet into her white Jacquemus Le Chiquito bag and hesitated before leaving her phone where it lay, charging on the nightstand. She had no one to call, no emails to answer, no notifications worth checking. She was scorned, but she was free. That had to count for something. What would a day be like without her phone? She was about to find out.

She forced herself not to look at Aly's house as she walked to the car. *Be calm*, she thought. *Be cool. Be casual. You are a hot babe going into town. She doesn't need to see you checking to see if she's looking.*

Still, as she slid into the passenger seat, she couldn't help it—she snuck a peek. All she got were drawn curtains and pretty roses. If Aly was watching, it was from a vantage point Lola couldn't see.

"Maybe she's still sleeping," Ryan said, reading her mind.

"Who?" Lola said, fiddling with the seat belt while Ryan rolled his eyes.

He drove them to Sant Ambroeus with the top down. Warm salt air tangled Lola's hair, and she put the radio on, finding the local pop station. Ryan turned the volume up. It was all very dreamy. She could almost pretend that she wasn't here to recover from the implosion of everything she loved.

"Earth to Lola," Ryan said. "We're here."

He had already parked in front of Sant Ambroeus, the Southampton outpost of the trendy New York City Italian restaurant with green-striped awning against classic red brick. In the city, it was famous for its fashionable lunch crowd, iconic magazine editors picking at salads while models sipped their iced coffee. The out east location was sure to be just as fabulous.

"Sorry," she groaned, snapping out of her daze. "I'm so spacey today!"

It was almost 11:00 a.m., and the line already snaked out the door, guests queuing for the chef-curated seasonal menu and Italian seaside vibes. Girls in vintage silk slip dresses and Chanel sunglasses held hands with their boyfriends in polo shirts, everyone looking well rested and tan and—she noted with some annoyance—in love. Men and women nuzzled into each other. The Hamptons were romantic. Just not for her.

It was a weekday, but no one was rushing off to work—this was not the place for working nor rushing. It was a place for enjoying yourself, having a glass of wine before noon, indulging in the frivolity of summer without schedules and meetings and sinking follower counts. Lola hoped the atmosphere would rub off on her soon. Despite her refreshed start, something about the Hamptons suddenly felt like an ill-fitting skin.

As they walked up, Ryan shot her a sidelong glance. "Girl, are you trying to have a nip slip before lunch?"

She looked down. Her boobs seemed to be ignoring the boundaries of the neckline, desperate to break free. They looked great, though, and she didn't want to put them away. "You mad about it?"

"No, I love your gorgeous tits," he said. "But you look like you're going to the club."

"Life's a club," she said. "We don't need a reservation, do we?"

"We obviously have one."

"God, I love publicists." She paused, thinking of her own former team, then added, "Sometimes."

As it turned out, Ryan had booked them not just a table but the best one, in the corner, where they could see the whole restaurant.

As soon as they sat down, though, Ryan's phone rang. "Frozen cappuccino," he muttered to her before picking it up. "Katherine, hi," he said, automatically switching into his professional work voice, standing up, and mouthing *sorry* before walking back outside.

Alone in the restaurant, without her phone to scroll through, Lola surveyed the scene.

Conservatively dressed women as small as birds were picking at avocado toast while their children stared at screens and their gray-haired husbands talked to one another about golf. The waitstaff exchanged knowing glances across the room. The restaurant smelled of coffee and maple syrup and sunscreen. She scanned the room for familiar faces— with a sharp eye for one in particular—but came up empty.

That was when she noticed people were staring back at her. She was suddenly struck by the realization that she was not invisible. On the contrary, she was a canceled, Instagram-famous blond. Queen of the bland. Her heart sank in her chest. She wondered who around her had read Aly's article. If they'd sent it to their friends and laughed at her. If, later today, they'd go back to their rental homes and say, "You'll never guess who I saw at Sant Ambroeus."

Or maybe everyone was staring at her because of what she was wearing. She felt, all at once, too large for the café. She'd wanted to look sexy and important and instead only succeeded in looking like she was trying too hard. She glanced down at her dress, how it clung to her, showed too much body. The humidity was making her hair twice its normal size, and her skin glistened with sweat. *What were you thinking?* she asked herself. She'd dressed for revenge—a small part of her had hoped Aly might see her and feel bad all over again—but this was no revenge outfit. She had only succeeded in humiliating herself. Again.

Had she humiliated herself last night at Aly's too? Should she have been less of a bitch while Aly tried to patch up her foot? She wasn't sure how she should have behaved, given the circumstances. She did feel guilty for the crack about Aly's career. But Aly had *ruined her life.* Surely Lola's one comment didn't compare to that sort of damage. Still, she found herself wishing she'd been kinder. Maybe if she had, they could have parted as friends. Or at least as not enemies.

But why did she care if they were enemies? Aly had started all this, not her.

The waiter came. Thank god. She didn't need to slip further into her oncoming spiral.

She ordered their drinks and added eggs, toast, and pancakes, suddenly realizing she was starving.

Ryan reappeared and not a moment too soon. "Am I dressed like an escort?" she said as he slid into the booth.

"Yes," he said. "But sex work is work."

She flushed with embarrassment but quickly tried to shake it off.

It was not like she could change clothes at the restaurant. "How was your phone call?"

"You don't want to know," he said. "But I *did* get a text from Emmett. God, he's so dreamy." Lola registered this information, but it wasn't enough to distract her from the train of her own thoughts currently careening off their tracks. As though sensing that she wasn't paying attention, Ryan sighed. "What did I miss *here*?"

"Just thinking my thoughts."

He studied her face. "You were thinking about ARC."

"I hate that you think that."

Their coffees came.

Lola definitely did not need more caffeine, but she downed it anyway, feeling her internal organs start to jitter. "I bet she doesn't even come to places like this. I bet she goes to Golden Pear just to seem like a local even though their coffee tastes burnt."

Ryan sipped his cappuccino. "You're really putting a lot of thought into this."

"Well, you asked!"

"It's true. Okay, what's the plan for later? You got invited to the Mytheresa x Flamingo Estate pop-up, right?"

Before she could answer, the waiter reappeared, holding plates piled high with steaming, salty carbs.

Ryan laughed. "Jesus, did you order the whole menu?"

"Duh," she said.

In another life, the spread of food on the table would have made the perfect Lola Likes content. She would have captioned it "Lola likes BRUNCH!" *I really am bland.* A more honest caption would be more like "Holding it together by a thread—but with a cornetto!!!"

She shoved a piece of whole wheat toast into her mouth, not

bothering to swallow before she added, "And no, I did not get invited. Or rather I don't know because I'm not looking at my phone right now."

"I am sure you got invited," he said, trying to reassure her, but she didn't believe him. "And anyway, no one will care if you show up. Emmett will be there, and I promised him I'd stop by, so you can just be my guest, okay?"

"Fine," she sighed. "But only if I can buy something new to wear."

"East Hampton is your oyster," he said. "Let's plan to go around four, okay?"

She agreed.

The new Khaite store was just a couple of doors down, so they walked over after brunch. Lola felt mildly ill; she was a little too full from brunch and vibrating at a high frequency from all the caffeine. But she was determined to enjoy herself. If she couldn't be happy shopping, she wouldn't be happy anywhere.

Ryan held up a long, black dress, mouthing at her, *Ten thousand?*

So maybe the brand was a rip-off, but it didn't matter. She had money in the bank and wounded pride to heal.

The shopgirl sat at the register, scrolling through her phone. Without looking up, she said, "Let me know if you want to try anything."

"We will!" Lola chirped back with so much forced enthusiasm that the shopgirl tore her eyes away from the screen to peer her way.

"Lola?" she said.

Lola cringed, expecting the worst. "That's me."

The girl stood up. "Oh my god, you're here! Everyone else is going to be so jealous when I tell them. We all love you. You're the reason I moved to New York!"

"Wait, really?" Lola flushed. It had been a while since a fan was nice to her.

"Really. Let me know what you want to try on. My manager is going to be so upset she missed you."

Ryan gave her an encouraging smile, and she grabbed a pale-yellow jersey dress.

"This feels very me."

"Lola likes!" Ryan sang. "Try it."

She stripped down in the small dressing room, kicking the halter dress to the side and tugging the high-end piece over her head. It fell softly down the length of her body, the buttery fabric the color of lemon ice cream. *That's more like it,* she thought, pulling back the curtain. The only thing out of place was the bandage on her foot, a painful—literally—reminder of everything that had happened.

The shopgirl and Ryan clapped. "There she is," Ryan said.

Lola grinned. "I *need* it."

"And it's only going to be, what, seven thousand dollars? A steal. I'll meet you outside."

If Lola was the girl Aly had accused her of being—someone with no personal style who defaulted to whatever clothing brands were paying her to wear and post about—she would not have bought this dress. She would have emailed a PR girl and asked for a freebie in exchange for some promotion. She would've even consulted the company about what color they were trying to push for the season, maybe even curated what would look best on her Instagram grid. But she wasn't that girl anymore. She refused to be. She was her own person, who could make her own decisions, starting with this ridiculous splurge on a yellow dress that she just simply *liked*.

Of course, even Lola knew Aly's criticism of her ran deeper than what she was wearing and where it came from. But she had all summer to make over her soul. For now, she'd let herself focus on aesthetics.

She bought the dress, only wincing slightly as the salesgirl ran her card.

On their walk back to the car, Lola noticed the Isabel Marant store was overflowing with people, crowding the sidewalk.

"Oh shit." She pulled on Ryan's hand as she began to drag him toward it. "They're doing that French vintage pop-up again. Can we go?"

"I would never deny you vintage," Ryan said, though by the weary way he said it, she knew he was running out of patience for the Lola Show and would soon need to recharge by the pool.

"We'll go home after this, I swear."

On the sidewalk, racks overflowing with beaded gowns, old T-shirts, and leather jackets called to her. She touched each piece gently, like a lover reuniting with their muse. There was so much to play with—so many different works of art that just needed a few stitches here or there to make them modern.

A younger, more innocent, version of herself wouldn't have hesitated to buy it all, then hole up in her apartment for days creating custom pieces that would get her stopped on the street.

But what would the new version of her do? The anti-Aly version? Who was the new version of her anyway? Maybe it was time to revisit her old self. It was worth a try anyway. And she had nothing else to do, not for the whole summer. She could buy a sewing kit and see what happened next.

She left the pop-up with her arms loaded down with her haul, a tentative feeling fluttering in her chest.

"Okay, now we can go." She grinned at Ryan.

———————

Back at the house, Ryan immediately fell asleep by the pool, and Lola retreated upstairs to try on her secondhand finds.

She'd found a polka-dot Moschino shift dress, green Issey Miyake pants, and huge brown Dior sunglasses; she'd scored a few thread-bare vintage T-shirts with various obscure logos on them from the dollar bin, plus an old silk floral scarf she was fairly certain was Gucci. She'd also grabbed some perfectly worn-in overalls with no label and a red leather trench coat with some rips at the hem. The final prize was a seventies maxi dress with long bell sleeves and orange flowers.

She had missed the smell of vintage, that musky giveaway that there had been previous owners, previous lives and stories. She tried to imagine the women who had worn these items before, what they'd been like, what they dreamed of.

She wondered, touching each soft piece, if she still had the knack for this or if she'd lost the gift over the years. It was entirely possible she'd just wasted a bunch of money for no reason. Her heart clenched, nerves racing through her. Maybe she wasn't quite ready for this step. She'd give it time. She had all summer.

She glanced at her phone. She had a lot of texts, most of which she ignored, though she did remember to send a message on the family group chat: Hi, Mom and Dad, I'm okay and alive. I love you. I'm in the Hamptons for the summer. It's for the best.

Her mom wrote back immediately: Have fun xx

Lola felt a little guilty that she hadn't called them back, but she knew they understood.

She returned her attention to the pieces before her. By the time she was finished trying it all on, the afternoon sun spilled through the window, creating soft shadows, and she realized it was almost time to go to the pop-up with Ryan. Still wearing one of her new T-shirts, she pulled on the vintage overalls and floated downstairs to find him.

He was nowhere to be found.

That was when she realized it was almost 5:00 p.m., well past when they were supposed to leave. It was odd that he hadn't waited for her or reminded her that they needed to go, but Ryan was always kind of passive-aggressive like that. Then she saw a note on the table. *Go without me. Love you.* She glanced out the front window and saw that the car wasn't in the driveway.

How annoying.

She sent him a text: You're not going?

I went already, he replied. I told you I was just stopping by. Emmett and I are going to dinner now.

She sighed. She didn't want to go without him, but she also didn't want to stay at home alone.

She could make an appearance. The party was just a bike ride from the house at least.

She checked herself in the downstairs bathroom mirror, dragging a bit of red lipstick over her lips. She didn't have the energy to change into the Khaite dress, so she fluffed her hair with her fingers and decided she looked like the kind of girl someone might call "chill." Hilarious, given that she'd never been chill about anything in her life.

It was breezy and a little cooler outside than it had been earlier, and on her ride over to the Mytheresa x Flamingo Estate party, she was thankful she'd worn pants. It was a beautiful ride, so different from her Manhattan adventures dodging pedestrians and taxis. With the ocean on one side and mansions on the other, the world became a blue-green blur as she pedaled, and she was grateful for the emptiness of the bike trail—it was calming. Despite her annoyance with Ryan and her mild dread about showing up alone, she felt a pleasant surge of dopamine. She should really get on the bike more, she realized.

The party was already spilling over into the parking lot when she arrived. Women were wearing silky gowns and strappy sandals; the men wore linen suits. Her stomach sank to the ground, a wave of dread washing over her.

She was completely out of step with the pace of the Hamptons—too dressy for brunch, too casual for the fashion party. She swallowed, trying to psyche herself up to turn on Professional Influencer Mode, or at least to prove that she still belonged to this world. Though who she was still trying to prove it to, she wasn't sure.

Herself, maybe.

She leaned the bike against the building just as a scruffy BFA photographer she recognized from some fashion week event or other materialized in front of her. "Hey, Lola," he said, raising his camera.

She posed for him—one leg slightly in front of the other, a hand on her hip, jaw relaxed, easy smile—falling into one of her tried and true angles. As the shutter clicked, she saw Monica Mollsbury, a beauty influencer she used to grab coffee with from time to time. She waved, trying to get Monica's attention. Their eyes met, and Lola smiled, willing Monica to come talk to her. But Monica only tilted her head to the side, as though considering whether to say hi. Then she turned on her heel and walked in the other direction.

So it's going to be like that, Lola thought, bracing herself for more awkwardness.

"Thanks, Lola," the photographer said and said, nodding at her.

He was cute, she noticed idly, though he wasn't really doing anything for her. She appreciated his tight T-shirt and his curly mop of hair but otherwise felt nothing. Not a jolt of interest. She sighed, suddenly missing the surety of Justin at her side.

"Honey lavender lemonade?" a server with a tray of drinks offered. She grabbed one, sipping it as she surveyed the scene and wondered who here would actually want to talk to her.

And then Brett Jennings, a guy she always tried to avoid, appeared before her and grabbed her by the arms. "Lola likes East Hampton!" he screeched in her face. "Girl, I haven't seen you since that messy Chanel party at Soho House. Rough summer, huh?"

Brett's brown hair was slicked back, and he wore an all-white linen suit. Lola couldn't really keep track of what he'd been up to recently; sometimes he had a magazine column, other times he worked in tech, but mostly he seemed to just be a hanger-on, following models around and stealing their clout. It was working; he had a million followers and the brand deals to match.

And he was still holding her by the arms. She hated when gay men thought they could get away with grabbing her like this.

"Don't worry, doll," Brett said, his smug smile making her want to scream. "You're no one until you get canceled. Welcome to the big leagues."

She wondered if he was going to ask to take a selfie with her—that was kind of his thing—but he didn't. Instead, he kept peering into her face, waiting for her to say something. Panic set in. She did not want to be associated with someone who thought getting canceled was a sign of success.

She needed to get herself out of this conversation, but she didn't know how.

As it turned out, she didn't have to.

Brett looked over her shoulder and then released her arms with a squeal. "Aly Ray Carter, live from the Hamptons! Take a selfie with me, doll."

Lola's breath caught in her throat. Not Aly. Not here. Not now.

Can I live? It seemed like the answer was no.

Lola forced herself to breathe normally, clearing her airway before she turned around slowly, her arms folded over her chest, trying hard not to look as shook as she felt.

Aly was wearing a white ribbed tank top, no bra. Sunglasses. Beige linen pants. Subtle adjustments to her Brooklyn vibe made her fit effortlessly into the Hamptons, like she was just slightly too cool to be here but participating in it all the same. Lola couldn't stop her jealousy from flaring. Of course, *Aly* didn't look underdressed. No, Aly made everyone else seem overly done up.

Aly grimaced through a selfie with Lola's new nemesis, who winked as he walked away.

She'd needed a lifeline, sure. There were few things worse than being faced with a judgmental cling-on. But did she really need Aly Ray Carter to save her? She resented it even while she appreciated the timing.

"Hi," Aly said, her expression unreadable behind her sunglasses. "I fucking hate that guy."

"Honestly, same," Lola said and then tensed as she remembered that she was supposed to hate Aly too. She searched for that swell of anger from yesterday, mentally giving herself a pep talk. *You hate her. You do.* Maybe it was the overalls making her soft, but she came up empty.

"How's the foot?"

"Like new," Lola said, which was a lie. It had been hurting her all day, though she'd been trying her best to ignore it.

"You look nice," Aly said, taking her sunglasses off. "Dressed down is a good vibe on you."

Lola bristled. She didn't want Aly to be sweet to her. It was so much easier when they were yelling at each other.

So she decided to be mean. It was safer.

"You look...comfortable," she said. "As always."

Aly laughed, surprised. "What?"

"I don't know, it's just... Have you ever put any effort into your appearance at all, or do nepo babies not need to get dressed up?"

"Oh my god, Lola," Aly said, a scowl gracing her face as she looked around to see if anyone was listening. "Can you just chill out for once?"

"Oh, *I'm* chill," Lola shot back.

"Did you bike here?" Aly asked, clearly trying to steer them into more neutral territory.

Lola nodded. "What, are you watching me?"

She couldn't be absolutely certain, but she felt pretty sure she saw a hint of pink in Aly's cheeks.

"I literally saw you ride up on your bike," Aly said. "We all did."

So maybe she wasn't blushing. Maybe she wasn't watching Lola as closely as Lola was watching her.

Unless...

No. Lola shook the thought off.

"What are you doing here?" Lola demanded.

Aly laughed. "What am I doing at a fashion party in the neighborhood where I, a fashion writer, am staying for the summer?"

Lola rolled her eyes. "I don't know, I feel like you should be drinking an Earl Grey somewhere, thinking about existentialism in Russian literature."

"I'm covering the event for *Nylon*," Aly replied tersely. "And you? Why are you here?"

"I'm canceled, not *dead*," Lola said. "I am allowed in public still."

What she wanted to say was that she was afraid if she stopped going to events, she'd be worse than canceled; she'd be forgotten. Showing up was a kind of self-preservation, a floatation device for her social status. But there was no reason to be that honest with Aly, not after everything.

"Oh, were you invited to this?" Aly asked, feigning innocence.

"Well, I…" Lola trailed off. She hadn't been. She was Ryan's plus one, and Ryan wasn't here anymore. How mean of Aly to call it out like that.

"I didn't think so," Aly said curtly. "I know the person who did the list. She's still mad about the lesbian chic thing, my article aside."

"I guess I will be apologizing for the rest of my life," Lola said, trying to sound more droll than she felt. Aly didn't need to know all the ways in which she was still beating herself up. It was more convenient to lay all the blame at Aly's feet.

"I think we are going to have to get used to running into each other," Aly said. "Otherwise, it's going to be a very long summer."

"I'm used to it," Lola said, giving her nothing. "This is not a big deal."

"If you say so," Aly said. A half smile played across her face. "Nice overalls by the way."

Any guilt Lola had felt for being too cruel last night was gone. Why did Aly have to be *so* fucking smug?

Her hands tightened into fists.

But then, as Aly walked away, Lola found herself wishing she'd gotten close enough to smell her.

After that, the seal had been broken. For the next three weeks, Lola saw Aly *everywhere*.

They bumped into each other at the wine store, reaching for the same bottle of rosé. They sat at nearby tables at the Crow's Nest for dinner, Aly with a mezze plate while Lola glared across the way until Ryan ordered her a steak, medium rare. In the mornings while she drank coffee in the kitchen, she often saw Aly going on walks along the beach. They sidestepped each other in line for the bathroom at Surf Lodge. They passed each other on Main as Lola went shopping. She saw Aly in her dreams too, but that was another story.

Aly was definitely a thorn in her side. But a rose was not its thorns, and Lola couldn't decide what was worse: seeing her or not seeing her.

At night, Lola retreated to the guest bedroom and indulged in increasingly raunchy fantasies—Aly tying her up, Aly fucking her in public, Aly teaching her how to squirt—all fueled by the running thrum of tension between them.

She wished she had brought her vibrator. She had a perpetual hand cramp.

In person, though, their interactions were less than desirable.

"What's up, Lola?" Aly said to her one afternoon as they passed each other in the produce aisle of Citarella.

Lola had a peach in one hand and an heirloom tomato in the other. She briefly considered chucking them both at Aly's head. Instead, trying to sound cool and aloof, she simply said, "Oh, you know."

"Those aren't really in season yet," Aly said, gesturing to the peach.

"I didn't realize you were the peach queen of Long Island," Lola snapped. "Any other hot grocery tips?"

Aly rolled her eyes. "Okay. Have a good day," she said, walking away.

Hot grocery tips? Lola spent the rest of the day trying to think of better comebacks.

Another time, Lola came out of the bathroom at Cowfish, a restaurant on the bay, to find Aly first in line.

"Fancy meeting you here," Aly said as though it was funny.

"Incredible," Lola said. "If I didn't know better, I'd think you were stalking me."

"Right." Aly nodded. "Because that's what I want to do with my summer."

"How else are you going to get your next headline?" Lola flashed her best fake smile as she squeezed by Aly to return to her table.

Each run-in, Aly tried to say *something*, as though she was enjoying watching Lola squirm, as though she liked constantly coming across as the bigger person. Sometimes Lola engaged. Other times she just laughed. It was getting ridiculous.

She was pretty sure she was losing her mind. How else to explain this complicated dance of one-upmanship she was engaged in?

She felt like she was seeing Aly more than she even saw Ryan, who was hardly even sleeping at Giancarlo's house anymore, always off to meet his new guy, whose name Lola had trouble remembering. She wanted to be happy for him that he seemed caught up in something romantic, but she was too resentful. Ryan gone meant she had no one to talk to, no one to bring her back down to earth.

––––––––

The big Goop event was on a Tuesday evening at the Parrish Art Museum, a charming, double A-frame building in a large, grassy field in Southampton. Precancellation, Goop had been one of Lola's biggest clients, and she assumed this was a pity invite. Still, she was determined to go. Perhaps by showing up, she could reclaim some of what she'd lost.

By now, Lola had figured out how the Hamptons worked: despite the relaxed beach atmosphere, you showed up on time and you wore nice clothes.

So she arrived at 7:00 p.m. on the dot wearing the yellow Khaite dress. And begrudgingly, she took an Uber instead of riding her bike.

It was a gorgeous, humid summer evening, the sky lavender with fluffy, pink clouds. The entrance to the museum was lined with candles, and PR people in all black were checking names at the door. Walking up, it was one of those moments when Lola—despite everything—was able to feel grateful for the things she had access to, for the beauty of it all.

Inside, women she recognized from the internet huddled in small packs, gossiping and taking photos. She beelined for the bar, ordering a spicy margarita that she sipped as she did a lap, pretending to be looking for someone. In reality, she was scouring the crowd, searching for just one friendly smile, one soft place to land.

A PR person materialized to usher the guests into another room, where a long table was lit with candles and decorated with dried flowers and herbs. String lights twinkled overhead. It was incredible Instagram bait, but Lola had deleted the app from her phone. There was still nothing she could post that wouldn't be met with the evil cries of delight from the trolls.

Pieces from the summer collection of G. Label were displayed around the room. Lola made a show of looking at some tunics before taking her seat. She always felt obligated to feign an interest in the product at a launch party, though for whose benefit, she wasn't sure.

A small card bore her name in calligraphy at a seat toward the end of the table, and she sat down, eyeballing the name cards next to her. On her left would be a fitness influencer named Rachel. On her right would be…

Of fucking course.

Aly Ray Carter.

Lola had accepted the fact that they were going to see each other everywhere, but that didn't mean she wanted to eat dinner next to the girl. She felt her pulse quicken as Aly appeared at her side, sitting down. She looked too pretty in the candlelight. Her pale skin had acquired the most subtle hint of tan. Her hair was down, hanging loosely around her face. The Hamptons looked good on her.

"Hello, Lola," Aly said. She sounded annoyingly professional. Lola had to remind herself that they were literally at work, and Aly *was* a professional. In many ways, Lola was the one who had turned this into a personal mess.

"Hi." She didn't want to be rude in front of all these people, but she also didn't care to be nice.

The rest of the table filled up quickly. She turned her back on Aly to say hello to Rachel, who immediately launched into a monologue about the weight she was trying to lose before September. "Have you tried the new all-natural GLP-1 supplements?" Rachel gushed.

Lola was nodding along at moments that seemed appropriate, but she wasn't listening. Instead, she strained to hear the conversation Aly was having with the people sitting across from them, who Lola gathered were other journalists.

"Yeah, I mean," she heard Aly say. "Sometimes I really don't think influencers should even be at press events."

Rachel was still midsentence, but Lola turned back to Aly. "What was that?"

Aly and the two well-dressed women across from them all stared at her.

She should be an adult. She should let this go. She should not make a scene in front of these notable writers and Goop; it was like she was spitting on Gwyneth herself. But lately, Lola hadn't been that great at doing what she should, Hamptons Zen be damned.

Maybe it was the tequila or the agonizing weeks of Aly run-ins, but she suddenly could not access Professional Influencer Mode. It was gone—it had evacuated due to the disaster of her career, running for higher ground. Which meant she was on her own.

She went full throttle. "You don't think influencers should be at press events? Who do you think is responsible for driving sales these days? You think anyone is actually reading the press? You think your little articles have more impact than one Instagram story from any of the girls here? You think print still has value?"

"Print still has value," Aly said in a voice that was frustratingly calm compared to Lola's questions raining down like shrapnel.

The problem with making this argument was that Lola *loved* print magazines. She still subscribed to all the major glossies and felt devastated any time another one became digital only, which was happening more and more these days thanks to—she knew—influencers like her. It was a horrible position to be in. She was partially responsible for the destruction of an industry that she loved, one she'd wanted so badly to be in that she'd created her own way to get there.

But she was absolutely not going to let Aly Ray Carter know they were on the same page about it.

Instead, she imagined flipping the table over, Teresa Guidice style.

A PR person at the other end of the table was clinking her fork on her wineglass and starting a toast, thanking everyone for coming. At the same time, cater waiters appeared, carrying plates of beautifully arranged salads, the first course.

Lola stabbed at her lettuce and frowned.

"How do you two know each other?" one of the women—the one with long, blond hair—across the table asked, as if to break the obvious tension that now blanketed them.

"I profiled her," Aly said, at the same time as Lola said, "She called me bland in *The Cut* and now my career is over."

"Oh," the other woman, a redhead, said, looking apologetic. "I did read that piece."

"And what did you think of it?" Lola asked tartly.

"Lola," Aly said. "We don't have to do this."

"No, really," Lola said. "I'm curious."

The two women glanced at each other. The blond one said, "I thought it was smart and largely harmless."

The redhead nodded, adding, "You know the news cycle. People were on to the next thing within a day."

"Well, this one seems to have had a longer tail," Aly said, stepping in. "There were some unintended consequences for Lola that I do feel badly about." She seemed to emphasize her words, her eyes drilling into the side of Lola's face.

Lola shot her a glare. "I'm sure you do," she said as sarcastically as she could manage.

"It was surprising to me that you even covered influencer drama," the blond said. "Not your usual beat."

The redhead was nodding. "Yes, that's true. What made you want to write it? Usually you cover much more serious topics."

"Yeah, Aly," Lola said, turning her whole body toward Aly, who looked like she was folding in on herself. "What gives? What did *I* do to earn the pleasure of your ire?"

"It was a good assignment," Aly said unconvincingly.

"Hear that, ladies?" Lola said. "Ruining my life was a good assignment."

Aly scowled in response.

"Are you going to stay on the influencer beat?" the redhead asked. "I'm sure it's lucrative, writing something so viral."

"No." Aly's voice was clipped now. "It was a one-off."

"Lucky me," Lola said. "So happy that you toe-dipped into my life specifically. I'm your unfortunate muse, I guess. Your one-and-done influencer chum! I feel honored."

There was a long, awkward silence. The women across the table stared at her. She was taking this too far, she knew.

"I think you and I need to have a conversation," Aly said to her. "Somewhere...else."

"Oh really?" Lola said before realizing Aly was serious—and was already standing. Lola's anger faltered. "Wait, what?"

"You don't *really* want to stay for dinner, right?"

"I mean, I guess not?" She had been looking forward to dinner, actually—steak was on the menu—but she'd lost her appetite the moment Aly had appeared.

She didn't know what was happening. She had not expected this.

Aly stood up and waited for Lola. And then, to Lola's complete shock, Aly placed a hand on Lola's lower back and guided her toward the exit. There was something almost chivalrous about it, and Lola gritted her teeth, as though that would protect her from Aly's charm.

"Do you want me to email you the one-sheet?" a publicist called to Aly as they walked out into the night.

"Yeah, thanks," Aly called over her shoulder. And then to Lola, she muttered, "I never read those."

"So rebellious," Lola whispered.

Aly smirked.

It was drizzling, and they were quiet as they huddled under the valet's umbrella, waiting for Aly's car. Lola was thrilled and terrified at the same time.

Would Aly shame her for her behavior? Collect more info to ruin her further? And where were they going?

There was nothing to do but surrender. Whatever was going to happen next was, apparently, up to Aly.

Chapter 9

THE VALET PULLED up in a vintage, green Bronco.

"Nice," Lola said, impressed despite herself. "What is that, an eighty-seven?"

Aly shot her a sideways smile, as though she was surprised Lola knew about cars. "Nineteen eighty-eight. My pride and joy."

It was raining harder now, and Lola held her bag over her head as she climbed into the passenger seat. Aly slid in next to her, one hand on the wheel as she pulled out of the parking lot and onto the road.

They didn't talk in the car. Lola kept accidentally holding her breath.

She eyed Aly's right hand, which rested lightly on the gear shift. She thought about holding it.

Aly was a good driver, with absolute control over the vehicle, which Lola always found to be a very hot quality in a person. It was a totally smooth ride. She loved being a passenger princess, even under these very weird circumstances.

Lola's indignation was petering out now that it was just the two of them in the intimate quiet of the car. There was no one to perform her anger for. Aly already knew how she felt. She didn't need to keep talking—or screaming—about it.

A few minutes later, they pulled up to Murf's, an Irish pub.

"How unpretentious," Lola remarked. "I'm surprised."

"I love a dive bar," Aly said. "I don't know who you think I am or why you've decided I'm so bougie."

Lola rolled her eyes. "Says the girl with a family home *out east.*"

Aly laughed, looking sheepish. "Shall we go inside?"

It was dark and quiet in Murf's, with a few sea-weathered locals hunched over tables. Aly and Lola sat at the bar.

"Do you have a chilled red?" Lola asked the leathery bartender, who could have been one hundred or twenty, but Aly interrupted her.

"We'll just take two Buds, please." And then to Lola, she whispered, "Trust me on this one."

Lola rolled her eyes, but being overruled like that made her stomach do a little flip.

There was a crack of thunder, and then the sound of rain dumping down on the roof.

"I think we're going to be stuck here for a minute," Aly said.

"Great," Lola said, and she wasn't sure she sounded as sarcastic as she meant to.

"Should we just have it out, then?" Aly turned to face her, and Lola did the same, wondering what Aly might do next. "You *have* to stop yelling at me in public."

"*I* have to stop *yelling* at *you*?" Lola forced a laugh to try to conceal how nervous she was. "Don't you think your article yelled louder than anything I could say at some stupid event?"

Aly winced. "Look, I'm sorry I wrote something that hurt your feelings. I'm sorry for the fallout. I wish it didn't have to be such a big fucking deal."

But Lola wasn't ready to accept the apology. "The fallout," she echoed. "Not a big deal? My entire team dropped me. I lost all my brand deals. And my boyfriend walked out on me." The roar of the rain grew louder, and so did Lola. "And even after all that, you *continue* to be *such a dick*. Why were you talking shit about influencers at what was essentially an influencer event?"

"You've been a dick too," Aly retorted. "All those comments about me being a nepo baby?"

Lola started to laugh but stopped when she saw the look on Aly's face—her mouth in a frown that said she was actually hurt by Lola's words. "I'm sorry," Lola said. "That was perhaps a bit too far."

Aly softened at Lola's apology. "I'm sorry too. I didn't mean to talk shit about influencers tonight. I just hate when I'm trying to write a story and no one will give me quotes because they're too busy making content. It wasn't about you."

"Was it not?" Lola didn't believe her.

"Okay, maybe it was a little about you. What you and I do professionally…it's not the same, you know? It's not similar enough to seat us next to each other."

"Yeah. What you do is so much more important than what I do."

Aly didn't have a response to this, perhaps because Lola had hit the nail on the head.

"Why am *I* the target here?" Lola demanded. "Those journalists at the event were right. I wasn't your usual beat. Out of the millions of girls in New York City posting on Instagram, why me? I know it's personal. It *has* to be personal. What did I ever do to you?"

Instead of answering, Aly crossed and uncrossed her arms. She tucked her hair behind her ear. For a brief moment, she looked like a little kid, unable to sit still.

"Oh my god, stop fidgeting," Lola said. "Just tell me."

"It's dumb," Aly finally said. She looked embarrassed, an emotion Lola hadn't realized cool-as-a-cucumber ARC could experience.

"Out with it."

"Laquan Smith, Fall/Winter 2019?"

Lola tilted her head, confused. "Huh?"

"You really don't remember?" Aly looked sheepish now.

"I really don't."

"You took my front row seat."

"I *what?*"

Aly looked like she was trying hard not to laugh at herself. Instead, she said, "Let me paint you a picture. I'm working on my first big *Vogue* story. I get stuck in traffic on the way there. By the time I fight my way inside, the lights are dimming. I have a ticket on my phone with my seat. A front row seat because, you know, *Vogue*. I run over to it, and it's occupied by this…" She trailed off. "This Amazon of a girl."

"*Amazon?!*" Lola cried, loudly enough that the bartender glanced down the bar mid-pour. "What makes me an Amazon?"

"You're, like, six feet tall, and you're built like you could kill a man." Aly smirked. "Just always taking up so much space. So anyway, there you were. And I said, 'Excuse me, I think you're in my seat.' Instead of getting up, you scooted over and said we could share it."

"I did?" Lola was still coming up empty.

"You did. So then we're, like, squished into this one seat, and the show is starting. I mean I was basically on your lap, and we couldn't stop laughing over how ridiculous it was. The PR girls even shushed us. I thought it was so funny and kind of charming while also totally insane that you would rather me sit on you than just get up and give me my seat."

Lola was stunned. "I feel like I should remember this."

"I feel like that too," Aly said, resentment and embarrassment warring in her voice. "I was shocked when you walked into Evelina for your interview and introduced yourself like we'd never met. Because I definitely remembered you."

They stared at each other for a few beats.

And then they both began to laugh.

Lola threw her head back and roared. Aly's shoulders shook as tears leaked out of her eyes, a silent hysteria. The more Lola looked at Aly laughing, the funnier it became until they were both hyperventilating.

They were making a scene, but Lola didn't care. Nothing had ever been more hilarious than Aly holding on to a one-sided grudge over something so minor and stupid.

"Water," Aly croaked, reaching for her glass.

When the laughter subsided, Lola felt lighter. It had been a release, getting everything out on the table.

She said, "So to get me back for not remembering, you told the world that I look like AI."

"No." Aly looked pained, her cheeks still pink from laughing. She briefly put her face in her hands. When she looked up, her brown eyes were wide and unblinking. "Do you want to know why I really wrote that?"

"Do I have a choice?"

Aly was quiet for a few seconds too long. She was clearly struggling with what to say.

Lola's heart started pounding in the silence.

Finally, Aly looked at her. "Because how you look..." She trailed off. "There's something unreal about it. Not in, like, a fake way. In a way where it's, like...hard to believe? Like, how do you even exist?"

Lola's mouth fell open. It occurred to her for the first time that her lust for Aly might not be one-sided. She felt like she was at the edge of a cliff.

Aly kept talking. "And there was no way to write that in the voice that people know me for. I had to add some snark to it so that it would still sound like me. But the truth? The truth is that I thought you were the most gorgeous girl I'd ever seen in my life, and the only explanation was that a computer generated you."

Lola's blood was rushing like Niagara Falls in her ears.

"And then, when we were talking, there were so many moments when you were so smart and funny and real. And I thought, *This girl is cool.* But then you'd pull back and come at me with this weird, fake shtick, and honestly, Lola, I found it really annoying that you were trying to be someone you weren't."

"Professional Influencer Mode," Lola whispered. How had Aly clocked it? As far as she knew, no one else ever had.

"Right. And I just wanted you to be *you*, to stop trying so hard. But you wouldn't. And that made me really frustrated because I liked you a lot, but it was like you wouldn't let me see the real you, and after our conversation, I was left with all these crazy mixed feelings. So I think, if I'm being totally honest, it's possible that I was so hard on you in the article because I was overcompensating for how I felt after we met," Aly said.

"How did you feel?" Lola could hardly breathe.

"The truth is I can't stop thinking about you."

Lola was both in her body and not. She felt the sticky seat beneath her legs and the pulsing between them. She felt the humid air and the warmth still on her skin. But she also felt herself zooming out, understanding that this moment was a major turning point, that when she'd look back on this time, she would remember this conversation at this bar with absolute clarity. There was a *before* this conversation and an *after*, and for a few seconds, Lola let herself luxuriate in the in-between moment. Everything was about to change.

Aly put a hand on Lola's knee. Warmth radiated up her leg.

She was glad she'd worn this dress, the material thin.

Lola wanted to say it back, to tell Aly how she'd dominated Lola's thoughts every moment since they'd met, but she couldn't. There was only one thing she *could* do, and that was slide off her barstool and take a step forward so that she was standing between Aly's knees.

"I'm going to kiss you now," she said.

Aly replied solemnly, "I know."

When their lips met, Lola forgot to be nervous that it was her first kiss with a girl. She forgot to worry if her breath was bad. She forgot that there were people in the bar who could see them. If someone had asked her name, she wouldn't have been able to say it.

Everything in the universe was Aly's soft mouth, her hands in Lola's hair, and the smell of her skin.

When Lola pulled away, Aly's eyes were soft and unfocused.

"Will you take me home?" Lola asked.

Instead of answering, Aly grabbed her by the hand and nearly sprinted out the door.

Chapter 10

ALY HAD LOLA up against the wall.

They had barely made it inside Aly's house. For the entire car ride, Aly's hand had gripped Lola's inner thigh, and at red lights, Aly had grabbed Lola's face and kissed her for so long that cars behind them started to honk.

The more Lola tasted of Aly, the more she wanted.

Aly's Double Chocolate Prada loafers had a bit of a platform to them, so when Lola kicked her espadrilles off in the foyer, they were the exact same height. When Aly's body pressed into hers against the wall, everything lined up. Their hips. Their chests. Their mouths.

Their pussies, Lola thought, blushing.

Hers in particular was feeling very…active. Desperate to join the party. Without thinking, she shifted so that Aly's leg was between hers and vice versa. Aly ground down into her thigh, just like in her fantasy, and let out a groan into Lola's mouth.

In response, Lola bit Aly's lower lip.

After everything that had happened between them—the article, the fallout, the cut on Lola's foot, the *weeks* of snarling at each other—she couldn't believe they were here. Doing this. Not in Lola's head while she touched herself alone in bed but in real life.

Aly pulled away from her and started kissing her neck.

Trouble, Lola thought.

She had no control once someone went for her neck.

Aly's hands slowly made their way up Lola's stomach until she was cupping Lola's breasts over the soft jersey of her dress. Aly's fingers found her nipples and grazed them lightly. Lola's breath caught in her throat, and Aly paused, noting the reaction, relishing it. Aly rolled them between her fingers. And then she clamped down and gave them a tug.

The noise that came out of Lola was unrecognizable to her. Almost a squeal, she realized with embarrassment.

But it made Aly grin.

"Kiss me," Lola panted, and Aly brought her mouth back to hers. She kept her hands on Lola's breasts, with Lola's nipples held tight between her fingers.

Lola wondered if now would be the time for her to touch *Aly's* boobs.

She certainly wanted to. But did Aly want her to? What did Aly want from her in general? Could Aly tell that this was her first time with another woman?

Was she judging her?

Was she wishing Lola would do something that wouldn't even occur to Lola?

What if she was only hooking up with her to be nice?

A pity fuck?

Suddenly, Aly pulled away. "You're freaking out."

Lola was out of breath. "I'm not."

"You *are*."

There was nowhere to hide from the panic. It was overtaking her. "I am," she exhaled, relieved to tell the truth. "I'm sorry."

"Is it weird for you that I'm a girl?"

To Lola's surprise, Aly sounded vulnerable, like she was afraid Lola might realize this was all a mistake and then leave. It had not occurred to her that she might have this power over Aly. She had only considered the other way around.

"Are you kidding?" she said, rushing to make Aly feel better. "I'm, like...*stoked* that you're a girl."

"Stoked," Aly repeated, a small smile twitching across her face, her previous tension relaxing. "Okay."

"Can we sit down, though?"

Aly guided Lola by the hand to the big couch in the living room.

"I think I am more nervous than I thought I'd be," Lola admitted.

"So you've thought about this?" Aly said, her voice wry. She arched an eyebrow, her whole body angled toward Lola's.

"You have no idea how much I've thought about this," Lola said. "The problem is I don't know what I'm doing." Aly's confident smirk warmed, and Lola felt the affection radiate toward her.

"You don't have to *do* anything," Aly said, pulling her close. "Allow me."

"Oh," Lola said in surprise, but then she couldn't think any further because as Aly kissed her, her hands dug into Lola's hair, and she pulled.

Everything ignited again. Unable to find the words to communicate how turned on she was, Lola bit Aly's lower lip. Aly grinned.

Then Aly's hands traveled down Lola's neck. She paused, feeling Lola's pulse race, and then traced Lola's collarbone.

Everywhere Aly touched glittered with electric heat.

Her hands moved down Lola's chest, grazing her nipples again before resting flat on Lola's stomach. She moved an inch lower, and Lola's body clenched.

"Can I take your dress off?" Aly asked, tugging her own shirt over her head in a decisive sweep. Lola felt dizzy, the simple act of Aly reaching for her own shirt hem, pulling expensive fabric from her own skin sparking a sharp desire in Lola's stomach. It was just so...*hot.*

Lola nodded and raised her arm so that Aly could unzip her, and then they both started laughing as they tried to wrestle Lola from the Khaite gown.

Once it was finally on the ground, they resumed kissing, sitting side by side on the couch, Lola in her matching black lace bra and thong and Aly in a Calvin Klein sports bra and black trousers.

Aly was a really good kisser. Perhaps she was even the best kisser Lola had ever encountered. It was like she could read Lola's mind. Their mouths melted together effortlessly. It wasn't too wet or too stiff. Aly didn't use too much tongue or too much caution in pulling Lola's hair or adjusting her chin just as she liked. It was the Goldilocks of making out.

Aly hummed happily, deepening the kiss as she skirted her hand along Lola's side, lingering and teasing Lola's bare skin. It was suddenly hard not to compare Aly to Justin. Justin was a good kisser too, but he'd always been a little forceful, a little too excited to press his tongue into hers. Aly was more controlled than that. More graceful, more giving. And Lola was no longer freaking out since the pressure to please Aly had been lifted. Now she could just enjoy each touch, sink into each kiss and lick and bite.

Aly unhooked Lola's bra with one hand. It fell to the couch.

Briefly, Aly pulled away and just looked at Lola, her eyes running up and down the length of her, eyes stopping in admiration, hands flexing where they were left against Lola's waist. Lola blushed, never having felt so bare.

"Damn," Aly said. "I know you know this already, but you're gorgeous."

"It doesn't hurt to hear it." Lola smiled.

"Oh, please. You definitely hear it on a daily basis," Aly teased, inching her hand up to Lola's collarbone again, stroking the soft skin just below her neck.

Lola shivered. "Not from you, though," she replied, head spinning from the goose bumps left in Aly's wake. "I never expected to hear it from *you*."

Aly paused, perhaps mulling over Lola's confession. "Then allow me to show you." Aly flattened her palm against Lola's shoulder, pushing her against the couch to climb on top of her.

Lola liked the feel of Aly's body on top of hers. She was light enough that it wasn't suffocating but substantial enough to be comforting. It was like being under a weighted blanket. A very sexy weighted blanket.

Aly's hair fell around them.

Holding herself up with one arm, Aly reached her other hand down so that it rested atop Lola's underwear. They locked eyes. Aly took one finger and pressed it right into Lola's clit, through the lace.

Lola tried to keep her eyes open, but she couldn't. They rolled back into her head.

Aly laughed. "Do you want more?" she asked.

Lola nodded.

"I need to hear you say it," Aly commanded.

Lola felt herself gasp, the demand sparking something deep and wanting. "I want more," she said. "Please. Fuck."

No one had ever made her beg for it before.

Aly slipped her hand beneath the waistband. Her fingers circled Lola's clit for a few seconds before landing on it. She began to rub Lola slowly, lightly.

Lola's heart was pounding so hard, she was pretty sure Aly could hear it. "Oh my god," she said. "Right there."

How did Aly know exactly how she wanted to be touched? No—how did she know *better than Lola* how Lola wanted to be touched? It certainly did not feel like this when Lola did it herself.

Aly started rubbing her harder now. Faster too.

"Let me take my underwear off," Lola said. Surely it would be easier for Aly to do this without that damn waistband.

"Keep them on," Aly replied.

"Fuck," Lola said, the only word she could remember. *"Fuck."*

She dug her hands into Aly's hair and pulled.

Aly made a sound that was halfway between a laugh and a groan, her eyes fluttering. "You can do that harder," she said, and Lola did.

Lola's back arched. Everything felt warm.

Aly dipped her fingers down into where Lola was wettest, not exactly penetrating her but deep enough to bring some of that wetness back up to her clit.

She craned her neck down and sucked Lola's nipple.

Game over, Lola thought. She was going to come.

She reached up and gripped a couch pillow above her head, anchoring her, everything pulling taut, every nerve alive. "Don't stop," Lola cried.

"I won't," Aly promised.

The moment Lola's pleasure tipped over, Aly slid two curled fingers inside her. Lola's moans became more like screams. She felt herself tightening around Aly's hand, as though her body was going to swallow Aly whole. And then everything crashed over her, the pleasure lapping in waves that had Lola writhing, that had Aly chanting her name, telling her, *yes, Lola, just like that.*

When Lola stopped writhing, Aly slowly pulled her hand away.

Aly kissed Lola on the mouth and then, still on top of her, nestled her head underneath Lola's chin.

Lola's muscles felt soft, immovable. Her head was empty. She felt like she had ascended to some sort of higher plane. And with the comfort of Aly's body tucked around her and the soothing touches of her hand skating across her arm, Lola let herself not think about what just happened between them, what might change now. Instead, she simply closed her eyes and gave in to the feeling of absolute peace.

———

They were still on the couch when Lola woke sometime later. Aly was on top of her, breathing in a way that told Lola she was in a deep sleep.

Lola craned her neck to read the wall clock. It was just after 3:00 a.m. She should go home. She had probably already overstayed her welcome. But there was no way to move without disturbing the surprising and almost terrifyingly sexy person sleeping atop her.

Aly lifted her head, feeling Lola shifting. "Oh shit," she said and then wiped some drool from her mouth and laughed. "I so did not mean to fall asleep on top of you."

"I'm so glad you did," Lola said, a warmth settling in her chest at the sight of the pink press on Aly's cheek. "But I should probably go home."

"You're going?" Aly asked. She sounded disappointed. "Was this too much? You *are* freaking out, aren't you?" Aly sat up, pulling away from her. She appeared to be shrinking into the couch.

Surprise hit Lola like a freight train, shaking the last bit of sleep from her thoughts. Cool, calm, collected Aly was *worried*. About her, about *them*. About what the two of them together actually *meant*. Lola grabbed Aly's hand, relishing the softness. "No, I just didn't think you'd want me to stay. *I'm* trying to not be too much."

"I want you to stay," Aly said, her voice taking on a more earnest tone than Lola had ever heard before. "It would be so sad in my bed without you."

"Then I guess I'm staying," Lola said. "God forbid you're sad in bed. And in the *Hamptons* of all places!"

Aly laughed, straightening again. "Exactly. I could get kicked out for my very sad, decidedly un-Hamptons -like behavior. They'd send me straight back to Brooklyn."

"Well, we can't have that, can we?" Lola stood from the couch, extending a hand down. She wasn't ready for Aly to leave the Hamptons. Not yet.

Not without her.

———

Aly's bedroom was painted the color of the ocean right before a storm. There were stacks of books on every surface. The bed was big and unmade, dark blue linens in an endearing twist. Lola briefly imagined a teenage Aly spending her summers here, brooding and rebellious, lazing on the bed reading Hunter S. Thompson and listening to some riot grrrl band that Lola had never heard of.

"Do you want to borrow clothes to sleep in? A T-shirt or something?" Aly asked.

"No." Lola grinned at her. "Though I will take some underwear. These are goners."

Aly laughed and tossed her a pair of Kallmeyer boxer briefs.

Lola went to the bathroom down the hall to change in a surprising rush of modesty given what had transpired between them on the couch. She pulled her thong off and placed it gingerly to the side of the sink, hoping she'd get to it in the morning before Aly noticed it. Then she used some of Aly's toothpaste on her finger.

She opened the medicine cabinet and surveyed Aly's products. It was the entire La Prairie line. She whistled under her breath. *Okay, Carter.* She didn't know why she should expect anything less than luxury taste at this point.

She washed her face with hand soap, though. It was probably too soon to break into Aly's prestige skin care.

Too soon. As if there would be a next time. She shouldn't get her hopes up. She swallowed and tried to remind herself of the very distinct possibility that this might never happen again, that Aly had put her in the hookup box. The one-night-stand box. The *it was fun, see you around New York* box. Once labeled, Lola knew it was hard to be moved into a different box, to convince someone to change their first opinion. It made her sad already. A weird kind of anticipatory heartbreak.

But when she got into bed with Aly, who was sleepy and warm in a soft tank top, Lola forgot about feeling sad at the thought that all this might be nothing. As soon as she was under the covers, Aly wrapped herself around Lola, becoming the big spoon.

ARC was a cutthroat journalist, an intellectual, a consummate cool girl. But Aly, the girl in bed? She was something else entirely. She was the embodiment of Lola's most secret fantasies. Dominant in bed but also caring and soft. Eager to please with flashes of vulnerability that made Lola feel understood. Funny, bright, and nonjudgmental, despite what Lola had previously believed. ARC might be a cool girl, but Aly? Aly was just cool. Cool to be around, cool to talk to. Very, very cool to kiss.

Lola fell asleep with a smile on her face.

———————

She woke up to Aly kissing the back of her neck. Soft morning light dripped golden through the window.

Aly's hands were caressing Lola's stomach, her breasts, her arms. Lola moaned sleepily and pressed her butt into Aly's crotch. This made Aly grip her harder. Lola turned her head back ,and they kissed.

She forgot to worry about her morning breath.

Before she even knew what was happening, Aly's hand was down the front of the borrowed boxer briefs. "Is this okay?" Aly whispered into Lola's ear.

Lola could only nod. She wanted Aly to touch her so badly that she didn't trust her voice to sound normal. She had always loved morning sex, the quiet intimacy of two bodies pressed together in a cozy fog of sleepiness, none of the pretense or performativity of nighttime hook-ups with lingerie, dim lighting, and candles.

How lucky that Aly was a fan too.

Aly kept her mouth at Lola's ear while she fucked her, and listening to the sound of Aly's breath quickening was almost more than Lola could handle. It told Lola how badly Aly wanted her. It was getting hot under the blankets, and Lola kicked them off. Aly was touching her more intensely now, so attuned with Lola's body that Lola didn't even realize she was going to come before she did.

When she could breathe again, she rolled over so they were facing each other.

Aly's eyelids were a little puffy, her hair a matted mess. She had pillow marks on her cheeks, a little crust around her eyes.

Lola was certain she'd never seen anyone so pretty.

"So," Lola said, smiling. "You're really into consent, huh?"

"What's sexier than consent?" Aly smiled back, but then she faltered. "I mean, you get why, right?"

Lola shook her head. She thought it was just Aly's thing.

"I'm gay. You're not. I would be horrified if it turned out I was making you uncomfortable or pressuring you in any way."

Lola had not considered this angle, and it gave her pause. She tried to see things from Aly's perspective. It made sense. Aly's desire for women was never in question. Lola was the wild card.

"Did I seem uncomfortable?"

"No," Aly said. "But I guess I needed reassurance."

"Did my dripping wet pussy not reassure you?"

The grin that splashed across Aly's face was as bright as the morning sun. "Good point," she said, clearly trying to downplay how thrilled this made her. She kissed Lola and then handed her a T-shirt. "So can I make you breakfast or what?"

Aly made scrambled eggs and sourdough toast while Lola, still wearing just Aly's underwear and T-shirt, sliced strawberries. They ate quietly at the kitchen island, their feet touching lightly under their stools. Lola wondered if she should try to make conversation but didn't feel pressed about it. There was something so nice about just sitting together. She didn't want to ruin it with small talk.

When they finished eating, Lola tried to bring the dishes to the sink, but Aly stopped her. "Don't you dare," she warned, taking the plates out of her hand. Then Aly kissed her for so long, Lola wondered if they were headed back to bed. She wanted to. She had nothing else to do anyway. Maybe they could have sex again and then take a nap. She felt herself grow wet anticipating it.

But then Aly pulled away and said, "I don't mean to kick you out, but…"

Before she could finish, Lola's pride swept in like the tide, snuffing out that early spark of interest growing in her belly. "No worries!" she chirped in her friendliest voice, masking the hurt, even though she knew it was silly. "Thanks for a super-fun night."

"Lola," Aly groaned, laughing. "*A super-fun night?* I just have a deadline this morning is all. *The Cut* wants a story on the Goop launch, and it needs to run this afternoon."

Chagrin swept through Lola, the explanation soothing that buzzy voice of anxiety in her head. It was as if Aly didn't want to play any games, wasn't into the whole mindfuck of the post-sex *will they, won't they*. "Okay," she said. "In that case, I had a great time."

"Yeah, me too." Aly nodded, opening the door. "Like, the best time."

They kissed in the open doorway, the warm morning breeze tickling Lola's hair. Aly grabbed Lola's hip, lightly smacking her ass with her other hand. Lola laughed into Aly's mouth.

"I'll be thinking about you all day," Aly said.

"Good," Lola said and forced herself to leave. Once she was in the driveway, she looked over her shoulder. Aly stood there with her arms crossed, wearing sweatpants and her sleep tank, grinning. Lola waved. Aly waved back. Lola promised herself she wouldn't look back again until she got to her own front door.

Which was when she realized that Ryan was there, in their doorway, his mouth open and his eyes twinkling.

"Hi, Aly," he called across the driveway.

"Hi," Aly said with a sheepish grin, closing her door. They hadn't been officially introduced, but Lola knew they'd seen each other across the hedges.

Lola reached Ryan, her face turning the color of a strawberry. "How much did you see?"

A lot, apparently.

Having a witness made it all the more real. *Holy fucking shit*, she thought. *I just slept with ARC.*

He grabbed her by both arms and yanked her into the house. Before the door was fully closed behind her, he shrieked, "LOLA LIKES PUSSY?"

"Oh my *god*," Lola said, annoyed that Ryan had already turned her night into a hashtag, but then she was struck by how funny it was, and before she knew it, she was laughing so hard that tears shot sideways out of her eyes.

Ryan was hysterical too, holding on to her as they both slid to the floor. When he could speak again, he said, "So after all that angry obsession, it turned out you just wanted to scissor her?"

"It would appear so," she said, wiping her face. "Sue me."

––––––––––

Later, after regaling Ryan with a thorough play-by-play of the past twelve hours and then taking a shower—reluctantly washing Aly's smell off her skin—Lola climbed into bed with her laptop and googled *how to make a woman cum.*

This, she knew, was slightly presumptive. It wasn't like they had made plans to see each other again. For all she knew, it was a one-and-done sort of thing. Maybe Aly hadn't enjoyed it as much as she had. But still, if it *did* happen again, she wanted to be ready.

But the search results were not super specific, too AI-generated to be helpful. She tried *how to have sex with a woman for the first time; how lesbians have sex; what does it mean if a girl doesn't want you to touch her back; how to tell if she likes me; diagram of a vulva.*

Then she typed *am I gay?*

She deleted it before even hitting search. She knew the answer—she wasn't. Her feelings for Aly didn't invalidate her feelings for all the men that came before.

Between each search, she checked her phone, wondering when or if Aly would ever text her. She kept having flashbacks to their night together: Aly's fingers curled inside her, Aly's hot breath on her ear. It was better than anything she had fantasized about.

Lola Fine, she said to herself as a vivid image of Aly pressing her into the door took hold. *You are down bad.*

Then she heard a knock. She checked the time. It was almost noon. "Ryan?" she called out. "Can you get that?" No answer. He must have left while she was in the shower, going to see that guy again. She wondered if she'd ever meet the mystery man or if Ryan was purposefully keeping him away from her. The thought left her mind as quickly as it entered, though. There were other things to worry about—like figuring out Aly's G-spot. And getting the door.

She was in a robe with her hair wrapped in a towel as she made her way downstairs, another knock quickening her step.

"Coming!" she yelled. She pulled the robe tighter around her chest as she opened the door. And froze.

"Bad time?" It was Aly. She leaned against the doorframe, the perfect picture of casual cool. Like she just *happened* to be here. In the neighborhood. Stopping by.

"Oh my god, hi!" Lola felt a rush of warmth.

"I realized I don't have your number," Aly said, smiling.

"Shit, that's right," Lola laughed. "And here I was waiting for your text." She immediately winced. "I mean…very casually waiting."

Aly laughed. "Well, if I'd had your number, I would have said that I really enjoyed our night together and would love to do it again soon."

Lola put a hand on her hip. "How soon?"

"What are you doing right now?"

Lola just about dragged Aly up the stairs.

In the guest bedroom, Aly sat on Lola's bed and watched as Lola took her wet hair out of the towel. And then, feeling only a little self-conscious, Lola untied her robe and let it drop to the floor. She stood in front of Aly completely naked.

Aly rose to her feet, wrapping her arms around Lola. Lola liked the feel of her bare skin against Aly's soft linen pants and even softer T-shirt. Aly ran her hands up and down Lola's spine as she kissed her.

"This is going to be a weird thing to say, but I missed you," Aly said.

Lola couldn't say it back because Aly's hands were already between her legs, rendering her speechless.

For the next three days, Aly and Lola did nothing but fuck, eat, and sleep. Or rather, Aly continued to make Lola come, and Lola quietly worried about whether she should return the favor.

Eventually, Aly turned her phone off and left it like that. The biggest event of each day was figuring out whose house to camp out at, an easier feat with Ryan being conspicuously absent from Giancarlo's, but other than that, they were bed bound. And shower bound and couch bound. And a couple of times on the floor.

The first time Aly went down on Lola, on her knees in the shower, Lola was pretty sure she understood why people believed in God.

She didn't know how anything could feel that good. Aly's tongue pressed into her with the exact right pressure. Then, as her lips encircled Lola's clit, she put one finger inside Lola while her thumb rested on Lola's asshole, and Lola sank to the floor of the tub, unable to hold herself up any longer.

"How are you so good at this?" she said when she could speak again.

"Not to sound like a jerk, but I've been a lesbian for a long time." Aly smirked. "You pick up a thing or two along the way."

After that, Lola required Aly's mouth on her. Sometimes Aly would drag it out, spending too much time kissing Lola's stomach while Lola squirmed in anticipation.

All the while, Lola wondered when Aly would be ready for Lola to return the favor. If she wanted Lola to return the favor. If Lola knew how to return the favor. The many, many favors.

Finally one afternoon, after Lola had come twice in a row in Aly's bed, she said, "I totally respect your boundaries, but I would very much like to touch you."

Aly turned pink.

"I'm sorry," Lola said. "I don't have to if you don't want me to. It's just starting to seem unfair."

Aly was quiet for a few seconds while Lola's heart thundered nervously in her chest. Finally, Aly said, "I am going to need you…to cut your nails first."

Lola blushed as she looked at her sharp, pink talons. "That's fair."

She flew to the bathroom and trimmed them down, doing a

horrible, uneven job. It was fine. She could get it fixed by a professional later.

But when she got back in bed, Aly's face was drawn. She'd pulled the covers up to her chin, like she was hiding.

Lola propped herself up on her elbow. "Tell me what's happening."

Aly groaned, but the faraway look on her face passed. "It's not that I don't want you to," she said. "I really want you to. It's just…my worst fear is that you'll be faced with my vagina and realize you're not into it. How would I ever recover from that kind of rejection?"

Lola's stomach sank as she realized that Aly was right to have that fear. She didn't know what would happen if—when?—she formally met Aly's pussy. She *hoped* she would like it. But that was just a theory, wasn't it? A theory that had never been tested. In the past, when she fantasized about sex with women, she didn't actually picture this part—or rather, their *parts*. All this time, it was as if Aly could sense it.

"Are you worried I'd be bad at it?"

"Good sex is about communication," Aly said. "And it's also about more than just orgasms. But I mean"—she paused, looking away from Lola—"the idea of someone not knowing what to do with my body is not necessarily a turn-on for me."

Lola's face fell. "Oh. Right."

Aly rushed to correct herself. "But I know you could learn. Shit, I'm sorry. I didn't mean to say that out loud. I guess I *am* freaking out a little."

Lola swallowed, trying to find the words to reassure Aly without being dishonest. "Obviously this is all very new to me," she started. "And I appreciate you letting me take it slow. But I can promise you that the way I feel about what we've been doing…" She trailed off. "You could probably have an alien living between your legs, and I'd be into it."

Aly laughed. "It's not an alien. It's a vagina. Isn't that scarier?"

"No," Lola said. She was continuously surprised by how much reassurance Aly needed, but she was down to give it. "Are you kidding? I have one too."

"I noticed," Aly said.

"I really, really want you," Lola said, growing desperate to build the trust between them. "I want to feel you. I want sex to be mutual. I don't need it to be all about my body."

"But I like your body," Aly said, still deflecting.

"And I like yours," Lola said, not giving up. "I'd really like the chance to get to know it better, though. Obviously, not if you don't me to. If that's not, like, your thing or whatever. But if there is any part of you that *does* want me to, please know that I am so down."

Aly sighed.

Lola could tell she was winning.

"If you're horrified, you have to tell me," Aly said.

"I promise I won't be," Lola said. "But sure, I'll tell you."

"Well, in that case," Aly said. "Go forth." She tugged off her underwear, leaving her sports bra on.

Lola reached down and touched Aly's soft mound of pubic hair. Aly moaned, and Lola grinned. This poor girl had gone so many days without release.

She tickled the hair lightly and then gave it a little tug before walking her fingers down, finding the place where Aly was open and swollen. Despite her nervousness, she found Aly's clit quickly. She wondered how anyone could miss such a thing; all those dudes who claimed to not know where Lola's was were clearly just not trying very hard. She flicked her fingers across it and then, imagining what *she* would want, began to rub it vigorously.

Aly immediately bucked, shouting, "OW!"

Lola pulled her hand back as though she'd touched a flame. "Oh my god, I'm so sorry. What did I do?"

Aly was laughing nervously, her hands over her face.

"Oh my god," Lola said again. Panic and embarrassment rushed through her. How had she fucked up so quickly? Should she quit while she was ahead, or would launching herself into the sea suffice as punishment? But no, Aly trusted her with this. She was going to fix it. "Tell me. Tell me what to do." She pulled Aly's hands down.

"Okay," Aly sighed. "I think we need an anatomy lesson."

"I think you're right," Lola said.

They lay side by side. "Okay, so all vaginas are different, right?" Aly said.

Lola giggled.

"I'm serious," Aly insisted, but she looked like she was trying not to laugh too.

"Okay, I'm sorry. I'm listening."

"So yours has a pretty substantial clitoral hood."

"It does?"

"Yeah," Aly said. "Feel it. Like, that piece of skin? It's like it's wearing a hoodie. So you like a lot of pressure, because your clit is underneath that skin, unless I were to pull it back while I fuck you, and then it would feel *really* intense."

"Huh," Lola said. She felt around herself. "I didn't realize that not everyone had that."

"Well, they do, but again, they're all different," Aly said. "As you may or may not have felt, my clit is bigger than yours. And it has less of a hood."

"Show-off," Lola said. "Big Clit Energy."

Aly rolled her eyes and smiled. Lola knew she really needed to stop making jokes, but she could feel the nervous energy bubbling up beneath the surface.

"Did you feel it?" Aly asked.

Lola shook her head. "I really wasn't on it for very long before I hurt you."

"Well, that's because it's *really* sensitive. It's totally exposed."

"Huh," Lola said. "I had no idea."

"I know," Aly said, a wry smirk on her face. "So how about you just do exactly what I say?"

Lola nodded quickly, obedient, nerves abandoning her as a rush of electricity shot to her core. *Hot*, she thought. She may not know intuitively how to please Aly, but she was good at following orders. She liked it in fact. A lot.

Aly said, "Don't touch it directly." She paused, looking at the ceiling. "With your hands at least."

"Oh." Lola's breath caught as she imagined her tongue on Aly.

Aly laughed, reading her mind. "One thing at a time. I'll tell you when I want you to go down on me."

Lola glanced down. Aly's pubic hair was trimmed into a perfect light brown triangle. Lola reflected on her own situation: a flawless Brazilian wax. She'd never considered how chic having a little bush might be.

Aly pulled Lola in, their mouths colliding. "Okay, that's enough class for today," she said. "Now show me what you've learned."

As it turned out, Lola was an excellent student.

She watched Aly's face as she touched her. Aly's mouth hung open in unselfconscious ecstasy. She was louder than Lola expected her to be, moaning like they were the last people on earth. With each wild cry, Lola felt more and more turned on. Giving pleasure to a woman was turning out to be as fun as receiving it. She wanted to fuck Aly forever. Her entire body ached with it.

"Go inside me," Aly begged.

They had not covered this in their lesson, but Lola felt confident she could figure it out. She slipped one finger inside Aly and then, because it felt like Aly wanted her to, another. Aly rocked on her hand, almost whimpering. All this time, Lola had thought she preferred to be submissive, but being in charge of Aly like this was powerful, intoxicating. Unbearably sexy.

"Can you hit my G-spot?" Aly said.

"If you tell me how to find it," Lola laughed.

"One inch up. Little spongy thing. Feels like corduroy." It was hard for Aly to talk in full sentences, which told Lola she was doing it right. She found Aly's G-spot quickly and pressed on it.

When Aly came, she screamed Lola's name.

It felt like flying.

On Thursday, Aly suggested that they go out to dinner. They'd been ordering takeout every day, existing on UberEats leftovers between meals, and Lola was nursing a low-level stomachache she was not ready to discuss.

"Like a date?" Lola grinned.

"Exactly like a date," Aly confirmed. "We can shower first and everything."

"I guess I'll go get ready," Lola replied. "Will you make a reservation?"

"We don't need one. Just come back here in an hour."

"Wonderful," Lola said, kissing her one last time before returning to Giancarlo's.

The house was dark and empty. It felt strange to be without Aly after so many days spent attached to each other. It was a little lonely, a little cold. But she knew it was good for them. Nothing killed a new romance like not having space from it.

God forbid we miss each other, she thought, stepping into the shower.

Her skin felt sensitive from Aly's mouth and hands all over her, and she was gentle as she scrubbed herself, pausing to examine the smattering of hickeys on her stomach. Aly had marked her that afternoon as they'd lain out on large towels in the sun, soaking in the afternoon heat while sprawled in Lola's backyard. It truly was the perfect summer afternoon—all pink skin and crashing waves and Aly's mouth again and again.

As Lola stepped out and wrapped herself in a fluffy white towel, she wondered what Aly thought of all this, if Aly had a habit of having sex with her subjects or with girls next door or if this was as new for Aly as it was for her.

She remembered what Ryan had once said, about Aly leaving a path of straight girls in her wake. She wondered anxiously if she was about to be one of them or if perhaps there was something special about her that made this different for Aly. She hoped there was. She couldn't imagine the alternative. Not now, with her skin humming in anticipation of seeing her again.

She dug a little black dress out of her suitcase and assessed herself in the mirror. Her cheeks were pink; her skin was glowing. She could go without makeup. She felt that there was something very French about wearing a sexy dress with a bare face. She scrunched her hair to encourage its natural waves. She couldn't remember the last time she'd felt so desirable.

The hostess at Si Si shrieked as Aly and Lola walked up.

"Aly Ray Carter, you get your ass over here," she cried, throwing her arms around Aly's neck. "You haven't been to see me once this summer."

"I've been a little busy," Aly said, glancing at Lola.

The hostess hugged Lola too. "Well, aren't you gorgeous," she said, and Lola blushed. "I bet you assumed I'd just have a table for you," the hostess said to Aly, glancing behind her where the dimly lit restaurant was packed with a growing weekend buzz. People on dates curled toward each other around small tables, slowly sipping martinis, cutting their mains with delicate hands. Larger groups of friends laughed around bottles of wine and seafood towers. Servers with their arms loaded with plates squeezed between tables.

"Do you not?" Aly's raised eyebrow calling the hostess's bluff.

"Well, of course I do." She grinned. "But it's rude to assume, you know."

"That's what friends are for," Aly said. "Assuming and free tables."

Aly held Lola's hand as the hostess took them to a corner table with a view of the bay. Lola was surprised by the easy affection. She hadn't been sure if Aly would be down with PDA, if she'd be okay with people knowing about their relationship. Or their situationship. Whatever this was.

The restaurant was oozing with charm. Leafy green plants snaked around rattan chandeliers. Just outside the windows, inky-black waves licked the white sand while boats rocked gently against a dock.

"Are you trying to impress me?" Lola asked.

"That depends. Are you impressed?"

"Very."

Aly grinned at her. The waiter came over before Lola had even opened the menu.

"We'll do a bottle of Sangiovese," Aly said. "And we'll start with a dozen oysters. Whichever ones the chef recommends. Then we'll split an arugula salad. She'll have the steak, and I'll do the fish. Oh, and a basket of bread, please."

The waiter nodded and left.

Lola was speechless, mouth left open and gaping like the expensive and—if Lola had to guess—delicious fish that Aly just ordered.

Aly looked up at her, noting her surprise.

"Is that not what you wanted?"

"No, I…" Lola paused. "It's exactly what I wanted."

Aly shrugged, looking pleased with herself. "I had a feeling."

"How?"

"I pay attention," Aly said. "I mean, how many times have we seen each other out to dinner at this point? How many meals have you posted on your Instagram? Which is totally cliché, by the way, but also proves very helpful when, let's just say, someone like me is agonizing about how to plan the perfect first date with someone like you." Aly winked her way. "I know what you eat."

"You insta-stalked me?" Lola asked, her mouth turning up in a dopey expression.

"I'm a *journalist*, Lola. It's what I do."

"You insta-stalked me," she said again definitively, her heart swelling into her throat.

So Aly *had* been watching Lola, just as Lola had been watching her.

And not only that but she had learned what Lola liked. Aly wanted to take care of her. To show her a nice time. It was startlingly romantic.

"I like your style, Carter," Lola added.

"I know you do," Aly replied.

"So tell me about coming here every summer," Lola said. "That must have been nice."

"It was nice and also lonely. There's not a lot for teens to do, and my parents' friends didn't have kids my age. I mostly just read books and felt sorry for myself. In hindsight, I was being a total fucking brat."

"I can see that," Lola said, fighting a grin. It wasn't hard to picture.

"How did you spend *your* summers growing up?"

"We had friends in Malibu," Lola said. "Which is kind of the Hamptons of LA."

"I liked Malibu the one time I went. It's crazy to see dolphins from the beach."

"My sweet little New Yorker," Lola replied.

Their wine came, and then the bread. Lola's stomach grumbled as she buttered a small piece.

"I heard that," Aly laughed.

"Good thing you got me the steak," Lola said. She was dizzy with the attention and the food. Eager to gorge herself on all things Aly, learn everything she could about the girl sitting across from her. "Okay, tell me more things. What are your hopes and dreams?" As the words came out of her mouth, she flashed back in time to her first encounter with Justin. This was a question *he* had asked her as they stood in that art gallery years before, slowly eyeing each other and updating their mental profiles from high school. Lola suddenly felt a pang of unease at how easily his question had slipped from her lips.

That being said, it seemed to work. Aly was smiling at her.

"My hopes and dreams," she repeated. Their calves brushed under the table. "I mean, sometimes I feel like I'm living my dream. Not many people get to make money on just their writing. Other times, I feel like I should be writing about more serious stuff. Not that I don't love fashion, but maybe politics or social justice issues. I don't know. And I do want to write a book. You were right about that."

Lola nodded, thrilled that Aly was opening up to her like this. "I had a feeling," she said. "I'm sorry I was so mean about it."

"It's okay," Aly said. "We were taking turns being mean. We can just chalk it up to foreplay." She reached across the table and held Lola's hand, a gesture so sweet and surprising Lola had to stop herself from melting. "Anyway, you tell *me* more things. What are *your* hopes and dreams?"

Lola swallowed. That *was* the question, just as it had been when they met for her interview. But she was unsure if she should reveal too much to Aly. She'd tried that once, and look where it had gotten her. How could she possibly articulate her identity crisis to the girl who had jump-started it all? But this Aly sitting across from her was not the same Aly who had interviewed her so many weeks ago. She couldn't be.

At least she hoped.

"Honestly?" Lola paused. She wanted to tell Aly about her dreams of being a fashion designer. But she couldn't get the words out. She was worried if she said it out loud, she might jinx herself. Or maybe Aly would turn around and write something mean about her again. No—Lola shook the thought off. She didn't really think that. Despite everything, she trusted Aly. Now that they'd spent a week in bed, she knew Aly wouldn't betray her like that again. But she still couldn't be totally honest with her, not about this. She wasn't ready. Instead, she said, "I don't know."

"You'll figure it out," Aly said, looking at her in a way that was so nonjudgmental and supportive, Lola felt warm all over.

After dinner—which Aly paid for—Aly said, "Have you ever walked around the hotel here? It's really pretty."

Lola shook her head. "Show me."

It *was* pretty. Pink and purple flowers wrapped around the resort, which had a pool overlooking the water and a dock lined with yachts. Their lights reflected golden swirls onto the inky-black water.

Aly pulled Lola's hand toward the beach, which was empty and dark. "Are we allowed down there?" Lola asked.

"Trust me," Aly said.

They kicked off their shoes when they reached the sand, which was cold and damp on Lola's feet. And then, before Lola really knew what was happening, Aly pulled her close and they were kissing. Lola shivered, and Aly held her tighter. They were in total darkness at the edge of the dock. They couldn't see or hear anyone else.

Which was how Lola justified putting her hand down the front of Aly's pants, where she found Aly was completely wet.

Aly hiked Lola's dress up around her thighs.

"How are we going to stay standing up?" Lola asked.

Aly started laughing and pulled Lola to the sand.

———

On Friday morning, Aly announced apologetically that she needed to turn her phone on.

Lola tried not to look over Aly's shoulder as reams of notifications filled the screen: texts, emails, news alerts, voicemails.

"Popular," Lola remarked despite herself.

She turned her own phone on. She had three texts in a row from

Ryan: **Wanna go to the beach?** followed by **Are you coming home tonight?** and finally **Going to Emmett's.**

She wrote back **Sorry sorry sorry! I'm at Aly's!**

Always a fan of brutal honesty, Ryan's read receipts immediately flagged that he had seen her text. He didn't respond.

But that was typical—Ryan was busy. Ryan was summering. Ryan would be fine.

"Sorry, I need to listen to some of these," Aly said, sitting up and bringing the phone to her ear.

"Totally fine," Lola said, while a sour, petulant feeling roiled through her. *Don't be so needy,* she chastised herself. *Just because you don't have anything going on doesn't mean she doesn't.* "I'll go make coffee."

Aly mouthed *thank you* before turning away.

By the time Aly joined her downstairs, Lola had made not just coffee but toast and eggs. She'd been singing to herself, trying not to wonder who had left Aly so many messages. Was it other girls, job offers, friends? Why did all of the above leave a small knot in Lola's chest? It would do no one any good for her to have a jealousy spiral. At least not before 9:00 a.m.

"Sorry about that," Aly said, perching on the same barstool where she'd once bandaged Lola's foot. "I totally forgot that I'm supposed to go to Fire Island this weekend. My friends kept calling me to be like, *are you alive?* And also to tell me I'm in charge of bringing hot dogs."

"Oh," Lola said, keeping her tone light. "Fire Island. Hot dogs. That sounds lovely." She wondered what she'd do while Aly was gone. She should probably try to make some plans with Ryan. The alternative (a house, alone; her hand, alone) was too pathetic.

"So you'll come? It's just for two nights. They got a big house in Cherry Grove. I'm supposed to leave later today."

Lola grinned, unable to hide her delight. "You want me to meet your friends?"

"Of course I do," Aly said, shaking her head and smiling. "Go pack. We leave at noon."

Ryan was home reading on the sofa when Lola burst through the door.

"What do people wear on Fire Island?" she said instead of hello.

"Tiny little Speedos," he replied casually, looking up from *A Little Life*. "Are you going with Aly?"

She nodded. "I have three hours to get ready to meet her best friends."

He sat up, concerned. "You're meeting her best friends after less than a week of fucking?"

Lola put her hands on her hips, annoyed at the accusation behind his words. "What's the issue?"

"Is that not… a little love-bomby?"

Lola was suddenly struck with the fact that she hadn't dissected Aly's invitation down to her every inflection. That she hadn't wanted to. Sure, things may be moving fast. But that was okay; Lola was into it—she wasn't shame spiraling and sad any longer. She was moving forward. She shook her head. "Do not plant the seeds of paranoia, puh-*lease*. I'm finally happy."

He sighed and lay back down. "Sorry. I don't mean to steal joy. Forget I said anything."

"Already forgotten," she sang, floating up the stairs.

And as Lola flung clothes into a weekend bag, she felt a needle of concern. Because she knew Aly liked her, that point had been solidified. But would Aly's friends be equally impressed by a fallen influencer crashing their little slice of summer paradise?

Or would they be so used to Aly bringing random girls to hang out with them that they wouldn't even register her presence?

Chapter 11

IT WAS AN hour drive to Sayville, where they'd catch the ferry to Fire Island, which, according to Aly, was the correct amount of time to prep Lola to meet her friend group.

"So it's Colette and Jess, and then Laurie and Lauren and their toddler, Clancy," she said, one hand on the wheel and the other resting possessively on Lola's leg in a way that Lola had quickly come to expect. "Colette and Jess are the most traditional butch/femme couple of the group. They're from another era. You'll see. And Laurie and Lauren are my bros. We call them the Laurs. They're my most normal friends. Laurie is a social worker and Lauren is a dentist. I love having friends who don't work in media. They're both LHBs. It's really cute. And they're both great, but Lauren is the sweet one. You'll see what I mean."

Lola's head was overflowing with information. "Wait, slow down. What's an LHB?"

Aly laughed. "Sorry. Long-haired butch."

Lola tilted her head to the side, considering this. "Is that what you are?"

"Mmmm," Aly said. "Not really. I feel like people always assume I'm more on the masculine spectrum than I am."

"The masculine spectrum," Lola repeated, suddenly feeling out of her depth. "Right. Okay. Are they all married?"

"Lauren and Laurie are. Colette says marriage is a tool created by the patriarchy to keep women at home."

Lola laughed, thinking of how she herself had balked at the idea of marrying Justin. "She's not wrong. And what do Colette and Jess do?"

"Colette is a literary darling. Her last novel was an international bestseller. And Jess is an associate producer, film and TV."

"Chic," Lola said. "Okay, tell me how you know everyone."

Aly launched into a story about how she met Laurie and Lauren at an all-lesbian pickup basketball game in Fort Greene, even though Aly hated basketball and was only there because her other friend was going through a breakup and needed company. Then she said, "And don't freak out, because it was a million years ago, but Colette is my ex."

Lola's mouth went immediately dry. "Why would I freak out? We all have exes."

"We sure do," Aly said in a tone Lola couldn't read. "But we're cool. It's been a really long time. We've both been with a lot of other people since then. And she's really in love with Jess."

"Great," Lola said, vowing to be reasonable. "I can't wait to meet everyone."

"They're going to love you," Aly said, kissing her at a red light.

"I guess we're about to find out," Lola said, her stomach twisting. She felt like she was about to take a test she hadn't studied for. "They know I'm coming, right?"

Aly waited just a beat too long before answering. "They know I'm bringing someone. Did I tell them it was *you* specifically? I mean, no."

Lola's stomach plummeted. "Oh good," she replied, unable to keep the sarcasm out of her voice. "I love providing the shock value."

Aly tightened her grip around Lola's thigh, not taking her eyes off the road. "That's not what's happening here, I promise. It's going to be totally fine. You'll see."

Lola sighed. She didn't want to ruin this perfect day with her nervousness. The sun shone high and hot on the car. The ocean was sparkling. Her bag was packed with ten different dresses and twelve pairs of underwear for forty-eight hours. She could get through this. If they didn't love her automatically, she'd force them to. She might even have a good time.

The rental in Cherry Grove was right on the beach. It was shabbier than the houses Lola and Aly were staying in for the summer but with its own kind of run-down charm; it had salt-weathered wood shingles and a huge porch overlooking the ocean. As they walked up, a toddler came bursting out the door, two gorgeous women with identical light-brown hair chasing after him.

"Clancy, get back here!" one of them yelled, sighing deeply before dragging her eyes up to non-toddler level, where she finally noticed Lola and Aly standing before her, holding hands with their luggage at their feet. "You're here!" she shrieked, allowing the other woman to retrieve the toddler from the sand.

Aly and the woman embraced tightly. When they pulled away, Aly said, "Lola, this is Laurie."

"So nice to meet you," Laurie said, a smile blossoming across her face. She was wearing cut-off shorts, a bikini top, and a trucker hat. Like Aly, she boasted a kind of understated beauty, like she didn't spend much time at the mirror because she didn't have to. She pulled Lola into a hug and then shot a look at Aly. "Well done," she said.

Aly smirked.

Lola wondered what Laurie knew of their situation or if the existence of a situation was simply implied.

To Lola, Laurie said, "That's my wife, Lauren, and the little monster is Clancy."

Lauren, who was shorter, equally pretty, and wearing an oddly similar outfit, materialized from around the porch, a squirming Clancy in her arms. "Hi, lovey," Lauren said to Aly and then gave her a one-armed hug, the baby wriggling between them. "And who is this?"

"This is Lola," Aly said.

"Hi, Lola, welcome." Lauren shook her hand warmly. Then she glanced at Aly. "You look like you could use some sun, Carter."

"You know how I feel about sunscreen," Aly replied peevishly.

Lauren rolled her eyes. "We know, we know. Sun protection is the only true antiaging product. Does she preach to you like this too?" she asked Lola.

Lola put a hand on her hip and assessed Aly keenly. "No, she actually has not, which is surprising, given that I'm a sun worshipper. I feel almost offended."

"Don't worry," Aly said. "I'm coming for you and your baby-oil habit."

"She probably just doesn't feel comfortable bossing you around yet," Laurie said, bumping her shoulder into Aly's.

Lola felt herself blush, and Aly grinned at her as if reading her mind. *Oh, they have no idea.*

Suddenly, Clancy started wriggling again, pulling Lola's focus as an alarming amount of snot dripped from his face and down his shirt.

"Oh, poor thing, does he have a cold?" Lola asked.

"No, he's fine," Lauren said, grinning. "What makes you say that?"

Lola didn't know if she was joking. "It just seems like a lot of mucus." She grimaced.

Laurie laughed, saving her. "Watch what happens when I try to wipe it." She pulled a tissue from her pocket. The second she got within an inch of Clancy's face, he started screaming, his face turning a reddish, ragey purple and his little eyes going all scrunched up.

"Got it," Lola said, swallowing the ick that rose in her throat. She had never been good with kids.

Lola heard the sound of a door creaking open on ancient hinges and followed Aly's gaze as she looked toward the house and grinned.

A small woman with a jet-black pixie cut and tiny sunglasses was walking toward them, a paperback in her hand. She was pale as a vampire with a see-through black dress and nothing but bikini bottoms underneath, her lips stark red with fresh lipstick.

"I cannot *believe* you got your hands on the *Intermezzo* galley before me," Aly cried.

"Sally sent it to me," the woman said, kissing Aly on each cheek.

"I've never been so jealous in my life."

Please don't be Colette, Lola thought as she watched the easy familiarity between Aly and the woman before them. *Please don't be Colette. Please. Don't be. Colette.*

The woman turned to Lola. "Colette," she said, sticking her hand out to shake. It was bony and cold in her grip.

"So nice to meet you," Lola said, forcing her best smile. She paused for a moment, searching for something more to say, something impressive. "Wow, you're so pretty," she blurted out instead.

Internally, Lola winced. Externally, she willed herself to keep smiling.

Colette did not smile back. "As are you, love."

Lola felt her anxiety, which had briefly quieted in the casual warmth of Laurie and Lauren, rise once again. The group stood there for a moment, awkwardly snared in the *what's next* of it all, when a fourth person burst from the house, waving her hand in greeting.

Jess, Lola reasoned, silently thanking the new arrival for the quick interruption. She looked like James Dean in a white T-shirt and blue jeans, her thick, brown hair slicked back in a pompadour.

Lola tried not to stare. Jess was very, *very* attractive.

She saw what Aly meant when she said the couple was from another era. They almost looked like Danny and Sandy at the end of *Grease*, all polished and sleek and hilariously juxtaposed against the weathered beach house.

Jess greeted Aly with a slap on the back so hard that Aly coughed.

"Let me take your things inside," Jess said to Lola after they were introduced.

"I got them," Aly said, but Jess had already gathered up all their bags and was heading inside.

Lola was surprised to see Aly roll her eyes. Was it jealousy? Did Aly not like being one-upped in the chivalry department? Did Aly prefer to be the only one taking care of Lola, or was it more about the performance of caretaking, and in that case, was it about what *Colette* thought? Lola felt unmoored in the new social dynamics, trying to understand years of friendship in a moment and how she fit in the mix.

They all followed Jess into the house, which smelled like Banana Boat sunscreen and the harsh chemicals people used to clean Airbnbs between guests. None of the furniture matched. Kids' toys were everywhere.

Toto, we're not in East Hampton anymore, Lola thought as she took in the cramped rooms, the shaggy throw blankets, and the half-open windows. The house was great. She had just grown used to Giancarlo's elevated beach decor and clean ocean view. Her summer thus far had been a bit more Amalfi Coast than Long Island. Not that there was anything *wrong* with Long Island. Lola could do Long Island. She could hear Ryan's scoff at the very thought. *Lola Likes Long Island, my ass*, she imagined him whispering conspiratorially in her ear. Lola shook her head, urging herself to stop being such a snob.

Aly and Jess took their bags upstairs, still in an odd standoff about who could carry the luggage up the fastest, while Lola followed the others into the kitchen. The counters were a mess, with bags of tortilla chips, dried fruit, nuts, LaCroix cans, and a few wine bottles strewn about, sprinkled in with sippy cups and scattered Cheerios. The art on the walls was cheesy and beach themed: paintings of seashells and sailboats, a large anchor hung on the pantry door. And somehow, as she looked from Colette to Laurie, Lauren, and Clancy, as they easily sank into their spots around the room—Colette perched against the counter, arms crossed; Clancy plopped on the floor with a toy truck; Laurie and Lauren quickly asking if she wanted a tour, handing her a cold glass of water—Lola realized just how much everyone fit here. How even Aly fit here.

She was the only one out of place.

Lola leaned against the sink, chugging the water. Her mouth was suddenly very dry.

"Do you want something to eat, Lola?" Lauren asked, popping open a bag of tortilla chips.

"I'm okay to wait until dinner," Lola said. The truth was she was too nervous to eat. She needed these girls to like her, and she wasn't quite sure how to accomplish it.

"So have you been out here before? To Fire Island, I mean?" Laurie asked, sitting at the table. She took her hat off and fluffed her hair with her fingers.

"Actually, no," Lola said. "Just the Hamptons."

"It's gay heaven," Lauren said, sitting on Laurie's lap, chips in hand. "I mean, like, gay *boys*. Cherry Grove is the one beach for the lesbians."

It hadn't occurred to Lola that the lesbians and the gay men would want their own beaches, and her face must have said so, because Laurie explained, "Different cultures. They're here to party. We're here with our wives and children to drink a glass of wine on the beach and then go to bed early. Not to be a total fucking cliché, but here we are."

Lauren said, "We have fun sometimes, I swear."

Lola realized, as Laurie was talking, that they had assumed she was not one of them. They were right, but it stung a little. She felt a twist in her stomach. She wished Aly would come back downstairs.

"Do you come here every summer?" she asked, trying hard to remain calm.

"We try to," Colette said. "The wild card is always Carter. Sometimes she has time for us, and sometimes she doesn't."

"One time, Aly met a girl at the bar down the road and didn't come back for a week," Laurie said.

Lauren gave her a light, playful slap. "Don't scare Lola," she said. "She just got here."

Lola managed a shaky smile. "No," she said. "I want all the dirty details." As she said it, she wondered if it was true. Did she want to know about Aly's sordid past? She *was* curious, but would it be better if she didn't pry? Could she remain in this blissed-out oblivion forever?

"Aly's the best," Lauren said. "Don't listen to us. And besides, we were all young and dumb once. Don't forget the year Jess got so drunk, she went to the wrong house, passed out on the couch, and woke up to that one queer punk band having a nice midmorning brunch around her."

She held the bag of chips out to Lola, who caved and took a handful.

"So, East Hampton, right?" Colette, who had inched closer, now leaning against the fridge, asked. "Next door to Aly?"

Seems they did know something of who she was.

Lola nodded. "Giancarlo's house," she said, her mouth still full of chips.

"I *love* that house," Colette said breathily. "I'm convinced no one has better taste."

"I agree with you," Lola said, swallowing. "Though personally I'm a little sick of minimalism. If I had my own house, I wouldn't have the restraint needed for an all-cream color palette."

Clancy abruptly threw the truck to the side and started wailing.

"Uh, yeah, same. Beige doesn't look good with Fisher Price, does it, Clancy?" Lauren said, swooping in to pick him up before sniffing his bottom. "Oof, looks like someone needs a change. Laur, some help here?" She strolled into the other room, talking softly and bouncing him as Laurie followed in their wake, leaving Lola and Colette alone in the kitchen.

The silence between them stretched.

Lola took another sip of water. She could feel Colette's eyes on her like a second skin.

"I *know* you," Colette said finally, taking her tiny sunglasses off. "You're the influencer from the article. The 'lesbian chic' heard 'round the world."

Lola felt the blood rush to her cheeks. "That's me," she replied, trying to sound casual. After a week of mind-blowing sex with Aly, she had almost forgotten it was the article that brought them together. Almost.

"Huh," Colette said, leaning against the counter, sizing her up. "Isn't this a plot twist."

"It certainly is."

"I mean, I guess it's not super surprising, given Aly's whole thing," Colette replied, waving her hand.

Lola could sense the bait dangling before her, but she couldn't help herself. "Aly's whole thing?"

"You know. Her thing for straight girls. I mean, you are straight, right?"

Lola was a good nine or ten inches taller than Colette, a fact that seemed to have no bearing on Colette's ability to make her feel small as the words hit her right in the chest. Lola shrank back, unsure how to respond.

At that moment, Aly walked into the kitchen, eyes flicking between Colette and Lola, her former lover and her current…what? "What's up, guys?"

"Colette just asked me if I'm straight," Lola said, trying to keep her voice light. "I haven't answered yet, because who cares?"

Colette laughed. "Sure. Right. Hey, Aly, what did your lit agent say about the article? Was the editor happy with how it did?"

Aly looked like she wanted the floor to open up and swallow her.

"What's she talking about?" Lola asked.

"Oh, you don't know?" Colette asked, feigning innocence. "Aly's trying to get a book deal. Cultural criticism. The editor at Knopf wanted her to have a couple more viral pieces before they sign on. Why else do you think someone like Aly would profile someone like…*you*?"

Someone like me?

"Colette!" Aly's voice was suddenly sharp. "Seriously?"

"What? It's not even a big deal—influencing and all that, it's all silly anyway. You said it yourself, so I'm sure Lola isn't offended. I mean, she's here with you, right?"

Lola's throat tightened. She felt the burn of tears behind her eyes. But there was no chance she was letting those free. She'd been to influencer parties and industry events; she'd had the most cutthroat things said to her with a smile and a swag bag. Colette wasn't going to make her crack because of a petty comment.

But boy did this one sting.

"Excuse me," she said. "I'm going to go get settled."

She kept her stride firm as she left the room. Aly called after her, but once she was out of sight, she flew up the stairs, finding their bedroom quickly, their luggage already on the bed. She saw there was an en suite bathroom and promptly locked herself in it.

Within seconds, Aly was knocking at the door. "Lola, can we talk?"

"Just give me a minute," she said and sat on the cold tile floor.

"Please," Aly said. "Let me explain."

Lola did not want Aly to explain. "I shouldn't have come here."

"Please don't let her get to you," Aly begged. "Please let me in."

Lola wanted to be left alone to try to untangle what the fuck had just happened. But she felt guilty for leaving Aly out in the room, so against her better judgment, she unlocked the door. She didn't get off the floor, though.

Aly closed the lid of the toilet and perched on it, her elbows on her knees.

"I was going to tell you," Aly started. "I mean you already knew I wanted to write a book. But I wasn't trying to use you to get a book deal. You *have* to believe me. I was just doing what my team wanted. I'm so sorry."

Lola cradled her hands under her chin. "I believe you," she said. "And I get it."

"You do?"

She nodded, a little bit vindicated that she was right—Aly *had* wanted to go viral. And she understood it, even if it stung. She even admired Aly's ambition. She was right to try to go viral to get a book deal. She just wished it hadn't been at her expense.

She already felt exhausted by this weekend, and they'd only been there thirty minutes. "It was more hurtful that she said you have a thing for straight girls." Though Ryan had warned her of this weeks ago, it hit harder coming from someone who actually knew Aly well. It made it more real—and possibly more true.

Aly sighed. "I'm so sorry she said that to you."

Lola looked at the ground. She felt too upset to look into Aly's deep brown eyes. She should have known that this whole thing wasn't about *her*—it was just Aly's pattern.

"So do you?"

"No!" Aly said. "I don't have *a thing for straight girls*. This has nothing to do with you and everything to do with Colette and the grudge she's holding."

At this, Lola looked up. "What's her grudge?"

Aly sighed and shifted her weight. "We were really young when we dated," she said slowly, clearly not wanting to tell this story. "And we broke up because I met someone else."

"That happens." Lola nodded.

"Well, the person I left her for had been straight up until we met."

"Ah," Lola said, the information starting to click into place. "So who was she?"

"She was a model," Aly said. "And I really loved her. I thought we were going to get married. We lived together for two years. We were kind of an it couple, though I hate to say it like that because it sounds gross. People were just constantly writing stories about us and taking photos of us. It was a whole thing. The relationship, in hindsight, was more about our aesthetic than our actual compatibility. Anyway, it turns out she was cheating on me with her ex-boyfriend. They're married now. They have two kids. They moved to the suburbs."

"Jesus," Lola said, her heart hurting for Aly despite how mad she still felt. "I'm so sorry, babe. That's awful."

Aly nodded. "So I guess Colette is mad about our breakup as my ex and, as my friend, worried I'm going to get hurt in the same way all over again."

Lola imagined what it would take for her to hurt Aly like that, for her to leave her for a man—for Justin, maybe. To have two kids with him and live in the suburbs. It felt impossible. It had felt impossible to live that life with Justin even before Aly was in the picture, but it was extra unfathomable now.

Lola rose to her knees and pulled Aly into a hug. "I would never do that to you."

"I know," Aly said, into her neck.

"But does it bother you that I'm straight?"

Aly pulled away and then gave her a funny look. "Do you really still think you're straight after the week we've had? You wouldn't say you're at least bisexual?"

"But I'm not bisexual," Lola said.

The truth was that Lola had never really considered it.

She knew that bisexuals existed, but somehow, in Lola's mind, it wasn't an option for her. Her ongoing attraction to men, she'd always felt, negated her occasional attraction to women. She hadn't bothered to think about the gray area, about whether her fantasies about women meant something larger about who she was. And whether that mattered.

Aly looked annoyed. "Whatever you say."

"I'm sorry," Lola said. "This is all so new." There was no use dragging this out, not when all Aly's friends were downstairs. "I'm going to take a shower, and then I'll meet you downstairs."

Aly seemed to understand that Lola needed a minute and finally left her alone.

In the shower, she turned the word *bisexual* over and over in her mind. She'd never considered it before. She had always just assumed she was a straight woman who was sometimes attracted to other women. If that made her bisexual, it was news to her.

The hot dogs were crisping to perfection on the barbecue by the time Lola reappeared downstairs. The tension from earlier seemed to have dissipated too. Whether because Aly told Colette to be nicer to Lola or she decided on her own, Lola didn't know and didn't care.

The sun had set and stars were twinkling into view, the moon a pale sliver in the velvety sky. Fire Island was greener than East Hampton, and the trees were bending in the warm breeze. It was a beautiful night, and Lola felt ready to relax into it. She didn't want to fight with Aly. She wanted to enjoy this new place, these new people—Aly's whole world and how she fit in it.

"Can I make you a drink, Lola?" Lauren asked. "We're all having negronis."

"That sounds perfect," Lola said, taking a seat on the balcony beside Aly, who put an arm around her and kissed her on the cheek.

"You look cute," Aly whispered in her ear, and Lola gave her a reassuring smile.

"Where's Clancy?" she asked.

"Sleeping," Laurie and Lauren said at the same time before quickly grinning at each other.

Lauren chimed in, "He goes to bed at seven on the dot. Otherwise, we'd go insane." She mixed Lola's drink and handed it to her.

Lola took a sip, struggling to swallow.

Aly said, "Too strong?"

Lola winced as it went down. "No, it's great."

Lauren laughed. "Sorry. I have a heavy pour."

"It's fine," Lola insisted. "God forbid I loosen up a little."

They all laughed. "Don't be nervous," Lauren said. "We're happy you're here."

"We are," Aly said and kissed her on the cheek again.

"I'll take a cocktail if you're still making them," Laurie said, handing her empty glass to Lauren, who smiled wearily as though this was her lot in life.

"Anyone else need a refresh?" she asked the group. Everyone handed her their glasses, and Lauren declared them all useless before trailing into the house, empties stacked and tucked in her arms.

"So, Lola, where are you from?" Jess inquired, leaning forward in her seat.

Lola flushed, finding Jess just a bit too stunning to look directly in the eye. Aly seemed to notice and smirked her way. "LA," Lola finally offered. "You?"

"No way, me too," Jess replied. "Whereabouts?"

"Laurel Canyon!"

"Altadena," Jess added, raising her hands in preemptive surrender.

"So you know that's hardly LA," Lola teased, "but I'll take it."

"I know, I know. The mountains were my backyard. But still. You and I have more in common than us and any of these East Coasters."

"Amen to that," Lola said. "So what brought you to New York?"

"Love." Jess eyed Colette, whose steely expression dropped momentarily. "We met when we were living in Los Feliz, and then Colette decided she wanted to be part of the New York lit scene. I followed her."

Colette rolled her eyes. "It was a little more complicated than that. It's hard to break out as an author when you're not near the publishing industry. In LA, everyone just wants to know about your screenplay."

"I get that," Lola said.

"Do you?" Colette asked, her voice curt.

There was an awkward pause as Lola grappled with what to say next. Sure, she may not be on the forefront of literary fiction, and sure, she didn't get hand-delivered books from Sally Rooney herself, but *still*, she at least knew what *Intermezzo* was. And Lola would pick up a smutty romance here and there. It wasn't like publishing and media were that disconnected. Lola squeezed Aly's leg under the table, a silent plea for help.

"Colette, can you be nicer?" Aly asked.

"I'm being nice." Colette pouted. "I just didn't realize Lola knew anything about the literary scene."

Lola stopped herself from rolling her eyes. It was bad enough that she was the only straight girl in the group—now she also couldn't be taken seriously because she didn't subscribe to *Kirkus*? Great to know.

Lola ignored Colette, turning back to Jess, who seemed to be watching the interaction like a mildly entertaining tennis match. "Do you think you'll ever move back?"

"I'm back and forth a lot for work, but it's hard to see myself there at this point. Maybe when we're ready for a slower life," Jess said. "What about you?"

"I can't imagine wanting to," Lola said, agreeing. "New York City is my whole personality at this point."

"I know exactly what you mean," Jess said. "I can't believe I ever lived anywhere but Brooklyn. But sometimes I do miss the mountains."

"Yeah. The natural beauty isn't really the same here. But…" Lola gestured at the ocean. "This is pretty beautiful."

Lauren returned to the table then, passing out fresh drinks before launching into a story about a mutual acquaintance that quickly pulled the four friends into a rousing gossip session. Lola raised her eyebrow at Jess, the plus-ones left to bond over their mutual West Coastness as Aly and her friends caught up. That was fine; Lola liked Jess a lot. She was funny and friendly and kind, so unlike Colette.

And it was a relief to talk to someone who had no baggage around Lola's very existence.

"So what do you do?" Jess asked.

The question was a gift; it meant Jess didn't know who Lola was or what Aly had written about her. She briefly considered lying, inventing a persona, but knew she wouldn't be able to keep up the ruse.

"I'm a content creator. I mean, an influencer. I used to be a fashion blogger."

"Oh, cool." Jess nodded. "What's your, like…" She paused. "Your thing? Sorry, I'm not asking this right. What do you influence people to do, I mean?"

"Buy clothes," Lola said, chagrined for a moment before adding,

"Vintage is my specialty." That wasn't necessarily true anymore, but maybe she could speak it back into existence.

"Oh, that's really cool," Jess said, like she was genuinely impressed. "I love vintage. You'll have to tell me where you go in New York. I need some new spots."

At this, Lola realized she didn't have any recommendations. Didn't have any new spots or freshly designed thrift finds to speak to. She suddenly felt struck by the fact that her plan for a soul makeover had paused the second she and Aly kissed, the pile of vintage she'd impulsively bought that first week in the Hamptons remaining in a neglected pile in her room.

It wasn't just the clothes themselves, of course; she knew that. It was what they represented. A different path—one where she was more creative, more independent, more free. Could she still take that path? Or had she been so busy distracting herself with Aly that she'd missed the boat?

No, she thought. It wasn't too late. The summer wasn't over yet.

Right?

"We'll compare notes," she said to Jess. "I'd love your recommendations too."

After a dinner of hot dogs and salad and cold pasta, everyone started to drift to their separate corners of the house. Aly took Lola by the hand up to the bedroom, closing the door.

"Would you like to have very quiet sex with me?" Aly asked.

That was, in fact, the last thing Lola felt like doing. She'd eaten too much, for one, but mostly she was just overwhelmed. Even when they were all being nice, meeting Aly's friends had left Lola's brain waterlogged, her eyes tired.

"Honestly?" Lola asked. "Could we just spoon?"

"Of course." Aly nodded. "I know this is a lot."

"It is. But it's also good. I'm glad I came." Lola offered a smile, leading Aly to their full-size bed, a downgrade compared to the king mattresses they slept on in the Hamptons.

Lola appreciated the size as Aly pressed against her back beneath the thin quilt.

Anxieties swirled in Lola's head, dulled only slightly by Aly's warmth and the negronis. She wondered if she was doing a good job getting these women to accept her. If she was fitting in despite the fact that she wasn't one of them. If she'd ever be one of them. If Aly minded that she wasn't. If Aly had brought her here as some sort of test. If she had passed.

"I can feel you freaking out." Aly's voice interrupted the quiet, and Lola sighed.

"Sorry, I'm just spinning."

"Try not to overthink it," Aly pleaded. "Let's just have a nice time."

"Okay, let me just flip my chill switch," Lola said, her voice flat.

Aly laughed into her hair. "Lola, please."

"Fine, it's fine. Switch flipped. I am chill, I promise."

She hoped this could turn out to be true.

———————

Lola woke up to the sound of a toddler screaming. She groaned and reached for Aly, but the bed was empty.

She looked at her phone. It was a little after nine. She texted her: **I'll give you a million dollars if you bring me coffee.**

There was a buzzing sound. Aly's phone was still on the nightstand.

Lola sighed heavily and prepared herself to go downstairs. Lying in bed, she went back over everything that had happened yesterday—the

awful things Colette said in the kitchen; what Aly had confessed to
her about her past; how nice Lauren was to her; how much she liked
talking to Jess; how special it felt, even though she wasn't part of this
group, to observe their bond.

As though watching a tape, she rewound to the part where Aly told
her about her ex, the one she'd left Colette for.

Aly hadn't been on Lola's radar when this relationship took place,
so Lola didn't have a mental image of the couple.

She googled *Aly Ray Carter and model girlfriend.*

The search results were flooded with Getty and BFA images, articles, and social media posts. The model ex-girlfriend, Raina, was a
light-skinned Black woman with long, shiny curls and a septum piercing. She was very tall and reed thin, which told Lola she wasn't just a
model but a *runway* model. Clothes simply hung off her in a way that
Lola envied. She dug deeper into the search results: Aly and Raina
photographed leaving fashion shows, at parties, on red carpets. Aly
and Raina linked together at restaurant openings and literary events.
Lola zoomed in, trying to figure out if Aly looked happier with Raina
than she did with her.

Aly wasn't smiling in any of the photos. Whether that was because
she was too cool or because she was unhappy, Lola could only guess.

She clicked further into Raina. She'd married her agent, a guy who
looked twenty years older than her. *Gross*, Lola thought. Their kids
were cute, though. Raina seemed to have left fashion altogether to be
a trad wife. Her entire Instagram was her making elaborate meals from
scratch wearing puff-sleeve dresses. Lola wondered if this was the life
Justin had imagined for the two of them. Despite how pretty Raina
was, she wasn't making it look appealing. So many fucking mason jars.

She was going to make herself crazy doing this, and finally the promise of coffee proved too powerful. She cleared her search history and forced herself to get out of bed.

Everyone was sitting around the kitchen table, nearly empty plates revealing the remnants of blueberry pancakes. Clancy was in a high chair, the floor around him covered in crumbs. Lola felt intimidated by the intimacy of the scene. Five friends who had known each other forever, enjoying each other's company first thing in the morning. She didn't belong here. She was intruding. She fought the urge to flee.

Aly saw Lola in the doorway and jumped to her feet.

"She wakes," Aly announced, bringing her coffee and ushering her to a seat.

"Lola, we were just making a plan for the day," Laurie said. "What do you feel like doing?"

"Me?" Lola asked, trying to caffeinate as quickly as possible. "Oh, no. It's whatever you guys want. I'm on *your* vacation."

"No, no," Lauren said. "We can find something everyone wants to do."

"We could go on that nature walk," Laurie said.

"I didn't bring sneakers," Colette said.

Colette looked like she didn't *own* sneakers.

"What about beach volleyball?" Jess said. "There's a net a little ways down."

"I hate volleyball," Aly groaned.

Lola sat up straighter. "Actually, I played in high school."

"Aly can watch Clancy while we play," Laurie said. "How long does everyone need to get ready? Five minutes? Three?"

There was some laughter. "Let's meet in the driveway in an hour," Aly said, nodding toward Lola. "Some of us are still waking up."

"I mean, it's a clothing optional beach." Laurie shrugged. "How much time do you need to get naked?"

The beach was already filling up with couples and groups of friends rolling out towels and blankets and picnics as their crew headed to the net. It appeared to be a younger, more diverse crowd than the beaches of East Hampton, and Lola appreciated it. In the Hamptons, everyone was thin and white; all the women had the same long, balayaged hair. Things were much more interesting out here. No two bodies looked alike; there were curves and cellulite and muscles, top surgery scars and tattoos and all kinds of piercings. Skin of every color. People had hair that was long, buzzed, cut into mullets. She tried not to look at all the bare breasts that shone in the sun. She didn't want to be a creep.

"Never been to a nude queer beach before?" Laurie asked, as though she could sense Lola's wide eyes.

"You know, I haven't," she said. She wished everyone would stop calling her out for being so new to this world.

To Lola's relief, despite the beach's clothing policy, all the girls in their group had their bathing suits on; Laurie and Lauren in simple one-pieces, Colette in a witchy Chromat bathing suit that tied into the shape of a pentagram, Jess in board shorts and a UV-safe tank top, and Aly in that black one-piece that showed off her long, pale legs.

Anytime Lola had been in a group of girls in New York, it had been in a work context: going to a fashion event together or agreeing to like and comment on each other's posts as a pod. She hadn't ever had a group of friends with such history and intention, and though she knew she wasn't really one of them, it was nice just to be around them and their fondness for one another.

Laurie produced a volleyball from her tote bag as they assembled themselves around the net, the waves crashing merrily in the background. Aly and Clancy flopped down into the sand and immediately began digging, making Lola's heart momentarily swell. Even though she wasn't technically a "kid person," she could appreciate how endearing it was to see Aly making Clancy giggle on the beach.

Jess and Colette declared themselves team captains, and Lola tried to prepare herself to not get picked for a team.

To her surprise, she was chosen first.

"I pick Lola," Jess shouted. "Team Bisexual!"

Lola wasn't sure if it was better to be called straight or bi by these women. Each felt like a potential minefield.

"You're bi?" Lola said, joining Jess on her side of the net.

"Does that shock you?"

Lola nodded.

"Because I'm masc?"

Lola treaded carefully. "I just don't think I've ever met a bisexual butch before."

"That you know of," Jess pointed out. "But the truth is I prefer the term *queer*. I feel like it encompasses more. It's not just that I'm into women and men. It's that I'm kind of into…everyone." She flashed Lola a blinding smile. "Transpeople, nonbinary people, just… people."

"I get that," Lola said, and she did. She felt it resonate deep in her bones, but she wasn't ready to go there. "But I don't think I'm bi. I think I just like Aly."

Jess shrugged. "Sure," she said. "Maybe for right now. But what about who you'll like *after* Aly?"

After Aly? Lola swallowed. She had not considered that there would be people after Aly. Despite the summer-fling vibe of whatever was going on between them, it was impossible to see beyond it.

Before Lola could answer, Colette's voice rose over the beach wind. "Stop flirting and pick your next team member."

"Flirting?" Lola cried, laughing at how ridiculous it was. "Who the fuck is flirting?"

"Ignore her," Jess said, laughing too. "She hates when I talk to pretty femmes."

So maybe they *were* flirting? But Lola hadn't meant to. Jess was just so easy to talk to and... Okay, she was definitely getting in her head now. She wasn't used to being in a situation where bonding with another girl could be misconstrued as sexual; she didn't know what to make of the teasing (or tormenting, coming from Colette). She eyed Aly, who seemed engrossed in building Clancy a sandcastle, and vowed to stop laughing so loudly at Jess's jokes, though she also had a feeling there was nothing she could do, no way she could act that Colette wouldn't have some sort of problem with.

"We don't need another team member," Jess called. "Let's do three on two. I have a feeling you're going to want the extra support."

Everyone agreed that Lola should serve first. She said a silent prayer that her muscle memory would kick in as she threw the ball in the air and then missed it entirely, slamming her fist through empty air as the ball dropped on the ground.

There was a pause before everyone began to laugh.

"Jesus," she exclaimed, heat rising in her cheeks. "I swear I've done this before!"

"You got this," Jess said from beside her, taking her spot on the sand, as Lauren called a chirpy, "Go Lola!" from across the net.

Lola picked up the ball again, mentally psyching herself up as she spun it in her hand. Across the net, Colette folded her arms, as though she didn't expect to need to use them.

How annoying.

Lola threw the ball in the air and then slammed down on it with a closed fist.

It flew over the net, and Lola's heart soared. That was until it rocketed square into Lauren's stomach with force, sprawling her on her back.

Laurie and Colette looked on in shock from both sides.

"Oh fuck," Lola cried. "Fuck, shit. Oh my god."

"Lola, what the fuck did you do?" Colette said as Laurie knelt down beside her wife.

Lola and Jess ran to the other side of the net, apologies spilling incoherently from Lola's mouth. That was when she saw Lauren bent in half, clutching her stomach, laughter racking her body. The knot in Lola's stomach loosened.

"I'm so sorry," Lola said, kneeling next to her. "Are you okay?"

Lauren wiped tears from her face, her infectious belly laugh catching as she burst out, "And to think, I've been so nice to you!"

Lola let out a groan. "You really have. I can't believe my aim was that off. I swear I was once good at this."

"It's okay. I'm fine. It mostly just surprised me!"

Laurie pulled Lauren up and then tossed the ball back to Lola.

"Try again," she said easily, a grin across her face. "And this time, try not to kill my wife."

Lola eyed Colette, her perfect lips twisted like she didn't want to smile. Lola gave Laurie a thumbs-up in return. "Right, aim for Colette next time. Got it."

Lola heard a loud laugh sound from the sidelines and turned her head, seeing Aly watching gleefully from her spot on the beach. Laurie and Lauren looked at each other in surprise before bursting into laughter again.

"Exactly, Lola. Exactly." Laurie nodded, stifling her glee as she patted Colette's shoulder.

They went back to their places, and Lola tried again.

On the next serve, she nailed it—a perfect volley. Lauren lobbed it back over the net to Jess, who set it over to Lola.

Okay, Fine, she said to herself. *You got this. This is just a normal game of beach volleyball. Do not overthink it. In fact, do not think anything. No thoughts. Just ball.*

Her mantra worked as she hit the ball clear over the net once again. For the rest of the game, she and Jess found a rhythm. The Laurs and Colette, on the other side, struggled to make three players work. They ran into each other; they missed easy passes. Jess and Lola were beating them so severely that, soon enough, they stopped counting points.

Lola felt, as they played, like she wanted more of this: trips to the beach and volleyball games and wine-soaked dinners under the stars— with these people, with Aly. Even if Colette was there, it held appeal. It was kind of dreamy to imagine how life might stretch out if she and Aly continued doing what they were doing. She was fitting in, despite her trepidation. She was even having a great time.

It was getting hotter out now, the sun high overhead, and eventually everyone drifted away from the net and into the sand, exhausted and starting to burn.

"Good game," Colette said to Lola.

Lola raised her brow, waiting for the *but* to drop.

"I'm serious," Colette said, stretching out on a towel. "I'm impressed. And ashamed. I suck at anything involving a ball."

"Or balls," Laurie said, smirking.

"Thank you," Lola said, accepting the compliment. "It's the only sport I've ever been able to play."

"That can't be right. I mean you're just so tall," Jess said.

"I bet you'd be good in our basketball game," Lauren added. "You should consider it when we all get back to the city."

Lola's stomach did a happy flip. Lauren thought she'd be around long enough to hang out with them in Brooklyn, to play basketball at the famous pickup games.

Aly passed Clancy back to his moms and then grabbed Lola by the hand and ran down to the water's edge, where the frothy Atlantic washed over their toes.

"How are you?" Aly asked. "Is this all okay?"

"I'm good," Lola replied, and she was.

Aly traced a finger down Lola's arm. "I love how your arm hair turns golden," she said.

"I know you do," Lola said and kissed her on the mouth.

Dinner that night was an early reservation at a pizza place with yellow umbrellas. Lola hadn't had pizza since leaving the city for the summer and couldn't stifle the groan when the melted mozzarella dripped hot oil onto her tongue.

"I heard that," Aly laughed.

"I think I just came," Lola replied, her mouth full.

Aly reached over and wiped the grease from Lola's chin.

"You're as bad as Clancy." Aly pointed. The toddler, too, was covered in pizza.

Tired from the long day in the hot sun, Lola was content to

sit back and let everyone else talk. She swirled her natural wine and looked out at the water, laughter rising and falling around her. For the first time in what felt like a long time, she thought of Justin. They were supposed to be in Capri by now. Or at least she felt fairly certain. She never could remember the exact dates of that trip.

And if she had been with him instead of here—if he hadn't abandoned her in her lowest moment as he had—she would probably be happy, just as she was now. But then she'd also never know the feeling of Aly's body on hers. Would she have spent her whole life wondering about other women, or would someone else have eventually caught her eye and lured her away?

It was strange to think how close she'd been to living a totally different life, how every decision had such a huge impact.

"Earth to Lola." Aly nudged her. While Lola spaced out, they had paid the check, and a girl with blue hair was cleaning up the table. "Let's go get in bed."

"Yes, let's," Lola said. They were the last to leave.

"Thanks for coming," the server said. "You guys make a really cute couple."

Their clothes were in a trail from the bedroom door to the bed. Under the covers, with the lights dimmed, they clung to each other.

"I have to tell you something," Aly whispered, between kisses.

"Anything."

"I like you."

Lola laughed. "I thought so."

"No. Like, I *like* like you."

"What is this, seventh grade?" Lola asked, trying to downplay the giddy rush she felt. "I *like* like you too, Carter."

"Thank god," Aly whispered in return.

What did it mean, Lola wondered, that she and Aly admitting to liking each other—no, to *like* liking each other? Did it mean she was safer? That Aly was less likely to leave her behind after this Hamptons summer, trample her heart on the way out?

She kissed Aly's neck, breathing in her skin. Her hands wandered down Aly's stomach. She certainly felt safer than she had in the beginning—than she had at the start of this weekend, even.

She flipped Aly onto her back and climbed on top of her. Aly laughed in surprise but stopped when Lola kissed her, hard and deep. Aly dug her hands into Lola's hair, pressing herself into Lola's leg. Lola could feel how much Aly wanted her, how vulnerable she was too.

Despite her reputation as a heartbreaker, she was just as soft as Lola, just as hopeful for love, trusting of it. Lola liked knowing this.

She kissed down Aly's neck and then her collarbone.

Aly's breath quickened.

Lola kissed down her chest, stopping briefly to flick her tongue across Aly's nipples, and then made her way down Aly's long stomach, dusted with beauty marks and freckles. She had the sudden urge to take a picture of Aly's torso so she could study it, memorize each spot.

She reached Aly's hipbones.

"Lola," Aly said.

"Shh," Lola said, grinning, and then gave Aly's left hip bone a hickey.

Aly squirmed beneath her.

This was fun.

She came eye level with Aly's underwear and kissed her over it before pulling it off.

"Are you sure?" Aly asked.

"Of course I'm sure," Lola said. "Now shut up. Please."

Aly nodded and gave in, closing her eyes and arching her neck.

Lola put one hand on each of Aly's small, lovely tits before sinking her open mouth onto Aly.

Remembering her lessons, she tongued Aly gently.

"Fuck, oh my god," Aly said too loudly, but Lola didn't care. Let them all hear her make Aly come.

And they did.

––––––––––

In the morning, everyone gathered in the kitchen to say goodbye.

"Thank you so much for including me this weekend," Lola said, not caring if she was coming off too earnest. "It was so nice to meet you all. I had the best time."

Jess pulled her in for a tight hug. "I don't know what I'll do without my teammate. It felt so good to kick their asses, you have no idea," she said.

"Until next time." Lola grinned. She turned, and there was Colette standing before her.

"I'm sorry for being such a cunt when you first got here."

Everyone laughed, including Lola.

"It's okay," she said. "Did I pass the test?"

"You did. And the truth is I've been following you on Instagram for years. I used to love your vintage how-tos. You should bring those back."

"Wow," Lola said, trying not to show how flattered she was. "Thank you. I know, I really should." If Colette thought she should bring back her vintage content, other people probably thought so too, which meant it didn't have to be a pipe dream. She could do it for real. She added, "I can't wait to read your novel."

"You'll like it," Aly jumped in, though it occurred to Lola that Aly had no idea what kind of books she liked.

"I'm sure I'll love it," she said, agreeing.

Lola hugged the Laurs goodbye, squeezing Lauren's arm for a second longer. "I'm sorry again for the volleyball incident."

"Oh please," Lauren said. "It's already forgotten. It was so, so nice to meet you. I hope we see you again."

"I hope so too," Lola replied, truly meaning it as she took in the group for a last time.

Lola and Aly left hand in hand. As the house faded into the background, Aly looked over her way.

"Did you really have a good time?"

"I did," Lola said. "And I liked getting to see you with your friends—your real friends, not people you know from the fashion world."

Aly nodded in agreement. "It's a different vibe. I'd love to meet your non-fashion-world friends too."

Lola frowned. "You can come over and hang out with Ryan whenever you want. Beyond that, the friendship pool is a little light these days. A certain takedown piece that a very hot, very high-profile journalist wrote took care of that." She bumped her shoulder against Aly's, teasing.

"Oh, Jesus, really?" Aly said. They were approaching the ferry now, and the air smelled like fish and fuel. "I'm so sorry, Lola."

"No, stop, seriously. It's not just that," she said. "I mean, I've never really needed more than one or two close friends. But the impact on my career, I think it's worse than you think it is."

"How so?"

"I couldn't tell you about this in our interview because of my NDA, but who cares at this point? I designed a line of dresses for Shopbop. They were going to be announced soon. But they killed the deal after the article. They don't want to be associated with blandness."

Aly looked pale. "So I ruined your dreams."

"It's okay," Lola said, suddenly uncomfortable. "I can find other dreams."

"No, you can't. You've wanted to be a fashion designer your whole life, and I took that from you." Aly dropped Lola's hand.

"Well, you don't have to make me feel worse about it," Lola said.

"And now I'm not saying the right thing either."

"Jesus, don't get so defensive," Lola said. "I'm the one whose life got ruined, not you. I'm allowed to have feelings about it."

"Yeah, but are you going to hold it over me forever?" Aly asked. "How many times do we have to go over this?"

"I didn't realize you were so sick of talking about it," Lola said, dismayed. "We've barely scratched the surface, and anyways, you're the one who brought it up, not me."

"Barely scratched the surface?" Aly repeated, her voice sounding angry and unfamiliar. "All you did was scream at me about it for my first month out here."

"But that was before," Lola tried. "Before we...knew each other." She didn't understand why this was turning into a whole thing.

"Yeah, but we were still us," Aly replied, short and sharp.

"Oh my god. Can you not start a fight with me after we just had such a lovely weekend?"

"I'm sorry," Aly replied, voice clipped, as they walked up to the queue. "I guess I'm just in a bad mood. Introvert overload. I don't do well when I don't get any alone time."

"I'm the one who spent all weekend getting tested by *your* friends," Lola said. "If anyone deserves to be in a bad mood, it's me."

"Were they really testing you, though? They just wanted to know if you're bisexual or not."

"But who fucking cares?" Lola said, so loudly that people turned to look at them. She lowered her voice but only by a little. "I don't understand why this feels so...political. I want *you*. It's not more complicated than that."

Aly's eyebrows raised. "You don't understand why *queerness* is *political*? What do you think it means to be a queer person in this country right now?"

Defensively, Lola said, "Why don't you go write an article about it?"

Aly rolled her eyes. "I know this is new for you, but what do you think my life, as a gay person, has been like? Some of us don't have the luxury of just liking who we like. It's who we *are*. It impacts our *rights.*"

"Please don't yell at me," Lola whispered. She suddenly wanted to cry. She felt like she was being lectured or talked down to or both.

"I'm sorry," Aly said before repeating, a bit quieter, "I'm sorry. I'm being an asshole. I think I need a snack or something."

They were silent on the boat. Lola stared angrily at the horizon while Aly sulked next to her. It was awkward in the car too. Aly didn't put her hand on Lola's thigh at all. Instead, she put NPR on and turned the volume up.

Lola spent the entire drive fighting back tears. Aly had been so cutting out of nowhere. After Lola had spent all weekend sucking up to her friends, it didn't seem fair to be treated like that. She was disappointed in Aly, but more than that, she was disappointed in herself.

Because the whole point of coming out to the Hamptons was to figure out who she was. And instead of doing that, she'd just jumped into an Aly vortex, where there was perhaps no room for her at all.

When they pulled into Aly's driveway, Aly finally faced her.

"Lola, I'm so sorry," she said. "Sometimes I do this thing where I push people away."

"No shit," Lola said, her arms folded across her chest.

"Please, listen to me," Aly said. "It's always been easier for me to do the hurting than to get hurt. And you could really hurt me if you wanted to."

"Great. So you decided to go first."

"It's what I do. But I'm trying to change. I want to change. I want to be a better person for you."

Despite herself, Lola's anger lifted an inch. It made sense. It was Aly's reputation, after all.

"We've got a good thing going, Carter. Don't ruin it."

"I know. I don't want to."

They kissed, and Lola pulled away first. "I think we both need some alone time," she said. "Come find me tomorrow."

"I will," Aly said and kissed her again.

As soon as she got inside, Lola let the tears fall. Slowly first, hot, thick drops dragging sunscreen down her face, and then harder as she sat down on her suitcase and began to sob. Everything that had been building all weekend came rushing to the surface—every snide comment, every dynamic she didn't understand, every single time someone reminded her that they all had something in common with each other and not with her.

"Lola?" Ryan was running down the stairs. He knelt beside her and put his arms around her. "What the fuck happened? Were the lesbians mean to you?"

"How did you know?" she said, laughing through her tears.

"Aly too?"

Lola nodded and sniffled. "She didn't mean to be, though."

Ryan rolled his eyes. "I'm sure. So *The L Word Takes Long Island* wasn't a dream, huh?"

"How long have you been waiting to make that joke?"

"Since the moment you left."

Lola wiped the last of her tears on the bottom of her T-shirt. "They gave me a lot of shit for being straight. Or for being bi. Or for not being gay. It was actually really hard to follow what they were giving me shit for in the end. And I thought Aly was on my side, but then when we left, she totally laid into me about it. And I still don't know what I'm doing with my life, and it's like I don't even really care because I just want to be doing whatever it is with her, you know?"

Ryan stood up and pulled her with him. "I hope you didn't let it get to you. You're allowed to just enjoy your new situationship without turning it into an identity."

"That's what I think!" she cried. "Why do I need a label? What does it mean if I'm just attracted to attractive people?"

"Honey, I think it means you're *alive*," he said, putting his arm around her.

She rested her head on his shoulder.

She wished being alive didn't have to be so painful.

Chapter 12

WHEN ALY DIDN'T respond to her first text, Lola wasn't all that worried, even though they hadn't spoken for twenty hours—a new record for them. Lola was surprised to find she really missed her.

The previous night, after she'd stopped crying about Fire Island, she and Ryan had caught up on *Love Island* for more hours in a row than she cared to count. She'd finished off a bottle of red wine while Ryan sipped a single beer. She had no memory of him going to bed; at some point, she simply found herself alone. She then ordered a whole chocolate cake on Postmates and ate most of it.

She crawled under her duvet around 1:00 a.m. with a stomachache but slept like the dead.

In the morning, she forced herself to down some chia seeds (surely that would balance out the cake) and even toyed with the idea of doing a Yoga with Adriene (the "Yoga for Overthinking" episode sounded relevant), though ultimately decided against it. Instead, she lay by the pool, tugging her bikini straps down to avoid getting tan lines, and took out her phone.

Hey you, she texted Aly. Lola was not a prideful person. She didn't mind sending the first text after a fight. Besides, they had made up yesterday. Aly had apologized, had even promised to come find her today.

While she waited for a response, she remembered the pile of vintage still sitting in the corner of her room. It was easier *not* to think about it, but with Aly not writing back, she couldn't avoid it.

She forced herself to focus on what she could do with the pieces. She could start wearing it as is, but most of it wasn't really on trend. Or, she thought, she could do what she used to do best: reimagine the pieces, tailoring them into something new. The thought made her heart race, though she wasn't sure if she was feeling excitement or dread. Her fingers itched to touch the fabrics, to arrange them into new shapes, but at the same time, she wasn't sure she still could. What if she'd forgotten everything she knew? What if she didn't have the right vision anymore? She thought of Colette urging her to do her vintage content again. If someone as chic as Colette wanted Lola to try, that had to mean something.

But more than that, with now nearly a whole day away from Aly, she finally had the brain space to think again. She wondered what it meant that, with Aly around, she couldn't see her own goals clearly. But this was normal, she told herself. Falling for someone new was distracting for everyone, all-consuming in a way. Wasn't it?

As if to prove to herself that underneath the layers of obsession and lust, she was still in there somewhere, she pulled up Amazon Prime and ordered a sewing machine, clicking the option for same-day delivery. It wasn't *that* expensive, and at the end of the summer, she could simply leave it at Giancarlo's house, a thank-you for letting her stay in his home.

Twenty minutes later, still no response from Aly. It was now noon.

You up? she tried.

Nothing.

Lola tried not to panic. She headed inside and went about her to-do list with one eye on the phone. She painted her nails; she made her bed. She went downstairs and did their dishes from last night, taking one final bite of cake before throwing the last piece out.

Still nothing.

Aly?

An hour went by.

She wandered down the hallway to Ryan's room and knocked.

"Yeah," he called, which she took to mean *come in.*

He was on the floor doing sit-ups when she pushed the door open, his muscles glistening.

"Give me ten," he said, and she wasn't sure if he meant minutes, seconds, or reps, but soon enough, he rolled to the side, splayed out on the ground and panting.

Ryan's room was larger than hers, with space for a king-size bed and a small sofa. It was only fair, she supposed, though she briefly regretted how quickly she'd taken the smaller one.

"You don't need more abs," she said.

"Counterpoint: I *always* need more abs," he said, catching his breath. "What's up? Why do you look like your dog died?"

"Aly's not texting me back. Should I walk into the ocean?"

He grimaced. "No suicide today, please. Sometimes people are just slow to text. It happens." He chugged some water, while Lola paced his bedroom.

"She hates me," Lola declared. "It's over."

"Hey, I have an idea," he said, arranging himself into cobbler's pose. "Why don't you come to dinner with me and Emmett tonight? Somewhere nice. It'll be a good distraction."

Lola stopped pacing. "Who the fuck is Emmett?"

He dropped his water bottle, eyebrows in an angry, straight line. "Seriously?"

She racked her brain. She was pretty sure she didn't know anyone named Emmett.

"Lola, the guy I've spent *all summer* falling in love with?"

By the way he said it, she knew she had fucked up. She tilted her head to the side, thinking. And came up empty.

"Are you sure you've told me about him?"

"Oh my fucking god," he groaned. "I'm sure! We analyzed his profile before we even got here! You've just been on Aly Island and clearly not paying attention to a word I've said for weeks."

He was right.

At least he must have been, because Lola had no memory of ever hearing about this guy, save for the notes Ryan left her when he vanished for days on end.

"Fuck me," she exhaled. "I am so, so sorry."

"I bet you are," he said, still sounding annoyed.

"There's just so much going on, you know? I'm pretty sure I'm losing my mind. This girl doesn't text me back for a few hours and I'm considering offing myself? Clearly something is really, really wrong with me."

He shook his head, but Lola could feel him loosening. "We already knew that."

She laughed, mildly relieved, but it was cut short by her own freakout—she wanted to meet this Emmett; she wanted to spend time with Ryan and work on her soul makeover and feel good again. She wanted to make clothes and gain back the trust of her followers. She wanted to influence (right?) and come out of this summer better. She even wanted to prove to Justin that her plan was the right one.

But she also wanted Aly. She didn't want Aly to ignore her. And she was worried that the latter wants felt…bigger. More demanding. And was that right? Was that supposed to be how this was? She could feel her panic stirring high in her chest.

"You can make it up to me by meeting him," Ryan said, interrupting her brain chaos, "and being really, really nice to him."

She nodded, eager to make it right, though she could still feel her worry about Aly trying to take hold of her brain. "Yes, let's absolutely have dinner. I am dying to meet him."

She hoped she could remember one single detail about Emmett first.

Ryan pulled out his phone. "I'm pulling strings to get us a reservation at Le Bilboquet," he said. "Seven. Okay? Don't dress like a hooker."

She flinched. He was kidding, but it stung.

Was that who she was without Aly? Still that same post-breakup, post-career, post-life-having poser who overthought everything, embarrassed herself in the wrong outfits, and made the wrong choices? If you took out the Aly piece of the summer, was Lola still in the same place as when she first arrived in East Hampton? She wasn't sure. And that was what scared her most of all.

"I'll be there," she promised. "Wouldn't miss it for the world."

A few hours later, Lola went to the downstairs window and peered out at Aly's house. There were no signs of life. Maybe, she thought with a sudden panic, something had happened. Maybe Aly had slipped or choked.

She should go over and check, she decided. Aly was a single woman in a huge house, alone. Which could be dangerous.

Still clad in just her bikini, she made her way to the neighboring house, where she knocked on the door and waited.

No answer. The lights were all off.

That was when she realized Aly's car was gone. *Huh*, she thought. She wondered when Aly had left. The car had definitely been there this morning. She wasn't sure how she'd missed Aly's departure. Maybe when she was painting her nails? Had Aly seen her texts before she left?

There were a few places Aly could be—lunch, not looking at her phone, having some sort of work meeting maybe.

Or hiding from Lola.

Maybe she even went back to Brooklyn to avoid her.

Maybe they would never see each other again.

Maybe Lola would be left on read forever.

The rational and irrational parts of her brain warred with each other as she went back to Giancarlo's and paced the living room.

She was not usually this girl. She didn't freak out when someone didn't text her back. Come to think of it, though, she was also not used to being ignored. Men in the city had just about lined up to date her. And Justin was a lot of things, but he wasn't toxic like that.

Was Aly toxic?

Maybe, she thought. But she also knew that her privacy and poise, that cool girl veneer, were what made Aly so attractive.

Or maybe Lola was the toxic one.

That still didn't mean she deserved to be ghosted.

Just as she was about to totally lose it, she finally got a text back.

Sorry, can't talk.

Sorry, can't talk?

What the fuck?

Lola wanted to throw her phone into the pool. She'd never been blown off so thoroughly. She didn't know how to respond. Should she say nothing? No, that wasn't an option. Aly owed her an explanation.

She wrote back Why not?

The three dots appeared and then disappeared. Appeared and then disappeared. Lola wasn't breathing.

Finally: Just give me some time, okay?

Lola felt like vomiting.

Never before had anyone requested time away from her.

Well, no, that wasn't true.

Justin had requested the whole summer off. Had she pushed Aly away in the same way? Was she just so unlovable that no one wanted to stick around? Was that why her followers were so eager to abandon her too?

Her phone buzzed with another text from Aly. Sorry. I am mind-fucking.

Lola's fingers flew over the keyboard. About what??

I just wish you weren't straight.

Her heart thundered in her chest. This again? she sent. Where are you?

Aly replied, Can I please have some space? I have a lot to process.

Lola flopped on the cream bouclé sofa. She gave Aly's text a thumbs-up and forced herself not to send another text.

Then she did the one thing she knew would make her feel better. She called her mom.

"Lola!" Jeanette answered on the first ring. "There you are."

"Hi, Mom," Lola said, feeling herself relax.

"How's my East Hampton girl?"

Lola paused, and in the pause, her mom heard everything. "What happened?"

"I like someone," she said, starting to cry. "And I think it got all fucked up, and I'm not sure how to fix it."

"Slow down," Jeanette said. Lola could hear the sound of the French doors sliding open as her mom went into the backyard and sat in her favorite rattan chair. Picturing it made Lola ache with homesickness. "You like someone? Not Justin?"

Lola was usually good about keeping her parents in the loop of her life. She flushed as she realized she hadn't even talked to them after Aly's article came out.

"I have a lot to tell you," she said.

"Well then, you better start," Jeanette laughed.

They'd read the article, of course. Jeanette gasped as Lola detailed the aftermath, how her team had dropped her. She made little noises of empathetic support as Lola described her breakup with Justin, how he demanded marriage and then walked out on her. She murmured appreciatively at how Ryan had taken care of her, and she laughed as Lola described the luxury and beauty of the place she was staying for the summer.

"Let's get to the fun stuff," Jeanette said. "Who's the new guy?"

Lola's eyes filled with tears again. She had not imagined this sort of conversation. Not a coming out conversation but not *not* that either. It wasn't that she expected her parents to shun her; they were her role models for acceptance. It was just that it was always hard to tell your parents something new about yourself when you've spent a lifetime as one kind of person.

"It's a girl," she whispered.

"Oh!" Jeanette didn't miss a beat. "You know, I dated a girl once."

Lola sat up, wiping the tears from her eyes. "You *what*?"

Jeanette laughed. "After college. Before I met your father, obviously. She was this superhot, really butch babe. I was powerless against her charms. Powerless!"

"So what happened?"

"Oh, you know. We had a lot of fun for a few weeks. But as it turns out, I'm not gay."

Lola slapped her knee. "See, that's exactly it! Why do you have to *be gay* to have a relationship with another woman?"

"Is that not the definition of the word?"

Lola groaned. "Mom, not helpful."

"Sorry, honey. I know your generation is a lot more fluid than mine was. It's different for you. You're not as caught up with labels as we were."

"Well, *some* of us aren't caught up with labels," Lola said. "I think that's why she's not speaking to me. Because her friends wanted me to say I was bisexual, and I wouldn't, and I think she got in her head about it."

"Well, who cares what her friends say? She should just trust her feelings for you and your feelings for her. Otherwise, what's the point?"

"*Thank* you," Lola replied, finally vindicated.

"So what do you want? What's your ideal situation?"

"What do you mean?"

"I mean, do you want to *be with her*? Or is it just a fling?"

"I don't know," Lola said. Yes, she'd considered a future with Aly, but she hadn't exactly landed on anything definitive.

Her mom laughed warmly. "Oh, honey. My sweet girl. Being in the moment is one of your great strengths. But when other people are involved, you do have to think about the future. It's not nice to be with someone you don't see a future with. It's a waste of their time, you know?"

Lola cocked her head to the side. That was exactly what she'd done to Justin.

She imagined her and Aly in bed together, holding hands on a date, making dinner in Aly's kitchen. There was nothing better.

It didn't feel like just a fling. It felt like something she could sink into. For a long time, at least—maybe forever? She considered it, and it didn't freak her out. Which had to mean something.

She *did* want to be with her.

She grinned into the phone, relieved to finally feel sure.

"Just be yourself," her mom added. "Everyone who knows you loves you. I think if you just start prioritizing Lola and the things *you* want to be doing, you'll attract the right sort of energy."

It was so LA to talk about things in terms of *energy*. She was really overdue for a visit home, she realized with a pang. But already, Lola's mind was stirring with ideas—she needed to find Aly, to tell her what she wanted—Aly.

"Speaking of which," her mom said, "are you doing anything to take care of *you* this summer? It's been a hard couple of months."

Lola's train of thought crashed to a halt. She hesitated. "I mean...I ordered a sewing machine," she said. "I was thinking of maybe trying to get back into designing."

She could hear her mom smiling. "I think that's great, honey," she said.

Lola smiled, albeit a little shakily. Taking care of herself was a nice thought, but it seemed beside the point. The point was Aly—she needed to make things right with her.

"Okay, tell me about you and Dad. What are you guys doing this summer?"

While her mom talked, Lola put her on speakerphone so she could redownload Instagram, not to post—she wasn't ready for that yet—but to see if she could find out where Aly was.

She logged in, gritting her teeth as she ignored the barrage of notifications and DMs, and searched for Aly's profile. They did not follow each other, but luckily, Aly's profile was public. She only had 9k followers, which Lola found endearing. Someone should really create a social media strategy for the poor girl. She couldn't stay mysterious forever.

Aly's most recent post was a flyer for a group reading. Lola zoomed in. It was that night. At Bookhampton. Lola had one hour before it began.

For a brief moment, she allowed her feelings to be hurt that Aly hadn't invited her. Then she shook it off. She understood why Aly didn't tell her about it. She would fix this. She had to.

Lola was hatching a plan when Jeanette interrupted her thoughts again. "Honey? Are you still there?" She realized she'd missed everything her mom had told her.

With a pang of guilt, she said, "Sorry. I lost service I think. Can you start over?"

Flowers. Lola needed flowers. And big ones too.

She probably wouldn't have time to come home after going to the florist, so she got ready for the evening as quickly as she could, showering so fast she might as well not have showered at all. Knowing Aly liked her dressed down, she wore her Levi's and her softest T-shirt. She pulled her hair into a topknot and kept her face bare but for some tinted Chapstick. At the last minute, she remembered deodorant.

Then she hopped on her bike and flew down the street.

It took her ten minutes to get to East Hampton Florist, narrowly avoiding getting hit by several cars along the way. She leaned
the bike against the store and burst inside, startling the florist,
who looked up at her through reading glasses and said, "You okay,
honey?"

"Great!" Lola said, panting and sweating. "I need a big bouquet
of roses."

"What's the occasion?"

Lola paused. "Telling someone I want to be with them."

The florist smiled. "Lucky guy. What color and how many?"

"Girl!" Lola corrected so loudly the florist jumped. "She's a girl."

"Good for you," the florist replied, nonplussed. "Color? And how
many?"

"Red," Lola said, trying to calm down. "A dozen. Please. No, two
dozen. Is that crazy?"

The florist shrugged. "I've heard crazier."

———

Lola followed Google Maps to Bookhampton, her bike basket overflowing with roses. The wind teased strands of her hair loose from
her topknot. Sweat stains began to form under her arms. But it didn't
matter. She just needed to get to where she was going and fast.

The charming, little, brick bookshop was sandwiched between a
Starbucks and an Italian clothing boutique. A crowd of bookish-looking
summer people gathered in the dappled light of the sidewalk outside it,
dressed simply in linens with branded canvas tote bags and oversized
glasses. Lola didn't *not* fit in, in her jeans and T-shirt, though she got a
few side-eyes as she entered the bookstore with her enormous bouquet
of roses. That was fine, though. Let them look. She was on a mission.

Inside, there were rows of folding chairs arranged facing a microphone. Lola planted herself in the front row and waited.

Aly was nowhere in sight, but that was okay. She was probably in some sort of green room, if bookstores had green rooms. Lola wasn't sure. She couldn't remember the last reading she'd been to or if she'd ever been to one at all.

She heard Colette's voice in her head accusing her of not being literary.

It wasn't untrue.

But everyone had to start somewhere, right?

She pulled the flyer for tonight's event back up, taking in details she'd missed before. It was all women writers. Aly was third in the lineup. The theme was "Stories of Summer." Lola didn't recognize the other names, but that wasn't surprising. This *really* wasn't her scene.

A bookseller walked to the front and said into the microphone, "If everyone will take their seats, we'll start shortly."

The room filled up, though no one sat next to Lola. She blamed the roses.

She had trouble concentrating on the first two readers, older writers with glasses, one of them wearing a big statement necklace that made her look more like a nineties art teacher. She nodded along anyway, though, participating in the performance of listening, all the while looking for a flash of Aly.

The bookseller returned to the microphone. "Our next reader comes to us all the way from the big city," he said to some scattered laughter, then began reading off his phone. "Aly Ray Carter is an award-winning journalist. Her bylines have appeared in *New York Magazine*, *The New Yorker*, *The New York Times*, *Vanity Fair*, the *Los Angeles Times*, and more. She's working on a book, but who isn't?" The bookseller paused, looking up at the crowd. "Obviously, Aly wrote her own bio." There was some scattered laughter at Aly's self-deprecating words. "All right, everyone. Please welcome Aly."

Applause.

Lola held her breath.

Aly, who must have been sitting in the back this whole time, walked up to the front, her eyes landing on Lola and then on the flowers.

Lola waved and then felt herself redden.

Don't be such a fucking dork.

Aly smiled uncertainly at her and then looked away, speaking into the microphone and addressing the audience. "Thanks, everyone, for coming, and thanks to Bookhampton for having me." Lola was surprised to hear her voice shake. Aly? Nervous? To read? It seemed unfathomable.

"You got this," someone called from the back, and the audience laughed. So did Aly.

"Thanks," she said. She pulled a piece of paper from her pocket. "I'm going to read something new. It's about…" She trailed off and then grinned. "It's about the girl in the front row, actually. Who, for the record, I didn't know would be here. But it's too late to read something else." Lola felt all eyes on her and beamed. "This isn't the kind of thing I usually write, so…go easy on me."

Aly took a breath and then began.

"You wanted to spend the summer in isolation—no plans, no friends, no obligations. You had a vision of yourself writing by the sea. You were going to drink wine on the dock while inspiration took hold, finally start that fucking novel everyone expects you to have published by now, find a therapist who will see you on Zoom, apologize to your mother for the way you've acted for the past twenty years. You were going to get in shape, get a tan, stop eating gluten." She paused, and the audience laughed.

"You came here to find yourself, and instead you seem to have lost your mind."

She looked up then, right at Lola, before continuing.

"It was like the world was drained of color. You deleted the apps. You didn't smile back at beautiful women. You closed yourself off to the idea of…" She paused for a long time before saying, "Love."

Love? Lola's heart felt like it was about to jump out of her chest.

"Sorry." Aly paused, breaking character. "This is unedited and unfinished." She flashed a nervous smile and then continued. "But love doesn't care what you had planned to do for the summer. It just wants to pin you against the door and hold you there until you're not sure if you've passed away from want. Love wants to come meet all your friends and pick fights with you the entire time." She stopped, looking at Lola again. "Love, I guess, wants to show up with too many roses after you've asked for space."

There was laughter. Lola's heart sank. She wondered if this was a mistake. She couldn't be sure where Aly's reading was heading. Foolish of her to think Aly would want her here when she hadn't been invited. When she had asked to be alone.

But then Aly kept going: "Love wants to insist you talk to her because you're doing what you always do. The truth is that you're terrified. The truth is that you're not sure you can survive getting your heart broken again. But she doesn't care about your reasons. She doesn't care about your summer plans. She doesn't care if you eat gluten. She demands to be taken seriously. And now that you've felt love, even if you totally fuck it up, you'll still never be the same. So you might as well stop being a pussy and give it a chance."

It was an odd and abrupt ending, and for a few beats, the audience was still, waiting for more. Then they realized it was over and broke into supportive applause.

Aly took the seat beside Lola and put her hand on Lola's knee.

I'm sorry, she mouthed.

In reply, Lola rested her head on Aly's shoulder, snuggling into her.

She didn't hear a single thing that was read after that. All she could think about was Aly's body heat, the smell of her skin, and the way she'd kept saying the word *love*.

While Aly thanked people for coming, Lola waited in the cookbook section, the roses growing heavy in her arms.

"Come here often?" Aly said as she finally made her way back to Lola.

Lola laughed. "Actually, no."

They kissed lightly, as though they were slightly unsure of how to act around each other now that Aly had bared her soul.

"I rode my bike here," Lola said.

"I can ride on your handlebars."

"That is literally *so* unsafe," Lola cried. "I'll just walk it back."

"Up to you." Aly shrugged, a mischievous grin on her face.

They were quiet on the walk back to their street. Lola ran through things she could say—*where have you been all day* or *I liked your reading* or *please don't ignore me anymore*—but everything felt trite. Aly seemed to feel the same way. Every now and then, they smiled at each other but quickly looked away. It was like a first date.

Finally, they reached their two houses. "Yours or mine?" Aly asked.

"Mine," Lola said and stashed the bicycle against the side of the house. A big box from Amazon sat on the porch. Lola was confused for a minute before remembering it was her sewing machine. She pushed it to the side and held the door open for Aly.

In the living room, they sat on the sofa side by side, only a few inches between them.

"Lola, I—" Aly started.

But Lola cut her off. "Me first, okay? You already had an audience."

Aly laughed and gestured for her to go on.

"I like you so much," Lola said. "I can't remember the last time I felt like this."

"Same," Aly interjected, and Lola shushed her.

"I want you in every way possible. I don't care that you're a bitch when you're moody or that you're still friends with your gorgeous, tiny, *super*-mean ex-girlfriend. I don't care that you ruined my life once already. I just want you. I want to be with you."

Aly raised an eyebrow. "Be with me, or be *with* me?"

"*With* you," Lola confirmed. "But you have to accept me for me too. And I'm sorry that I'm not a lesbian. I'm sorry I'm not even bisexual. I know it would be easier for you if I were. It might be easier for me too, or at least less confusing. But it's not like I want anyone else. And shouldn't that be what matters?"

Aly was quiet, her hands folded in her lap.

Lola continued, "Maybe one day, I'll feel differently. Maybe there's a word for me that I haven't encountered yet. But all I know is how I feel, and how I feel is that I can't lose you. I won't."

"You're not going to lose me," Aly said. She took both of Lola's hands in hers. "And you're right. It doesn't matter. I know that you care about me. I don't need you to be someone you're not."

"Really?" Lola said, in shock that Aly had agreed so quickly. "Are you sure?"

Instead of answering, Aly kissed her, long and deep. Lola leaned into it.

Aly whispered into her mouth, "I'm sure."

Lola pounced on her, happiness filling her body, coursing through all those places that had been empty and sad all day, knocking them both backward onto the couch. She kissed Aly's neck while Aly gripped her ass. "I've never wanted anyone the way I want you," Aly said, and then she flipped Lola over and pulled her jeans off.

She kissed up Lola's legs, her hands tight on Lola's thighs. Lola didn't bother trying to be quiet.

When Aly finally put her mouth where Lola was wettest, it was all Lola could do to keep from screaming. Aly's tongue swirled into her with the exact right pressure. But she didn't want to be the sole recipient of pleasure. She wanted Aly to feel what she was feeling while she was feeling it. She sat up.

"What are you doing?" Aly asked.

Wordlessly, Lola arranged herself so that Aly could keep going down on her while she did the same.

"Fuck," came Aly's muffled voice from between Lola's legs.

Don't come, Lola told herself while she licked deeper into Aly. *Don't come don't come don't come don't come.*

Aly's thighs tightened around Lola's head. *Okay*, she thought. *Maybe now I can come.*

They both did.

Just in time to hear the front door open. And then a scream.

"Lola, what the absolute fuck?"

Aly and Lola flew to opposite sides of the couch, scrambling for their pants.

Ryan stood in the doorway, horror painted plainly on his face.

"This is what you missed dinner for? So y'all could sixty-nine on Giancarlo's twenty-thousand-dollar sofa?"

Dinner?

Then it hit her.

Dinner. With Ryan and Emmett.

"Oh my god, Ryan," she started to say, but he cut her off.

The words were tumbling out of his mouth faster and faster. "You are out of control. This entire summer, you've been so selfish. You've been binge-drinking depression wine, you haven't done anything to salvage your career, you've been entirely absent from my life, and you've just been here using me and my house and my access."

"Jesus," Aly said.

Ryan ignored her. "It's always about you. It's always the Lola show."

"I don't *want* it to be," Lola cried. "You know that!"

"I *do* know that. Why else would you bury your head, actually literally I guess, in a new lesbian-chic relationship instead of dealing with your own fucking shit!"

The truth slapped Lola right in the face.

It was exactly what she didn't want to deal with, stated so plainly by Ryan, who always had known her best. And he was right. Because Lola was so sick of herself, sick enough she was willing to get totally lost in a relationship so she wouldn't have to face her own thoughts. But she couldn't say that. Not with Aly here.

"Ouch," she said quietly.

Ryan wasn't done yelling at her. "Oh, poor me. I'm Lola. I didn't mean to say it. I didn't mean to do it. I didn't mean to sleep with the woman who ruined my life. But, like, you *did*. And you're an adult. You have to take accountability."

"I should go," Aly said, starting to stand up.

"No, no, by all means," Ryan said. "Stay at my client's house and jizz on his white sofa. Really. I don't care at all."

Aly sat back down, as though stunned by his crudeness.

"Ryan, I'm sorry I missed dinner," Lola said, trying to keep her voice from breaking. "I was so freaked out about losing Aly that I just totally spaced."

"And what's your excuse for every day leading up to now?" he shot back. "First we hate her, then we love her, then we hate her, then we love her. Meanwhile, I've been here all summer, on *my* summer trip, waiting for you to come back down to earth. At a certain point, the problem is *you*."

Lola did start to cry then.

Aly jumped in. "Hey, man, it's none of my business, but don't you think you're being a little hard on her?"

"You're right. It isn't any of your business."

Aly held her hands up in surrender.

Ryan continued, "And what the fuck is that huge box outside?"

"A sewing machine," Lola whispered.

"A *sewing machine?*" Ryan repeated. "How the hell do you plan on taking it back to Soho?" He paused for a beat and then laughed cruelly. "Oh, I see. You're just going to leave it here and make Giancarlo deal with it. Sounds familiar."

"Ryan, stop!" she cried. "Just stop. Okay? I'm sorry. I'm sorry for everything. I'm sorry I let it get to this point that you had to yell at me like this for me to hear you. But I hear you, okay? I really, really hear you."

And she did. She knew he was right. She'd come out here for a summer of friendship and introspection and had instead become totally obsessed with the enemy next door, ditching both Ryan *and* herself in the process. How quickly had she kicked aside that sewing machine on the doorstep? How easy had it been to forget how terrible she felt even before Aly's article tore down her life?

"I'm so sorry that I forgot about meeting Emmett and that I haven't let you tell me about him all summer."

Ryan threw his hands up in the air. "How long have you known me? Twelve years? And how many guys have you seen me with over that time? A dozen? A hundred? Have you ever heard me say anything about being in love before?"

"No." Lola frowned.

"No," Ryan repeated. "This is a wholly new situation, and you just…you bailed on me for it. I really needed my best friend."

Ryan was softening. Lola could see it.

"Can we reschedule?" she begged.

"It's not even about the goddamn dinner," he said. "It's about you not being here for me at all, ever. Sure, fine, we can reschedule the dinner. But we can't reschedule all the times you've flaked on me since we got here. All the times I was talking to you and you literally didn't hear a thing I said or when you were just gone completely, nowhere to be found for days and days."

"I know," she said. She felt like her heart was breaking. The thought of hurting Ryan—who had been with her through the toughest shit of her life—was too much to bear. "I know I won't get a do-over. All I can do is promise to do better starting now. And I do promise."

He looked at her warily. "I don't want to get my feelings hurt again," he said. "It's easier to just expect nothing from you."

Lola felt the hard truth scrape through her middle. How had she let herself become this person? She had to fix it. She would.

"I won't let you down again," she said, her voice strained with desperation.

"What if we all had dinner at my house?" Aly offered. "I'll cook. We can do it tomorrow."

Ryan had always been dying to be friends with Aly. He'd never pass up an invite for dinner at her house, regardless of how angry he was with Lola.

"It's kind of last minute," he said, feigning hesitation. "I'll have to check my calendar."

"Please do," Aly said. "And let me know. I would love to have you all over."

"It'll be like the fucking Gay Straight Alliance," Ryan said.

There was a tense pause, and then they all started laughing.

Lola flew off the couch and pulled Ryan into a tight hug. "I'm sorry I'm the worst," she said.

"You really are," he said, hugging her back. "And I can do tomorrow," he added, not having checked his calendar.

Lola grinned. "I had a feeling."

He pulled away, a smile tugging his mouth up. "Oh, and I do have some pants that need hemming. Since you have a new sewing machine and all."

"Whatever you need," Lola said, and she meant it.

"I think *you* need to take a shower," he said, his voice clipped. "You smell like pussy."

She could tell he was still mad at her. But she'd win him over. She had to.

———

In the morning, Aly drove Lola to the farmers market.

Lola didn't love being up before 8:00 a.m., but she was committed to doing whatever it took to get Ryan to forgive her. And if that meant getting to the stalls early to get the most perfect produce on Long Island, well, she'd do it.

Not that there was anything for her to do once they got there. Aly, it seemed, was friends with every single person running each white tent; she knew where to get the best of each item too. Lola stood back and watched her charm the entire farmers market.

They returned to the car with their arms loaded down with dark leafy greens, heirloom tomatoes that looked like Loewe, ripe peaches, fresh mozzarella, an entire chicken, and a bunch of basil. It really was a shame that she wasn't posting to Instagram anymore.

They gently put everything in the trunk.

Climbing into the passenger seat, Lola said, "I've never been so aroused by the way someone buys groceries."

"Should we have sex?" Aly joked, turning the car on.

"Not *no*," Lola said.

But as Aly pulled out of the parking lot, the windows down and a warm breeze tickling Lola's neck, things felt less urgent between them. Instead, a tender intimacy had settled. They held hands while Aly drove them back, NPR playing softly from the car speakers.

"He'll forgive you," Aly said. "Everyone fucks up sometimes."

"Yeah, but I *really* fucked up," Lola replied, leaning her head back on the headrest. "It's really hard to balance falling for someone and... well, anything else."

They came to a stop at a red light, and Aly looked at her. "So you're falling for me," she said.

"I mean, what would you call it?" Lola grinned. But then she realized she was doing it again: she was talking about her and Aly when the focus should have been on Ryan. Her smile faltered. "I don't want to be a bad friend," she said. "He's really been there for me forever.

And he's right. He's never been in love before. The least I could do is remember the guy's name, and I couldn't even do that."

"I get it," Aly said. "But from an outside perspective, it seems like he wants to make up. Being mad takes so much energy. And he's clearly dying to talk to you about this guy. Friendships like yours don't disappear because of one fight."

"I hope you're right," Lola said. "Thanks for listening."

The light turned green, and Aly drove onward. "I'll always listen to you," she said. "I like when you tell me how you're feeling about things."

It was such a simple thing to say, but it made Lola's heart soar.

———————

At 7:00 p.m. on the dot, Aly's doorbell rang.

Aly was in the kitchen wearing a brightly hued Dusen Dusen apron over her best black linens, stirring a big pot of pasta.

"I'll get it," Lola offered from her perch at the island.

She opened the door to Ryan and Emmett. She and Ryan hugged while she assessed Emmett over his shoulder. He was cute, which was no surprise; he had thick, black hair, olive skin, and broad shoulders. He was a little bit shorter than Ryan, wearing a blue henley and khakis.

"Lola, Emmett; Emmett, Lola," Ryan said.

"Can I hug you?" Lola asked.

"Please," Emmett said, opening his arms. "It's so nice to finally meet you. The best friend. And wow, you are just as gorgeous as Ryan said you'd be."

Lola laughed. "I like him already," she said.

She led the couple into the kitchen, enjoying getting to watch Ryan take in the exquisite details of Aly's space.

"We *have* to talk interiors," he said to Aly, kissing her on both cheeks. "And this is Emmett, my boyfriend."

Lola couldn't help it. "Boyfriend?" she shrieked.

Ryan laughed. "How's that for a hard launch?"

Emmett grinned and grabbed Ryan's hand.

Lola felt competing emotions: thrilled for Ryan that he found someone he loved enough to put a label on and absolutely riddled with guilt that she hadn't been there for it.

"Why do you look like you're going to cry?" Ryan asked her.

"Sorry," she said, laughing as she wiped a tear from her eyes. "I'm just so happy for you. And so sorry for being the worst friend in the world."

"You're not the *worst*," he said.

Her heart did a little happy jump. It almost felt like forgiveness.

Aly refused to let anyone help cook, so the three of them sat at the table and waited for her to serve them. Delicious smells were wafting around them, making Lola's stomach growl. Boygenius played softly from hidden speakers, and the lighting was soft and warm. Lola felt like they were auditioning to be the Spotify playlist picture for Dinner with Friends.

"Emmett, I'm going to need a full bio," Lola said. The table was lit with candles and decorated with a huge bouquet of sunflowers.

"Well, I'm a talent manager," Emmett said. "I'm from Brooklyn originally. I'm a cat dad of two. I don't usually come to the Hamptons, but my mother insisted I take a vacation, and I always listen to her. Oh, and I'm in love."

Ryan was blushing, something Lola had never seen before.

"A talent manager, huh," she said. "I don't know if Ryan told you, but I'm in need of a whole new team."

"Lola," Ryan warned.

"Sorry, sorry." She smiled, sheepish. "I am supposed to stop making things about me."

She felt a flash of guilt remembering how she'd stood up their dinner the night before. She couldn't believe how selfish she'd been, not giving Ryan room to talk about the perfect man at the table across from her. It clearly *was* serious.

"I'm happy to give you some names," Emmett said, nonplussed. "I just don't represent friends, and I have a feeling you and I are going to be *great* friends."

She felt warm all over.

"So I saw the sewing machine," Emmett said. "Seems like there's a story there."

Lola eyed Ryan, waiting for him to get pissed about her large purchase, but he just nodded at her to talk.

"I used to make clothes," she said. "Or at least I used to rehabilitate secondhand items, give them new life. I was thinking about getting back into it. I mean, what else am I doing? I can't work with brands right now, might as well do my own thing."

"I think that's a great idea," Emmett said.

"Do you think that as a talent manager or as someone dating my best friend?"

"Both," he laughed. "You do have to keep moving forward, you know? The spon con will come back. It always does. Meanwhile, it's a great time to reestablish your own brand, remind people who *you* are and why they follow you."

"I love him," Lola said to Ryan.

"Right?" Ryan beamed.

"And a cat dad to boot. Are you sure you don't want to marry me instead? My life has been sorely lacking cat children."

Ryan flicked his napkin her way, and Lola grinned.

Aly finally left the stove and came to the table, putting a hand on Lola's shoulder. "Okay, guys, I've got pasta with homemade tomato sauce, sautéed kale, and roast chicken. Give me your plates."

"You're going to *plate* for us?" Ryan gasped.

"Of course." Aly nodded, solemn in her role as chef. "Just tell me what part of the chicken you prefer."

"Lola likes breast," Ryan said.

Aly's neck turned pink. "I know she does."

Each plate Aly brought back to the table was artfully arranged and steaming hot. Lola uncorked the red wine and gave everyone a generous pour. Finally, after they all had food in front of them, Aly sat down.

"Eat," she said. "Don't let it get cold."

Lola gave Aly's knee a squeeze, and they exchanged smiles. "Thanks for cooking, babe," Lola said.

"Seriously, thank you," Emmett said. "It's so nice to not be at a restaurant for once this summer."

"I'm so sorry for yesterday, Emmett," Lola said. "I feel like such a dick."

"Girl, it's fine," Emmett said. "Sometimes you really do just need to sixty-nine on a priceless piece of furniture."

Aly nearly did a spit take, struggling to swallow her wine.

"Ryan!" Lola screamed, but she was laughing.

He shrugged, then flashed a wicked grin. "You shouldn't have done it if you didn't want me to talk about it."

"Fair enough," Aly said. "Okay, I want to know everything about both of you."

Dessert was peaches, which Aly grilled in the yard while the rest of them lay on her lawn furniture and looked at the stars.

It was a clear, warm, perfect night. The full moon looked like an opal in the velvet sky. Just a few yards in front of them, the ocean roared in and out, washing away the day's footprints.

"I really like him," Lola whispered to Ryan.

"Right?"

"He's so nice and smart and seems really..." She searched for the word. "Like, normal? As in not crazy."

"I know, right?" Ryan said. "Can you believe there are still normal guys out there?"

"I can hear you," Emmett said, and they all laughed.

Aly fetched a pint of vanilla ice cream from inside and then made them all put two scoops on top of their grilled peaches, which she served in white ceramic bowls.

"And to think, we could have been having chic dinner parties all summer," Ryan said. "Instead of whatever Greek tragedy you two have been involved in."

"I think the tragic part is over," Lola said. "I'm ready for things to be good from here on out."

"Me too," Ryan said. "And I'm so glad to have you back."

"So you forgive me?" Lola asked.

"I forgive you," he confirmed. "Besides, it's hard to stay mad when I'm in love."

Emmett leaned over and kissed him on the cheek. Lola kissed the other cheek. "You guys!" Ryan cried, laughing. "This is too much PDA. But thank you. I feel very special."

"You're the most loved and the most special," Lola said. "I'm so happy we're all here together."

Lola was pretty sure she'd never felt so happy. Everything suddenly felt possible; she didn't have to disappear into Aly in order to have a relationship with her. She didn't have to abandon Ryan in the process. She could have both friends *and* a love interest *and* her own wants and needs. Her mom was right: all she had to do was be herself.

It made the future feel exciting too, despite everything that had happened. For the first time in a long time, she was looking forward to whatever might come next.

"There are five weeks left until September," Aly said. "Let's make them count."

<hr />

When Ryan and Emmett left, after the dishes were cleaned and the food put away, Aly took Lola by the hand up to her bedroom and said, "I was wondering if you'd be interested in trying something."

"Anything," Lola said. She meant it; something felt different between them. Perhaps it was because Aly had seen her through this major conflict with Ryan, had been part of the milestone now labeled *Ryan falling in love*. They weren't just two people fucking anymore. They were two people who cared about each other, who were becoming friends with each other's friends. Aly was starting to see the real her and, she hoped, vice versa. A new sort of trust hummed between them, and she felt eager to prove it.

"Well, don't agree just yet," Aly said, laughing. She looked nervous as she opened her nightstand and produced a silicone dildo attached to a leather harness.

When it came to sex, Lola liked to think she was hard to shock, but her mouth fell open. The dildo was purple and sparkly and on the small side.

"Oh," she said. "I..."

Aly raised her eyebrows. "It's okay," she said. "Never mind."

"No, no, no, wait," Lola said, grabbing the dildo from her. "Listen, you know that I like dick. I just don't know if I want one inside me right now. I've been kind of enjoying sex without it."

Aly cocked her head to the side. "Oh, no," she said. "I don't want to wear it."

Again, Lola found herself shocked. "You want *me* to wear it?"

Aly nodded.

"To fuck you?"

Aly nodded again.

"You want me...to be the top?" Lola felt proud that she knew the lingo.

"Not permanently," Aly clarified. "But it's fun to switch things up, no?"

Lola allowed herself to imagine it—taking control, penetrating Aly with something she'd wear. It was a surprisingly hot visual, surprising because of how submissive she tended to be and hot because, well...the idea of dominating Aly—of Aly *wanting* to be dominated by her—was not something she had considered before.

Stepping out of her comfort zone was good, she knew. She'd been doing so much of it lately. She felt like it was making her a better person, or at least a more interesting one. Whereas the Lola of six months ago never took risks, the Lola of this summer was all about them.

She couldn't conceal her nervousness, though. "What if I'm terrible at it?"

"You won't be," Aly said. "But if I don't like what you're doing, I promise to tell you."

"And if you like it?"

Aly smirked. "You'll know if I like it."

Lola imagined Aly overcome with pleasure because of the way Lola was fucking her and felt her skin heat. A rush of anticipation flooded her body.

"Besides," Aly said, "haven't I proven to be a good teacher?"

"You have."

"So?"

"Okay, Carter," Lola laughed, getting used to the idea. "I get it. You want to ride my dick."

Aly laughed too and then groaned. "Have I created a monster?"

"Maybe," Lola replied. "But a monster who is about to fuck you."

They undressed, and Aly showed Lola how to pull the straps into place. Lola felt like a nervous teenage boy. It was not something she'd ever fantasized about, having a dick, using it to have sex with a girl. She wasn't sure if she'd like it, but she was determined to be a good sport. Still, she felt a little silly, looking at it hanging there between her legs. *Dangling.*

Aly handed her the lube.

Lola said, "I feel like I'm about to lose my virginity."

"You aren't not."

She worried briefly if this was some sort of test, if Aly was trying to see how committed to the bit she really was, if it was a bit at all, or if it was actually serious. She was determined to prove herself.

Aly lay back, and Lola crawled on top of her. Together they guided the dildo inside Aly, who made a little gasp when it was fully in. Then they were joined, their bodies fitting together in a new way. Abruptly, Lola's concerns vanished. There was nothing *not* to like about this. The base of the dildo pressed into Lola's clit, and as they moved together, she found she liked the sensation of being in total control. It was nice for them both to be hands free too.

She was setting their pace—slow but intense. Her hips moved like liquid.

Aly was soft and pliable under her, following her lead, her eyes half-closed in ecstasy.

"Do you want to get on top?" Lola asked.

"Not really," Aly said, and they both laughed.

Lola went back to thrusting. Her abs were growing tired with the effort, her arms a little shaky from holding herself up in a forearm plank, and she felt a new appreciation for every man who'd ever fucked her in missionary. It was a lot of work. But it was worth it.

"Are you sure you've never done this before?" Aly whispered into her ear. Her breath was hot and damp.

"Maybe in another life," Lola replied.

Chapter 13

JULY GAVE WAY to August, the days melting into each other like ice cream dripping off a cone. Life for Lola became a hallucinogenic whirlwind of sunshine, Aly, the beach, oysters, Aly, wine, lobster rolls, Aly, orgasms, Aly, Aly, Aly.

Lola *wanted* to keep in mind that she'd vowed not to lose herself in Aly, but Aly was making it very hard. Finally, she gave herself a deadline: by the end of the summer, she'd figure her shit out.

But for now…

Every night, they fell asleep together, tangled and spent, and then Lola would dream about Aly until waking up to her face. The world smelled of salt air and pheromones. Her lips were permanently swollen from being bitten and sucked.

The obsession seemed mutual, much to her ongoing surprise. Sometimes she'd catch Aly staring at her while she did the most mundane things like brushing her teeth or putting her hair in a topknot. Often when they kissed, she could feel Aly's heart pounding. She still couldn't believe she had this kind of power over someone so cool and confident, who only became more and more devastatingly hot with each passing day.

Once a week, she and Ryan did a girls' night, staying in to watch TV, do face masks, and gossip. That was their promise to each other, a way to make sure neither got so lost in new love that they couldn't find each other. But otherwise, Lola was happily camped out on Aly Island.

Sometimes, though, she felt small needles of panic about the life that awaited her back in the city—or rather the life that didn't. She didn't want to hide forever. She wanted to make a plan for herself. She knew she needed to. She knew it was the most important thing she was supposed to be doing. It was her *life*, after all. But then, there Aly would be, kissing her neck and whispering into her ear, and all would be forgotten.

Her clothes started to fit a little more snugly, now that the farthest she walked was to Aly's house. Their frequent picnics of bread, cheese, and wine on the beach certainly didn't help. But she also didn't care about the pockets of extra flesh that were softening her out. The more of her there was, the more Aly had to grab on to. The weight seemed to settle on her boobs and her ass, making her feel like a ripe peach. And Aly certainly didn't seem to mind.

As with every year, there weren't any work events in August; it was always as if everyone—the PR people and the influencers and the journalists and the marketers—had all signed a contract agreeing to slow down for four long, sun-drenched weeks. The product launches and collection re-sees would pick back up in September—New York Fashion Week too, followed by London, Milan, and Paris. The whole racket.

Usually, Lola grew bored in those final summer moments, restless in Soho waiting for life to pick back up while Justin was at work, their apartment too big for one person. This was the first year she allowed herself to enjoy the endlessly long days. The lack of obligations or reasons to put borrowed clothes on felt like a kind of liberation. Her only job was Aly.

Meanwhile, the sewing machine sat in the corner of Giancarlo's living room, unopened and collecting dust. She hadn't had a moment to even think about unboxing it. She'd even grown sick of seeing it, its looming shape a testament to how she'd ignored her own promise to work on herself. It was taunting her. She knew she should probably just send it back and figure out if she could resell all that vintage she'd acquired too. When she saw it all folded in the corner of her room, she sometimes felt a pang of regret that she still couldn't bring herself to fully go down that road. But the pang was quickly replaced by the very real pull to devote herself to Aly, get her fix again.

One morning, as she and Aly lay by the pool eating chocolate croissants and drinking iced lattes, Aly said, "Do you have a vision for what this looks like when summer is over?"

"I'm not really sure," Lola said, which was the truth. It was hard to imagine what would happen after they left this magic place. Or what she wanted to happen. She hadn't let herself think about it since Aly had gone MIA.

"*I* was thinking," Aly said and trailed a finger along Lola's forearm, "we could do this, for real. You could be my girlfriend."

"Your girlfriend," Lola repeated, tasting the word on her tongue and all it implied. Did she want to be Aly's girlfriend? She knew she wanted to be with her in the here and now, but despite her mother's advice in July, she hadn't pictured much more of their future.

She tried to imagine what it would involve. Cohabitation, maybe.

Monogamy, definitely. Meeting each other's families. Sharing bills. Dividing chores. Reminding each other of doctor appointments. The seriousness and stability seemed at odds with the experience of actually being together, which still, for all intents and purposes, made Lola feel more than a little insane, like at any moment Aly could change her mind and leave them in the Hamptons. She couldn't put a finger on why she felt like that. She just couldn't quite settle, so instead she chose the dizzying effects of their mutual obsession and left it there.

In a way, that was what made Aly so intoxicating, that layer of danger. But it also made it hard to imagine sustaining this. Surely it wouldn't be good for her blood pressure, long term.

Above them, fluffy, white clouds dotted a sapphire sky. The sun was growing hotter. Next to her, Aly was wearing her favorite black high-cut one-piece, her porcelain skin protected with SPF 50. Despite the surgeon general's warnings, Lola was slathered in baby oil, her skin turning a golden brown.

"I like you so much," Lola said, eager to provide reassurance while being careful not to say something she couldn't take back. "What if we just continue to see what happens?"

"I can work with that," Aly said. Lola tried hard to detect the hurt in Aly's voice, but she couldn't. Instead, Aly leaned over and kissed her. "And I don't want to pressure you. But you should know that if you turn me down, you'd be missing out. Fall is *really* my season."

Lola loved when Aly was cocky. She felt something light up in her, an ember of flirtation quick to stoke. "Oh yeah?"

"I mean, it's canonically lesbian—beanies, flannels, boots, leather jackets."

Lola laughed. "Apple picking, pumpkin carving."

"Hot apple cider with whiskey," Aly added. "Fireplaces. Hudson Valley Airbnbs. Hiking. Just think about it."

"I will," Lola promised. "You're very convincing."

Aly was right: summer *would* end. Sooner than Lola would like to think about. Then she'd have to go back to the city and face her life or what was left of it. Despite the promise of autumn's sapphic wonders, the truth was that how Aly would actually fit into Lola's world was unclear.

She wasn't even sure where she'd be living next month, if Justin was permanently moving out or if she was. She'd need to figure out a new income stream if her influencing career was truly and permanently over too. And she needed a whole new team. There were so many big things to sort through. She didn't know how she could do that while being Aly's girlfriend. When Aly was around, all she could think about was hibernating together, getting back in bed and never escaping.

If Lola could freeze time, she would have, forever suspended in their bliss bubble.

But even in her delirious haze of hormones and lust, Lola knew that all bubbles eventually pop.

Toward the end of August, on a day so hot it made the air feel like soup, Ryan and Emmett invited Lola and Aly to go to Wölffer Estate Vineyard for a wine tasting.

Getting out of the house sounded good. Lola donned a cozy white nap dress. Aly wore an oversized blue-and-white-striped poplin button-down, just slightly elevated from her usual plain T-shirt.

Emmett drove the four of them in his convertible with the top down. In the backseat, Lola and Aly held hands, the wind whipping their hair around, turning them into blurs of brunette and blond. All four of them wore different variations of very expensive sunglasses: Aly in her Tom Ford aviators; Lola in a round, white Marc Jacobs pair; Emmett and Ryan both wearing thick black Balenciaga frames. The sun beat down on them. The car stereo was blasting Chappell Roan. Lola couldn't stop grinning.

It was a quick drive down the verdant Route 27, past mansions hiding behind green hedges and the occasional deer along the road, past the tennis club Lola would never go to and Levain Bakery with its long line of people waiting for a three-inch-thick chocolate chip cookie. Then they turned off 27, and suddenly it was like being in Tuscany. The vineyard stretched in all directions, surrounded by grassy fields and tall, skinny cypress trees. The estate itself was a charming, white farmhouse.

"Chic," Lola said as they pulled up.

"Only the chicest for you," Emmett replied, extending a hand to help her out of the car.

———

At a small, wood table in the outdoor tasting room, which overlooked endless neat rows of lush grapevines, Lola sipped a rosé and tried hard to taste the alleged notes of brioche.

Their wine was being poured by a young server who looked like he'd walked straight out of a nineties J. Crew catalog, complete with a thick mop of hair, ruddy cheeks, and an athlete's body.

"I'm getting rose petals," Ryan said, swirling the pink liquid in his wineglass and smelling it. "And maybe some brine?"

"It pairs well with oysters." The server nodded before moving them on to a chilled red.

Under the table, Aly's knee pressed into Lola's. Around them, middle-aged, white women in straw hats talked loudly with Long Island accents.

The server splashed a thimble's worth of red into their empty glasses. "This is our classic blend, with an earthiness and minerality that gives it that intense mouthfeel."

To Lola, wine was wine. But she enjoyed the ceremony of the tasting, the swirling and sipping and guessing at the notes.

"Notes of cedar?" Ryan guessed.

The server was impressed. "You're a natural," he said.

Lola raised an eyebrow. "You looked at the menu ahead of time." She knew him too well.

Ryan laughed, guilty. "Can you blame me for trying to impress this guy?" He nudged Emmett.

Emmett grinned at him. "Babe, you don't need to know about wine to impress me."

Lola watched them kiss, her heart full. Next to her, Aly was smiling too.

"You guys are really cute," the server said, his ruddy cheeks turning redder. "It's so nice to get a table of gays in here for once."

Lola's mouth opened and closed as she considered and then reconsidered asserting that she wasn't gay.

Instead, she allowed herself to feel what it was like to be included in the category. She knew that there was likely no universe in which someone would see her out of context and read her as anything but straight. But as Aly's date, with Emmett and Ryan making out across from them, she fit it. She was one of them. She was not the straight girl tagging along with her gay friends. She was...

Well, she still didn't know what she was. But that was okay. Best not to overthink it.

Meanwhile, the server seamlessly moved on to telling them about a more full-bodied red.

When they'd made their way through every sample of wine on the menu, they continued to linger at the table, tipsy and rambunctious.

Other groups were leaving, presumably to go to their dinner reservations. On her way out, a woman stopped by their table. She had the look of a publicist; she wore a black jumpsuit despite the heat, her brown hair pulled into an aggressively tight ponytail.

"Ryan!" she squeaked.

"Jessica," Ryan gasped, standing up to hug her. "I am gagged to see you."

Jessica grinned. "Summer Fridays, huh?"

"Guys, this is my work wife, Jessica," Ryan said, introducing everyone. Lola was only slightly jealous that Ryan had another wife.

Jessica's eyes settled on Lola. "I've heard *so* much about you," she said. "I want you to know that we all think what happened to you in the spring was ridiculous. Everyone has just lost their minds these days. I'm sure it'll be forgotten by New York Fashion Week. Paris at the latest."

"That's nice of you to say," Lola said, her skin feeling warm.

"It's simply the truth. I know you'll have the perfect comeback. What brands are you working with?" Jessica asked.

"Lola doesn't need to worry about all that right now," Aly chimed in, putting a protective hand over Lola's. Lola's stomach sank. She felt suddenly very small.

Lola knew Aly was trying to be protective, but how it felt was... dismissive.

She *did* need to worry about it right now. Summer was rapidly reaching its conclusion, and she was no closer to making a plan than when it started. The wine in Lola's stomach roiled, and instead of setting her wineglass down, she took a healthy swig.

It was easy for Aly to say that Lola didn't need to worry when Aly's career was on such a clear upward trajectory. Aly had no idea what it felt like to need to start over. Aly had a dream, a clear vision, support to get her there. She was…happy, happy with where it was all going.

A low-grade panic started to froth in Lola's gut, and she wanted to drown it out. Telling Lola not to worry wasn't supportive. It was encouraging her worst instincts.

"Oh, wow, you're ARC." Jessica eyed Aly, putting two and two together. To Lola, she said, "I see you've made peace with the enemy."

Aly laughed. "I'm hoping that I'm not the enemy anymore."

"What happens in East Hampton." Lola shrugged, forcing a smile.

Aly squeezed Lola's hand under the table and then whispered in her ear, "I would really like it if this didn't stay in East Hampton."

"I know," Lola replied. "I'm still thinking about it."

Jessica was walking away, waving goodbye. "God, I love that bitch," Ryan said. "So weird to see work people out here, though. Really reminds you there's a whole world waiting for us in New York."

"I think we can pretend there isn't for a little longer," Emmett said. "At least I plan to."

"I will cheers to that," Ryan said.

"We're out of wine," Lola pointed out.

"Should we get another bottle?" Aly asked.

They all agreed that was for the best. The server suggested a prosecco.

———

When the Uber dropped Aly and Lola off—they'd had to call a car instead of driving back because of all the wine—it was a little after 6:00

p.m., the summer sun still hours from setting and the muggy air only getting hotter. Lola climbed out of the car, saying goodbye to Emmett and Ryan, who had set a second destination in the app, claiming they were going to a party. Lola had a feeling, though, they were just going back to Emmett's to jump in bed.

"I'm starving," Lola said, as they walked up to the house, feeling wine soaked and fuzzy. "Should I UberEats something? Pasta, maybe?"

"I have steaks in the fridge," Aly said. "I'll grill for us."

"Dream girl," Lola sighed.

"But first," Aly said, and then instead of finishing her sentence, she kicked off her shoes and headed straight for Giancarlo's pool, unbuttoning her shirt and throwing it to the side, then slipped out of her pants, leaving an expensive trail of designer clothes in her wake. She dove into the pool in just her bra and underwear and then bobbed up to the surface. "Come on," she called to Lola, who was enjoying the show. "It feels great."

Lola shimmied out of her nap dress. And because she was feeling wild and free and more than a little buzzed from that final bottle of wine (plus the glass she'd chugged in Jessica's presence probably), she took her bra off too. She cannonballed into the pool in just her underwear.

She found Aly in the cool blue water, and they kissed, enjoying the feeling of their submerged bodies pressed together, nearly naked and wine drunk and sunburned. Skin slid against skin. The earth was tilting around her; she was off-balance, but she couldn't fall down in the water, not with Aly's arms around her. Aly's hands traced the outline of Lola's body. Lola's pulse quickened. They could do it in the pool if they wanted. There was no one stopping them.

But Aly pulled away and said, "Lola Fine, do you not know how to dive?"

Lola grinned, treading water. "What gave me away?"

"You almost killed me with that cannonball, for one thing," Aly replied. "Shall we teach you?"

"You can try," Lola said, splashing her. "No one has ever been able to help me. I'm a lost cause."

"We've already established my teaching skills," Aly said with a smirk. Then she dragged Lola out of the pool and made her stand on the edge. She positioned Lola's body, trying to explain the technique. Lola was only half listening. She knew she didn't have the right proportions for a graceful dive. No one with huge boobs did.

Aly made her try it anyway. Lola took a breath and then did the world's largest belly flop. When she pulled herself to the surface, Aly was laughing hysterically.

"I fucking told you," Lola cried, trying not to laugh for fear of drowning.

"Try again," Aly said.

She did. And again and again. She wondered if she'd be better at it if she were sober. She doubted it. The physics just didn't make sense.

Aly brought her portable speaker out and put on a Phoebe Bridgers album. The light was turning gold. From this moment, it didn't seem possible that summer would in fact ever end.

"Bend your knees a little more before you jump," Aly instructed.

Lola liked Aly coaching her, even if she knew it was futile. She idly wondered if anyone could see them, naked and jumping in and out of the pool, but the truth was she didn't really care. Let them see two gorgeous women falling in love, having the time of their lives, splashing around in the perfect turquoise water under the setting Hamptons sun.

Finally, after a dozen or so attempts, something clicked. With her arms above her head, Lola launched herself off the edge of the pool.

She knew this was the one. She could feel it—the way the ground gave way, the way she cut through the air.

The world appeared to flip upside-down as she completed the mid-jump arc down into the water.

And there, walking up to the pool, was a man.

She caught a glimpse of him just as her body sliced down into the pool. She stayed under for a few moments longer than necessary, looking up at his blurry figure through the chlorine, her heart pounding.

She knew who it was, but it couldn't be real. Perhaps her alcohol-soaked brain was making her see things—or maybe she'd fallen asleep in a lounge chair and was having a nightmare.

When she couldn't hold her breath any longer, she burst to the surface.

"Lola?"

It was Justin.

Aly was sitting on the edge of the pool with her legs dangling in the water, her face registering shock. Lola looked at Aly, then back at Justin, then at Aly again.

Drowning would perhaps have been a more pleasant experience than having the two of them come face-to-face like this.

Justin had a suitcase and a backpack. He appeared rumpled, like he'd just gotten off a plane, but gorgeous too; his perfect skin shimmered with sweat in the golden-hour light. Something in Lola ached at the sight of him—and those big, strong arms.

Fuck.

For a moment, looking at each other, it was like nothing had changed—they'd never broken up, he'd never left her. All the love in the world was written on his face.

But then Aly cleared her throat, and Lola was brought back to earth. She blinked the water out of her eyes. "What are you doing here?" He took his sunglasses off. "Why don't you have a bathing suit on?" Anger quickly replaced the ache. "That's what you want to say to me?" Aly stood then and approached him stiffly. She stuck her hand out. "Aly," she said, not smiling.

"Nice to meet you," he said. "I'm Justin."

Before she could stop herself, Lola blurted, "Aly's my neighbor."

Aly's my neighbor? That was really how she wanted to explain the presence of Aly Ray Carter, the life-ruiner she'd been fucking all summer, to Justin, the boy who'd broken her heart?

But what else could she possibly say?

She wished the drunkenness would lift. This would be a hard situation to navigate *without* the fuzzy feeling coating her brain.

Aly shot a sidelong glance at Lola and tilted her head to the side, her brows lowered. She looked like she wanted to say something, but she didn't.

Instead, she shook Justin's hand—it looked like a firm squeeze too—and then, without another glance at Lola, turned on her heel and walked across the lawn to her house. She left her clothes on the ground. There was nothing notable about her gait as she walked away—not too slow, not too fast. If Lola didn't know her, it would have read as casual. Aly seemed to be in complete control of herself, seemed to simply be giving two exes space to sort out their shit. But Lola knew better.

"Aly, wait," Lola called. But Aly didn't stop walking, and she didn't look back. She opened the door to her family home and then closed it quietly behind her.

Lola's heart twisted in her chest. This was bad. This was *really* bad. A door slam would have been better.

What must Aly think of Justin showing up like this? Of Lola not saying *this is the woman I'm seeing?* But how could she say that? How could she come out to Justin of all people?

There was perhaps an alternate universe where Lola ran after Aly and left Justin standing in the yard. Where she told Aly that she had nothing to worry about, that she would make Justin leave, that she even wanted to be her girlfriend and nothing could change that, not even her former great love showing up out of the blue.

But in this universe, Lola let Aly go.

She did not chase after her.

At least for now.

Instead, she told herself she'd triage the Aly situation later and deal with Justin first.

Justin, who didn't seem to pick up on the complexity of what had just happened.

He didn't seem to recognize Aly at all. Which was a relief. Lola wasn't surprised that he hadn't googled her. He was never petty like that.

Instead, he simply said, "She seems nice."

"Sure," Lola said.

She climbed up the ladder out of the pool, her hands over her nipples as she went to retrieve her nap dress from where she'd thrown it on the hydrangeas.

Before she got to it, Justin said, "Lola."

Something about the way he said her name made whatever was wound so tight inside her come undone. There was a painful sensation in her throat as a sob fought its way out. It was too much. Justin, here, after all this time. Aly, gone back to her own house. Lola didn't know what to do with herself. She felt totally unmoored.

He could tell. "Come here. Please."

It was like someone else was controlling her body, making her walk toward him. The muscle memory taking over in a moment, rewiring her circuits.

She stepped into his arms, which he wrapped around her so tightly she could barely breathe.

Her wet breasts pressed into his T-shirt as he held her, burrowing his head into her sopping wet hair. She clung to him.

Justin.

Here in his arms was the safest place in the world. She'd spent five years luxuriating in the feel of him, the smell and the taste of him, the absolute comfort and stability he provided. Half a decade. Those feelings didn't go away overnight. Or over one summer, even.

"I missed you so much," he said. "I'm so sorry."

It all came rushing back—all the feelings she'd been hiding from; the way she couldn't face the ruins of her career or figure out how to move forward; the way she instead did what she always did, hiding herself in romance when what she really needed to do was focus on herself.

She was furious with herself for all of it.

And it was easy to blame Justin.

"You left me," she said. "How could you abandon me like that?"

"Can we go inside and talk?" They were still holding each other.

Lola nodded into him. "Can I put clothes on?"

He laughed, the warmest, best sound. "Sadly, I think you probably should."

In Giancarlo's kitchen, her hair dripping onto her dress, Lola poured two glasses of water from the Brita pitcher.

"This house is amazing," he said, looking around. He ran a finger along the marble island.

"I had a feeling you'd like it," she replied. She eyed his luggage. "Where did you come from?"

"LAX to JFK," he said. "And then I Uber'd out here. You can imagine how the driver felt about that."

"Wow," she said, surprised that stable, logical Justin would spend money on something so frivolous as an Uber from Queens to the Hamptons.

"How was LA?" she asked, assessing him. His gray T-shirt had pit stains; his hair was a little longer than he usually liked it. Soft stubble shadowed his jaw. For Justin, who typically never had one single wrinkle on his clothes, this was the aesthetic equivalent of a total breakdown. She'd never seen him so unkempt.

"Lonely," he said, taking the water from her. "Everyone was so worried about me, but no one could say anything to help."

Lola was annoyed by this. He'd done it to himself. Still, the thought of Justin alone and brooding at his parents' house also made her chest hurt.

They sat next to each other at the kitchen table. Lola felt competing urges: she wanted to climb into his lap and she also wanted to throw her water in his face.

She wondered, too, what Aly was doing. If she was watching them through the window.

Please don't ask about Aly, she thought, eyeing Justin. *Don't ask if I've missed you.*

"Did you sleep with anyone?" she blurted out, immediately chastising herself for asking. She'd just wrenched open the door she was trying to keep closed.

He started to answer, and she stopped him. "Actually, don't tell me. I don't want to know."

He nodded. "I quit my job," he said.

"You *what?*"

"I couldn't focus. I was a wreck. I had to get out before I ruined my reputation."

"Oh, babe," she said. He must have really been a disaster to risk his career like that.

"I want to find something with better hours," he said. "A family practice maybe. Something that would allow me to have more of a life. To spend more time with the people…" He trailed off. "No, with the *person* I love."

The present tense of what he'd just said felt very loud. *The person I love.* So he still loved her. She didn't know what to say.

Into the silence, he said, "Tell me about you. How was your summer?"

"It was…full of self-discovery," she said, which of course wasn't exactly true. She'd discovered that she loved having sex with a woman, but as far as self-discovery went? She had still come up short. Not that she could say any of that. He didn't deserve to know.

"I saw you haven't posted at all. That must have been a nice break."

"It was." She nodded. "All kinds of breaks for me this summer. And you? How was your summer?"

"It was hard," he said. He looked pained. "I knew I made a mistake as soon as I walked out the door, but it took these months away from you to really let it sink in."

"I'm listening," she said.

"I freaked out," he said. "I was hurt by what the article said. I took it to mean you didn't want to be with me, and I lashed out to protect myself."

"You hurt me so that I wouldn't hurt you," she said.

He nodded. "I left before you could leave—my stupid fucking pride."

This made sense to Lola; in fact, she'd heard it before from the girl she let walk away. She nodded. "You could have just talked to me about it."

"I don't know if I could have," he admitted. "My ego was too bruised."

"You walked out on something really good," Lola said. "And I don't know if we can get it back. It changed me, your leaving. I'm different now."

Justin frowned, the corners of his beautiful mouth tugging down. He put a warm hand on her arm, and she shivered. His touch shouldn't have felt as good as it did.

"You didn't even call," she said. "Or text. Or email."

"I know," he said. He looked at his hands.

"You've had months to reach out."

They were quiet for a few moments. The vintage wall clock ticked; a seagull shrieked outside. Finally, he looked at her. His face was open and imploring.

"Look, Lola. The truth is I don't care if we ever get married," he said. "It doesn't matter anymore. It shouldn't have ever mattered."

He was like a bleeding wound, just so raw and vulnerable. She'd never seen him like this. He leaned toward her. "I just want to be with you, and I'll take whatever I can get. If you want to go back to exactly how things were before, I would do it. I would do it *forever*. Lola, I love you. You're the love of my life. I know we can fix it."

She didn't even realize that tears were pouring down her face until they hit her bare knees.

She'd waited so long to hear him say these words. She hadn't thought she ever would. And now here he was, asking for her back.

He reached out and tucked a strand of her hair behind her ear.

Just like he used to.

Like he'd never left.

"Justin," she said. Her voice caught in her throat. His hand lingered at her face, and she pressed her cheek into it, catlike.

Then he pulled her onto his lap like she weighed nothing. She curled into him.

"I'm so sorry," he said, holding her tightly. He was crying too. "I can't lose you. I can't."

He smelled like himself—like sandalwood and amber and sweat.

But she couldn't bring herself to offer him words of comfort in return. Despite how good it felt to be held by him, she didn't know what she wanted anymore.

This was a world she could slide back into. She could see it all so clearly, how they'd simply go back to Soho and pick up where they'd left off.

But she wasn't sure she wanted to be that girl again—the girl out partying at vapid brand events while her partner saved lives at the hospital. The girl who had racks and racks of gifted PR products that didn't even mean anything. The girl who never had a scathing article written about her, who never met Aly at all.

And what would it mean for Aly?

Or was Aly already gone, spooked by the specter of Lola's heterosexuality?

Lola nestled deeper into Justin, where she was safe from thoughts of the girl next door.

"Do you mind if I stay here tonight?" he asked. "I know it was short-sighted, but I didn't really make a plan for what to do once I got here."

"Of course." She nodded. "Do you mind sleeping in one of the other guest rooms, though?"

He looked pained. "Yeah, that's fine. I have no expectations," he said, as though he could hear her confusion.

She hoped this was true as she led him upstairs.

While he was in the bathroom, Lola sat on the bed and checked her phone.

She had a text from Aly.

She held her breath while she opened it.

The worst part is that I'm not surprised.

There were a thousand meanings layered into that one sentence. *Fucking writers*, she thought, her stomach seizing up with too much wine and not enough food. She wondered briefly if she was about to throw up. It felt possible.

Justin emerged and assessed the look on her face. He still knew her so well. "What's wrong?" he asked.

Lola knew this was her chance to tell him about Aly, who she really was and who she'd become to her, but she still couldn't. She wasn't sure how he'd react, and beyond that, she wasn't sure how *she'd* react to his reaction.

"Nothing," she said. She placed her phone upside down on the nightstand and tried to put Aly out of her mind.

He tugged his shirt off and then dug around in his backpack for a clean one. "I'm sorry if I stink," he said.

"You never stink," she replied. "Don't worry about a shirt."

She lay down on top of the blankets, and he lay next to her, her in her damp dress and him in just his sweatpants.

"This isn't the guest room," he said.

"I'll show you where it is," she said, but neither of them moved.

It wasn't that she wanted to sleep with him.

But his warm presence in the bed next to her just felt so familiar.

He took her hand and held it between both of his. "Are you going to make me beg for you?"

She considered this, looking at the ceiling. "It's not about begging," she said.

"I know," he replied. "I'm sorry. This is just…" He trailed off. "Terrifying."

"For me too," she said.

"Can I hold you?"

She considered it. Aly would definitely freak out if she saw them cuddling in bed. But Lola needed to be held. She and Justin had a history. And an ending that was somewhat unresolved. This could be part of the work of resolving it.

She nodded. He curled around her.

She felt his hot breath on her neck. She had the sense that she could disappear into him, that if he just held on tightly enough, she would go up in a puff of smoke. It didn't sound so bad.

Justin seemed to want everything to go back to how it was, which, for Lola, would mean a return to influencing—if that was even possible, given how it had all fallen apart. Still, it stood in stark contrast to what Aly wanted her to do, which seemed to be give up influencing entirely and do something with more purpose, or at least do something with a purpose that Aly believed in. Either way, they both *wanted* something from her, wanted her to be someone who she wasn't sure she was.

And how could she possibly know who she was with both of them pulling at her like this?

"I can feel your heart pounding," Justin said.

"This is just a lot," Lola whispered. "You, in this bed."

"I'll go to the other guest room," he said, untangling himself from her. "I'm assuming it's down the hall?"

"Yeah." She nodded. "Second door on the left."

"Okay, Lola," he said. She didn't move to watch him go. Instead, she lay there, holding her breath until she heard the bedroom door open and close, followed by his footsteps down the hall.

She exhaled, relieved that he was gone even though she missed his warmth.

She tried to concentrate on her breathing instead of her spiral. Inhales and exhales. Inhales and exhales. Gradually, her heart rate slowed.

She fell asleep like that.

Chapter 14

LOLA WAS AWAKE, but she didn't want to be.

She was wrapped like a burrito in the soft, warm linen sheets, a cool breeze from the open window tickling her one exposed foot. She felt cloudy with sleep, as though she'd been in a coma for a hundred years. Her temples throbbed. For a few minutes, she didn't even open her eyes, just nestled deeper into her cocoon.

She heard sounds from the kitchen below—heavy footsteps, then the sink running and dishes clattering. Someone was cleaning.

She stretched an arm out.

It landed on an empty pillow. That didn't feel right.

Her eyes flew open.

The events of the night before came rushing back.

Justin had been here. *Was* still here, somewhere.

At least they hadn't had sex. Maybe some cuddling. Then, to her credit, she'd made him leave.

Was that him cleaning downstairs?

And where was Aly?

Fuck. *Aly.*

Lola bolted upright.

She remembered herself saying *This is my neighbor.* And then the confused look on Aly's face, followed by the horrible, calm way she'd turned and walked out.

Lola flew out of bed, then caught a glimpse of herself in the mirror.

She looked…terrifying. She was still wearing her nap dress, now wrinkled to shit, and her underwear, which definitely smelled like the pool. Her hair was stiff with chlorine. Sheet marks lined her face. Her chapped lips were stained wine red. She could shower before going downstairs and facing her life.

She *should* shower.

Especially if that *was* Justin making so much noise in the kitchen. He preferred her clean, and old habits died hard.

She quickly stripped, and then, under the hot water, as she scrubbed her skin raw, she tried to think about what she actually wanted to happen next.

The problem was that she hadn't planned for any of this.

She had not expected Justin to show up and beg for her back.

She had not expected to have to introduce him to Aly.

She had not expected Aly to want to be her girlfriend.

Her mind was swirling with what other people wanted from her. But what did *she* want? She combed conditioner through her tangled hair and tried to picture her perfect scenario, given all the factors. But she couldn't.

She hated that his body in bed had been so comforting.

He wanted to get back together. What a plot twist. But did she feel the same way? On some level, she thought, sure, there was a world in which she still wanted him. Five years' worth of feelings didn't just disappear.

She tried to picture it—she could slip back into a relationship with him easily, go back to the way everything had been, minus her career, of course, though that felt less pressing in this moment. But she could just as easily run over to Aly's house and apologize, finally tell her that yes, she did want to be Aly's girlfriend. She didn't want this to be an either/or situation, though. She didn't want to choose between them. If she was being honest with herself—and she was really, really trying to be, for once—the problem was that she wanted both of them.

But she had a feeling neither of them would be down for a throuple. And she didn't actually want that either; she couldn't imagine juggling two relationships at once.

What she wanted was for there to be two different Lolas, two separate versions of her, one who could date Justin and one who could date Aly. Then no one would have to get hurt.

Barring an alternate universe, she had no idea what an actual solution would look like.

She stayed in the shower a little longer than necessary, letting the mirror fully fog up, until she couldn't put it off any longer. Reluctantly, she turned the water off.

She dried herself off, pulled on jeans and a T-shirt, and walked barefoot downstairs.

Justin sat at Giancarlo's kitchen table with a glass of orange juice and his phone. He looked neater than he had yesterday, back to normal in a wrinkle-free T-shirt.

"Hey," she said, "did you find everything you needed okay? You want cereal or something?"

He looked up from his phone, frowning.

"Oh god," she said, assessing the look on his face. "What?"

"Lola, what is this?"

He handed her his phone.

She held her breath as she took it, her heart already thundering in her chest. *Now what?*

It was Stepped Out's Instagram, a celebrity gossip and meme account known to their 1.7 million followers for their ruthlessness, irreverence, and breathless coverage of notable people stepping out. Not a super on-brand page for Justin to be looking at.

He had it open to their most recent post: a grainy photo of two women holding hands and walking through a restaurant. One was wearing a skimpy, black dress with long, wild, blond hair; the other, a brunette, was in black linen pants.

It was her and Aly.

"What the fuck is this?"

"Just read it," Justin said. His voice was eerily quiet.

She bit her lower lip and began to read.

@steppedout: Lesbian chic? More like lesbian SHRIEK! Canceled bland princess Lola Fine has been seen all over East Hampton this summer with none other than rising sapphic star Aly Ray Carter, and they've been looking more than a little cozy. Ironic, given that Lola was canceled for being homophobic on main, and if you recall, Aly was the one to twist the knife with that damning, viral profile in The Cut. ARC, of course, is known for being somewhat of a lesbian Casanova (anyone else remember the Raina era?) so it's not surprising that she has this kind of pull—what's surprising is WHO she pulled. All this begs the question: If Lola is queer, did we cancel her for nothing? Or is this just a PR strategy to rehabilitate her image? And if she IS queer, why not just come out? So, readers, tell us what you think: Is this for real, or is it the greatest queer bait of all time?

Oh, and quick PSA: Stepped Out does not condone the outing of any-body, unless of course that person has a documented history of homophobia, in which case we consider them fair game.

With shaking hands, she swiped through the carousel.

Blurry, zoomed-in photos showed her and Aly at Sí Sí, their first real date. Someone at a nearby table must have taken them. They were looking adoringly at each other, holding hands across the table, not paying attention to the world around them.

Clearly.

The phone fell out of her hands, clattering on the floor.

"Justin, I…" She sank to her knees to retrieve it.

"Lola, what the fuck?" he interrupted her. "Aly Ray Carter is the girl I met yesterday? *Your neighbor?* I'm so confused. Please, *please* tell me you're not fucking the person who ruined our lives. Literally anyone but her."

Lola stayed on the ground.

"That's your idea of a rebound? *That woman?*" He was yelling now.

"She's not why we broke up," Lola said, finding her voice at last. "You cannot blame everything on Aly."

"Can't I? Lola, this is so fucking humiliating. After I crossed the country to get you back. You haven't missed me at all. You've just spent all summer sleeping with the one person you knew would hurt me the most."

The words shot through her, a knife of clarity. Once again, he'd made it about *him.*

She looked up at him: his crisp blue jeans, his pristine sneakers, his stainless-steel TAG Heuer watch. He always looked extra handsome when he was angry.

And then she *really* looked at him.

Here was the man she'd spent so many years loving. It had been hard to see him clearly when they were in their little bubble, having amazing sex and eating $500 groceries and lying around their penthouse. But from this vantage point—not just where she knelt on the floor but with over two months of distance between them—she saw who he was.

He was a good person in many ways. Noble, even.

But in others, he cared about the wrong things. He couldn't see outside his own ego, his own image. He never could. And maybe that was why she had once been so perfect for him.

Once.

A strange sort of calm settled over her.

"Has it occurred to you that it has nothing to do with you?" she asked, her voice quieter than both of them expected it to be.

He looked startled by it. As though he'd wanted her to scream back. "My parents are going to freak out," he said.

"Your parents?" she repeated. There it was. She had once loved how much his family meant to him. Now, though, she realized that he'd never be able to prioritize her over them. "That's who you're thinking about right now?"

"My whole entire family knows I'm here," he said. "They're all waiting for me to call them and tell them that we're back together. And now I have to tell them—well, you tell *me*. What should I tell them, Lola? That we're not getting back together because you're a lesbian now?"

"I'm not a lesbian," she said matter-of-factly. "But you know what? If I were, it wouldn't be any of their business. Nor yours, for that matter."

Justin's mouth hung open. She had never asserted herself like this before.

"You lost the right to know what's up with me the second you walked out our door," she added.

"I told you I wanted to take a *break*," he said. "Not break up. There's a difference."

"I'm not sure there is," she replied, everything clicking into place at once. "You could have stayed so we could work through our differences *together*."

"Lola, I asked you to *marry me*," he said.

"Yeah," she said, incredulous at the memory of it. "You called it a proposal, but it was more like an ambush. I was clearly not in the head-space to make any major decisions, and instead of understanding that, you held it against me. When things got hard, you literally bounced. You left me alone to pick up the pieces of my life."

Just then, Ryan burst through the front door and came crashing into the kitchen. "LOLA!" he screamed. "Stepped fucking Out?" Then his eyes landed on Justin. "Jesus, fuck," he cried. "Not you."

"Hi, Ryan," Justin said, his voice flat and unfriendly.

Ryan ignored him. "Lola, are you okay?"

"Oh, I have no idea." She tried to laugh, but what came out of her mouth was more like a sob. "I can't believe this is happening."

Ryan shot Justin a look. "Which part can't you believe?"

"Don't worry," Justin said, getting up. "I'm leaving."

Lola and Ryan were both frozen in place while Justin pushed past them, pausing only to take his phone from Lola's hands. He made his way upstairs, thundering up each step.

Justin? Ryan mouthed at her. *What the fuck?*

She shook her head, gesturing for him to stay quiet.

They listened as he gathered his things and then returned, suitcase in hand, standing in the doorway looking bereft.

"Justin," she started but trailed off. She didn't have that much left to say to him.

"I'm sorry I showed up like this," he said. His shoulders slumped forward. "I know it wasn't fair to surprise you. For what it's worth, I do want you to be happy. I just wanted you to be happy with *me*, I guess."

"I know," she whispered.

"I love you so much," he said, his hand gripping the handle of his suitcase. "Everything I said last night still stands. If you want to be with me, *be* with me. But if you don't, I need you to tell me sooner rather than later."

She nodded, her heart aching at the sight of him so undone, despite all her anger. "That seems fair."

"My Uber is almost here," he said. "I'll wait outside."

And then he was gone.

Lola, still kneeling, crumpled all the way to the ground.

Ryan sat on the floor next to her. He wrapped his arms around her and pulled her close.

"Oh, honey," he said. "Fuck him. I promise you, we will get through this."

But Justin leaving like that wasn't what caused her to collapse.

It was the Stepped Out post.

She'd already been through Justin dumping her. She knew she'd survive whatever sort of breakup 2.0 they were having. But the post? The intrusion on her personal life? This Hamptons life she'd been living? She wasn't sure she could get through it again.

Tears streamed down her face. "I can't believe they outed me."

"It's bad enough being outed when you're actually gay." He nodded. "But you're still voting undecided. How dare they pull this crap? It's so unethical. Do you want me to call their lawyer?"

She wept into his shoulder, the embarrassment taking hold. "I wonder if Aly's seen it."

"Woof," Ryan said. "Maybe go talk to her?"

"I doubt she wants to talk to me."

He hesitated, and then it registered. "Ah. I gather she knows that Justin is here."

Lola was hit with alternating waves of sadness, regret, and fear. "That's why you shouldn't date your neighbor, I guess."

"He spent the night, I assume?"

"Yes," she said. "But nothing happened—except for me having to introduce him and Aly and totally messing it up."

Ryan winced. "I think the sooner you go over there and face her, the better. I'll wait for you."

"I know that you're right, but I don't think my legs work."

He laughed and pulled her up. "You can do this," he said and then gave her a little push toward the door.

Lola was so panicked about talking to Aly that she barely even registered the walk to Aly's front door. Suddenly she was just there, knocking.

And knocking and knocking.

What would Lola even say to her? She hadn't planned a speech, hadn't tried to imagine all the different ways this could go. For better or worse, Lola was in the present moment—facing it.

Or trying to. She kept knocking.

Aly's car in the driveway meant she was home, but all the lights were off.

Lola tried the door. It was open. Inside, the house was a mess. Cartons of ice cream crowded the coffee table. The couch was covered in tissues. An empty wine bottle rolled across the floor. But Aly was nowhere to be found.

Lola walked around the side of the house, then to the pool.

"Aly?" she called, rounding the corner.

"Oh, it's you."

Aly's voice came out hoarse and quiet. She was sitting at the edge of the pool, feet dangling into the sparkling turquoise water. She wore all black, a linen set from the Row that Lola had admired in Aly's closet just a few days ago.

She had her sunglasses on, but through the lilac lenses, her eyes were puffy, as though she'd been crying. As though maybe she hadn't slept at all.

"Come to break my heart?" Aly asked.

"Oh my god, no!" Lola said.

Aly stood up and walked toward her. She was holding a Starbucks paper cup of black coffee, no lid, the edges all chewed.

"Oh, Aly," Lola exhaled. She moved to hug her, but Aly dodged her arms, her coffee sloshing.

Despite how distraught she obviously was, Aly looked prettier than ever, her cheekbones extra defined, even her puffy eyelids giving her a kind of sensual, sleepy look.

Lola ached to hug her. Instead, she stayed put, trying to respect the clear boundaries Aly was projecting.

"Let's cut to the chase," Aly said. "I know he spent the night. I know you're here to tell me you're getting back together with him. Don't waste your breath." Aly leaned against the side of the house, as though she were trying to do that signature too-cool thing she liked to do. "I've been through this before. I know how it ends."

"No," Lola said. "You're wrong."

"About which part?"

"He spent the night, but nothing happened. I wouldn't do that to you. I'm here because of the Stepped Out post."

Aly folded her arms across her chest and started laughing.

It wasn't her real laugh, though. It was something meaner, colder. Lola wanted to recoil.

"Lola, who fucking cares about a Stepped Out post?"

Lola was stunned. "What?"

"You and I are *known*. We went out in public *together*. What did you expect?"

Lola was pissed off now. "I expected to have my privacy respected. I expected to be able to choose how we were talked about and analyzed, how I wanted to define this."

"Oh please." Aly rolled her eyes. "You're a public person. You gave up the right to privacy when you hit seven figures on Instagram."

"I…don't know if I agree with that," Lola said.

Aly put her hands on her hips. "I can't believe we're talking about a post from some stupid fucking meme account right now."

"It's not just a meme account!" Lola cried. "I can't believe you don't care more about this. It's my career. It's my life, being dissected by vultures, *again*."

"You don't even want to be an influencer," Aly shot back. "You hate that life. You haven't tried at all this summer to get back to it. You don't miss it at all."

"What the fuck are you talking about?" Lola said, fury hot in her chest. "The reason I haven't tried to work this summer is because I've been so busy falling for *you*."

"You don't get to blame me for the fact that your life lacks direction."

It was like getting slapped across the face. "My life doesn't lack direction," Lola protested, though she knew Aly was right—again. "You have no idea what I want."

"You don't either," Aly said.

"Wow," Lola said, her voice flat with anger. "So that's what you think."

"I think that I cared about you," Aly said simply. "And I care about the fact that I just wasted my whole summer on something that you threw away."

"I didn't throw anything away," Lola protested.

"*This is my neighbor?*" Aly said, mimicking Lola. "I know you never agreed to be my girlfriend, but I thought I was a little more than the girl next door."

Lola's vision blurred with tears. She wiped them away, not wanting Aly to see her fall apart. It was too vulnerable to cry when Aly was being so mean.

"Aly, *please*. I'm sorry. I don't know why that came out of my mouth. I just wasn't ready to tell him that I am in a relationship with the person who he thinks ruined his life. And anyway, if you cared about me, you'd care how much these photos have hurt me. This is the second—no, *third* time I've been majorly called out in one summer. People keep picking me apart in public. Using my life—my real, actual life, complete with my mistakes and my feelings and my relationships—as fodder for fucking clicks. Do you have any idea how bad that feels?"

Aly didn't seem to have anything to say to this. Instead, she looked at the ground.

Lola wanted Aly to understand how it felt like a slap in the face, how lost she felt, how, despite all the public criticism hurled her way, she was still the same girl with the same problems in the same place. But Aly didn't seem to hear her. Aly was being defensive, not trying to work through this with Lola.

Here Lola was, coming to Aly with an open heart, and Aly wasn't listening to a word she said.

She tried to feel empathy for Aly. She put herself in Aly's shoes: Aly had a history of dating women who left her for men. Because of that, she was expecting the worst. And maybe, because she expected it, she was pushing for it—a self-fulfilling prophecy, just like when Aly ghosted her after Fire Island. Lola *did* feel bad for her when she thought about it like that. But she could feel the ember of anger stoking in her belly. Because Aly was putting her personal history on Lola, a history that had nothing to do with her. It wasn't fair.

Besides, it wasn't like Aly was trying to have empathy for *her*.

Lola took a breath. "Aly, I know you are triggered by Justin showing up, and I want to honor that, but I promise you that nothing happened. I'm not Raina. I would really like for us to be able to process what it means that I've been outed. That we've been outed as a couple."

She felt proud of herself for stating her needs so clearly. She wondered if she'd ever had such clarity before.

Though it didn't matter how well she expressed herself if Aly was shut down.

"But we're not a couple," Aly said.

"Are we not?" Lola's heart thundered painfully in her chest. If they weren't a couple, then she didn't know which end was up. Sure, they hadn't used the word *girlfriend*, but they spent all their time together, and they weren't seeing other people. Wasn't that what being in a couple was?

"I think you should go," Aly said.

"Really?"

Aly nodded. "Please, Lola, just get the fuck out of my yard."

Lola wasn't ready to give up yet. "Do you still want me to be your girlfriend?"

Aly's eyes widened. "How can you ask me that right now?"

"I need to know if I'm fighting for us or if you've already made up your mind."

Aly threw her arms up into the air. "Lola, *I'm* the one who has *been* fighting for us. You're the one who just spent the night with your ex-boyfriend."

Lola was reaching the end of her patience. She could hear her own volume raising. "Justin and I were together for five years. This was the first time we've seen each other since we broke up. I owed him a conversation. What was I supposed to do, kick him to the curb? That's not how I treat people I've loved. I would hope that you don't either."

"That's fine," Aly said, though by the way she said it, it seemed anything but. "I understand. It's whatever. And maybe this would feel different if you'd committed to me. But you haven't. You're still thinking about whether you want to actually do this for real. And honestly, Lola, I'm tired. I'm tired of chasing you around. There are plenty of girls who would love to be my girlfriend."

That stung.

"I'm sure there are," Lola said, imagining an invisible line of beautiful women just waiting for the chance to get with ARC.

Was she still one of them?

She wasn't sure. Aly's cruelty was clouding everything.

"Let me know what you decide," Aly said. "You can't have us both."

Lola sighed dramatically. This was like having a conversation with a wall. Nothing she said was getting through.

"Okay," she said, giving up, "I guess I'll let you know what I decide, then."

Before she left Aly's backyard, she took one last look at the girl who had turned her whole life upside down. It suddenly occurred to her that she didn't know when she'd see her again.

Aly stood in dappled sunlight, leaning against the side of her house, her arms folded across her chest, her face was drawn.

"For what it's worth, I do really care about you," Lola said.

Aly didn't say anything at all.

———————

Back at Giancarlo's, Ryan was waiting for her in the kitchen.

He read the look on her face and then pulled her into a hug. "Tell me what you need," he said.

As they held each other, she looked over his shoulder at Giancarlo's flawless, cream-colored house. Sunlight streamed through the bay windows. She listened for the sound of the waves outside. It was stunning here. But it wasn't her home.

Summer was ending. Real life was calling her back. There was no hiding from it. Not even here. She had the feeling she'd overstayed her welcome in East Hampton.

Wherever you go, there you are, she thought.

"I think I want to go back to the city," she replied.

"It does feel like it's about that time, doesn't it?" He rubbed circles on her back. "Giancarlo comes back after Labor Day anyway."

"Maybe we could rent a car this time," she said. "So I can take the damn sewing machine with me."

"You better," he said, laughing. "And if you ask nicely, I'll even help you carry it."

Lola was too sad to laugh with him, but she appreciated the sentiment.

"I wonder if Justin will be in my apartment when I get home," she mused.

"If he is, you can just come stay with me," Ryan offered.

She pulled away and squeezed his arm. "That's really nice of you, but you don't actually want me living in your space."

"Maybe not long-term, but the offer still stands."

"Thank you," she said, overcome with appreciation for Ryan, her best friend in the whole wide world, who had seen her through so much. "I probably don't say this enough, but I literally don't know what I'd do without you."

"And you know what?" he replied. "You never have to find out."

Chapter 15

HECTOR HELD THE door for Lola with a warm smile on his face.

"It's *so* nice to see you, Ms. Fine," he said as she wheeled her suitcases through the threshold. "I hope you had a lovely summer."

"It was definitely full of surprises." Lola grimaced.

The Lower East Side lobby was exactly as Lola had left it: lit beautifully with mid-century modern wall sconces, the concrete floors pristine, a lit Diptyque candle at the front desk that smelled of bitter orange. It felt strange being back in this unchanged space when she had changed so much. Like a decade had gone by, not one summer.

Behind her, Ryan was struggling with the huge Amazon Prime box that contained her sewing machine, likely regretting his offer to carry it.

"Do you want us to have someone send that up for you?" Hector asked.

Ryan promptly put it on the ground. "That would be great," he said, wiping the sweat from his brow.

They were both a little gross from their journey; they'd hit horrible traffic on the LIE, and it had taken them nearly five hours instead of the estimated three. Ryan had wanted to drive the whole way, which was fine with her. They'd stopped for lunch at a truck stop Burger King, which Ryan made a fuss about and Lola secretly loved. She could eat fries forever. Back in the car, though, they both smelled like fast food.

Other than that, Lola had been surprised at how emotional the drive back to the city was. The moment she saw the skyline stretching out across the horizon, she felt a pull toward it. Like the city itself had actually missed her. Like it had been different because of her absence.

She forgot how good it felt to belong somewhere—how important to be grounded.

Ryan hugged her goodbye and left, saying he was double-parked. "Call me later," he said, blowing a kiss before disappearing.

She stepped into the elevator and, as she pressed the button for the penthouse, wondered if Justin would be there. Her heart pounded harder with each floor she ascended.

Emmett had had to go back to the city a few days before them, which meant Lola and Ryan had spent their last three days in East Hampton doing everything they'd neglected to do together this summer. They went kayaking in Montauk. They spent an afternoon walking around Longhouse Reserve, with its lush gardens and sculptures. They rented Jet Skis and zoomed around the ocean waves, racing each other. They ate clam chowder at a local diner, far away from Main Street's hiked-up prices.

She'd avoided Aly for those three days, which hadn't been hard—Aly was nowhere in sight. They didn't see each other across their respective lawns, didn't run into each other on the sidewalk. It was like Aly had gone into hiding.

Lola missed her terribly but was also too pissed off to reach out again. The ball was in Aly's court; Lola was fine to spend her final days with Ryan instead. With Ryan, she knew where she stood.

And then, when they'd exhausted all the tourist attractions and felt convinced they'd maxed out their time, they packed up all their stuff, cleaned Giancarlo's house, and Uber'd to the rental car place. She didn't try to say goodbye. There was no point.

Now, finally back home and ready to face her shit, Lola held her breath as she unlocked the door to her apartment, pushing it open with her shoulder and lugging her bags inside.

Justin's shoes were not by the door, the telltale sign of his whereabouts. She exhaled.

The apartment was empty.

It was also quiet. So clean.

She left her things in the entryway and entered the kitchen, running her hand along the countertop. She checked the fridge for food and found it was totally empty but for some artisanal ketchup and a half-empty bottle of Chardonnay, both definitely no longer safe to consume. She started a grocery order on her phone while absent-mindedly walking through each room. Justin was everywhere: his clothes in his closet, his water bottle near his gym equipment, his soap in the bathroom. The photos of his family still hung on the walls. It was like their break never happened, like he was just at work and would come home in a few hours to kiss her neck and cook her steak.

But it *had* happened. And she knew there was no going back.

She opened all the curtains, letting the light in.

There was a knock on the door. "Delivery," she heard a voice call.

It was someone who worked for the building, carrying her sewing machine.

"In here is great, thank you so much," she said, directing him to set it in the living room.

When he was gone, she sat on the floor and pulled it from its box. The heavy-duty, high-speed Singer was gray and not very aesthetically pleasing. But the pretty ones weren't as good, and this was the best one under a thousand.

She traced her finger along its knobs and dials. "Hello, friend," she said.

She placed it on the coffee table, where she could use it while sitting on the floor.

Lola knew she had more important things to do—deciding between Justin and Aly, for one and two, figuring out what the fuck to do with the rest of her life—but all she could think about was finally using that damn machine.

She opened her suitcase there in the living room and pulled out the vintage, polka-dot Moschino shift dress. It was good quality, but the sleeves needed to feel current. She dug around until she found the floral Gucci scarf. She would probably never wear the scarf if she was being honest with herself. But it could serve a different purpose.

The little voice in her head that liked to tell her she wouldn't know how to do this anymore was starting to whisper to her, but she shook it off. It wasn't helpful to hold herself back, to stand in her own way. Not now, when she had nothing left to lose.

Humming to herself, she retrieved the little bag from her office that contained scissors, pins, and thread and then plopped down on the floor. She cut the scarf in two and then created puff sleeves for the dress with it, pinning them on. She pinned the waistline in so it was less of an A-line and more form flattering.

Cute, she thought, pleased with herself. The floral silk looked nice next to the polka dots, and the silhouette now felt more like Hill House—nap dress but make it designer vintage. She could make the neckline a little lower too, she thought, cutting farther into the frock, maybe a square shape.

Lola loaded thread into the machine, feeling a happy rush in her stomach when it whirred to life. And then she began sewing.

It was like she'd never stopped.

As her fingers fed the fabric through, the needle moving in and out, she entered a sort of meditative state, and she thought of the current dilemma of Aly versus Justin.

There were pros and cons to both.

Justin, she had history with. She knew what to expect from him. He'd take care of her forever. But to keep him happy, she'd have to eventually cave to what he wanted: getting married, having kids, moving to LA. Otherwise, he'd be miserable, she knew, stuck in a life he resented, which would make him resent *her*. Was a happy marriage just constantly choosing between her misery or his? She didn't want to believe that. Her parents didn't live like that. They wanted the same things. Their life together was harmonious.

That was what Lola wanted too. It was what she knew she deserved.

Not to mention the little ways she'd always had to cave to Justin— the cleanliness, the aesthetic choices, the family vacations.

Plus, there was the way he'd left her when she'd needed him the most. She could forgive him for that, but she couldn't trust he wouldn't do it again. Besides, if Justin hadn't wanted her at her worst—her messy, figuring-it-out phase—why did he deserve her now, at her best? She always hoped that her true love would accept all parts of her, the bad stuff included. Justin only wanted her when she was okay. That was not a good foundation for a life together.

Lola didn't know what to expect from a life with Aly, who was moody and unpredictable. But Aly also pushed her to be better in almost every way, opened her eyes to a whole new world of people and culture and feelings. However, Aly wanted Lola to say she was bi and would probably never stop pushing for it. Lola hated the idea of someone else deciding who she was. And the way Aly hadn't cared at all about the Stepped Out post was unsettling.

If Justin cared too much what other people thought, Aly didn't seem to care enough. It was why she'd been able to write the article about Lola in the first place; she didn't think about its impact. No—she didn't *care* about its impact. Because Aly thought Lola's career and her aspirations were beneath her, and because of that, Lola hadn't been able to figure herself out during an entire summer spent with Aly. Would she be signing up for that dynamic for the rest of her life if she stayed with Aly?

Still, she could see a future with both of them. It would be as easy as picking up the phone and saying, "I want you. Let's do this." Either one would welcome her back, she knew.

But in each scenario, she was sacrificing part of herself to make them happy.

She turned the dress over and began sewing the other side.

She didn't want to have to appease Justin and his family by getting married and having kids. She didn't want to appease Aly and her friends by coming out as bisexual when the truth was she still had no idea what identity, if any, felt right to her.

She wanted to be herself.

She wasn't sure she could do that with *either* of them.

She stopped sewing as something abruptly clicked into place.

She'd been thinking about this as a choice between two people. But

Aly and Justin were not the only other two people on earth. She'd left out the third option: neither of them.

Or, put differently, she could choose *herself.*

Which would mean being alone, something that had previously been her worst-case scenario. Come to think of it, the whole reason she'd gone to East Hampton with Ryan was to avoid being alone in this apartment—alone with her thoughts, her existence, her future. Alone with herself.

But maybe being alone wasn't the worst thing. Maybe if she was alone, she could finally have the space to think about who she was.

Or maybe she'd been alone this whole time, regardless of who she was with.

Because what was more lonely than not being seen by the people you love?

And then, before she could think any further about what to do, she got a text from Justin.

Can I come by to talk?

She wondered how he knew she was home and then remembered the Ring camera he'd insisted they install on the front door. How annoying, to be kept track of like that. He must have gotten a notification, seen a recording of her coming home. Could he tell she had been holding her breath as she entered? Was her trepidation visible through the Ring's lens?

She didn't want to write back. She didn't want to stop sewing. She wanted alone time.

But she also knew it was now or never. She might as well get this over with. She put her pins down.

Give me a couple hours to shower and get settled, she replied. **But then yes. Come over.**

Just tell me when, he said.

———————

A few hours later, Lola's groceries—too many, probably—had arrived. She'd then taken a much-needed shower, blow-dried her hair, actually unpacked all the way, ignored the groceries and ordered a dinner of soup dumplings (which she ate standing up), and put her sweatpants on. Finally, she couldn't put it off any longer. She texted Justin.

While she waited for him to come by, she wondered idly if he'd knock on the door or if he'd let himself in. She already felt like he should knock, even though this was still his apartment too. Both of their names were on the lease.

With a pang, she remembered how excited they'd been to find it, how they'd walked into this empty, sparkling loft holding hands, mouthing *oh my god* at each other. They'd looked at a dozen or so places before finding this one, no apartment checking all their boxes until the Realtor called and said, "I think I have something perfect in Soho for you." She remembered how they'd carried their things in together, laughing as they knocked into the walls, then eaten pizza sitting on this floor surrounded by boxes and had sex there too.

She knew many people who stayed in relationships out of a need for good housing. It was a classic NYC conundrum and understandable, given the market. She did not want to be one of those people, though she also knew she probably shouldn't live in her dream loft by herself. It would be a colossal waste of money.

Maybe it was time to get some new dreams.

She was sitting on the couch in the living room when, within twenty minutes, she heard the sound of his key in the door. *So not going to knock, then.* That was fair, she supposed.

She wondered where he'd been staying—at a hotel, with a friend, or maybe with another girl? Though that last one felt unlikely after everything he'd said. Still, it was odd to imagine him with someone else, but if she was really going to go through with this, he eventually would be. Would he look at this new other person the way he'd looked at her? Probably yes. She'd find a way to be okay with it when there was someone new in the picture for Justin to love.

And then there he was. He looked a little out of breath, but otherwise not a hair was out of place, his pleated khakis crisp and his sneakers so white, it was as though they'd never been outside. He unlaced them and left them by the door before approaching her.

"Can I sit down?"

She nodded and made room for him.

"So," he said.

Out of habit, she put her feet in his lap.

He looked pleasantly surprised. "Oh," he said and clutched them, beginning to rub her feet between his hands.

It felt so good to be touched by him.

But she didn't want to send mixed signals.

She pulled her legs back. "Sorry," she said. "Muscle memory."

"Ah." He nodded. "So I guess I'm not moving back in."

She steeled herself to tell him the truth.

He frowned, bracing for it.

"This is really hard to say," she said, her voice cracking.

"Just say it," he said softly. "Please."

"What we had was really special," she began. "I think in a lot of ways, I'll always love you. But we want different things. And you shouldn't have to compromise what you want in order to keep me."

"But, Lola, love is about compromise," he pressed.

She was worried this was going to turn into an argument when what she needed was for him, for once, to hear her out. "To a certain extent, sure," she agreed, trying to be gentle so he'd stay open. "But I'm not sure you should be expected to compromise your entire lifestyle. And honestly, I wouldn't want you to. Because I don't want to do that either."

"Is this because of Aly Ray Carter?" he asked, his voice rising. "Are you in love with her?"

"It's not because of Aly," Lola said, sidestepping the second question. "Though it's not *not*, I guess. Being with her made me realize that I have so much to learn about myself. And I'm not sure I can learn those things while in a relationship."

"With me," he added.

"With anyone," she corrected.

"There's nothing I can say to change your mind," he said, less a question than an observation.

"I'm so sorry, Justin," she said.

"So you're breaking up with me." His voice was flat.

"I think we're breaking up with each other," she pointed out. "This was never on the table before you put it there."

He looked at his hands. "I'm really sorry," he said. "This is all my fault. I wish I could take it all back."

"It's not about fault," she said, a wave of relief coming over her now that she'd gotten the words out. "This was going to happen sooner or later. I'm glad it's happening now and not when we're, like, married with five children and living in the Valley."

"We would *never* live in the Valley," he laughed.

It felt good to hear that sound. It told her that he didn't hate her. On the contrary, he loved her and maybe even understood where she was coming from.

It gave her hope that even though their relationship was ending, she wasn't losing him. Maybe someday they could figure out a way to be friends.

"Can I hug you?" he asked.

She nodded, and he pulled her close. She nestled her face into his neck and breathed him in. His arms tightened around her.

Their cheeks brushed as she pulled her face back to look at him. His beautiful, familiar face.

She was really going to miss it. She looked at his mouth.

His lips parted. "Lola," he said.

She was surprised to find that she really wanted to kiss him.

She knew she shouldn't. They were breaking up, after all. It would be irresponsible. It would send the wrong message. It would be giving into the desires of her body and neglecting her heart—and her brain, for that matter. She had come so far. Was she really going to backslide like this?

Before she could spiral any further, *he* kissed *her*.

She should stop this. It wasn't right. But...

Their lips pressed together. She felt herself melting into him. Their tongues met. He ran his hands through her hair. He breathed into her mouth hungrily.

She pulled away. "I'm sorry," she said, breathless and guilty. "We shouldn't have done that. We're breaking up."

"I know," he said sadly. "I just wanted to say goodbye in a way that felt..." He trailed us.

"Like us," she said, completing his sentence.

"Like us," he repeated, his voice low and soft.

Tears sprang out of her eyes. She wiped them away and then realized he was crying too.

"If we do this, it doesn't negate everything we just said," she said. "We still need to end this before anyone gets more hurt."

"We *are* ending it," he said. "It's over. I can just leave if you want."

She shook her head. That wasn't what she wanted. "I want closure," she said.

"So breakup sex." He smiled, though he was still crying.

"I've never had it before," she replied.

"I've never had my heart broken like this before," he said. "First time for everything, I guess."

"I'm so sorry," Lola said. "I never meant to hurt you."

"I never meant to hurt you either."

And suddenly, they were kissing again. Tears mixed with saliva. She found herself in his lap, her legs wrapped around his waist. He stood up, holding her, and walked them into the bedroom.

When he lowered her onto the bed, she was still holding tightly with all four limbs. He lay on top of her and kissed her deeply. She felt him hard against her, and she lifted her hips into him.

He tugged his shirt off and tossed it on the ground. She ran her hands along his biceps, which flexed as he held himself up.

She wiggled out of her shirt and her sweatpants, and then she unbuttoned his khakis. Her hands grazed the stiff top of his dick, which strained toward her under the waistband of his briefs. He kicked his pants to the ground. His underwear too.

He stretched his neck down to suck her nipple, sending shock waves through her whole body. She gasped.

He brought his mouth back to hers, his tongue pressing into her a little too firmly, but she appreciated the urgency. She felt it too.

She guided him inside her.

She was wet as hell, and he slid in easily. It felt familiar and new all at once. It made her want to cry more, the feeling of him filling her up like this. She tilted her pelvis to make room for more of him.

He buried his face into her neck. He kept a slow, steady pace. So much self-control, always. She clawed his back desperately. He was swearing under his breath. She felt his heart thundering in his chest, a slick of sweat sliding between them.

Every time they'd ever had sex in this bed played like a montage in Lola's brain.

All their fun experiments—the handcuffs, the vibrators, the blindfolds, the body chocolate—and all their passion. Her on top. Him flipping her over. Them coming at the same time over and over and over. All the times he'd moaned her name. The way he sometimes lightly choked her. The sheets damp with their puddles of sweat. Soft caresses as well as bite marks, hickeys, scratch marks. The way she enjoyed the vanilla as much as the kink. How good it felt just to feel his skin on hers, his weight.

Not just sex in this bed, of course, but also whispered conversations. Making each other laugh until tears leaked from their eyes. Her waking in the night to feel him scooting up against her, warm and solid at her back. The smell of him on the sheets even when he was at work.

All of that was contained in this moment, her on her back, him above her, for what was probably the last time.

It was so, *so* sad. But there was also something so beautiful about it all. About being able to say goodbye in the same language they'd so often said I love you.

Something so final shouldn't feel so sweet, but it did. She could feel all the pleasure that had ever transpired between them at once.

Lola felt her orgasm start to build. "Justin," she cried. "Oh, fuck."

He bit her neck.

And then, finally, he started going faster and harder. She felt like she was going to go blind with how good it felt. She arched her neck back. She felt him start to throb inside her.

When she came, it was less like an explosion and more like the period at the end of a sentence.

─────────

When Lola woke up, it was dark out, and Justin was gone.

She turned the bedside light on. His closet door was open. Inside, a single velvet hanger swung. Otherwise, it was empty.

She sat up.

Had he taken all his things while she slept?

She made her way into the hallway. His photos were gone from the wall. She went to his office. It was surprisingly cluttered. Upon further inspection, she realized he hadn't taken anything with him, just moved it all in here.

In the kitchen, there was a note on the island.

I'll come back and get all my stuff when you're not here, it read in Justin's perfect blocky handwriting. *Sorry to leave while you're asleep. Easier this way. Let me know when to come by. I love you.*

She sat down on a stool, put her hands in her face, and sobbed.

Not because she regretted anything. She knew this was the right thing for both of them. She cried because she knew it was definitely, absolutely over. Even if they weren't meant for each other, she was really going to miss him.

She already did.

When she couldn't cry anymore, she took out her phone.

Might as well just get everything over with.

Can we talk? she texted Aly.

She wanted to hear Aly's voice while she explained to her why she so desperately needed to be alone right now. She owed it to her. She owed it to herself too. What happened between them was meaningful. It was maybe one of the most meaningful experiences of Lola's life. She wanted to end it in a way that honored its importance. If she couldn't do it in person—couldn't simply walk over to Aly's Hamptons house and ring the doorbell—talking on the phone would have to do.

She thought of everything that had transpired between them. The interview, that electric first meeting. The betrayal of the article. The shock of Aly next door. Them fighting all around East Hampton. And then the anger and tension giving way to something new. Lust. Affection. Love. Aly pressing her against the wall. Aly's hands all over her. Her hands all over Aly. The way touching Aly felt so different from anything she'd ever experienced but also so intuitive, like she was born to do it. Aly's dark moods settling in like a storm, then lifting, replaced by that wisecracking grin that made Lola swoon. Aly driving, Aly cooking, Aly asleep beside her.

Was she really ready to let it all go?

She was.

Because Aly was amazing. But she wasn't Lola's person. And Lola didn't want to be in another five-year relationship with someone who wasn't right for her, no matter how good it felt moment to moment. It would be selfish to do that to someone again. Besides, Lola didn't need another person. She needed herself.

Aly replied: So you've made up your mind about us.

Lola groaned. She really wished Aly could be slightly less Aly-like sometimes. I would really like to talk to you, she wrote. This isn't the kind of thing I want to text about.

Within a few seconds, Aly said, And that's my answer.

Lola didn't know what to say. Her fingers hovered over the keyboard. Before she could text back anything, Aly sent, **Have a nice life, Lola.**

For a second, Lola wondered if she was going to cry some more. Instead, she started laughing.

It was just so fucking ridiculous. And childish. It told her everything she needed to know about her decision: mainly, that it was the right one. Often, the way people act in a breakup justifies the breakup itself, she knew.

When she settled, she wrote, **This is such a stupid way to end things, but if that's what you want, fine. I hope you have a nice life too. Thanks for changing mine. I'll never forget you.**

Aly didn't respond.

Lola didn't expect her to.

So that was that. Nearly three months of falling in love, over with a text. It stung, even while she knew it was for the best. Aly might have been the best sex of her life—yes, she thought, even better than Justin—but it came at a cost, and that cost was that she also made Lola feel insane.

You don't end up with a person who makes you feel insane, she thought. You sleep with them until it's no longer fun, and then you get out while you still can—hopefully with your dignity intact.

She was a new Lola. She knew how she deserved to be treated. There would be no going back.

———

The next day, Lola started making clothes.

When the puffed-sleeved polka-dot dress was done, she moved on to the seventies maxi dress with long bell sleeves and orange flowers, which she turned into a mini dress and added lace trim. When that was done, she dove into her closet, pulling out sweaters she hadn't worn in years and pinning them into different shapes, finally deciding to cut them up and make a long, patchwork cardigan.

She left the house once to go to the art store, where she bought fabric paint and brushes, stopping at her favorite bodega for an iced black coffee and an egg-and-cheese bagel. God, how she'd missed a good, greasy egg and cheese. She ate it while she walked back to the apartment, grease on her chin and her mouth in a wild grin. The sky was a bright, cloudless blue, the birds chirping madly in leafy, green trees, the traffic a thrilling cacophony of honking and shouting. She was home, and everything felt new. Like she'd been flipped inside out and could feel for the first time again, nerve endings exposed. She was raw, stripped bare, totally vulnerable, and absolutely, completely alive.

She peered directly into the faces of everyone who walked by, filled with curiosity. Who were they? What were they like? What did they dream about? Who did they love? Some people smiled at her, and others averted their gaze, but it didn't matter. There was promise and potential everywhere.

She was, for the first time in a long time, coming unstuck.

When she got home, she took out the vintage overalls and began painting an intricate floral pattern up one of the legs: a pale green tendril with delicate leaves and bright pink flowers.

She lay her creations around her apartment on display.

She knew if anyone were to walk in, they would think she was having a manic episode. But they'd be wrong. Lola had never felt more sane in her life.

She tried everything on, taking a picture in the full-length mirror of each one. Then she texted them in a batch to Ryan.

What do you think?

I think you're a little rusty, he replied.

Oh my god, she responded, but she was laughing as she texted, **You're so mean.**

Sorry!!! he replied. I like that you're doing this. Honestly. I really think this is what you're meant to be doing. Proud of you bb.

She sighed.

Maybe she *was* rusty. It was always hard to tell the actual quality of her own creations because she loved them too much to be objective. But it was possible she had a lot to learn. She could see that.

She opened her laptop and pulled up the Fashion Institute of Technology website. Maybe, she thought, she could sign up for some classes. Brush up on her skills. Get back in the weeds of fabrics and designs.

Or maybe, instead of dabbling in classes here and there, she could enroll in a proper certificate program. Actually learn something all the way through, become an expert at it. Do it for real. FIT offered certificate programs in Haute Couture, Draping Techniques, Pattern Making, and more.

If Lola was being honest with herself—something she was too scared to be in the past—nothing had ever sounded more interesting. She wanted to learn all of it.

And then perhaps someday she could launch a line of dresses. Not as a collaboration with Shopbop nor even as Lola Likes but as herself. Lola Fine. A bona fide designer. Maybe eventually she could open up a little boutique somewhere downtown or even in Brooklyn, where she'd display her dresses and tailor pieces for clients in the back. Eventually, she'd show at NYFW or maybe even Paris instead, where all the cool brands were heading these days.

Instead of getting paid to wear clothing other people designed, she could get paid for other people to wear *her* designs.

Maybe someday when she was an accomplished, world-famous designer in her fifties, with a short, gray bob and tortoiseshell glasses, she'd get hired to be the creative director at a luxury heritage brand, putting her stamp on something that would be seen and worn by millions of people.

Lola had never bothered to try to picture herself at midlife.

Imagining it now made her feel tingly all over.

A few days later, she decided it was time, at last, to face her followers.

She couldn't hide from them forever.

Wearing her dress made from the Gucci scarf and polka-dot shift dress, she sat at her desk and turned her ring light on. She placed her phone on its stand. She didn't have a plan, but maybe, she thought, as she opened Instagram, that was good. Maybe she should just speak from her heart and not try to curate the truth.

She hit the little icon to post and then toggled over to LIVE.

Her face was reflected back to her, a nervous gloss of sweat on her forehead, her skin still tan from the summer. Behind her, her office was a chaotic mess.

She watched as ten people joined, then twenty.

"Hi, guys," she said. "I'll just wait for more people to get here."

She picked at her nails as she watched the count go up and up. When there were two hundred people watching, she started to talk.

"I totally understand why you all canceled me," she began.

Five hundred people now. Then six hundred. She forced herself to stop watching the number.

She continued. "I said something problematic. I deserved the criticism. If we can't criticize each other, there's no point to community, to any of this. I'm glad that I was given the opportunity to learn that what I did was wrong, and I'm even glad there are consequences to doing the wrong thing. I don't want to live in a world where people can say offensive things and not be held accountable." She took a breath. "Of course, I didn't imagine my life would fall apart in the way it did." She laughed nervously, briefly wondering if this was a mistake, but willed herself to keep talking. "Just for context, my boyfriend ended up leaving me. My team put me on pause. I thought my life was over. I didn't know who I was anymore. But when I started thinking about it, the truth is that I haven't known who I am for a long time."

She paused. A series of hearts fluttered up from the comments.

"The most unexpected part of all this was that after my life fell apart, I fell in love. With a woman. With the specific woman who called me out for losing myself. I'm sure you all read her article. What Aly wrote about me was true: I stopped standing for anything. I stopped being myself. And because she saw me, like really saw me, I fell for her. And what we had this summer was beautiful.

"But that experience is not my identity. I don't know what my identity is. It sucked to have our relationship leaked on the internet, because it robbed me of the chance to define it for myself first. I would really appreciate you guys giving me some grace here. I don't know if I'm bisexual or queer or just a straight girl with really good taste in women. But whatever the case, I think I deserve the right to figure it out away from scrutiny."

She paused, not wanting to get too upset. More hearts popped up from the comments. There were suddenly 10k people watching. She swallowed and then kept going.

"But I guess what I'm trying to say is that who I am is more than who I'm dating. And I've put off figuring that out for a long time. I hid myself in relationships and brand deals, and I lost sight of what I want and what makes me happy."

She felt suddenly like she was going to cry and blinked back the tears before continuing.

"Listen. Being loved is great. I was loved by someone for five years, and it was the best. And I was loved by all of you for so long. But ultimately love and adoration and money and brand deals and likes don't make you who you are. That's not enough to sustain a person. What sustains you is the fire inside you. And you need to keep that fire lit whether you have a girlfriend or a boyfriend or a million followers or one. My problem was I let that fire die. I forgot who I was. And I've decided that the only way to find myself is to be alone for a while. Otherwise, I think I'll just keep distracting myself with what other people want from me."

She imagined Aly hearing this. She hoped she would.

"I don't know if my life is supposed to be about sponsored content and brand deals. All I know is it stopped feeling meaningful. And I know that it's an incredible privilege to say that about something so lucrative. But it's the truth. I started to feel empty, and I don't want to live that way anymore. I want to do something creative. Something fulfilling. I feel like I'm starting over. We should all be so lucky as to get fresh starts sometimes, I think. So that's what I have to say. If you're all cool with it, I would love to start posting again as I figure out this new chapter of my life. But if not, I guess you'll let me know. Thanks for listening to me ramble. I hope this made sense. I hope that if you've experienced something similar, you feel less alone."

She wasn't sure how to sign off, so she simply ended the livestream.

Within seconds, her DMs started filling up.

But she felt afraid to read them. She didn't want to hear people yelling at her, telling her what she'd done wrong this time. So she simply flipped her phone over and went to bed.

––––––––––––

Lola woke up to the sound of her phone vibrating on her nightstand, a jarring, loud buzz.

She squinted at the screen as her eyes focused. It was a little after 8:00 a.m. Ryan was calling. He never called her this early.

Which meant someone was dead or in trouble. Her heart started pounding with fear.

"What's wrong?" she picked up. "Are you okay?"

He laughed. "Girl!"

Okay, so no one was dead. Then why the early call? "Oh my god, *what?*"

"They love you," he said.

"Who?" She got out of bed and opened the curtains. Light filled the bedroom.

"Everyone."

She felt a rush of bright, glittering hope in her stomach, putting him on speaker as she pulled up Instagram.

There were too many notifications for her to understand what was happening—likes, tags, follows, DMs, all of it.

"Can you give me a quick summary of what the fuck is going on?"

"Your confession last night was recorded and shared to TikTok," he said. "The youth have declared you iconic and uncanceled. Oh, and you're Mother again."

"Oh my god," she said, the gravity of this finally hitting her. "They forgive me?"

"They more than forgive you, babe. They stan an authentic

bicurious queen. They think you slayed your comeback. They *love* you. And I watched your video, so I know being loved by strangers is not the point. But isn't it a *little* exciting?"

"No, it's very exciting," she laughed. "I'm still me."

She looked out over Soho, bustling with rush-hour traffic. There was a whole world out there just waiting for her.

"A new version of you, though," he said. "Lola 2.0. Look through all your shit and then call me back. We need to celebrate."

She was too overwhelmed to properly examine her notifications. There were too many. Instead, she went into the kitchen and made a pot of coffee while she microwaved a bowl of oatmeal. Then, as she sat at the table and slowly ate her warm breakfast, she opened her email.

Her inbox, as usual, was a stressful disaster of press releases and newsletters. But there at the top were three messages that caught her eye. The first was from Todd, her former manager.

> Great video, Lola. I think the clients are going to love this rebrand. Let's talk.

She rolled her eyes.
Fucking Todd.
The next was from Veronica, her publicist.

> Lola Fine!!!! You are literally so major. We're all obsessed with what you said live last night. I've already gotten a mountain of NYFW invites for you. Are you still out east, or can I have someone deliver them to your apartment? Can't wait to get back to work. I think a comeback profile in the Times style section would kill. Or a spot on Tinx's podcast. Something big. Call me.

Lola perked up at the idea of NYFW invites but then felt annoyed. Veronica only wanted a piece of her when things were going well.

The third email was from... Her breath caught. Colette Boucher. *The* Colette. Aly's Colette. Lola's heart was pounding. She forced herself to read slowly enough to take in the words.

Dear Lola,

I was so moved by what you said last night. I think it's great that you're taking the narrative back. But more urgently, I loved what you were wearing. Clearly vintage, clearly reimagined. I'd know your style anywhere. Which brings me to why I'm emailing you. I'm going on a book tour next month and having a total clothing crisis. The book is about climate change, so I think it would be a really bad look to buy new clothes for it. I was wondering if you'd be willing to style me, using only vintage and secondhand clothes. Of course, I'll pay you whatever you want. I think we could have fun. I already checked with Carter, and she's fine with it. She thought it was a great idea. Also, I just wanted to add, don't worry about her. She'll come around. She has a pathological need to be friends with all her exes. Just give her some time. Anyway. Let me know what you think. I'd die to work with you on this.

xx Colette

"Oh my fucking god," Lola said out loud to her empty kitchen.

Her team reaching out was not surprising. They were a bunch of absolute vultures. But Colette? Wanting to work with her? Wanting to be styled by her no less? That was definitely not on Lola's bingo card.

Colette was potentially the chicest, most intimidatingly hot girl Lola had ever met. And she wanted *Lola's* eye for *her* style? Lola was pretty sure nothing had ever been so validating. The email didn't even *sound* like Colette. The *xx* sign-off? Insanity. Like an alien had hijacked Colette's brain. Unless…maybe how she'd acted on Fire Island was just a front. Or maybe she had been so triggered by seeing her ex with another straight woman that it brought out the worst in her. Lola had room to forgive Colette for being mean at first—especially after an email like this.

The part about Aly didn't hurt either. She hoped it was true, that someday they could be friends. That Aly would want that.

She finished her breakfast and retreated to her office. Important emails, she felt, needed to be composed on a laptop, not a phone, which she knew made her more millennial than Zillennial, but she was fine with that distinction.

She opened a new email, adding Todd and Veronica and her agents. There was no need to write them back individually, not when she essentially had one thing to say to all of them.

Hi guys, she wrote. She was smiling as she typed, sitting up straight. This was going to be *so* deeply satisfying. *Please feel free to fuck all the way off.* She immediately deleted everything. Too mean. *To whom it may concern.* Nope, she thought, deleting that too. Too formal. *What up, bitches! I hope you all rot in hell!* Too insane.

She deleted it and started over, taking a few deep breaths and trying to think of what a normal person might write in this situation.

Hi everyone,

Thanks for reaching out. I appreciate your support. However, I've decided to manage myself moving forward. I'm taking on a

personal styling client and going back to school. Your services are
no longer needed, but I wish you all the best.

There. That was it. Nice, formal, and just *a little* bit cunty. She
didn't need to burn bridges, but she did need them to know she was
thriving without them.

After she hit Send, she went back to Colette's email.

I'm so happy to hear from you, she wrote, not deleting anything this
time, because she knew exactly what she wanted to say. *I would be
honored to work on this with you. Let me know a good time to connect.
I'm back in the city and stoked to get started.*

For the first time in a long time, everything she was doing felt right.

She couldn't wait to see what would happen next.

Chapter 16

IT WAS LATE morning on her thirtieth birthday, and every surface of Lola's apartment was covered in flowers.

There were bouquets of roses, sunflowers, lilies, tulips, peonies, sweet peas. Every time she put a new bunch into a vase of water, there would be another knock on her door with a delivery for her. Soon the floor was covered in petals like there had been a parade.

Eventually the air became so thick with sweet pollen that she had to open a window, and as she pushed the glass up, the comforting, dissonant sounds of Soho traffic and pedestrians floated in on a cool autumn breeze.

Lola's heart felt so full, she wasn't sure it could be contained in her chest.

Some of the senders, she knew. Her parents had sent a particularly cute bunch of daisies and a card that said, "Happiest birthday to our favorite girl. Can't wait to celebrate you tonight. Every year you amaze us with your strength, heart, and creative soul. We love you so much."

Her team—well, her ex-team—had sent white roses and a simple card that read: "Happy birthday, Lola!" They were still so thirsty for her, despite the fact that they hadn't spoken since she broke up with them.

Other senders she had to strain to remember—old clients and other influencers that felt like they belonged in someone else's life.

She took a picture of her living room spilling over with bouquets and posted it to Instagram with the caption: *Goodbye 29, and thanks to everyone for the birthday wishes. I'm feeling like the luckiest girl in the world.*

She hit Post and then tossed her phone onto the couch, not immediately refreshing it like she used to in order to watch the likes and comments roll in. Instead, she went to the kitchen and began prepping to make her perfect birthday breakfast: French toast with strawberries.

Her mom had taught her how to make French toast when she was little, how to soak the bread in a mix of cream, eggs, and cinnamon before frying in butter. The warm smell made her homesick for lazy California Sundays with her family. She was so glad Ryan had invited her parents to dinner tonight and that they were actually coming. They'd arrive at JFK this afternoon and stay nearby at the Crosby Street Hotel, which Ryan had booked for them with his PR discount.

In fact, Ryan had put himself in charge of her whole birthday dinner too, which was his present to her. Not that there was much to do this time around other than make the reservation.

Last year for her birthday, Lola had rented out the downstairs of Jean's, a swanky secret club under a restaurant on Lafayette, and asked Veronica to blast the invite out to basically everyone who mattered in NYC, whether Lola knew them personally or not. A discerning publicist managed the list at the door. Lola, clad in a slinky, silver Rabanne dress that barely contained her curves, had gotten blackout drunk on vodka shots and thrown up in the Uber on the way home. Justin later held her hair back while she retched over the toilet. He had really been a good sport for that one.

She would not, she decided, flipping her French toast over, miss her twenties.

This year was more grown-up and intimate. They had a reservation at 7:00 p.m. at a nice restaurant. No private room. She'd wear a red silk Victoria Beckham dress that had been in her closet for a while. She would not, under any circumstance, be throwing up in an Uber. Or anywhere.

She was surprised by how excited she was to turn thirty, an age that once felt like it represented so much—like when you hit it, you were supposed to have checked all the boxes of adult milestones. She had, at the very least, expected to be married by now, to be settled in her career. And here she was, starting over instead. What an incredible gift.

Part of the problem, she thought, chopping strawberries and then sprinkling them on top of the golden-brown slices, was that to a young person, thirty sounds like the end of something—not just youth but its potential, as though you better have it all figured out by the end of your twenties, because nothing can ever change after that.

Of course, as Lola now knew, thirty was only the beginning.

Her whole life stretched out ahead of her, glittering with promise. She heated up some maple syrup and then drowned the French toast in it.

While she ate breakfast, she doodled idly in her new drafting notebook, a sketch of a dress design copied from one of her textbooks. She was still working up the courage to fully commit to fashion drawing, but what she'd created so far was encouraging, and her professors were enthusiastic about the talent she was already showing two weeks into her certificate courses.

She finished drawing the dress, and then, because it was her birthday, she drew a huge bow at its waist.

Lola spent the afternoon doing her favorite things. She went to the Beacon's Closet near NYU, trying on Gen Z's trendy castoffs; she got a manicure at Salon M, choosing Big Apple Red for her short, round nails; she got a blowout at Jenna Perry; she stopped into some of the interior design boutiques near her apartment, looking for inspiration.

Now that Justin had moved all his stuff out, her home felt alarmingly bare. She was *itching* to redecorate. She had filled several Pinterest boards with photos of other people's homes. She gravitated toward images with lots of rich colors and decadent patterns, power clashing. But she was also trying to be more financially responsible now that she wasn't taking on new brand deals. So for now, her walls remained bare.

It was not lost on her that she was spending the entire afternoon of her birthday alone, something that would have horrified her just a year ago. But it was exactly what she wanted. She loved the feeling of spontaneity, of following her instincts as she wandered in and out of shops, not having to consult with anyone else on the series of micro-decisions and content opportunities that make up a day. She felt free.

Finally, it was almost 5:00 p.m., and she couldn't kill any more time. She went back home to get ready for dinner.

As she did her makeup in the bathroom mirror, she got a text from Colette: Can't wait to celebrate you tonight!

Over the past few weeks, Lola and Colette had hung out so many times, she'd lost count. The first time was to meet over coffee to discuss their work together. They'd stayed so long, talking about everything from their childhoods to their dating histories to their favorite designers, the coffee shop asked them to leave because it was closing time. After that, they simply got together to walk around different neighborhoods, popping into little vintage stores as Lola began to assemble Colette's book tour looks.

Colette apologized several times to Lola for her behavior in Cherry Grove. The first time, while they walked down Mulberry Street drinking oat milk lattes, Colette said, "I think I was so mean to you at first because it freaked me out to see Carter with another girl who looked like a model. It really had nothing to do with you. I just kept thinking, if that's her type, why did she ever date *me?* Did she even like me at all? I couldn't stop comparing myself to you, and I'm really sorry."

Lola had already forgiven Colette, but it was nice to hear. "It's really okay," she promised. "For the record, you *do* look like a model. But I get it. None of us should be judged by our worst moments."

Colette had narrowed her eyes at Lola and then grinned. "You're kind of wise," she'd said.

Colette apologized two more times after that, until Lola told her to stop. "I'm not dwelling on it, and neither should you," Lola said and hugged her.

Lola had never really been a girl's girl, and she was starting to realize how much she'd missed out on because of that. Having Colette as a friend was one of her favorite parts of her new single life.

Even Aly was okay with it. I had a feeling you'd become friends, Aly texted Colette after Lola had begged Colette to get Aly's official blessing on the situation. Lola felt weird about them hanging out so much without Aly knowing. Aly had added: It makes me happy. Don't worry. Have fun. Maybe someday I'll tag along too. I'm not ready yet, but I hope someday I will be.

"See?" Colette had waved her phone in Lola's face, showing her the texts. "She's much chiller than she makes herself seem."

Lola had laughed. With the worry about Aly's feelings lifted, they became even closer.

Now, she texted back, Thanks, love. See you so soon!

———————

Lola wore her pink Miu Miu flats so she could walk the ten minutes to Café Altro Paradiso without getting blisters.

It was one of those perfect September evenings when it's finally cool enough for a leather jacket but warm enough that you're not shivering. She'd recently scored an oversized black motorcycle jacket from L Train Vintage in Williamsburg, one of the only destinations that could make a trip into Brooklyn worth it. She thought it looked cool with her red, bias-cut silk dress; it signaled that she was chic, but she was still *fun*.

The sun was setting over Soho, reflecting off the concrete in gold and lilac. Lola couldn't help smiling to herself as she walked up to the blue awning of the restaurant, and people walking by her smiled back. It was contagious, this kind of joy.

A handsome man with thick, black hair and dimples leaving the restaurant held the door for Lola with a twinkle in his eye. She smirked at him, her face growing hot as she entered, but didn't turn to look back at him once she was inside because there, in the center of the dining room, at a long table lit by candles, were the people she loved most in this world.

Her parents wore their reading glasses as they peered over a menu together, her mom in a purple knit cardigan and her dad in a blue button-down. Across from them were Ryan and Emmett, holding hands, looking fashionable as hell in their designer T-shirts. Down the table, Colette, in a black slip dress, was there with Jess, who wore a navy chore jacket.

Lola took a sly picture of them before approaching. She wanted to remember her friends and family like this, waiting for her.

All throughout the restaurant, groups of people were leaning toward each other, laughing warmly over bottles of wine and plates of pasta. The golden light from the sunset trickling through the big windows combined with the candlelight on the tables gave the space an enchanted feeling, like anything could happen here. The air itself seemed to sparkle. Every face that Lola's eyes landed on was more beautiful than the next.

"There she is!" Ryan cried, leaping out of his chair and hugging her. "The birthday girl has arrived."

She kissed his cheek. "Thank you so much for organizing this," she said.

He waved her gratitude away. "Anything for you."

She hugged both her parents at once, letting them envelop her with their softness and warmth.

"You look great, honey," Jeanette said.

"So do you," Lola said. "Was the flight okay?"

"Totally fine."

Her mom's hair was dyed auburn and cut into a chin-length bob; her reading glasses hung from a chain on her neck. She smelled like Chanel No. 5 and Dove soap—like home.

"Happy birthday, kiddo," Roger, whose graying hair had receded significantly since the last time she saw him, said. "The big three-oh.

Jesus. Last I checked, it was your mother's thirtieth birthday, so I'm really not sure where the time went."

Lola laughed. "Mom still looks thirty."

"No, I definitely don't." Jeanette grinned, her face full of deep laugh lines that told a thousand stories.

Lola hugged Colette and Jess. "I'm obsessed with your parents," Jess said.

"Me too," Lola replied.

After Lola finished hugging everyone around the table, she finally sat down and then eyed an open chair.

"Ryan, who is that for?"

"Oh, I totally forgot to tell you," he said sheepishly. "I hope it's okay. Giancarlo's in town and wanted to have dinner with me. I told him I could only see him if he came to my best friend's birthday, not thinking he'd actually come, but..." Before he could finish, an older man with salt-and-pepper hair, wearing a perfectly tailored suit and Prada loafers, approached.

"Giancarlo!" Ryan said, standing up to shake the man's hand. "I was just telling Lola you might come."

"Happy birthday, Lola," Giancarlo said, sitting next to her. "Thanks for letting me crash your dinner."

"Wow, hi," Lola said, grinning. "I feel like I'm meeting a celebrity."

He laughed. "Why's that?"

"Your East Hampton house. It's amazing. Thank you so much for letting us stay there this summer."

"Oh, it's my pleasure," he said. "I was glad it was occupied by someone I trust." He patted Ryan's arm.

"What are you doing in town?" Lola asked. "Ryan said you live full-time in..." She trailed off, unable to remember where he called home.

"I wouldn't say I'm really full-time anywhere these days," he replied. "But my husband's work keeps us in Los Angeles mostly. I'm here with our daughter. She just graduated college and insisted on moving to the big city."

Lola's parents perked up. "Sounds familiar." Jeanette smiled. "They always want to go as far away as possible, don't they?"

Lola rolled her eyes, but she was smiling. "It's not my fault California and New York are on opposite sides of the country," she said.

"Where is she moving to?" Emmett asked.

"Well, that's the thing," Giancarlo said, taking a sip of water. "We spent all day looking at one-bedrooms downtown, and I swear, this girl is Goldilocks. Nothing was *just right* for her."

"What is she looking for?" Ryan asked. "I'm sure between everyone at this table, we can ask around. Sometimes in New York, you just have to know the right people."

Before Giancarlo could answer, the waiter came over and took their drink orders. Lola ordered a bottle of champagne for the table and a round of martinis for everyone.

She wasn't going to get blackout drunk, but that didn't mean she wasn't going to have fun.

When the waiter left, Giancarlo said, "She thinks she's going to be able to find a roomy loft in Soho with natural light, in a doorman building. Imagine? In the year 2024, finding something like that?"

Lola tilted her head to the side.

"A loft in Soho," Colette echoed. "That sounds like where Lola lives."

"Oh, you'll have to give me your Realtor's info," Giancarlo said.

Lola nodded. "I will," she said, though even as she said it, she felt another idea brewing.

Their drinks came, and the champagne was poured around the table.

Lola clinked her fork on her flute and everyone looked at her. "Thank you all so much for coming," she said, beaming at the people around her. "I love you all so much. I know I've been a lot over the past year. Well, maybe I've always been a lot."

Her parents laughed.

"The truth is I've always been so afraid to be alone. But looking at all of you here, what I'm realizing is that I've never been alone, and I never will be, no matter what."

Her mom took her reading glasses off to wipe a tear away. Across the table, Colette beamed at her. Ryan squeezed her knee.

"I'm pretty sure *we're* supposed to be making toasts about *you*," her dad said, raising his glass. "To Lola. Who is only just getting started."

Lola's throat constricted like she might cry, but it was canceled out by the warm, floaty sort of glow she felt in her chest.

They clinked their glasses, every combination of people making sure to look in each other's eyes as they did for good luck, and then they all took a sip. Bright, sweet champagne bubbles fizzed in Lola's mouth.

"So what are you two doing while you're in town?" Colette asked Jeanette and Roger.

"Lola is going to take us to all her favorite places," Jeanette replied. "So I think we're about to spend a lot of money."

Everyone laughed. "It's not my fault I have good taste." Lola shrugged, amused. She loved going shopping with her mom.

"And maybe a museum or two if there's time," Roger added. "And we also have some old friends to see, so we won't be in Lola's hair for too long."

"I want you guys in my hair," Lola said, though she also appreciated that they had their own plans.

The waiter came to take their food orders. Lola let Ryan handle it.

While Ryan talked to the waiter about the specials and everyone's various dietary restrictions, Jeanette asked Colette about her book. Emmett and Giancarlo talked about work. Roger and Jess discovered they had mutual friends in production. And Lola simply sat there, vibrating with happiness just looking at all of them together.

When the meal was done, the waiter brought a slice of flourless chocolate cake with a single lit candle in it and placed it in front of Lola.

"Don't worry, we're not going to sing," Ryan said. "You do have to make a wish, though."

Lola closed her eyes.

The only wish she could think of was that her thirties would be full of as much joy as she felt in that moment.

She blew the candle out.

Everyone clapped, including a few people at nearby tables. She grinned goofily at an attractive woman with short, brown hair sitting at the table next to them, who smiled back and then held her eye contact for a few seconds longer.

Colette, clocking the exchange, gave Lola a friendly nudge under the table.

Lola was blushing as she pushed the cake into the center of the table. "You guys do have to help me eat this," she said. Then she turned to Giancarlo. "So would your daughter be interested in a sublet?"

Ryan gasped.

Giancarlo looked interested, tapping his fingers on the table. "Tell me more."

"I've been thinking of moving somewhere more modest while I'm in school. But I don't want to give up my loft altogether. It's a dream apartment. I'd love to hang on to the lease until I feel like it's financially responsible to live there again."

"I'm sure we'd love to come see it," he replied. "How's tomorrow?"

After they made plans for Giancarlo and his daughter to come by in the morning, Ryan said, "Where would you move to?"

"Brooklyn?" Colette suggested.

At the same time, Ryan and Lola said, "Not Brooklyn."

Jess snorted.

"I was thinking maybe Alphabet City," Lola said.

"What about Dimes Square?" Jess asked.

"Oh, I am *so* not hip enough for Dimes Square," Lola replied, shoveling a forkful of cake into her mouth.

"I don't know about that," Colette replied. "You're about to be an up-and-coming fashion designer. You're cool, Lola. Get used to it."

Lola shrugged, quietly thrilled. She liked the idea that she was cool enough for Manhattan's hippest downtown neighborhood, but she still didn't want to live there. She didn't want to be in an area where she was constantly trying to prove herself.

Her parents insisted on paying for dinner, despite the fact that every single other person at the table offered to handle the bill.

Afterward, everyone hugged goodbye, and Lola felt an old pang watching all the other couples break off and go into the night together. She shook it off quickly. This was what she'd wanted. And she didn't feel bad for herself, not really. She loved herself. And until she found someone who would love this new version of her too, that was enough.

———

When Lola got to her building, Hector was not at his usual post by the front door. She yanked it open herself, and when she got inside, she saw him, the super, and a few of her neighbors gathered around the front desk, looking at something she couldn't see.

She approached them. "What's that?" she asked, and someone moved over to let her into the circle.

On the desk was a cardboard box. It was lined with a rumpled plaid shirt.

And full of kittens.

"Oh my god." Lola's heart swelled.

There were six of them, each a different color. Black, gray, calico, tabby, orange, white. A couple were sleeping in little balls, but the rest were wiggling around, meowing at each other and the people who gazed down at them.

"I found them in the basement," the super told Lola. "Mama Cat nowhere in sight."

"Animal control is on its way," Hector said.

"Animal control?" Lola gasped. "They're not going to kill them, are they?"

"No, no," Hector reassured her. "They're taking them to a shelter."

Lola leaned her face closer to the kittens and made eye contact with the calico one. And then, out of nowhere, it pounced on her, landing on her chest.

"Oh," she exclaimed. "Hello, little friend."

The kitten rubbed its face under her chin and began to vibrate.

"I think you just got claimed," one of the neighbors, a younger woman in yoga pants and a ponytail, said.

"Well, shit," Lola laughed. The kitten continued to burrow into her, purring. "I think you might be right." She rested her hands on its warm, little body. She was overcome by the affection. By how small it was. By how much it seemed to need her and how good that felt.

She could not imagine putting the kitten back in the box and walking away.

She knew, in no uncertain terms, that she would be going through the next fifteen to twenty years of her life with this kitten—well, cat soon—curled up next to her. The cat would see her go through life's ups and downs, experience things she couldn't even yet imagine. The decision made itself.

Hector beamed at her. "Happy birthday, Lola."

She tickled the kitten. "What do you think, pal? You want to come live with me?" The kitten dug its talons into her dress, which she took to mean yes.

"I guess I'm a cat mom now," she said. "Or what are we saying these days? A childless cat lady?"

The neighbors laughed. The kitten let out a high-pitched meow.

She zipped the kitten up into her jacket, where it nestled itself into a little ball, purring the whole elevator ride up to her apartment.

In the morning, after Giancarlo came by, she'd take it to a vet to make sure it was okay. Then she'd scour the city for the best pet products. A litter box. All-natural cat food. Some sort of scratchy tower so it wouldn't destroy her couch. She'd name it something cute. Tabitha, maybe.

She'd set Zillow to show her pet-friendly apartments in Alphabet City, and when Giancarlo's daughter sublet her apartment—as Lola knew she would; the loft was perfect, even for Goldilocks—she and Tabitha would move in somewhere cozy and start a new life together.

She lay on the couch and felt the kitten's little body melting into hers. This tiny creature, so trusting of her that it had leapt into her arms. The kitten wasn't afraid of love. Lola wasn't either. On the contrary, she was wide open to it.

After a few minutes, she got up, gently placing Tabitha on the sofa. The kitten glanced up at her before curling up in the corner and falling back asleep.

Lola went to the window. The city sprawled out below, thrumming with the promise of a new beginning. She should probably go to bed soon, but she was too wired to sleep, too happy.

Then, remembering she had an assignment due Monday morning, she went to her sewing machine and resumed working on a ruffled blouse she'd be presenting for critique. It was a more complicated design than she'd ever tried, and she'd already had to start over a few times before getting it right. She still wasn't sure this version would be the final one, if it would fall the way she wanted it to, if it would feel both classic and unique. But if not, she'd just start again. It was more important to get it right than to declare it finished just for the sake of being done. At any rate, she loved the process. She realized she was smiling to herself as she flipped the garment over to sew the other side.

She wondered as she worked what she would tell herself at twenty-two if she could go back in time and give herself advice. If she would tell herself to focus on a career that made her happy, not what was making her money the fastest; if she would tell herself not to date someone who wanted different things. But if she'd known all that in her twenties, she'd probably have less gratitude for where she'd landed at thirty. As it was, she knew how lucky she was, how hard-won the layout of her life was.

So, she thought, finishing the blouse's left shoulder, she supposed that meant that even if she could, she wouldn't change a thing about her life so far. Not even the hard parts. The hard parts had made her who she was. She was at once stronger and more vulnerable than she'd been when she was younger. And she was so thankful for all the heartbreak that had broken down her walls and allowed her to rebuild herself as someone better. She hoped the rest of her life would be full of such opportunities for change and growth. She had a feeling it would be—as long as she was open to it.

And she was.

Acknowledgments

To Gabrielle Korn. Thank you for being the most fabulous collaborator ever. Thank you for your nonjudgment. Thank you for the talent and creativity.

I'd like to thank my mom. Thank you for making me so brave. I wouldn't be able to do anything without your endless support. Thank you for every word of encouragement, every late-night phone call, every house-sit, every article sent. You are the most fabulous person, and I love you endlessly. I would be nothing with you.

Thank you to my dad for the work ethic and private school education. I hope you are proud of me.

Thank you to my brother. Hanging out with you is the opposite of loneliness. You are the funniest person I know, and I would die without you.

Thank you to my best friends. To Pig, for being the silliest best friend ever. When I'm sad, I remember I am on earth at the same time as you, and I feel so happy and lucky. To Lucas, for everything. So many of the happiest memories of my adult life are with you. To Dena, for getting me into romance novels!! To Ashley, for being so kind. To Chloe, for being so Diane. Thank god we found each other. To Jyoti, for a lifetime of sisterhood.

Thank you to Lauren. I would be lost without you.

To Viche and Miso for the joy and entertainment.

To Allison. I am sorry I am so insane, but at least you're entertained.

To Margaret and Alyssa, for answering every manic call and generally believing in me.

Thank you to every boyfriend I've ever had, even the bad ones. You shaped me one way or another. There are parts of you in me. No longer physically, thank god. But metaphorically.

Thank you to my followers. You are an endless fountain of inspiration, and everything I do is for and because of you. May this book awaken new depths of your mind. I love you.

About the Author

Christina Najjar—popularly known as Tinx—is a content creator and *New York Times* bestselling author, known for her real-talk dating advice and "Rich Mom" satire. Tinx, whose wit and candor have established her as a resounding voice for women, is also the host of the hit podcast and live radio show It's Me, Tinx. Tinx's undeniable impact on social media has earned her the distinction as one of *Forbes'* Top Creators. This is her second book, following her *New York Times* bestselling debut, *The Shift*.